THE
SIBERIAN INCIDENT

GREIG BECK

SEVERED PRESS
HOBART TASMANIA

THE SIBERIAN INCIDENT

"We know more about the face of the moon than we do about the Blue Eye of Siberia (Lake Baikal)."

Old Siberian saying.

We Were Never Alone

PROLOGUE

Lake Baikal, Southern Siberia—100,000 years ago

The object entered the southern part of the nearly 400-mile long lake where it was deepest, at 5,300 feet—just over a mile down to where it was darker than night with crushing depths and a permanent, unbearable cold. Its ferocious impact shattered and melted the lake's ice layer, and the flash and sonic boom created a pressure wave so great it flattened the trees around the lake for dozens of miles and generated a 50-foot displacement wave that washed inland, turning most of the low-lying shoreline into an impassable bog.

Huge air bubbles continued to boil to the surface for days, and the colonies of rare *nerpa* freshwater seals refused to leave their dry perches until near-starvation finally forced them back to the water.

Homo sapiens had been in Siberia for over 250,000 years, and one small band observed the phenomenon. That night, huddled together in their cave, they felt the need to document what they saw on the walls around them. But their curiosity was both a gift and a curse. The following day, a small band of warriors set off toward the lake to investigate.

Many days later, of the six warriors that departed, only one returned. He wasn't the same man he'd been when he left. It became clear that something terrible had found them.

That evening, the ground shook. The clan huddled in the rear of their cave, unable to act as their world collapsed around them.

Seasons came and went, and eventually, the scars on the landscape healed. The animals returned, new plant growth sprang up, and the lake's water settled and cleared. The ice closed over the impact site like a scab over a wound, and nature forgot. But down in the pitiless, sunless depths, the lake never did.

EPISODE 01

CHAPTER 01

INTERACTION: *Southeastern shore of Lake Baikal—2nd century B.C.*

The war had raged for nearly 200 years, bloody battles fought between the Chinese Han dynasty and the Xiongnu confederated state. But in a final assault, Huo Qubing of the Han had marshaled one of the greatest armies seen in over a century.

He marched over 1,000 miles to engage the forces of the Xiongnu's Worthy Prince of the East, and Huo's army quickly encircled and overran their enemy, killing over 70,000 men in a single day and scattering the rest.

Huo's military leaders assembled and General Jinx Wei bowed before he spoke. "You have won, my lord."

Huo Qubing grunted and then looked out over a near-endless plain of broken corpses. The cold trapped the smells, but steam still rose like tiny departing souls from the torn bodies.

"I didn't come here just to win, but to annihilate our enemies for all time." He turned back to his generals. "Kill them all."

And so, the remnants of the Xiongnu army were tracked all the way to the shore of an icy, inland sea that would one day become known as Lake Baikal. And there, the last few thousand Xiongnu warriors were slaughtered to a man.

Before returning home, Huo Qubing ordered supplies to be taken from the forests: deer, bear, Xiongnu horses, and even wolf meat.

But over the coming days, the men became restless, and rumors spread of great disturbances out on the frozen lake. Cracking sounds, water falling in the darkest times of the night, and then men started to go missing—a few at first and then many, and always when the night was darkest. Soon hundreds of Han warriors had vanished.

"Deserters," Huo Qubing proclaimed. "They are to be executed on sight."

But the warlord knew this was just to placate the men's nerves, as none of the disappearing men had ever been found. And then there were the tracks.

He had been shown the strange marks leading from and back to the lake where the ice was broken open. Huo had posted more guards, but then two of his most trusted men vanished and he personally joined in the search, following their bare footprints—until they found the final abomination.

Huo Qubing swallowed hard and worked to control his expression as he stared at the piles of human intestines and organs on the lakeshore. He had seen the insides of men before, but the inexplicable thing was that the men's tracks proceeded into the dark water as if they had been disemboweled and then simply kept on going as if nothing had happened.

The great military leader knew then that his men were being taken and drawn down into the frozen, inky depths by something evil. He could make war on any army and win. But he couldn't fight against something they couldn't even see.

He ordered the army to immediately break camp and they marched away from the lake. No one spoke of what happened. And after a while, no one wanted to.

CHAPTER 02

Boca Ciega Ave, Madeira Beach, Florida—Today

"*Yes!*" Marcus Stenson put the phone down and turned to his wife, grinning from ear to ear.

Sara balled her fists. "You got it?"

Marcus waited for a second or two, building the suspense before yelling: "W*e go-ooot it.*" He sucked in a huge breath and let it out. "Five-year rolling contract, with worldwide rights. No one else but us."

Sara leaped in the air. "Yay!" She ran and jumped into his arms, kissed him, and then held him at arm's length. "So what's next from here?"

"Now, we spend money… lots of it." Marcus mentally ran through the business plan in his head.

The five-year contract was for farming the endangered Beluga sturgeon in the pristine, freezing, and secluded waters of Lake Baikal in southern Siberia. The ancient fish was slowly going extinct, and the Russian government was looking for solutions to resurrect the species. Marcus had put in a proposal that described a breeding program that would pay for itself within five years, and also be able to create a healthy population of fish for both restocking the lakes and for ongoing farming.

He had already spent hundreds of thousands of dollars of his own money, first on securing an old disused paper mill and its surrounding lakeside property. Then more on navigating the labyrinthine bureaucracy of the Russian public service, and ensuring political donations, special fees, and gifts were all funneled into the right hands.

He turned and held up a finger. "Step one, we now need to lock in our suppliers of eggs and breeding age Beluga sturgeon, and formalize all those promises that were made to us."

"How long have we got before…?" Sara raised her eyebrows.

He smiled and knew what she was asking: how long has *she* got until they both needed to go over and live there, perhaps permanently.

Marcus puffed his cheeks and blew air between pursed lips. "Well, I need to go next week to get the ball rolling. The sturgeon can't arrive until we have the pens set up, and they're not built yet. In fact, next to nothing is built yet. I'll need to find and engage local tradespeople, as part of my proposal submission was to create jobs for the local community." He counted off another finger. "Plus, we need to find suitable pen sites that are clean and secluded to ensure there is no cross-contamination from the local sturgeon species that can be riddled with parasites and infections."

"And what'll you do in your next week?" Sara grinned.

Marcus laughed and held his arms wide. "Go fishing, of course."

Truth was, there were a million things he needed to do, and it all seemed so achievable on paper. Now that he needed to press the button and execute his plans, he felt a bit overwhelmed.

"Once I've got the basics set up, then you follow."

"How long?" She lifted her chin.

He bobbed his head. "Maybe three months." He looked up at her. "Is that doable?"

Sara studied to be a biologist but was enticed into corporate life early on. Now she ran a marketing consultancy business, and he knew she had already floated the idea of stepping back from hands-on control and letting her second-in-charge run it for her. Even though he was the specialist marine biologist, he needed her with him—she was smart, decisive, and as well as being an excellent scientist, she was the one with the business brain. He was a dreamer, and she was the one with the eye for detail and clarity.

"Three months?" She nodded. "Yeah, doable, easy." She tilted her head. "Will we still be staying at the mill house?"

"Yes and no. Not in the mill house itself, but the manager's residence. By the time you get there, I'll have transformed it into a palace." He grinned and tried to look confident.

"Palace, huh?"

He nodded slowly. "Yep... and fit for a queen."

She crinkled her nose. "Can you at least make sure it's warm?" she asked with a half-smile.

"As Florida?" His brows shot up. "Well, I'll do my best."

Marcus knew she was still a little concerned by the cold—after all, it was Siberia. In summer, the lake weather was mostly warm and mild. Down on the southern tip, people even went swimming, although they did so with gritted teeth and blue lips.

Unfortunately, where they would be living and working was more north, where the lake area climate remained both freezing, the lake's surface frozen for most of the year. And in winter, when it *really* got cold, he'd heard reports of the lake's ice layer growing to 10-feet thick.

He saw that Sara was turned to the window and looked out over the lush green lawns to the sparkling blue water of the Gulf of Mexico. Madeira Beach was beautiful, and she was a beach girl through and through, so he knew where they were going was going to be tough on her. She turned back with her hands on her hips.

"Well, as long as the roof doesn't leak, and it can be heated, then I'm in. But just remember, buster, we're from Florida, and the mill is in

Siberia."

"Of course, don't worry." He hiked his shoulders. "And when have I ever let you down?"

She tilted her head, smiling. "Well, firstly, there was that time…"

"Okay, okay." He grabbed her hand and pulled her close. "Enough about me." He kissed her, deeply, and then continued to hold her close. "It'll be hard, but we can do it."

She felt down between them. "I think it's hard already." She smiled with heat in her eyes.

"I thought you'd never notice." He kissed her again.

CHAPTER 03

30,000 feet over the Pacific Ocean

Marcus sat in the window seat of the business-class cabin. There was enough room for his six-foot frame to stretch out with just a touch of luxury. On the tray table beside him was a cold beer and he hummed softly as he flipped through his marketing proposal. Sara had put it together for him and it was a great summary of the work that needed to be done and even a description of the fish stocks he'd be managing.

He knew one of the advantages he had in winning the bid was in part due to the work he had previously done on a similar breeding program at home, on the endangered sturgeon in the Great Lakes basins. Given sturgeon can live to be 120 years old and are not even sexually mature until they're 20 to 25 years old, it would be a generational program unless he added in a few extra DNA marker changes for speeded maturization. His success was a world first and he had patented the process.

"And that's where the magic comes in," he said softly and hummed a little more.

Still, there were years of work before them, and Russia understood that and was looking more to the long-term preservation of their prized fish and not for fast returns.

And their agreements reflected that: if he could meet certain performance targets within five years, he'd be granted a non-competitive 99-year license—it'd be a family business that made him and his heirs rich for a century.

He flipped a page of his notes, finding the fish's background information and quickly skimmed through it again. He smiled; there was so much work to do, but he looked forward to every minute of it.

The airline steward appeared with the drinks trolley, and he grabbed another beer, and this time, instead of the usual dried nuts in a foil pouch, he was given a small cheese and fruit plate. *Nice*, he thought, and cleared the plate in just under a minute.

Marcus slumped back in his seat after he finished his beer. He closed his eyes and let the alcohol and his good spirits transport him away.

*****

Marcus woke as the plane juddered upon landing and he groaned as he sat forward, rubbing a stiff neck. There was dribble all the way down one side of his face, and he quickly looked about with puffy eyes to see if anyone had been watching while quickly wiping it away.

He bent down to look out the small oval window at early morning Moscow—grey, misty, and exactly as he remembered it. It was busy, modern, and just as crowded as any other big city airport.

He checked his watch and sighed. He had another flight to catch to Irkutsk, then a train to the ancient township of Listvyanka.

Marcus had spent months learning basic Russian and could navigate most conversations. In Moscow, many spoke English, but once you went further outside the city, then without language skills or an interpreter, you were on your own.

He finally arrived by evening and when he did, he'd been on the move for nearly 42 hours. He was still fairly young at 35, and fit, but by then he felt 100 years old and every bone, joint, and muscle in his body was making him pay.

He stood in the main street of Listvyanka and breathed in the cold air that prickled the inside of his nose and escaped as a ghostly plume from his lips. In summer, the fields surrounding the town were magnificently green, and the clean sunshine made the pastels of the buildings stand out like a schoolroom pencil drawing. But today, with the light fading and a slate-grey sky overhead, the grass was brown and dry, and the lake glinted like bitter mercury in the setting sun.

In another few minutes, Marcus found his hotel—the Belka—and dragged his bags in through the door, instantly greeted by the luxurious, hot breath of internal heating. It made him relax and feel immediately sleepy.

The hotel was modern inside, and fairly empty now. While he waited as an efficient young woman checked him in, he could see that off to the side was the bar and restaurant. He took a few steps back to peer in.

"*Privetstvuyu g-na Gollivud!*"

Marcus grinned and the receptionist looked up at him. Yuri Revkin's jovial, and loud, address of: "*Greetings, Mr. Hollywood,*" was his usual joke about Marcus' good looks, but he bet that every American the big Russian met weathered the same ribbing.

Marcus turned and gave him a wave and the man held up a beer and pointed at it. Marcus was dead tired and the next morning they wanted to leave early, but he felt he could still deal with a bite to eat, a beer, and a catch up with his friend and new site manager.

He pointed at his bags. "I'll dump these and come down." He held up five fingers.

"Good." The big Russian clapped his hands together and yelled to the barman to pour two more beers, plus a shot of vodka each for the cold.

Marcus grabbed his key and lugged his bags up the steps, found his room, and shouldered open the door. Inside, it was neat and clean, with a window looking out on the lake. He dropped his bags and headed for the bathroom. He leaned on the sink and stared at his visage—red-rimmed eyes, pale, greasy, and tired-looking—basically, exactly how he felt.

He quickly washed his face, changed his shirt, and headed back down to see his friend.

Marcus walked into the bar room that smelled of cigarette smoke, fish, old and new beer, and a popular Russian, pine forest smelling aftershave that he knew from experience burned like fire. His friend jumped up and opened albatross-wide arms.

Marcus grinned. "Comrade."

Just as Yuri said every American came from Hollywood, Marcus teased Yuri about everyone in Russia being an old commie. The big man grabbed him in a hug, and literally sat him down and pushed a jug-sized Yarpiro beer toward him, plus another glass full to the brim of oily looking vodka.

Marcus didn't really feel like it, but what the hell, he was going to pass out within an hour anyway. He raised the vodka first.

"*Nasdarovje.*"

Yuri did the same and downed his in one. He slammed the empty glass down, slapped the table, and ordered another. He raised his eyebrows at Marcus, who shook his head.

"Just a beer; I want to wake up tomorrow."

He grabbed his huge glass, lifted it in a toast, and then gulped. The Russian beer was strong, earthy with hops and with a hint of something like cinnamon. It was good, and he then gulped a third time suddenly feeling the dehydration of the long travel followed by the dry atmosphere outside.

"So." Yuri sat forward. "You win?"

Marcus put his glass down. "Yep, we got it; five-year contract. After that…" He held up a hand with fingers crossed.

Yuri waved it away. "You will win again… and then 99 years." He raised his glass again and drained half his beer.

"Maybe," Marcus said.

"No maybe. Together, we unbeatable." Yuri nodded confidently, but then raised bushy eyebrows. "And when will princess arrive?"

"Princess Sara arrives in three months. Gotta have the house spick and span before then." Marcus pretended to grimace.

"Good plan; it will be summer, lake at its best. Nice and warm." Yuri nodded his big head, but then his mouth turned down. "She won't like it so much now."

Marcus sighed and sipped again. "Before the fish, we need the people, and before the people, we need somewhere to house them. We need the hatchery up and running; plus, the laboratory, the pens, and the cabins—a lot to do."

"We look tomorrow. Then I can have people start working by end of the week." Yuri's vision seemed to turn inward. "More people there the better. Better for…" He bit down on the words and then just shrugged. "You sleep better."

Marcus tilted his head. "Something else?"

The big Russian grumbled deep in his chest for a moment and then shook his bear-like head. "Just too much vodka, I think." He raised his glass. "To tomorrow morning."

"So, you still have a boat?" Marcus asked.

"Sure, sure. But lake is frozen, so no boat now." He grinned. "But I also have a truck."

"We're driving, and it's safe, right?" Marcus' brows went up, as he hadn't actually tried driving on the ice sheets yet.

"Yes, we are driving on the lake." Yuri toasted Marcus again and downed it in one.

Marcus didn't hear his reply on the safety question.

CHAPTER 04

Listvyanka, Lake Baikal—main wharf

The next morning, Yuri was waiting at the dock, and Marcus had changed into more formidable cold-weather clothing of his bright orange SeaWorld jacket, boots, and gloves. Even though he expected it wouldn't be a boat he'd be traveling in but the cabin of a truck fitted with spiked ice tires, he knew when they were out on the open ice sheets that the cold was going to be like a living thing, trying to get in at them any chance it got.

To begin with, Yuri would be coming back and forth for supplies as they were setting up, but then he too would situate permanently at the mill house compound. On one of his trips, he'd return with the boat on a trailer, and also a pair of bobcats, powerful little snow sleds that were like motorbikes on ice.

Marcus was lucky to have found the guy, and he'd interviewed plenty. Yuri was a successful manager and jack-of-all-trades, involved in fishing, construction, and probably half a dozen other things Marcus didn't want to delve into too deeply. However, the bottom line was, the guy was honorable, dependable, got things done, and was an all-round good guy— good enough for Marcus, and after working with him now for two years, mostly via the phone, he knew he'd be lost without him.

Yuri pushed open the truck door. "You Americans like to stand out, yes?"

"It's my favorite jacket." Marcus threw his bags in the back and jumped in. He gave him a thumbs-up, and then pulled his collar down from his chin. "So cold," he said.

"This? This is nothing." Yuri reached across to slap his shoulder. "Wait until teeth of winter. She bites hard." He roared with laughter and then started the truck.

Marcus groaned and turned to watch the town of Listvyanka grow smaller as they departed. Save for smoke lifting from chimneys, it looked deserted, bleak, and frozen in time.

Marcus settled back and stared out at the lake's icy surface; it was like driving on an endless white plain that was dusted in sparkling sugar crystals. He knew beneath that ice, the water was crystal clear, and in some places impossibly deep.

They had a long way to go, and Yuri had sandwiches—fish, of course—several thermoses of coffee, and plenty of spare fuel. The surface of the lake, either driving over or boating, was the fastest way to traverse it, but even at top speed, it would still take them the entire day traveling along the coastline.

Marcus fell into a form of trance as the shoreline flew past. They needed to travel up past the staggering, over-sized Olkhon Island. It was the largest island in Lake Baikal, which was 44 miles long with a landmass of 280 square miles. It was covered in thick forest and even had its own community of people living there.

It was the size of everything around here that staggered Marcus. Everything about this place was enormous, ancient, and remote. It made Marcus feel tiny and insignificant, and a modern creature out of place in an alien land.

It was probably why these areas suited the sturgeon. Their evolution dated back to the Triassic some 245 million years ago. And since then, they'd undergone remarkably little morphological change—basically, evolution liked what it did with the fish and decided to freeze their form—and why not? They had a lot going for them: they could tolerate tropical warm or freezing water, salt or fresh, they grew big and therefore didn't have many predators, and they were also armor-plated, having four rows of scutes that were the bony projections you see on alligators, and were even present on some dinosaurs.

The truck bounced on an ice fold, jolting Marcus from his trance. He saw that the morning was just a pale-orange blush on the horizon, and the sky a watery-blue. But ahead of them, the ice still seemed endless.

Yuri had told him that in winter, the Russian also took the heartier divers out in his truck and cut holes through the ice so the divers could drop in, or he would lower motorized cameras as miniaturized submersibles. Marcus had seen some of the photographs from under the ice, and it was a strange world of a sky of blue ice above and inky blackness below.

In those dark depths, they needed to find fish pen sites that were close to the mill, with a depth of between 200 and 500 feet, and preferably not too far out where there was a chance in summer months that the pens could be run over by any boating traffic, or lashed by some of the fierce storms that can kick up in a Siberian summer.

Where the mill site was located, much of the lake was frozen most of the year and that was a good thing for storm protection.

Marcus held a plastic mug of lukewarm coffee and sank back in the seat next to Yuri. The two men became lost in their own thoughts. Already he missed Sara. She was his rock, his soul mate, and his sounding board. Yuri was good company, but Marcus' wife always seemed to bring out the best in him.

He sipped the dregs of his coffee and sucked in a deep breath, feeling a hint of nerves deep down in his stomach. There was so much riding on this. He had already spent close to a million dollars buying the mill and equipment, and hiring Yuri—even travel expenses were significant. And there would be no returns for years. That end-of-the-rainbow pot of gold was piled high, but getting there was fraught with risks, challenges, and mountains of damned hard work.

Marcus felt like a gambler who had a great hand and pushed all his chips into the center of the table, while the other players just smiled. He couldn't shake the feeling there was something he didn't know or was missing.

He turned to the left to watch the landscape go by. They were well past any settlement areas now, and the land moved between endless plains of brown, spiky grass to forested thickets coming right down to the water. There were also crags of weathered stone, some rising hundreds of feet into the air.

The land was wild, ancient, and mysterious. It was a place of secrets, mystery, and it was no wonder it held legends within its watery depth and dark forests. Modern people had been here for centuries, and before that there was cave art, telling stories of the land stretching back tens or even hundreds of thousands of years.

He passed by a waterline rocky outcrop where a few seals raised their heads to watch them speed by. Yuri had told him they'd be living off the land wherever possible to save money, and they could eat the local nerpa seals. Marcus didn't think he could do that, as they reminded him too much of shiny dogs.

However, on one of their last visits, they'd encountered several of the massed seal colonies in the water. Though the beluga sturgeons were far too big and lived too deep for the seal to predate them, they would certainly make a meal of younger sturgeon. Added to that, his potential netted pens would prove no problem for the seal that would simply slide or dive over the top of the mesh.

When Marcus had remarked on the risk, Yuri had lifted his jacket and produced a handgun. Before Marcus could object, he fired twice into the air. Like magic, the seals vanished.

"Around here, we the boss, not the seals." The big Russian had grinned and pretended to blow smoke from the muzzle.

Marcus shook his head and laughed. "When in Russia, I guess."

"No, worse; you in Siberia." Yuri slapped Marcus' thigh and laughed hard enough to make his seat squeak like a tortured mouse.

Damn right, Marcus thought. But he did wonder why Yuri needed a handgun.

At around 4 pm, Yuri half-turned to him. "Not long now." He pointed.

"Just around bend."

However, the bend was still in the far distance, the day was gone, and the ice was now turning a burnt orange from the setting sun. And as soon as the sunlight started to bleed away, the temperature plummeted. It would be well below zero before they knew it.

Marcus pulled his thick pullover collar up over his chin as the cabin heater struggled against the cold outside. His breath steamed again, and he picked out landmarks he remembered from his previous visits.

Even though he'd been here many times before, he felt a tingle of excitement in his belly because this time his ambitious project was in motion.

He smiled as they started to round the final bend. The mill site was as secluded as it got, and access was mainly by boat to its own private wharf. Another peculiarity of the site was that communications around some areas of Lake Baikal were spotty at best. Some days were fine, and others it was nothing in and nothing out.

Marcus had been there at various times of the year, and he knew the lakeshore area was magnificent—the lake was a white desert in winter and most of spring-autumn, but when it finally warmed, it was a wildflower wonderland. And by then, the summer lake was so glass-clear that you could see the bottom in 150 feet of water.

The compound and surrounding land he now owned was huge, and on it was the manager's residence that was almost a mansion, as well as a number of smaller cabin-style buildings for the staff. The main factory building, that everyone still called the mill house, he'd be converting into a fully functioning hatchery and laboratory.

Marcus' smile broadened as he imagined him and Sara sitting on a front porch in the evening, sipping mulled wine, and looking out over the crystal water. His smile broke into a grin—he could think of worse places to start a family. He just hoped Sara thought the same.

The night was catching them quickly, and as they rounded the bend, the first thing Marcus saw was a light on. "Hey, somebody's home."

Yuri grinned. "Maybe the ghost of previous owner." He turned theatrically, raising his eyebrows. "I think this is where headless horseman used to live. You go in first; I scared of ghosts."

The truck slowed as he came in toward an icebound wharf. When they were beside it, Yuri gave a few more revs as the truck moved up the slope from the lake's icy surface and onto the land, and then stopped.

He jammed his pipe in his mouth, leaned out the window, and looked up toward the lit houses.

"Who is it?" Marcus asked.

Yuri shook his large head. "I don't know." He then wiped his hands on his heavy knit pullover and shouldered open the door with a scream of hinges. "So, now we find out who your guests are."

"I think they've found us." Marcus could see four people appear and come down along the path toward them. He and Yuri stood their ground, and he saw the big Russian surreptitiously feel for the revolver in its holster on his rear hip.

Marcus watched and waited, and Yuri let his arms hang by his sides.

"*Privet*, Mr. Stenson!" The lead man waved.

"*Zdravstvuyte*," Yuri responded and then half-turned to Marcus. "They know you. Might be okay, local accent."

Marcus nodded. Yuri didn't need to translate as he picked up the greeting loud and clear. The men looked slightly Asian or Mongolian, with high cheekbones and folds over their eyes. And whoever they were, they were here to see him.

"*Zdravstvuyte, zdravstvuyte*." Marcus stepped forward, and the lead man marched up and stuck a hand out. Marcus took hold of it and the guy pumped his hand like he was trying to draw water.

"Congradlins on unclose mill, you, *ah*..." He looked skyward as he seemed to think over his words, and a younger man, who looked remarkably similar, came forward to join him.

"My father says, congratulations on reopening the mill." He put a hand on the older man's shoulder. "My name is Nikolay Grudinin, and this is my father, Pavel."

Marcus nodded. "Thank you."

Pavel shrugged. "My English is better, the, *uh*, more I use." He turned and spoke in rapid Russian to his son, who listened and then nodded. He stood back and motioned to the other men with him.

"With us are Mr. Dmitry Melnikov and Mr. Leonid Luhansk. We have come here to help you, work for you, Mr. Stenson." Nikolay smiled.

News travels quickly, Marcus thought. He could have Yuri dismiss them immediately, but he noticed that they had already begun to clean the site up, and obviously weren't averse to hard work.

"First, I need to know whether I can use you." He addressed Nikolay, but let his eyes travel over each of them. Once again, Nikolay did the talking.

"My father is very good with wood, carpentry, and with machines. Our family has been living in this area for many generations and knows the lake well." He pointed to the men standing behind him. "Dmitry and Leonid are both experienced sturgeon fishermen, and *ah*, Jack-all-trades, own their own boats, and also know the lake."

The one called Leonid took a homemade-looking wooden pipe from between his teeth and saluted with it.

Not bad, Marcus thought. Exactly the sort of people he would have been looking for. "And what do you do?"

Nikolay bobbed his head and grinned. "I just finished my economics degree at Moscow University. Unfortunately, there is no work for me right now. But I am strong, and smart, so..." he shrugged.

Marcus nodded. *Strong, smart, and language skills were also useful*, he thought. "Well, I will need a laboratory assistant for the breeding work we'll be doing. Do you learn quickly?" Marcus raised his eyebrows.

Nikolay nodded solemnly. "Oh yes, very quickly." He pointed to the main building. "We went all over the mill and cleaned it. It is still in very good shape, structurally sound, and any hazardous material was removed years ago. We think we can get it up and running very fast."

"Good." Marcus nodded, quietly impressed.

Yuri leaned in close to him and spoke just behind his head. "I think they are Turkic, maybe Yakut. Good, honest people. Hard working." He leaned back and shrugged. "Your choice."

"Okay." Marcus turned back to the men. "I'm not saying *yes* just yet. But let's get our stuff unpacked and we can chat some more over dinner."

"Very good, Mr. Stenson." Pavel clapped his hands together. "And please, we join for dinner. We make, *uh*, we make you stroganoff for eat." He winked. "Reindeer."

Marcus chuckled. "Well, okay then. In that case, I can tell you that your interviews are going very well so far."

Marcus and Yuri squared away their supplies and equipment, inspected some of the cabins and the manager's house, and then met the group inside the main mill house for dinner.

He was impressed with the amount of work they'd done already— inside and out of the mill, small buildings, main house, and surrounding property was near spotless, with some minor repairs already undertaken. In addition, they had partially stocked the larder.

These guys really wanted a job, and he guessed if times were lean, then he was happy to help out. Plus, he always planned to try and create employment for the local people.

He was going to task Yuri with doing a background check on them, but so far, Nikolay had already shown him his degree, and he noted he had passed with honors, so the kid had plenty upstairs. Besides, how much could they find out about the others if they didn't even own computers or have records online anywhere?

The six of them chatted for hours, getting to know each other. They talked about their backgrounds, their lives, and their desires. Yuri was right, in that they were all Yakuts, an ancient local people who had populated this area since the 7th century. As Marcus suspected, the Yakuts had Mongolian heritage and today they were still largely hunters, cattle herders, and fishermen. But they were also intelligent, fierce, and tough.

Marcus liked all of them, and in turn, he told them of his plans and hopes for the fish farm.

Leonid took his wooden pipe from his mouth. "And you hope to breed the fish, and sell their eggs, the Beluga caviar? In five years?"

"Yes and no." Marcus held his arms wide. "The Beluga sturgeon produce millions of eggs, and large individuals have been known to carry several hundred pounds of caviar. It's true that the Beluga sturgeon caviar can be worth as much as U.S. $3,500 a pound, but the problem is, it's in such demand that the Beluga are vanishing."

"I think you will do it," Pavel said. "Our people sad and happy when mill closed. Sad because we lost work, but happy it go, as it was making the water unclean."

The other men nodded, and Pavel held up a fist. "But this is good, so we will help you be success."

The others agreed, and Yuri poured a round of vodka. He lifted his glass. "To your success."

"To success," Dmitry said. "And to keeping you safe."

The men drank and Marcus sipped and then lowered his glass. "Safe?"

The men fell silent, and Dmitry looked down at the ground. 'I mean, happy."

"Safe from what?" Marcus pressed.

The Yakut Russian muttered something but didn't look up.

Marcus exhaled and put his drink down. "Okay, guys, what am I missing here?"

Dmitry finally looked up, his brow creased as though struggling to choose his words. "There are people, bad people, who… can make things, hard, for new businesses."

Marcus stared for a moment until the light went on in his head. "Oh, I see; you mean like the local mafia?"

"They are called *bratva*." Yuri grunted dismissively as his mouth turned down. He faced Dmitry. "They operate even out here?"

"They operate where they want to operate," Dmitry said. "They usually just want *arenda*, rent. To keep things all good."

Marcus groaned. "Protection money."

The men nodded solemnly.

"Just great." Marcus sighed and held his glass out to Yuri who splashed some more vodka in it.

Yuri refilled his own glass. "You make a cake, there is always someone who wants a slice."

"For free," Marcus added. He sighed; he'd heard of them, and knew how despicable and unrelenting they could be.

Thinking of them made his mind turn to his only relative, his older brother, Carter. Marcus stared at his cup as his vision was turned inward. Carter was the proverbial black sheep of the family. He'd done a tour of Afghanistan in the Special Forces. He never spoke about it, but he came back a little screwy. Then one night he ended up hurting two guys real bad in a bar fight. One of them was connected to the police chief, and Carter ended up doing time.

When he got out, he just withdrew, from everything, and now he ran a small bar somewhere in the Midwest. But that wasn't the whole story. The thing was, Carter was dating Sara before Marcus was. They both loved her, but Carter was gone so long, and one thing led to another, and the next thing he knew, it was him dating her and then eventually won her hand.

Marcus felt like shit and felt he also deserved a beating. But the worst aspect was his brother never complained. He seemed to realize he could never be there for Sara like Marcus could and just wanted her to be happy—both of them to be happy, and he was glad they had found each other.

And that made Marcus feel like the asshole from hell, which caused an eternal awkwardness between all three of them. To this day, he never knew if his relationship with Sara was the real reason Carter vanished.

Marcus sighed and leaned back. Thing was, he could have used his brother's help now as he knew some parts of Russia were still like the Wild West, and Carter was a fearsome individual, having the skills to back it up.

He shifted in his seat; maybe he could think of a way to employ him and also some of his old team buddies for security.

As he mulled over the logistics, he raised his own red flags; the problem with Carter was that he was like an elemental force. Sometimes you pointed him at a problem and he could obliterate it, or he could make it worse. He was just as smart as Marcus was, but tended to solve things with his fists rather than his head.

Marcus sucked in a deep breath and lifted his head, sighting on Dmitry. "Anything else?" he asked.

Leonid bobbed his head for a moment.

"Okay, what?" Marcus sat forward.

"The lights," Leonid said softly out of one side of his mouth while holding his pipe in the other.

"Lights?" Marcus' brows rose.

"The lights," Leonid repeated. "Under the water."

"Submarines? Divers?" Yuri asked.

"I don't think there are any submarines working the lake anymore." Marcus had done his research on the lake. "There was a team of scientists in 2008 or maybe 2009 who tried to reach the lake bottom in a pair of mini-subs, and stayed down for five hours, half of that the descent and return. But they didn't make it; didn't get deep enough. They never tried again."

"Something frightened them down there?" Leonid nodded.

"No, I think it just wasn't enough preparation," Marcus replied.

"They fell short by about 500 feet," added Nikolay.

Marcus sat back. "No one down there now; not that I know of."

"I don't think these are submarine or diver's lights," Leonid said. "My father told me he had seen them himself when he was a boy. One night, when it was very dark and he was out late on the lake fishing with my grandfather. He said that down deep, there was something glowing, green… and moving. Submarines not here then."

Yuri tilted his head as he turned to Marcus. "What about those fish with lights on their head. Is deep and dark enough down there."

"No, there's no bioluminescent fish in Baikal's depths that I know of," Marcus replied. "In fact, it's something that has puzzled scientists for years—why exactly bioluminescence hasn't evolved in freshwater."

"Because the ocean is far older," Nikolay added. "This specialty must take a long time to evolve."

"I think so too," Marcus said, impressed with the young man. "And good answer."

"So, no sub, no diver, no fish with lights on their head." Yuri bobbed his head. "Then can only have been one thing."

Everyone turned to him, and Yuri began to grin slowly as he lifted the vodka bottle and shook it. Marcus chuckled, but no one else did.

"My father was sober," Leonid said levelly. "He never drank while he fished."

"I have heard the stories too," Pavel added. "About the lights, and the people not coming back. But I think mainly when ice is gone. Perhaps sometimes the ice traps… them."

"*Them*?" Marcus was becoming a little exasperated. "Has anyone here seen the lights? I mean personally. When they were out on the water or even from the land?"

Leonid looked up. "No one goes out fishing on the darkest nights. Maybe no one *wants* to see them."

"Well, I'm sure there are boats out there on those darkest nights. If you're not out there, you just don't see them," Marcus replied.

"I don't think so," Leonid said. "Even the seals stay out of the water. And sometimes the colonies move off their rock perches to travel into the forest for a few days."

"There are bears and wolves in the forest." Yuri frowned. "That's stupid."

"Perhaps they think this is less of a threat than what is in the water on those nights." Leonid lifted his chin. "They know more than us."

"Good grief." Marcus ran both hands up through his hair, before fronting the men again. "There is nothing that can't be explained by science... eventually."

Leonid waggled a finger at him. "Not these legends."

"Legends; we all have them," Yuri added softly.

"You know about this?" Marcus asked his manager. "Tell me everything."

Yuri opened his arms wide. "People go missing." He leaned forward. "They used to call this place the haunted mill." He threw his head back and laughed. "But, of course, just superstitious people in Soviet-era times."

"But not now, huh?" Marcus saw that none of the Yakut Russians agreed with him. "Look, the water is freezing here, plus there's snags, and the lake is so big that it has tides and currents. Anyone falls into it, especially at night, then they have about 30 seconds to get out, or..." Marcus shrugged. "They go missing."

"Except people go missing when walking along the shoreline. Not canoeing, not swimming, or even fishing." Nikolay leaned forward. "Mr. Stenson, did you know that just a few years after the mill commenced operation, everyone vanished?" He nodded slowly. "*Everyone*; the workers, the managers, even the boat owners."

Marcus groaned. "Yes, I read about that. They were having problems, industrial, and the story goes they all just walked off the job."

Nikolay slowly shook his head. "That was just for the public. They never got home. They vanished. I think they never even tried to get home. Or they tried but couldn't."

Marcus sighed. "I see."

He knew all large bodies of water had their secrets, and most were promulgated by superstitious locals, or for the benefit of gullible tourists. There were the lake monsters, the fish men, the things that rose from the stygian depths on a full moon, no moon, or half-moon, and even of the things that couldn't be seen at all, that just left tracks behind.

"The lake knows; it has memory." Leonid kept his eyes on the fire.

"*Ozero pomnit*," Pavel intoned softly.

"The lake remembers." Leonid's brows came together. "What does that mean?"

No one answered.

Marcus sighed and got to his feet. "On that note, gentlemen, I'm turning in. We can all talk more tomorrow. Goodnight."

Marcus headed for the main house and climbed the few steps to the front veranda. It was a large wooden two-story cottage, and on the top step, he turned and looked out over the frozen lake. Out here, there was little background light save from the stars and the current crescent-shaped moon. Right now, it looked like an endless plain of frozen ink.

Marcus let his eyes travel slowly over its surface for many minutes. As he expected, there was nothing out there.

He pushed open the front door and stepped inside. He had a lot of work to do, and he wasn't going to let ridiculous old village stories about the local bogeyman get in his way.

"Tomorrow's another day," he said and kicked the door shut behind him.

CHAPTER 05

The Mill House Compound, Lake Baikal—first morning

Marcus woke just on dawn to a silence that was so unnerving it felt unnatural. He lay there, just staring up at the ceiling. Back home at Madeira Beach, there would have been gulls greeting the approaching sunrise, the sound of surf breaking on golden sand, and if he was lucky, maybe Sara up and about already making coffee.

But by the lake, it was like the inside of a tomb. He blinked a few times and felt the cold on his nose. The house wasn't properly heated yet, and he dragged back the covers and threw his legs over the side of the bed.

"Oof." He lifted his feet back off the ground and wished he could crawl back under the covers. Even better, crawl back under them with Sara; he missed her terribly already. He had tried to call again last night but had no phone reception as the signal had vanished once again. It was a weird feature of the area that whited-out radio, satellite, and probably even smoke signals.

He placed his feet carefully on the floor again, stood, and padded to the window that looked out over the lake—it was like an iron-grey desert that was as calm and serene as a sheet of dirty glass. Small wisps of cold vapor hung over it, and from here, it was easy to see why early explorers had thought that when it was thawed, it was a sea, as there was no shoreline visible on the other side. Marcus thought it was as vast and endless as any ocean he'd ever been on.

As he watched he saw two men—Pavel and his son Nikolay, he suspected—moving across the grounds, gathering firewood. Both had hoods up over their heads and their breath steamed like a pair of racehorses in the still air.

Marcus' vision turned inward as he tried to think through the enormous amount of tasks he needed to accomplish, and now that he was here, it was time to expand and prioritize them. The cleanup, renovation, and lab setup were a priority—he needed his facilities to be in top shape before the Federal Agency for Fisheries and Conservation released the fish. And before they did that, they'd want to pay him a visit.

He kept thinking he had this deal won, but there were several hurdles along the way, and if he stumbled on any one of them, the entire project could be delayed, penalized, or even canceled. He doubted very much there'd be any compensation for funds expended if that happened.

"Not much riding on that." He snorted. "Just, everything."

From one end of the mill compound, he heard chopping wood, and as he doubted it was Yuri, he bet it was another of the local Russians. He decided to offer the men ongoing employment—perhaps a three-month probation to really feel them out to begin with.

After all, he could certainly use them, and even after just a few hours, he felt they were trustworthy and quite likeable, even though a little superstitious.

Besides, he could throw them straight into the rebuild jobs from today. Yuri could organize further professional tradespeople for the more complex work as and when they needed them. He'd also need to bring in specialists for the lab setup... another thing on his "urgent" list.

Marcus blinked crusty eyes, urging himself to get on with the day, so he crossed back to his bed where there was a dish of water and a small towel waiting for him. He stood looking down into it for several seconds, before finally dipping his fingers in, scooping up a double handful of freezing water and splashing it on his face—it was as cold as he expected and it quickly jolted him into full wakefulness. He dried his face, feeling refreshed, but still couldn't bring himself to wash his body with the water, and instead just dragged on a thick pullover.

Marcus jogged down the steps to the front hall, whistling, and pulled open the door to be immediately assailed with wood smoke, biting morning air, and the sound of branches being broken up for a fire.

He stepped out onto the wooden porch and tugged his collar up a little higher. In the early morning light, he looked over the grounds. The mill house compound gardens had withered away to spindly dead trees, grasses like hay, and everything else covered over in snow. But he was sure that Yuri could source some fruit trees, and as his wife wasn't arriving until late spring, their blossoms might even be out in time to add some color and perfume to the air.

Then came the butterflies and birds—*our Russian Garden of Eden*, he thought and smiled again. Sara would love it. If there was wildlife, then Sara the nature lover was at home.

Marcus paused to smile at a memory. He remembered when she found a small green bird that had stunned itself after hitting one of their windows back home. She opened her cupped hands and it sat there, looking at each of them, and then it simply nestled down as though content in her warm, safe hands. *She was nature's friend, all right*, he thought.

He saw there must have been more snow overnight as everything had a layer of gleaming white powder. Further down, he could see trenches, ankle-deep, that had been pressed into the snow by the Russians going to and fro on their morning tasks.

He squinted down at the snow right in front of his house—there were more tracks, but weird ones that he didn't recognize at all.

Marcus stepped down a few of the front steps and saw that they came right up to the landing where he stood now. He wasn't much of an outdoorsman but they sure looked like nothing he'd ever seen before. They were about two to three feet apart, and in twin lines, as though the legs on each side of the creature were spread wide. And they must have been sharply pointed, making him think they were more like those of an insect or crustacean than a land mammal.

Marcus tried to think what it could be but knew classification was always going to elude him. He scratched his chin. *Tiny hooves or paws on skinny legs*, he wondered. *Or maybe something like a stork*, which he immediately rejected, as it was the wrong time of year.

He didn't mind the wildlife venturing into their compound, as long as it wasn't bears, wolves, or something he couldn't verify as being non-dangerous. He gave up trying to work it out and made a mental note to ask Yuri about it later.

Smoke billowed across the open compound and he could see the big Russian placing a grill over the open fire, edging a metal pot of coffee onto its center. They'd brought some stores with them and for now had plenty of eggs, bacon, and some bread for toast, and he was looking forward to a hearty breakfast.

Yuri had also brought a tank of diesel fuel for the generator, and one of his tasks was to get the thing up and running so they had power. If the generator worked, he'd still order a backup one. If not, he'd have to order two—it was already built into the budget, and it was something that was an absolute necessity. If he was to have a viable and reliable laboratory, the one thing he couldn't abide from a risk-management perspective was the power going out—if it did, then all his samples, eggs, sprats, and anything else he needed to keep at a controlled and constant temperature would be destroyed.

He headed toward the fire and Yuri looked up and grinned.

"*Dobroye utro.*"

"Same to you, big guy," Marcus replied.

Yuri pushed more logs into the fire, causing the pot to quickly boil, filling the air with the delicious smell of dark, strong Russian coffee.

He hoped Yuri would wait until the flames died down a bit before trying to cook anything with the cast iron skillet, but coffee was always the first order of business.

The smell also attracted the other men, and from around the grounds, Dmitry, Pavel, and his son Nikolay, plus Leonid, waved and approached.

With a coffee each, they sat around the fire, and Marcus proceeded to hand out the day's jobs—Yuri would check the generator, the men would see what work needed to be done to the cabins, and Leonid would be tasked with clearing more of the mill house compound's grounds.

In another 10 minutes, Yuri was pushing the steel pans onto the fire, cracking eggs and nudging bacon around the pan in speckled duck fat. Marcus didn't know if it was the bracing air or not, but the smell was intoxicating and made his mouth water.

Bread was poked onto sticks and held close to the fire to toast, and Dmitry pulled out a large jar of amber honey that he had collected himself in the summer from a local hive. In it floated honeycomb, twigs, and what looked like the remains of bees that had been a little too slow to escape his collecting prowess.

Breakfast went on longer than expected, and Marcus found he really liked the group of men who would be working with him. All seemed to have experience, a sense of humor, plus good connections with the local Yakut community—valuable, as he needed to be on good terms with all his neighbors.

One thing Marcus had wanted to do while the weather was still with them was walk to the prominent rocky hills a few miles further up the coast. He planned on scaling it and getting a bird's eye view of the lake, and maybe conclude some options for pen sites—what he'd be looking for was somewhere close in and sheltered. Then he and Yuri could take to the ice, cut into it, and verify the depth with cameras and aqua-topology mapping.

In another 20 minutes, breakfast was finally over, tasks set for his team, and so Marcus loaded up a pack and prepared to set off. Yuri stopped him.

"Please, let me come with you." He bobbed his head and lifted his coat, showing the revolver on his hip. "Bears."

"Thanks, but I'll be fine. Besides, priority one is to get our generator working... and that's on you, mister." He went to turn away, but felt the big Russian's hand alight on his shoulder.

"Then take one of the men, please, Marcus."

There was real concern on Yuri's face and that worried him enough to give him pause. "Bears, *huh*?"

He sighed, thinking a local guide wouldn't hurt. He turned to see Pavel's son Nikolay sliding another pot of coffee onto the grill over the still-hot coals. Given that he planned to have the young guy as his trainee lab tech, an enormously important role, it wouldn't hurt to conduct a more intensive interview.

"Nikolay, are you up for a bit of hiking today?"

The young man nodded enthusiastically. "Sure, I love hiking. When?"

"Now," Marcus replied. "To the high cliffs up along the coast."

"I know them." Nikolay held up a finger. "One moment."

He scurried off, probably to inform his father and grab his own pack. In a few minutes, he returned with a loaded backpack that he opened.

"I have biscuits, dried meat, and an extra bottle of water for us." He grinned.

"Well done." Marcus also noticed he now had a 10-inch hunting knife on his belt. Maybe that bit about bears from Yuri wasn't just an attempt to give him pause for concern.

Marcus checked his watch—it was just coming up to 8 am. He waved to Yuri. "Back mid-afternoon. If not back by nightfall, send a search party." He grinned, but Yuri just looked grave.

"Have good luck." Yuri finally waved and continued to watch the pair depart all the way out of the compound.

CHAPTER 06

Marcus and Nikolay had been trekking for about four hours when Marcus called a halt to take a drink from his canteen. Even at midday, it was still only about 10 degrees, which was extremely mild for this time of year, but the cold sucked the moisture from the air, so dehydration quickly became a problem.

He gulped his water, trying hard not to take too much as he was mindful of the long, dry trek back. Added to that, the brisk pace had warmed him up to the point of feeling slick under the arms and on his lower back.

The countryside wasn't too rugged and fairly flat as they went along the coastline. But then they needed to turn inland where the land rose toward the high stone edifice that would give him the vantage point he was looking for. It was just under a mile or so ahead, but already they could see the large up-folding of the Earth's crust.

They pressed on, as Marcus wanted to be there with plenty of time to look around, and then be back at the mill before sundown.

It was another full hour before they came to the start of the mini mountain. It rose from the landscape like the snout of a massive stone whale breaching the surface of the land. The climb would be fairly easy, and only in some places Marcus thought they might need to do some actual rock scaling.

Nikolay set off first and even though Marcus was only in his mid-30s, the younger man made him feel like a geriatric with the way the kid leaped and bounded up the steep incline.

In life, Marcus tried to stay fit, but after just 20 minutes, he was puffing and was exhausted. He climbed another large rock and found Nikolay waiting for him.

"Caves," he whispered while pointing. But then put a finger to his lips. "Quiet, maybe bear."

"*Shit*," Marcus replied softly. Looks like Yuri might have been right— Russia was home to some big-ass bears, with the Kamchatka brown bear growing to nine feet tall and weighing as much as a grizzly. He suddenly wished he accepted Yuri's offer of a gun.

Marcus reached into his pocket and pulled out his only weapon—a black Swiss army knife he'd had since he was a teenager that even had his name written on the side. He and his brother were given one each by their dad. He pulled the three-inch blade out and waited.

Nikolay eased along toward the cave and quickly looked in and pulled back. He waited for a second or two and then peered in again, staying there this time, and only later Marcus found out he was actually sniffing and not looking. He finally turned.

"I think okay."

Marcus came closer and also peeked in—he then drew a small flashlight from a pouch pocket and shined it into the cave, still gripping his small blade, hard. It was fairly small and shallow, with the remains of plenty of plant debris littering its floor so it could have been used at some time in the past as a nest or den.

"Come on," he said to Nikolay as he folded the knife away. "We've still got a ways to go."

Marcus looked up and saw that there was a lot more climbing of the rocky face yet. The outcrop was mostly a solid piece of granite, but there were huge slabs that had been broken off in the past laying like decks of cards up against the cliff's face.

They came to one particularly large slab lying on a flat area of the small mountain. It didn't look all that passable, and Marcus thought they might need to backtrack and see if there was another way up.

"I'll check it," Nikolay said.

"Good idea." Marcus stepped back.

"Up, please." Nikolay lifted a foot.

Marcus meshed his fingers and allowed the young man to step into them. He lifted and Nikolay launched himself to spring higher. He began to climb as Marcus stepped back and shielded his eyes. As he scrambled higher, he dislodged a loaf of bread-sized rock. Marcus stepped out of the way, but on its bouncing way down, it struck a larger boulder that also began to roll out, that in turn finally pounded into one of the huge slabs laying up against the cliff face in front of Marcus.

The slab was rocked backward and hung perfectly upright for about two seconds, before falling back in slow motion.

Marcus dived out of the way as the huge rock thumped down, making the ground shake beneath him. Snow clouds roiled around him.

"Mr. Stenson?" Nikolay scrambled down. "Mr. Stenson, are you okay?"

Marcus sat up and spat dirty snow and grit. "Yeah, yeah, I'm fine." He got to his feet as Nikolay leaped down and ran to help him up.

"Just glad I wasn't standing any closer. Or else I'd be a human pancake right now." Marcus dusted himself down.

Nikolay wandered closer to the rock face. "I think we just found another cave."

Marcus turned. "What?" He followed him, and as the snow-dust now settled, he saw there was a cave exposed that had been hidden behind the huge slab of stone.

"I think is old," Nikolay said, craning forward. "Was sealed, so no bears."

Marcus looked at the broken slab. The exposed edges were discolored and were now fairly smoothed, meaning it had been exposed to the elements for tens of thousands of years. And by the amount of degradation to the edges of the super-hard rock, Marcus guessed maybe a lot more.

"Hidden for at least 50,000 years old, possibly 100,000, or maybe even more." Marcus lifted his light. He'd done a bit of caving in his youth, and though this was not why they came, a brand new cave was too hard to resist. "Just a quick look." He ducked inside.

The dust motes floated in the glowing pipe of his light beam, but further in, the air was still and settled. The cave was deeper than he expected, probably six feet to the roof, and about 10 feet wide in some places.

Nikolay walked along one wall, and Marcus the other, sweeping his beam back and forth. Up ahead was an alcove, and he crouched before it. It led onto another cave, but this one much shallower.

"Bones," he said.

"People," Nikolay said in a hushed tone.

"They once were," Marcus agreed.

Inside were the remains of several bodies, and by the look of the bone discoloration, they looked very old. Marcus eased in and lifted one of the brown skulls. It was small, but didn't have the heavy brow ridge and receding jaw of the Neanderthal, and looked more modern shaped.

The skeletons were all tangled or on top of one another, as if they had been all huddled together.

"I think they must have been trapped by the rockslide," Nikolay said.

Marcus nodded. "The poor guys; all of them were locked in and could do nothing but wait to die."

Marcus cast his beam around, noting the remains of animal hides, tools, and even some shining items that might have been crude jewellery. "All their worldly treasures," he whispered.

He'd report it when he got back, as it'd be a treasure trove to local archaeologists. As Marcus eased back out, Nikolay was shining his own light on the far wall.

"They painted."

Marcus lifted his light and then joined him. The wall here was flat, twenty feet long, and covered in cave art that had been protected from the elements for however long the cave had been sealed off.

The picture colors were ochre, brown, red, yellow, and charcoal black, and the skill and artistry was magnificent. He could easily pick out deer, bear, wolves, and many animals that were now long-extinct like mammoth, giant bison, and even something that looked like a massive bird.

There were also the handprints, some small, some adult-sized, and anthropologists believed these were like signatures, a form of: "*I was here,*" or "*I did this,*" statement.

Marcus held up a hand close to one of the largest of them; his own hand was so much bigger than the race of people who had done the work. He then moved his light further along to where some of the paintings seemed to have been overwritten.

Here, there was a single set of images—the dark sky, with a moon, and a long ochre yellow streak. In the next was the lake, and then something striking it, followed by what had to be a depiction of a huge wave.

"Did they see something?" Marcus pointed. "Something hitting the lake?" He could be wrong, but that's what it sure as hell looked like they had been depicting.

Marcus lifted his phone and took a few pictures. If anything, the artist had done a fairly good job of rendering landmarks, so if he got to his lookout spot atop the peak, he might just be able to see exactly where this event occurred.

He turned to Nikolay. "What do you think?"

The young Russian shrugged. "Maybe it was the last thing they saw. Maybe the wave or aftershock was what collapsed their cave and sealed them in."

Marcus turned back to the picture and then faced back toward the small alcove that housed all the bodies. "Yeah." He hadn't thought of that, but it seemed very plausible. Maybe the group had even drawn the images by burning torch, as a way to tell whoever came after them that this is what happened. "Well, we'll leave it all to the scientists. They'll have a field day with this."

"I think there's more paintings." Nikolay pointed to the depths of the cave.

Marcus checked his watch and saw that it was already two in the afternoon, and they still hadn't even got to the top yet.

"Maybe we can check them out later, or come back another time. Come on, we need to get moving."

The rest of the climb was just as arduous, but in another 45 minutes, the pair clambered up on a shelf of stone that was the highest point on the small mountain with a view across the frozen lake.

There was a natural stone seat and both men sat and looked out at the vast inland sea that was Lake Baikal. Marcus could trace the coastline, north and south, but to the east, there was nothing but frozen water for as far as he could see.

"The sea, once it casts its spell, holds one in its net of wonder forever." Marcus smiled and turned. "Jacques Cousteau."

"I know of him." Nikolay nodded. "Did you know he came to explore the lake in 1997. A great adventurer, yes?"

"Yes, a great man of the sea." Marcus pulled out his phone and looked at the pictures. The drawing by the cave people was raw and faded, but holding it up and looking from it to the actual landscape, he saw a similarity to the landmarks up and down the shoreline.

Up north, there was another rocky headland, and in the far distance yet another plug of stone, and in front of it a vast expanse of frozen water—exactly like in the image. It was a weird feeling to think that the people who had been trapped in the cave below may have stood on this very spot perhaps 100,000 years ago, looking out at the same vista as he did now.

Marcus lifted his gaze to the sky and tried to visualize seeing whatever it was come down and strike the water. *Would it have made a sound? A screaming, a whistle, or a booming like distant thunder?* he wondered.

He would have been scared shitless, and he couldn't imagine what the primitive humans would have felt. He turned back to the ice sheets.

"I think whatever came down is still in there," Nikolay said and turned to him. "Maybe buried down deep on the lake bottom."

"Probably nothing but a big ugly chunk of stone. Hey, maybe it was magnetic as well; that's why electronic communications are so screwy around here." Marcus stood up and walked closer to the rock ledge. He quickly looked at the images and at the one depicting the huge wave—if this was their vantage point, then the wave looked to be a good 100 feet high and would have been absolutely terrifying. He grunted. "A very, very big ugly chunk of stone."

They stayed for another half hour, and Marcus took around 50 more pictures. There were a few sites that he thought looked ideal for pens—in fairly close to the shoreline, but out far enough where he suspected the water would be clean and deep.

The shoreline wasn't flat, and in some places was a sheer cliff face, which was perfect—they didn't expect to have too many visitors or campers, but that was today. If the lease ran for 99 years, he didn't want some time in the future for it to be accessible so they needed to worry about contamination from settlers or campers from the shoreline.

Marcus felt the trip had been well worth the exertion, and he promised himself he'd bring Sara back here in the summer. He got to his feet, stumbling for a moment on some loose scree.

"Damn." His flashlight fell free, and Nikolay grabbed it before it rolled off the cliff edge.

The young Russian handed it back. "Time to go?" His eyebrows were up.

"Thanks." Marcus stuck the light back in a pouch pocket. "Yep, we've seen enough for now. We've got a long trek and let's hope we make it by dinnertime."

Nikolay headed off and Marcus went to follow but paused for a moment. He looked back out over the near-endless lake. *No deep lights today*, he thought.

As a man of science, he didn't believe in fairytales, myths, or legends. But he certainly could get how a land as remote and ancient as this one could have so many working their way into the local villager's history.

Nothing to fear, but fear itself, he thought and turned away to follow the young Russian down the side of the rocky outcrop.

*****

On the ground tucked in beside the stone where both men had sat to enjoy the view, sat Marcus' black Swiss army knife. Now, another lost relic in a place lost in time.

CHAPTER 07

The Mill House, Lake Baikal—2 months later

Marcus carefully put the paintbrush down, wiped his hands on a rag, and stood back to admire his work. He'd been touching up some of the woodwork, picking out the skirting boards and door panels with a light blue color that he knew Sara loved. The basic walls inside were done in an off-white, and he had also managed to buy plenty of good solid antique furniture to populate the house.

"*Hm-hmm.*" He nodded, really liking how it was all coming together.

The other smaller cabin-type houses had been repaired and upgraded, and he had both a primary generator and backup one with an auto-transfer switch should the first shut down for any reason. The grounds were growing in nicely as the weather warmed up a few degrees, and their crowning glory was the mill house.

He hummed as he glanced around the room. There were two homes Sara would be spending a lot of time in, and they needed to be in top shape—this one, her home-home, and the laboratory.

The huge building had been totally gutted and was now immaculate inside and out, had full power, and was divided by shatterproof glass into several rooms, comprising of laboratories, hatchery, bio-study, plus workshops and a loading dock—from both land and water.

Though they'd had battalions of tradespeople onsite, it had been Yuri and the local Yakut Russian guys that had worked themselves to near exhaustion.

It was just three weeks until Sara arrived, and he felt he was not only working to his schedule, but he dared to believe he might be even just ahead of it.

Marcus unnecessarily dabbed his brush at the freshly painted wood. There were a few major things still to come in the next few weeks, and that was the adult Beluga sturgeon, plus 200 pounds of fertilized eggs, as well as, and most importantly, a visit from the ministry officials to check if he and his operation was ready. He was confident that he should pass that test easily so there should be nothing standing in his way.

From outside, he heard an SUV pull up and guessed it was more deliveries that one of the guys had ordered. The car's horn tooted, long and loud.

"Done and done." He balled the rag and tossed it onto the sheet that held his tins of paint and brushes, and stood, turning slowly and admiring all the work. He grinned. Sara would love it, and he had just left enough unfinished so she could stamp her own final touches to it.

"Joint effort," he announced to the empty room.

His reverie was broken as the car horn sounded again, longer and more insistent. He looked over his shoulder.

"Come on, guys, someone get that."

Marcus shook his head and muttered as the horn blared again.

"Oh for fuck's sake."

He bounded down the steps and pulled open the door. There was a single SUV pulled up, big and new. Four hulking men lounged around it, with another, smaller and better-dressed guy standing in front of the car.

Yuri, Pavel, Nikolay, Dmitry, and Leonid all stood in a line as though waiting for inspection from the headmaster. Marcus looked to Yuri, who shot him a glance that could have been a warning. Marcus was immediately on guard.

"Can I help you?" he asked.

"Mr. Marcus Stenson?" The snappy dresser grinned wide, showing a pair of stained front teeth, obviously trying to impart friendliness, but he just came across like a sharp-suited barracuda. He stuck out a hand.

In turn, Marcus pretended not to notice and jammed his in his pockets. "Like I said, can I help you?"

The man nodded as he dropped his hand. He looked over the grounds. "You have done good work here. No one ever expected this old place would ever be anything but a roost for owls, and maybe home to a few bears."

He grinned wider, displaying a brilliant gold side-tooth. "But now, it is almost ready, and as soon as your fish and eggs arrive..." He paused to grin again, and maybe to study Marcus' face at his insightful delivery before going on. "... then this business will be booming, yes?"

"We've still got a lot of work to do, Mr....?" Marcus lifted his chin.

"Ah, of course, I am so rude. Introductions..." He half-turned to point toward his huge and leering colleagues.

"Mr. Drago, Mr. Volodin, and the big ugly ones are Borya and Egor Orlov... they are twins, but not so alike, yes?" He touched his chest and bowed slightly. "And I am Arkady Tushino, manager and emissary of Mr. Gennardy Zyuganov, the local area director of... *business*."

"Director, *huh*?" Marcus snorted. "Of the bratva."

"No, no, no." Tushino maintained his grin. "We are professional people who provide services to many businesses—guaranteed product delivery, laborers, and of course, security." He looked from under his brow. "You know there is a lot of bad people around, and we can ensure they never bother you."

Marcus chuckled. "You don't say?"

"Yes, is true." Tushino seemed to miss the sarcasm.

"You know, I think we'll be okay for now." Marcus walked forward. "But if you leave a card and I think of anything, I'll call, okay?"

Tushino's smile fell away, as he seemed a little surprised. He then waved an arm around at the compound.

"This place used to be paper mill. Made water very dirty a few years ago. I hear some of those chemicals may still be around. May still even find their way back into the lake. That would be very bad." Tushino turned to fix cold dead eyes on Marcus. "If that happened, it would kill everything; every fish, every seal, everything alive." He smirked. "And I think then it would kill your business."

There it is, Marcus thought. He lifted his chin. "Listen, buddy. I'm running on fumes and I won't make any money out of this place for five years. Come back then." He began to turn away.

Tushino didn't budge. "I think you won't be here in five years. Maybe not even five months."

Marcus stopped and slowly turned back. The Russian tilted his head.

"You are not from around here, Mr. Stenson." Tushino drew in a deep breath and his chest swelled, his lips turning down. "Foreigners do not get much help from the local police. Sometimes crimes do not even get reported. And without security, you risk everything." His grin returned. "When did you say your pretty wife was arriving?"

Marcus' jaw clenched and he squared his shoulders. Yuri also straightened, but so did Tushino's goons. The tension suddenly became so heavy it was like a living thing.

Finally, Yuri broke the spell, by belly laughing and clapping his hands. Only Tushino and Marcus continued to glare at each other.

"So, we will think over your suggestions, okay?" Yuri rubbed big hands together. "Some very good ideas, thank you." He shook each of the mafia men's hands. "Thank you, thank you." He began to turn Tushino away. "Thank you for coming." He guided him back to his car, holding onto his arm. "We will let you know. Don't worry. Leave with me, we work something out."

Tushino and his men climbed back into their SUV, and the man's window glided down so he could lean out. He looked past Yuri.

"Mr. Stenson, you do a lot of hard work here. *Lot* of work. Don't waste it." He grinned. "We hear from you… soon." He pulled his head back, and his grin was gone and in his flat stare, a warning.

As the car left, his team visibly relaxed, and Marcus exhaled. Yuri came and raised his eyebrow.

"Thanks. Was going to get ugly, *huh*?" Marcus asked.

Yuri bobbed his head. "Maybe not this time."

"So, what do we do? Do you believe him when he said that the police might ignore any crime out here?" Marcus hated to hear the worst.

Yuri hiked his shoulders. "Some people pay the bratva, and some people get paid off by the bratva. I wouldn't like to see whose side the police took if there was a crime committed out here and it was reported... by a foreigner."

"Well, that's just great." Marcus sat down on an old tree stump that might have been lopped down a hundred years ago and was now weathered and grey. "What do they want, *ah*, I mean, how much would they want?"

"Want?" Yuri went and grabbed an old wooden chair that had been beside the fire pit and sat down heavily. "Here is problem." He opened his hands wide. "To them, all Americans are rich, so..."

"Yeah, from Hollywood, right?" Marcus scoffed. "So they're going to ask for a lot." He sighed. "We haven't budgeted for any of this. We'll end up broke before we even turn a dime, or rouble." He rubbed both hands up through his short, blond hair. "*Shit*."

Yuri held up a hand. "I will meet with them, and I will explain how things are. Maybe I can negotiate a very small payment, perhaps monthly. Hopefully, that only starts in a few years, when you are making some money."

"And if we don't pay?" Marcus sat forward. "I'd rather hire extra security than give in to these assholes."

Yuri bobbed his head for a moment. "These are serious people. If he says your fish might get poisoned, I believe him. Or maybe house burned down, or mill, or the boats." He looked into Marcus' eyes. "Or someone gets hurt. *Very* hurt."

Marcus waved over his team who were talking amongst themselves. "Pavel, Nikolay, Leonid, Dmitry, what do you think? Please speak freely. Have you seen these people before?"

The four talked again amongst themselves for a few rapid seconds, before Nikolay turned to face him.

"Not these men, but there are bratva even in Listvyanka. Also many who work for bratva are there who will inform for them. Nothing goes on without them knowing."

Marcus snorted. "They want payment, protection money we call it. It's a rip-off."

Nikolay nodded. "Yes, but everyone pays."

"And I'll ask again; what if you don't?" Marcus asked.

Nikolay turned to talk to his father in soft Russian for a moment, and Pavel pulled at his chin as he listened. He responded slowly and Nikolay nodded and then faced Marcus. "My father says there was a man in the town, a shopkeeper, who said he couldn't afford to pay. Then his shop burned down. With shopkeeper in it." He smiled ruefully. "So now everyone pays."

"Kill a chicken to scare a monkey—and everyone else gets the message." Marcus exhaled. "Okay, Yuri, meet with them, and find out what's the absolute least we can get away with. And I mean, the rock-freaking-bottom."

CHAPTER 08

Listvyanka—Proshly Vek Bar

Yuri Revkin drove into the town and pulled up at the end of the single long street. He sat for a while in the cabin with the engine off, and felt like he had a small sack of sand in his gut. He wasn't feeling confident.

He was due to meet Arkady Tushino as Marcus Stenson's emissary to discuss their future relationship. But he knew the bratva, and they were no benign business partners. In fact, they had no qualms about bleeding a business dry until it, and its owners, were nothing but lifeless husks. After all, there were always more businesses to feed off.

Yuri's objective was to convince them to be patient, and maybe secure a smaller but longer-term payment system. Then as the business got on its feet, they could pay a little more.

To begin with, he'd off them 30,000 roubles per month, which was about 400 U.S., and a little less than the average monthly wage. *Not bad for doing nothing*, he thought. He'd also be prepared to negotiate up to 500 dollars per month as a fallback if need be.

Yuri reached down beside his hip and felt the butt of his gun. He left his hand there for a moment, and then exhaled slowly as he unclipped the holster from his belt and stuck it in the truck's map compartment—the bratva would have guns, more of them than him, and probably be better shots. He liked Marcus Stenson, but wasn't yet ready to die for him. So there was no use trying to provoke something that he could never win.

Yuri wasn't a particularly religious person, but he always prayed to anyone who was listening when he thought he needed some divine help. He inhaled deeply, and then blew air through his lips with a growl.

"You can do this," he said into the rear-view mirror, and then elbowed open his door and headed for the bar.

The men he would meet weren't from this village, but were just doing their monthly sweep through all the local villages, collecting payments. They were just bagmen, and local warlords.

The big boss would be situated in Moscow and have political connections all the way to the top of business and government. The bratva had been around for hundreds of years and would be around for hundreds more. The upside was they weren't dumb, and very quickly spotted good business opportunities. Yuri was hoping what he presented was exactly that—an easy way for them to make ongoing money by doing very little.

He pushed open the bar door. It was just gone 11 in the morning and there were few patrons. The large woman behind the bar with the Slavic folds over her eyes indicating strong Mongolian stock sized him up in seconds and nodded to a door at the rear. He crossed to it, knocked once, and then waited, calming himself.

It was pulled inward and he was met by heavy blue smoke hanging in a layer just above his head—everyone in Russia smoked, and you either smoked yourself, or sucked in the next guy's chimney-like exhalations.

"Comrade Revkin."

Tushino grinned his golden shark grin but didn't stand. Four men sat around a table, and Yuri recognized them as the small gang of muscle from their visit to the lake.

Yuri nodded. "Mr. Tushino... and esteemed colleagues." He gave a small salute. "A nice day for a meeting."

"Every day is a good day for a meeting with friends." Tushino motioned to a vacant chair beside him.

As Yuri sat, one of the huge Orlov twins slid an empty glass in front of him and then half filled it with clear fluid—it was good quality vodka, and Yuri doubted it was available at the bar outside.

Tushino lifted his glass. "*Proust.*"

Yuri nodded and lifted his glass in return. "Proust." And downed it in one. It was *very* good quality and finished with a smooth burn on his palate.

Tushino put his glass down, and his smile turned to that of a favorite uncle. "Now, my friend. What does Mr. Stenson say to our offer of security and guaranteed product delivery services?"

Yuri opened his hands and shrugged a little. "Of course he wants to have a good relationship with the local businesses." Yuri pulled on a look of mock concern. "But as his cash flow is weak right now, he can only pay what he can afford. The upside is we hope the relationship is a long term and mutually beneficial one."

Tushino didn't blink. "How long term our relationship is depends on what he offers—now, here, today."

Yuri nodded. "We think we can afford 30,000 roubles a month."

"Four hundred American dollars a month?" Tushino burst out laughing and was joined by his goons. He lifted a hand and slowly twirled the finger in the air. "This little bar in the middle of nowhere pays that much." He lowered his brow. "Your millionaire American friend was joking, I think." He leaned forward. "Because that would be an insult, and one I would not dare telegraph to my boss." He tapped the table with one finger. "Now you tell me what he is *really* offering."

Yuri felt a little ball of panic begin in his stomach. He didn't think the offer was that small, and he didn't have all that much further to negotiate.

"Maybe we can go to 35,000 Roubles, $500 a month, if we push ourselves." He drew on his poker face and waited.

Tushino lifted his tiny glass of vodka and held it up to the light. "Stolichnaya Elit. Made from Russian Alpha Spirit distilled from winter wheat and then filtered through quartz sand, Siberian birch charcoal, and then cloth fibers." He continued to hold the glass in his fingertips and turn it, catching the light through the clear liquid. "It is then flash-chilled to -5 degrees and finally passed through ion-charged filters to ensure its purity." He threw it back into his mouth and then put the glass down. "I drink a bottle a day, at a cost of 80 dollars. That's 2,400 dollars per month."

Tushino slapped the table as his gang sniggered. "So, maybe you need a little help with this *pushing yourself* thing. I think you can afford a little more than $500 a month." Tushino's face dropped all pretense of good humor. "You will pay $1,000 per week… to begin with. After a year, it will be $2,000, then the year after $4,000, and so on." Tushino sat back and shrugged. "Inflation."

Yuri felt his heart sink in his chest—they were miles apart, and this wasn't negotiation, but extortion. He suddenly felt stupid thinking he could ever have bargained with these people.

"We cannot afford this. Mr. Stenson will be bankrupt before he has made single rouble. We offer a long-term partnership, where you don't need to do anything other than collect your pay. I even bring it to you."

Tushino sat staring back for a few moments as his brow knitted slightly. "Dear loyal friend, you do not know what potential you have in that business." He poured himself another drink, and then one for Yuri. "The real value in your business is not a simple fish breeding program, but the *results* of that breeding program. You have good contacts with the Federal Agency for Fisheries and Conservation, but more importantly, you have a formal contract for the supply and receipt of Beluga caviar."

A smile began to spread on the man's face. "Beluga caviar, which they call black gold. Which is now so very rare and in demand that it can trade for up to $5,000 per pound."

Tushino downed his vodka. "So, if some of those eggs were diverted for sale, and only some for hatching, we could all be rich very quickly."

Yuri's eyes widened. "This is not possible." He held his hands up flat and sat back. "Not possible at all. Mr. Stenson will never agree to this. His business will remain honorable and committed to working faithfully with those who have put faith in him at the highest levels." Yuri frowned. "Mr. Stenson is an honorable man."

"Oh, I see." Tushino nodded and his brow creased. Then he snapped his fingers as though he had a sudden thought. "I know; I have an idea where you get to pay nothing."

Yuri waited, knowing this suggestion wasn't going to be any better, and probably far worse.

Tushino meshed his fingers together on the table. "We take over half of your business. You run the farming, and we run the export of Beluga caviar. Mr. Stenson gets to remain honorable, and we get to be rich—good deal for everyone, yes?"

Yuri's mouth gaped for a moment. "There is no—"

Tushino lunged and swept a hand across the table, wiping the glasses from it to shatter against the wall. His face was terrifying as he leaned closer to the bigger Yuri, a finger pointed gun-like into his face.

"This is what will happen. You scurry back and tell this richy-rich American bastard that if he wants to do business in Russia, and have a long and healthy life for himself and his pretty wife, he will accept us as a business partner. If not, then his business is dead, only option is to pack up and go home… while we let him."

Yuri sat there blinking for a moment, trying to process the implications. He knew his boss would never agree to what the bratva had demanded.

"Maybe we can—"

Tushino made a small sound like spit, and waved him away. "Show him out."

His goons got to their feet and stood behind him. A huge hand fell on Yuri's shoulder and he slowly rose. He walked stiff-legged to the door and when he got there, Tushino called to him.

"One week, you come back, with Mr. Marcus, and you sign agreement with us as your new business partners." He made a small jerking motion with his chin, and Yuri was pushed outside the room.

The meeting was over.

*****

"*What?*"

Marcus' mouth hung open and his brow was so deeply furrowed it looked like someone had taken an axe to his forehead.

He threw his hands up as he got to his feet. "We have to tell someone." He paced. "The police, or secret service, or what's the equivalent of the FBI over here?"

"The FSB, the Federal Security Service of the Russian Federation," Yuri said glumly.

Marcus spun back and pointed. "Exactly. These guys can't get away with this. We've done everything by the book and have the government on our side."

"Marcus." Yuri sighed long and deep, and his shoulders slumped. "This is not America. This is Russia, and things move very slowly here. If, and that is big *if*, the FSB looks into this, it'll take them months to even get moving."

"Months?" Marcus ran hands up through his hair. "We've got to respond to those thieves by next week. It's fucking extortion… a crime." He began to pace again. "We've got to stall them somehow. I can tell them that I need a lawyer to look over the documents. Then we throw a lot of legal questions at them."

"They have lawyers; lots of them." Yuri shrugged. "Corrupt ones."

Marcus turned, and Yuri went on.

"And doctors, and police, and politicians, and just about everyone they need. In Russia, they are another form of government."

"Well, it's not happening. It can't." Marcus folded his arms. "We need to use our good contacts at the highest level in the Federal Agency for Fisheries and Conservation, which is surely in a direct line to the Kremlin." Marcus rubbed his chin. "But I can't call from here and have the damn lines drop out. I need to be there myself. Make my case personally." He quickly looked at his watch.

"We have seven days until we're supposed to meet. I can be in Moscow in just a few days and then be back by the meeting date." Marcus rubbed his chin for a moment before spinning back to the big Russian. "I can do it, if I leave right now. You take me to Listvyanka and I'll grab a train."

Yuri grimaced. "This is very bad idea. They might be watching the stations and airports. These people are dangerous because they're ruthless, and also because they are smart. We need to think about this, please, Marcus."

But it was impossible to think clearly. He was also more pissed than he'd ever been in his life. These assholes came out of nowhere and threatened his livelihood, his business, his life, and that of his family as well? *Like hell*, he thought.

He had zero choice; it was a no-win situation he needed to take head-on before it totally owned him.

"I have thought about it." He faced his friend again. "We don't have a choice; there's too much at stake."

Yuri nodded slowly. "Yes, there is a lot at stake, but…"

"Then it's done." Marcus turned toward the house, planning to pull a bag of clothing and toiletries together. He half-turned as he ran up the hill. "There's more than a lot at stake; there's *everything* at stake."

CHAPTER 09

52 miles outside of Listvyanka

"Done and done." Marcus disconnected his call. As he hoped, Listvyanka had little problem with phone reception like at the mill house compound, and he was able to secure an early meeting with Mikhail Ivanov from the Federal Agency for Fisheries and Conservation.

For some reason, just getting the meeting from the senior Moscow bureaucrat lifted his spirits. Something was going right for a change. *And about time*, he thought.

Marcus nestled back in his seat and pulled up the hooded collar on his orange SeaWorld jacket; he had the train carriage to himself, and it rattled and shook as he barrelled toward his destination. It was ink-dark outside the window and resting his head facing it, all he saw was his image reflected back at him—he looked tired, and also a little worried.

The train ride would take many more hours yet, and the rhythmic rocking and clackety-clack of the steel wheels on the iron rails was lulling him to sleep regardless of the shaking.

His eyelids grew impossibly heavy and he started to drift. He smiled as he saw Sara in his dream; it was that time again where she had the little green bird nestled in her hands that had stunned itself after hitting one of their windows. He looked down as she opened her cupped hands, showing him the small animal sitting there, looking up at him. It shook itself and then settled back down. It seemed to know it was safe in her hands.

The train slowed and then stopped. Marcus frowned and looked out the window. They weren't close to any station and he guessed someone was getting on or off.

Weird, he thought. "Siberia." He snorted. "Hey." He lurched forward, smiling. "You idiot; don't waste the reception... and hang the cost." He dialed the numbers for home and waited impatiently as it rang, and rang, and then:

"Hello?"

He exhaled, feeling warm all over just at hearing her voice again. "Hiya, beautiful."

"Marcus!" She near shouted down the line. "How are things going at the mill? How's the weather? How are *you*?"

He smiled and closed his eyes, hunching over to talk softly even though he was alone in the carriage. "Ah, you know, a few teething problems, but nothing a week on a tropical island couldn't fix."

"I can't wait to see what you've done." She rushed her words now. "I've developed some great new techniques for the breeding programs, plus a synthesized food that'll promote growth. I'm getting squared away so will be there soon."

"You're my champion. And I miss you so much." He chuckled softly. "But maybe you should hold off for a few more weeks. Just until I bed down some last-minute things."

"What? No. I can help." Her voice became serious. "What is it? What's wrong?"

His head came up as he heard the carriage's rear door be pulled back. Then came the sound of footsteps as a man with a phone to his ear went past, briefly glanced at him, and then kept on going out and through the door to the next carriage. Marcus thought little of it and turned back to the window.

"Nothing serious. Just the unexpected complexities of working in Siberia." He laughed softly. "Bureaucracy; nothing I can't handle."

"Is it the fish and egg deliveries? The pen sites? The compound? What can I be doing from here?" she implored.

"You just being you, is all I need right now." It was times like this he felt homesick. He traveled a lot, and though he always missed Sara, it was when things were going bad, or he was lonely, or sad, that missing her became unbearable. And right now, he missed her calm intellect, her face, her body, her smell, her love, and every other damn thing about her. He wished she were here right now.

No, on second thought, he was glad she was far away until he had all this bad shit sorted out. But he needed her.

"Well, okay, but I know you and something's up," she mused.

The rear door of the carriage opened again, and this time, there were multiple footsteps. He was about to turn, when the front carriage door opened and the guy who went through a few minutes before reappeared. But this time, he closed it and just stood there, back to the door and blocking it with his body. His amused eyes were on Marcus.

"Ah, shit. Bratva," he breathed out. Now he knew who got on the train a while back.

"What?" Her voice had an edge. "Marcus?"

Immediately, alarms started to go off in Marcus' head and he swung around. That was when his heart sank. Tushino and his henchmen were sitting in seats a few back, grinning or giggling.

"Hello again, Mr. Stenson. Small world, yes?" Tushino got to his feet and came to sit across from Marcus. "Who would think we would both be going to Moscow at same time, *hmm*?"

"Who's that?" He heard her say as he lowered the phone from his ear. He faced the men while working to keep his expression deadpan. "Yeah, lucky me."

"Lucky, yes." Tushino sat forward. "So, where would Mr. Stenson be going today? Visit relatives, maybe?" He chuckled and turned to his men. "Maybe he has little old babushka hidden away in Moscow."

His men brayed and Tushino's face became serious. "Or maybe you have friend in Agency for Fisheries and Conservation?" He pointed at the phone. "You talk to them now?"

Marcus shook his head, realizing Sara was still on the line. He expected that he was in for a beating and would cop it. But he didn't want Sara to know. He'd had fights before, and even though he was outnumbered, he'd sure as hell let these assholes know they'd been in a match.

"Just my accountant." He put the phone to his ear. "Okay, Lenny, call you back later."

"*Marcus... Marcus...*"

He hung up, cutting Sara off.

God, he wished his brother were here. He and Carter would wipe the floor with all of them, twice over.

He'd tell them nothing and only give them enough so that they thought they still had a chance of securing their black money. "Just need to get some supplies myself. Lab equipment, that sort of stuff." He folded his arms and sat back.

"Really?" Tushino raised thick eyebrows. "Funny thing about Russia is that everyone likes a little bit of extra money. Whether it's the postman, the shopkeeper, the police chief, or the politician. You see, my boss, Mr. Gennardy Zyuganov, also knows people in the fish ministry, and they mentioned you had made an urgent meeting plan with their chief scientist." His brows went up. "Just for supplies?"

"Yep." Marcus yawned. "I'm a little tired now and want to get a few hours' sleep. Do you mind?"

Tushino shook his head slowly. "No sleep for you this night, I'm afraid." He reached into his pocket and pulled out a folded document. "This is contracting to give Mr. Zyuganov a 51% controlling stake in your company." He flattened it out and also took out an expensive-looking pen and opened it. "No need to read it; just legal stuff." He handed it over. "Sign, and we'll get off next stop. And we all stay friends."

Marcus made no move to take it from him. His mind worked a mile a minute as he tried to think of responses to put the guy in hibernation. Right now, he was alone, outnumbered, and outflanked.

"That's not the way we Americans do contracts. Let me take it to my lawyer, check it out, and then see if we can come to some sort of agreement. I can guarantee I'll have an answer by the meeting you called, next week."

Tushino's grin was back. "I don't care how you Americans *do* contracts. You're not in America now. And in Russia, business is governed by Russian law." He exhaled with theatrical exasperation. "This is the problem with American arrogance; you always think that you are the ones who are in charge. Even if you are not in your own country."

Here goes nothing, Marcus thought. He shook his head. "Sorry, buddy, not signing anything today."

Tushino's eyes were half-lidded. "Well, if you sign today, we will own 51% of your company. If you sign tomorrow, it'll be 61%. The day after, 71%. You see how this works? Better to sign today." Tushino held the pen and contract out.

Marcus shrugged. "I can't anyway. The business is in both my wife's name and mine. Even under Russian law, it requires both of us to approve something this significant."

Tushino's eyes flicked to one of the people behind Marcus momentarily, before he eased back in the seat. He seemed to think it over for a minute. "Yes, it would be better if only one person we need to negotiate with."

Marcus suddenly had a horrible thought. "Forget it; my wife's not coming now. So you get to deal with me and me only."

Tushino tilted his head. "But your wife *is* coming. And I think once you get to Moscow, you may tell her not to come. But if you *don't* tell her not to come..." He smirked. "Then she'll come, and when she sees you have already signed, then she will sign."

The Russian's eyes flicked to just over Marcus' shoulder and he gave a near-imperceptible nod. Suddenly, a strap went over his head to catch him around the neck. Immediately, a crushing pressure was applied and it happened so quickly he had no chance of getting his fingers under the leather.

Marcus threw a punch over his shoulder but was grabbed by two other sets of arms as he thrashed and kicked. But his head began to pound and his throat was on fire. He quickly ran out of oxygen and felt his eyes bulging as his strength ebbed away.

Tushino's face started to become blurry as the man simply sat and smiled as his life was being taken from him. The Russian held up a hand and the pressure eased. He slid the contract forward.

"Easy choice; sign or die."

Marcus coughed, his voice hoarse. "You need me; you can't kill me."

Tushino nodded again, and one of the huge men holding his arm quickly reached forward and grabbed a finger, jerking it backward until it snapped like a dry stick.

Marcus howled from the excruciating pain.

"Sign." Tushino's gaze was amused.

"You... son of a bitch." Marcus grit his teeth.

Tushino nodded again, and a second finger was grabbed.

"*Wait...*" Marcus yelled.

He didn't, and the finger was jerked backward and broken like the first. Tears ran down Marcus' cheeks, and he saw his hand with the two largest fingers sticking up at wrong angles.

"Number three?" Tushino jeered.

'No, no, I'll sign." Marcus needed time to think, and he had none here.

"Good, good." The Russian slid the contract forward and held out the pen once again.

Tushino's goons released his arms but stayed hovering at each shoulder. Marcus lifted the pen and scrawled on the page. He dropped the pen.

"Fuck you."

The Russian bratva leader ignored him and turned the contract around and scrutinized it. "Good; thank you, Mr. Stenson. And now, my business with you is concluded. Goodbye." He jerked his head to the side, and Marcus was pulled from his seat.

"*Hey, hey.*" He was dragged down the center of the carriage aisle to the exit, and once in between the old carriages, he was immediately assaulted by the deafening sounds of steel wheels on the iron tracks and also the freezing wind howling like a thousand banshees.

One of the thugs said something to him in Russian, laughed cruelly, and then threw him off the moving train.

*****

Marcus trudged alone for hours, his collar on his SeaWorld jacket pulled up, cradling the mangled hand in his other hand. His shoulder felt like it was dislocated, his face was scraped raw, his phone gone, and he couldn't feel his nose and tips of his ears. But he was alive.

There was no moon, and he walked as close as he dared to the train tracks, hoping that he'd make it back to Listvyanka in the next few hours. The temperature was dropping, and he would have given anything for a hat that pulled down over his ears, as he bet by now the tips would be blood red, and then if he was out much more, the tips might even turn black.

The temperature dropping also meant he might be closing in on the lake, and he remembered that the train line passed close to the water for a few miles as it pulled out of the town.

Not far now, he hoped.

The upside of the cold was his fingers had stopped throbbing. He hated to look down at the twisted contraption that used to be his hand. He'd head home to get it repaired so the fingers knitted properly. He needed his hands.

"Arthritis central, here I come." He chuckled and the sound was sucked away by a bitter wind.

In another few hundred yards, he thought he saw the dark sheets of ice signifying the lake surface, and then moments more he spotted a glow, green, and coming from just behind the tree line. It didn't look right.

"What's that?" he asked aloud, perhaps to bolster his own confidence.

The wind seemed to die away, and he felt he was walking in a vacuum. The only sound came from his feet as they crunched down on the snow. Then he heard it, the other footsteps. They were heavier, and he bet, larger.

He looked over his shoulder, but saw nothing. Then looked left and right, contemplating crossing the train tracks.

Marcus felt the fluttering of nerves in his stomach. The campfire tales the Yakut Russians told rushed back into his mind, and he suddenly knew how the superstitions took hold. He looked back again.

"Keep it together, buddy," he whispered and turned back just as the shadow loomed over him. He had to crane his neck to look up at its face, and when he saw, his breath caught in his throat.

Marcus could only stare, open-mouthed. He knew what was coming, but didn't think of himself. Instead, he thought of Sara holding her cupped hands out to him. She opened them, showing him the small green bird that had been nestling there, nestling all this time in his memories. Except this time, it suddenly flew away.

His scream was cut dead as it took him.

EPISODE 02

CHAPTER 10

INTERACTION: *Northern shore of Lake Baikal—1602*

"What was that?"

Vasily sat up in the dark, grabbing his shaska, the special, curved Cossack sabers both men carried. Kurbat was also instantly awake and sat listening for a few moments. The sound came again—a cracking like splintering wood, or…

"Ice breaking."

Vasily frowned. "Can it be thawing?"

"No, not this time of year," Kurbat replied. "Something else."

The pair listened some more, and sure enough, the cracking sound came again, this time accompanied by the sound of water falling. Kurbat stoked the fire up and in a few minutes, it was blazing and the light created a glow around the men for fifty feet.

The deep cracking continued, louder, and seemingly even closer. Kurbat Kolesnikov and Vasily Ivanov had been friends for over a decade and in their lives they'd encountered giant bear, wild tribesmen, wolf packs, and vicious weather, and prevailed every time. They didn't scare easily.

"We take a look." Kurbat lit a lantern and also grabbed a spear.

Vasily followed with a burning torch and his weapons. Kurbat was first to the shoreline, holding his lantern out and craning forward.

"See, the ice is broken open."

Sure enough, a huge swathe of ice, looking around four feet thick, was pushed up and back like the folds of a giant's blanket.

"I see a light," Vasily whispered. "It seems to be coming from under the water." He stood slowly, but stayed behind a tree trunk. "How can fire burn beneath water?"

"No fire that I know. But maybe black magic." Kurbat also stood.

"I don't like this. I think we must leave, *now*," Vasily insisted.

"Not yet," Kurbat replied firmly.

The pair crept nearer and saw the snow near the water was dry and though none had fallen for a while, it was like a smooth blanket—mostly—because just to the left of where they hid, there were lines of tracks leaving the dark lake.

"Something came out of the water," Vasily whispered.

Kurbat held his lantern up. "Seals maybe."

Kurbat edged closer and crouched to examine the marks—whatever it was, it looked to walk on spindly legs, many of them, that were wide apart.

"Some sort of new animal," Kurbat mused. "Let's follow them."

In just a few minutes, they came to a mound of something wet that still had steam rising from it as it rapidly cooled in the freezing air. Kurbat edged forward toward the mass.

"What is this?" He prodded it with his spear.

Vasily grimaced at the massive pile of viscera. Something had been slaughtered and disemboweled, and given it was still hot, it had all happened quite recently.

"Wolves, or maybe hunters," Vasily surmised. "Gutted a deer."

"Bigger than a deer," Kurbat said and backed up. "And why didn't we hear it? There should have been screaming like the devil himself was being tortured." He continued to back up behind Vasily.

Vasily continued to study the pile of steaming red guts just as there came the snap of a dry twig behind them.

From behind, Vasily Kurbat screamed. Vasily spun. The monstrous bear that loomed over him was around seven and a half feet tall and it froze him to the marrow. However, even though its huge mouth hung open, displaying finger-long teeth, no sound escaped that deadly maw. Its face was slack and the eyes milky as though sightless.

Vasily backed away with his spear. "*Heyaa!*" He waved his torch in its face, but the thing took another step, and Vasily yelled a war cry and jabbed his spear into it. He pierced its chest, and it still made no sound, but where he had stuck the massive creature, light emanated from the wound like there was some sort of fire inside it.

Vasily slashed downward over the gut, enlarging the wound and finally, there came a noise, a scream, unearthly, but not from its mouth, but confusingly, from inside the belly of the beast. He pulled the spear free and held it up in front of himself.

He felt his sanity slipping away, because as he watched, gore-coated spiky legs and lashing fibers whipped out to grip each side of the wound and pull it closed like an old man drawing a cloak around himself in the cold.

There was something in there—something alive—and something that wasn't bear.

"*Demon*," he yelled.

The massive creature's sagging face never changed, and he jammed his spear in again and again. The bear thing finally turned from the attack and lumbered away, barging small trees from its path.

There came a human scream from the forest.

"Kurbat." Vasily ran toward the voice, looking for his friend's lantern. He could just make out the light heading toward the shoreline. He sprinted after it to find it abandoned there.

"*Kurbat?*" he yelled again. "No, no, no." Vasily began to panic.

He followed the tracks all the way to the black water where the ice was broken open. His friend was gone, leaving nothing but mad tracking and splashes of blood. Far out on the ice, he thought he could make out a receding glow of something below the ice—like a greenish fire.

Vasily lowered his torch as the silence closed in on him. His friend was gone, and he was alone.

CHAPTER 11

USA, Florida, Madeira Beach

"Hello? Marcus, *hello*?" Sara gripped the phone so hard her knuckles went white. She immediately called his number back, but it rang out unanswered.

Something had just happened, and she tried to replay what she heard in her mind—Marcus on a train to Moscow talking normally one minute, and then some people had come into his carriage. The voices, sneering, and then he had pretended she was someone else. *Why would he do that?* she agonized.

She called him over and over, without him picking up, and then she had called Yuri Revkin, his site manager. This just produced a lot of ear-splitting static.

"*Fuck*," she hissed out, feeling her stomach roil with nausea.

Sara Stenson walked to the window and stared out over their garden. Her favorite hibiscus was in bloom, and its crimson, dinner-plate-sized flowers had shared their blooms to be tucked behind ears at many a party. As she watched, small colorful birds flitted from tree to tree, and a few landed on the emerald green grass to argue with each other momentarily, before flitting away.

It was all so calm and normal. Sara stood for a moment more, indecision and panic beginning to short-circuit her thinking.

She began to pace, but then stopped at the mantlepiece to look at their picture frames. From one of them, she and Marcus grinned at the camera from a tropical Fijian island. In the background was a sandy beach, water the color of crushed sapphires, and two spread beach towels. They both looked tanned, fit, and high on life. She continued to look at his face—large blue eyes with long lashes, straight nose and strong jawline.

She damn well wasn't going to let anything happen to him. She called the police, and then the FBI, and after an hour of rising agitation and impatience, she was politely but firmly told that neither of them had the jurisdiction to do a damned thing. The most they could do was give her the number for the local police in Moscow and a suggestion to call the State Department.

She'd called the State Department first, who were cordial, but did little more than record her details and gave her a promise to pass it on to the embassy. Then she tried the Russian police, and after 30 minutes of laboring through an excruciating call, she had been told they would look into it in a few days, as no one was classed as missing in Russia for the first 48 hours. She had the feeling that the policeman didn't even bother to write any of her details down.

"That's too late, that's too late," she muttered as she paced some more. Her eyes traveled again to the mantlepiece where there stood a photo of Marcus as a boy. With him were his dad and his brother, Carter.

She walked toward it as if in a trance. She'd dated Carter before Marcus, and where Marcus was the heartthrob, Carter was the brutally handsome one. Where Marcus was smooth and cool, Carter was fire and dynamite—her choice had been danger or security—and in the end, she had chosen security.

But the thing about Carter was, he didn't play by the rules. She hadn't talked to him in years, and she knew he owed her nothing for the way she had treated him. But right now, following the rules was getting her nowhere. She still had his number.

Fuck it, she thought and dialed.

CHAPTER 12

USA, Iowa, Hawkeye—The Sanctuary Bar

Saturday night was always crowded down at the Sanctuary Bar. The place was full of bikers, truckers, and men and women in checked shirts rolled up at the sleeves and sweat-stained cowboy hats. The music was loud and the place smelled of beer, whiskey, and good times.

The regulars knew how to look after themselves, and even though the bar was tough and rough, it was generally safe. The patrons all operated by the oldest code going around —*don't start shit, won't be shit.*

The other reason a crowd of the big and bad behaved themselves was that the one thing they respected and feared more than each other was the guy who ran the place.

Carter Stenson was six-three, ex-military, and looked like he had been carved from solid granite. If you pissed him off and you just got thrown out on your ass, you should go buy yourself a lottery ticket. On a bad night, if you decided to make trouble or take the guy on, then you just might just go home without your front teeth and your nose under your ear.

Carter was behind the bar, stacking dirty glasses into the rack ready for the machine as he let his bar staff do their thing. He looked up, seeing the pictures of his mom and pop, both now long gone, and also one of his little brother, Marcus and his wife Sara. There were several more of them, of he and Marcus, from when they were on pushbikes, to then being at school, and then next thing he was at his brother's wedding. He was proud of the kid.

When the fork in the road came about, Marcus was smart enough to take the high road. Unlike Carter who took the low road, and kept going, down. *Thank God one of them made it up and out*, he thought.

He couldn't help his eyes going back to the image of Sara, and he felt the familiar pang in his chest. She was so beautiful.

Let it go, he demanded for the hundredth time.

Behind him, there was the sound of glass smashing and voices raised. He glanced to the side and into the reflection of the mirror over the bar and saw the small group of out-of-towners trying to bump chests with a few of the local boys. The regular guys backed up, not because they were scared of the out-of-towners, but because they knew the rules.

Carter sighed, undid the apron from his waist, and lifted it over his head. He rounded the bar, with many watching him. They already knew how this was going to go down.

The rules were simple: the locals stayed cool, and in return, he'd take out the trash. He looked at the new group—three of them—big, young, and looked like they'd stopped a few punches in their time. Maybe they were hard-heads, a street gang, or maybe even budding MMA fighters. They looked hard, but the thing was, these guys might know how to fight for money or drinks, but Carter had done it for a living and had needed to fight to the death in his past. There was a huge difference.

As he came round, he rolled his shoulders and many of the locals gave him space, grinning in anticipation. A few even began to slap money down on the bar as they took bets.

Time to go to work, Carter thought, as he closed in on the trio.

"*Carter*."

Carter paused at his bar manager's voice.

Maxine held up the wall phone. "Call for you; says it's important."

"*Argh*." He grimaced and looked from the three troublemakers who glared back at him to Maxine. "Coming."

He rounded the bar and grabbed the phone where she had left it. "Stenson."

"Carter." It was Sara's voice, and in that single word, she sounded broken up—bad. He was immediately on edge, and the delight in hearing her voice was tempered by apprehension.

"Sara, are you and Marcus okay? What's happened? Are you hurt?"

"No, I mean, I'm fine, but..." The words tumbled out fast then. "*Marcus, in Russia, sturgeon farming, phone call, something happened, I don't know...*"

"Slow down, slow down." Carter concentrated. "Tell me slowly, firstly, where is he?"

"Okay, okay." He heard her suck in a breath and let it out. "He went to Russia, Lake Baikal in Siberia, to open a fish farm. To farm the sturgeon's caviar." Her voice was becoming a squeak as if her throat was closing up and she seemed to be only just stifling tears.

"And you said he's missing?" Carter waited. If it was him, it'd be so what. He went missing all the time—a booze bender, a woman, just gone fishing or hunting and not made it back on time, or a hundred other reasons. But his brother was as reliable as the sun coming up.

"Yes, no, not really. He was on a train headed to Moscow for some reason. I heard some people get on, with Russian accents, and everything changed. He sounded worried." She took a few deep breaths. "He said one word: *bratva*."

"Bratva," Carter whispered, straightening. *Shit*, he thought. He'd had to deal with criminal gangs before. Then, he'd won, because he had nothing to lose, and he also didn't bother playing by the rules. But a guy like

Marcus would have been a soft target.

"The local police said I'm supposed to wait for two days before worrying. But I think something bad has happened to him." Her voice was barely audible. "He pretended I was his accountant. He didn't want them to know it was me on the phone."

Carter closed his eyes and leaned his forehead against the wall. He knew of the Russian mafia; they were as brutal as they were cunning. If they had taken an interest in his brother, it was no good thing.

Carter drew in a deep breath and let it out slowly. "Where are you?"

"Home, Florida. But I'm going over to Russia as soon as I can."

"No," he shot back. "Just, wait, until I come over so we can make a plan."

He heard her make a noise in her throat. "That plan better include travel to Russia." And then. "I'm scared, Carter."

"I'll be there tomorrow morning. And Sara, don't worry, we'll find him."

Carter said his goodbyes and stood frozen for a moment, just staring at the tiles on the wall, but his mind was already a thousand miles away. He'd find his brother, and bring him back safe. And if anything had happened to him, by anyone's hand, he'd fucking kill 'em all.

The phone was still in his hand and the plastic case started to crackle as his fingers compressed. Carter's teeth ground so hard his jaw began to ache, and he felt the muscles bunch in his neck and shoulders. He suddenly began to smash the phone receiver onto the hook, once, twice, three times, before holding it up and glaring at it as though he wanted to strangle it.

Behind him, a glass smashed on the ground, and he spun to see the three guys still acting like assholes.

Carter hung up the phone and rounded the bar in a rush. The first guy saw him coming, widening his stance and shaping up. When Carter closed in, the guy threw a straight right, with all his shoulder behind it.

Carter dodged, grabbed the arm, and pulled it downward, throwing the guy over his shoulder. But he hung onto the arm. The elbow is a strong joint, but a heavy man's bodyweight and bending the limb backward means something's gotta give… and it's always the elbow joint.

Carter left him howling from a now very-ugly broken arm and dove in among the next two. He allowed his fury to be vented with a flurry of punches, kicks, and a head butt that flattened one opponent's nose to his face. The other he delivered a flat strike across his lips, caving in all his front teeth. He was out cold before he even hit the ground.

Looking down on one of the broken guys, he had the urge to stomp down on him, but only just held it in check. Instead, he quickly dragged all three out into the carpark and left them there.

He then wiped his hands on a bar towel and fished in his pocket for the bar keys.

"Max."

"Yo." The woman lifted her chin.

He held up the keys and then tossed them to her. "Take over until I get back."

"Trouble?" she asked. "How long?"

"Family issue. Might be days, weeks, longer." He headed toward the door. "Give yourself a pay rise; you're the boss. I'll be in touch."

Maxine started to come around the bar. "But…"

Carter was already out the door and moving fast.

CHAPTER 13

Listvyanka, Lake Baikal—the Belka Hotel

Yuri Revkin had a sense of déjà vu as he sat in the same hotel bar waiting on Mr. Stenson. This time it wasn't Marcus, but his older brother, Carter.
He still felt sick and guilty for allowing Marcus, his friend, to travel to Moscow. Thinking back now, of course the bratva must have anticipated the last option he had was to try and appeal to the only senior political or government people he knew in the capital. And how else was he going to get there? 90% chance it was going to be by train, and he would start from Listvyanka. All they had to do was stake out the station and wait.

Maybe he's just a hostage, he thought as he then threw back the large vodka. He laughed cruelly and had to choke it off before he wept. The chance of that was next to zero. He knew in his belly his friend was probably dead.

And now, Marcus' brother was arriving to most likely be thrown into the same meat grinder as well. He had debated whether he would just leave and go back to taking out fishing tours for a living. Pay was crap, but it was an uncomplicated life.

To the side of the bar, the doors opened and he heard the low talking of a man and a woman as they headed to the front desk. Yuri looked through the doorway, just as a figure came and stood in it, searching the bar room, he knew, for him.

Yuri felt a small shock of recognition—the resemblance was so strong it could have been Marcus. But Marcus if you added another two inches in height and 30 pounds of muscle. Also, if you made the face less pleasant and more brutally handsome, probably due to him having taken his lumps over the years. This man was no Hollywood American.

The final difference was where Marcus' eyes contained the sparkle of boyish enthusiasm, this older Stenson, Carter, had eyes that were hard as flint and had probably seen things that normal men probably weren't meant to see. Yuri knew eyes like those—there'd been violence in this man's past, both received and inflicted.

Those eyes now fixed on Yuri, and the Russian lifted his hand to wave. Carter nodded in return, but it was less a greeting and more an "I see you" motion. He disappeared for a moment, and then in a few minutes he was back with a small blonde woman. He said something to her and she immediately picked Yuri out and came toward him.

"Yuri? Yuri Revkin?"

Yuri got to his feet so quickly he nearly knocked over his chair. "Yes, yes, and you must be Ms. Sara." He shoved out one large paw.

"Sara, just Sara." She took hold of his hand, and he felt how tiny it was and still cold from outside. The fingers were soft and delicate. She looked up into his face, smiling, but her brow was creased with concern and her eyes were filled with worry.

He motioned to two spare seats he had ready and sat. Just like when Marcus had arrived, he had small glasses of vodka and beers on order. Sara watched his face, and when Yuri offered Carter a drink, the big man just shook his head slowly.

It was obvious he wasn't here to make friends, a long-term relationship, or anything other than getting answers. And to that end, Carter sat forward and placed two enormous hands on the table.

"You said in your messages that you believed Marcus may have fallen foul of the local mafia. What have the police said?"

Yuri shrugged. "They said they have no proof that foul play had occurred. They simply said that maybe he has run away, because he was under business pressure."

Yuri saw the muscles in Carter's jaws work and knew exactly what he was thinking. He went on. "You must remember that the local police have been touched by the bratva. Men working in remote places with little pay. They get offered money to look the other way sometimes." He shrugged. "And if it is a foreigner, then looking the other way is easy."

"So, we can forget about any help from the police." Carter edged forward, now placing both forearms on the table. He clasped his hands together. Yuri noticed they were huge and had calluses over each of the knuckles, making them stand out like knobs of bone.

"And I'm guessing there's no CCTV footage or witnesses," Carter said.

Yuri just shook his head. "He got on the train, and then he disappeared."

Carter stared for a moment, his eyes boring into Yuri's. "But you know the men that turned up at the mill?"

"Yes and no. I know their first names, and I know their faces. But I don't know them personally. I met with the local boss named Tushino to try and make a deal. It didn't go well. They all work for a man named Gennardy Zyuganov in Moscow, who is connected to all arms of government, business, law enforcement, and politics. He is a powerful man and his tentacles reach everywhere."

"All the way to Lake Baikal," Sara said and turned to Carter. "Can we find Marcus? Get him back? Maybe they've taken him hostage and want some sort of payment."

Carter laid his hand over hers and squeezed momentarily before turning his gaze back on Yuri—the glance between them told Yuri that Carter knew that his brother was probably dead already. It also told him that the man wasn't really here for criminal justice. He was here to clean the stables.

"Do you know where we can find these men?" Sara's brow creased. "We can pay them off."

"They don't want anything... now." Yuri sighed.

"Why?" Carter leaned forward.

Carter made him feel nervous and Yuri sat back a little "I, ah, attended the meeting that they requested, after Marcus had gone missing to try and find out where he was. They wanted to know when you were arriving." He shook his head. "They told me that Marcus had signed over 51% of the business to them."

"*What*!" Carter's teeth were bared.

Yuri rocked back in his chair, and the other bar patrons turned. The Russian could have sworn in that instant Carter's eyes actually burned red as if all the pure hate of hell itself was inside the man. Yuri held up his hands, waving the big American down.

"They can't do that," Sara added.

"I didn't see it, the contract. But the urgency of their demands had abated, and they told me they would wait on the wife of Marcus Stenson to countersign and make it formal." Yuri's mouth turned down. "They said they had no idea where Marcus was, and don't care. But, their smirks told me that they knew what had happened to him."

Yuri turned to Sara. "They need you to sign as well. This ugliness hasn't gone away, it has just been transferred over to you."

"Those bastards." Sara bared her teeth for a moment. "If I find out they were involved in anything happening to Marcus, I'll..." her lips moved as if she was trying to form words, but then her face crumpled. "Oh Marcus."

Carter stood and took her hand. He helped her to her feet. "This is tough, and it's all so raw right now. Why don't you go upstairs while I finish up with Yuri here? Then we can catch up after for some dinner. Deal?"

"Sorry. I'm stronger than this." She wiped her nose. "I just want him back."

"I know, me too," Carter said softly.

*****

Carter walked her to the door of the bar and let her go. He watched her for a moment more, and then turned back to Yuri. The big Russian looked nervous, and Carter bet he knew more than he was letting on.

He sat back down. "We need to talk to these men you mentioned. They'll never leave Sara alone, and never leave any of you alone unless they've got what they want, or you're out of business, or you're dead. I've dealt with crime gangs before; they have a head, hands, and a body. Sometimes, you only need to sever the head. But other times, just cutting off one or both of the hands sends enough of a signal to back off."

Yuri looked down at the table and blew air between his lips. "Mr. Stenson, this is not something that…"

"*Hey.*" He banged a huge fist down on the table, and Yuri's head jerked up.

Carter glared for a full 15 seconds. "Marcus believed in you, trusted you, and took a chance on you. If it's true that Marcus signed over 51% of the mill to them, then they don't need him anymore. That means he's probably dead." He leaned forward another inch. "He died trying to protect his and his family's livelihood, but also you and your jobs. He was the sort of guy that would lay down anything to protect those he loved. Don't you fucking dare throw that sacrifice away."

Yuri threw his hands up, cursing Carter's pigheadedness and stupidity in Russian.

Carter craned forward and now laid both huge fists down on the table. "*Bud'te ostorozhny s vashimi slovami!*"

Yuri's head snapped up. "I, *uh*, sorry. I'm just angry." He shrugged. "I didn't know you spoke Russian."

"I speak lots of languages. And I've dealt with the Russian bratva before," Carter replied evenly.

"Yes, as you say, I should watch my words." Yuri nodded. "The thing is, Mr. Carter, you are American, and when things get too hot for you, you can simply go home. But myself and the others at the mill have to live here. Anything you do might end up being inflicted on our families and us for years to come. Some of these hard hitters are in town right now. They watch and see everything."

"In town right now?" Carter grunted and sat back. "Look, all I want from you is information, and a little logistical help. I do not expect you to fight or be involved in anything that puts you at risk." He lifted his chin. "But when I find the people responsible for this, then…" He sat back. "… then, perhaps you'll never need to worry about them again."

Yuri nodded. "That would be good, thank you." He half-smiled. "So what do you want to do?"

"Tomorrow morning as planned, you take us out to the mill to meet the team there, and we can assess what needs to be done."

"Okay." Yuri brightened.

"I also want you to show me these hard hitters." Carter smiled cruelly. "Once I speak to one of them, I can work my way up the chain from there."

"When?" The Russian frowned.

"Tonight." Carter smiled grimly. "Straight after dinner."

CHAPTER 14

After dinner, Carter said goodnight to Sara and watched as she headed for her room down the corridor. He then entered his own room and changed from his shirt into a black pullover, plus a black, woolen beanie. He took with him his camera with the telephoto lens, plus a small pair of binoculars. He put them in a dark, slim backpack, as well as a long Ka-Bar blade, laser sharpened, with a dark, non-reflective finish.

In another few minutes, he was down the stairs and waiting out front for Yuri to show up. Carter wasn't yet sure if he could really trust the guy; he certainly agreed when he said that the bratva had their tentacles everywhere, and for all he knew, it was Yuri that set Marcus up.

But then again, Sara had said that Marcus trusted him and had a good working relationship with him, so, for now, he'd give him the benefit of the doubt.

Yuri was going to take him to a small village on the outskirts of Listvyanka; it was here that Yuri had his meetings with the local bratva. The Russian had told him that a few of the local men still hung out here, but the lieutenants like this man named Tushino only came on certain occasions—to conclude business or to inflict pain and suffering on their targets, he guessed.

Yuri soon showed up in a dark roll-neck pullover that looked thick enough to stop a shotgun blast. Carter bet his last dollar that his mother probably knitted it for him 20 years ago.

"Hello." Yuri smiled but looked nervous.

"You okay?" Carter asked.

"Fine, fine." Yuri's head bobbed.

"You said there was a bar that they hung out at. So that's where we'll go first," Carter said.

"The bar? We go in?" Yuri looked panicked.

"No, don't want to show my hand just yet. But I do want to get a look at these guys. We'll just wait outside, and see who goes in and out. Your job is just to point them out to me."

"Oh, good." Yuri looked relieved, but then looked up briefly. "Will be cold."

"Not a problem," Carter replied. "Let's go."

As they walked, Carter chatted to the Russian, trying to find out a little more about him. He was a big man, probably the same height as Carter. But where Yuri was like a slightly overweight bear, Carter was assembled from blocks of iron.

Carter turned to him. "I'll need you to get some things for me. Things I couldn't bring with me."

Yuri grunted. "I'm guessing a weapon."

"Yes, is that a problem?" Carter asked.

"Not if you have money," Yuri said. "What do you need?"

"Glock 17, single stack, or even better a Glock 19c gen4," Carter replied smoothly. "Can you do it?"

"Yes, yes. But if you want quickly will cost extra," Yuri said. "New or second-hand?"

"Get the gun; price is not an issue. But make sure it's new, no history."

"Okay." They trudged through the freezing night in silence for another 15 minutes, before they came upon the first of the scattered dwellings. Yuri motioned with his head.

"Here we are, town central."

The entire village consisted of two main streets with all the shops and businesses crowded along just one of them, and then with the houses spreading a little wider out like satellites. There was nothing over two stories high, and at this hour, all was quiet and calm.

They headed in and Yuri led him along the back of houses with the smell of wood smoke and cooking fish hanging in the air. Finally, they turned down a lane where he took Carter up a hill that overlooked the bar.

Carter knew they could have gotten in closer, but two guys standing in between houses was far too unusual and suspicious—especially in a village where everybody knew everybody else.

Up on the hill, they were on a rise that overlooked a roof and directly down onto the bar's front door—a little further out than Carter would have liked, but no problem with a telephoto lens.

Carter handed Yuri the binoculars and the pair lay down on the cold, hard earth to wait.

Carter slowed his breathing that also took his heart rate down. He'd been out on night patrols before, in the cold, and also with a burning anger in his soul. But he needed to be calm and cool and refuse the imps of impatience that tried to force things to happen. He'd either spot one or more of the men tonight or not.

Beside him, Yuri kept the field glasses to his eyes and was continually shifting to try and get comfortable. He finally took the glasses away from his face.

"How much longer?"

"How late does the bar stay open?" Carter replied evenly.

Yuri checked his watch. "Midnight; another hour."

"Then, another hour… and a half." Carter smiled and turned. "I appreciate it."

Yuri sighed and went back to watching.

Right on midnight, the front light went out, and then the door opened. An old guy staggered out and wobbled down the street twenty feet before coming to a doorway, stopping and opening his pants to take a piss.

Then from the bar came two men, big and wide, with hands jammed into their jacket pockets. Yuri reached out and gripped Carter's arm.

"That's them." He squinted. "I remember these two came to the mill and were also at the meeting I had. *Uh...*" he seemed to think on it for a moment. "Yes, now I remember; the twins, Borya and Egor Orlov. I don't know which is which."

Carter lowered the camera. "*Very* good."

Yuri looked to him, perplexed. "You not take pictures of them?"

Carter shook his head. "Not yet, later maybe." He watched as the pair of men turned to the pissing man to yell something at him and then laughed darkly. They then headed off down the street, probably to their lodgings.

"How long do Tushino's men usually stay in town?" Carter asked.

"One, two days." Yuri shrugged.

"So, they could take off soon." Carter half-turned. "Thank you, Yuri, you can go now."

"But..." He frowned.

Carter nodded to him. "It's okay. I'll see you tomorrow for the run out to the mill, but I'll take it from here." Carter turned away. "Goodnight."

Yuri sighed theatrically and got to his feet. "Be safe. But remember, this is not America."

He vanished in the darkness, and Carter turned back to spot the men ambling down the street and rose to follow them. What Yuri probably didn't know was that bad things, very bad things, happened in America as well. Evil wasn't the sole domain of any one country, and when you inflict hell on someone, sometimes you attracted the attention of the devil himself— and then he came to pay you a visit. Carter closed in on the men.

He tracked the pair of beefy Russians to a small lodging at the end of the street; they entered and then slammed the door. He quickly followed and gave them a few minutes to get fully inside. He expertly picked the front lock and stood inside the dark entrance hallway for several moments, just listening.

He could hear the men moving around upstairs, and he rolled his woolen beanie down over his face to become a balaclava, and kept his gloves on. There were probably other lodgers, and the building was old, primarily wood, and reeked of onions, cooked fish, and stale tobacco smoke.

He crossed to the steps and began to climb, being careful to only tread on the extreme outside of the risers where there would be little give, and therefore, little squeaking of old wood.

Once on the upper landing, finding the twins' room was easy, as he could still hear the men laughing and talking loudly. They sounded good humored, boisterous, and still a little drunk.

Carter got to the door and gently tried the handle—locked. He'd been lucky; he had no doubt they were the local muscle for the bratva and probably weren't in town all that often. Here, in this small village, they would have been immune from police interest, from any pushback or retribution of any kind.

That was the reality for these men and others like them. He stood back two paces and sucked in a huge breath—their reality was about to be changed forever.

Carter kicked out at the door right over the lock and it exploded inward. In one smooth motion he was inside, catching the two huge men sitting at a table, bottle of vodka in one of their hands and mouths gaping open.

In two rapid steps, he crossed to the twin closest to him as they both began to rise, and struck out with a flat hand to the nose, crushing it back into his face to explode wetly in a spray of blood. The strike would be extremely painful, disorientate him, and send tears to his eyes, blinding him for several seconds. It was all the time he needed.

The second twin was out of his seat and a Christmas ham-sized fist swung at Carter's head, accompanied by several bellowed Russian curses. Carter easily ducked under the blow and sent a chopping strike to the man's Adam's apple with enough force to ensure the windpipe was compressed, but not crushed.

The man grabbed at his neck, bending forward, hacking, and Carter followed it up with a brutal uppercut to the down-turned face, sending the man's head rocking back on his thick neck. He fell back like a sack of bricks.

Carter then quickly crossed to the door and pushed it closed, jamming a chair up against it. He listened for a while but heard nothing—maybe the other residents knew better to complain about anything they heard coming from the twins' room.

Carter then went to the groggy twin whose throat he'd smashed and lifted him back into his chair. The other twin still had his head down on the table, out cold and leaking blood.

He searched the room and found several lengths of power cord and ripped them from the wall. He then tied both the unconscious brothers to their chairs. He went back to the throat-crushed guy and went through his pockets, extracting a wallet. He opened it and read the ID—*Borya*—then he looked at the other guy. "So that makes you Egor."

He then got in close to the guy and grabbed his already-bruised throat. He squeezed it and moved it sharply from side to side, feeling the damaged cartilage unkink. Borya screamed in pain, but his air pipe was now fully open again.

"Hey, wake up," he said in fluent Russian as he slapped the man's face. "*Hey!*" He slapped him again harder.

"Wha...?" The man winced and rubbed his eyes and then held his throat. "Who are you?" He blinked a few times and caught sight of his brother. He went to launch himself from his chair, but Carter was ready and punched down hard onto the bridge of his nose. More blood splashed onto the table and Borya howled and held his face.

"You are a dead man," the Russian said through red teeth, as blood and mucous dripped from his chin.

Carter punched him again. Then again. The man held up a hand. "Fucking stop."

Carter smiled and rubbed his fist. The guy's bonehead felt like hitting a bowling ball. "Borya, yes? I think you misunderstand your position." He drew his long-bladed KaBar and slammed it down to stick in the center of the table. Carter placed a hand on either side of the blade and leaned forward.

"I have some questions."

"Fuck you." Borya looked dead ahead.

"Oh, you like pain?" Carter straightened.

"Fuck you. I give you nothing." The man spat a bloody gob onto the table in front of Carter.

In a single fluid motion, Carter whipped the knife from where it was pinned to the table and chopped the sharp blade down on the outstretched hand of the man's unconscious brother. Egor's two smallest fingers were cleanly severed and flew off the table.

The unconscious Egor was smashed awake from his stupor, but as his arms were tied to the chair's armrests, he could only howl and stare at the damage.

Carter stood back. "Borya, those two fingers of your brother were for you. The next two will be for me. *His* fingers first, and then yours." He held the bloody knife up. "I think it's going to be very hard to collect cash for Gennardy Zyuganov when you both don't have any fingers left, yes?"

The glaring Russian's eyes widened at the sound of his big boss' name.

Carter scowled at Egor still yelling from the pain of his finger amputations and lashed out with a fist across his jaw to shut him down. His head bounced from one side of his neck to the other before it fell forward.

Carter then grabbed Egor's bloody hand and laid it down flat again on the tabletop. He looked to Borya. "Now, two more fingers from Egor, or maybe the first two from you? You choose."

Borya began to laugh and shut his eyes. Carter leaned forward on the table. "I have plenty of time, and once I finish with your fingers, I may start on your toes."

Borya shook his head and grit his teeth hard for a moment, his eyes still shut. "What do you want?" he asked, seething.

"That's better," Carter said. "Let's be clear before we begin. If you die tonight, it won't be me that kills you, but your own stupidity. *Da?*"

Borya opened his eyes to glare. Carter grinned.

"I'll take that as a yes." He straightened and stared into the man's face. "An American has gone missing. Marcus Stenson. Do you know of him?"

"Never heard of him." Borya's eyes were half-lidded.

Carter lopped off the slumbering Egor's thumb. The man howled and Carter punched him again to shut him up.

"Your brother is going to blame you, you know."

"Stop." Borya bucked in his chair.

"Then try again." Carter's voice was emotionless. "The guy that owned the fish farm, the American."

"I know of him, but I don't know what happened…"

Carter lifted the blade.

"No…" Borya shook his head. When Carter paused with the blade held aloft and over his brother's two remaining fingers, he exhaled and shook his head. "He was alive when we saw him. He was on a train going to the authorities, in Moscow, to make some noise. We threw him off the train." He bobbed his large head. "Maybe 10 miles out from Listvyanka."

"So you stopped him?" Carter waited.

Borya slumped, dropped his hands below the tabletop, and began to nod slowly. "Yes, we stopped him. But not kill."

"Then where is he?" Carter asked flatly, using every ounce of self-control to stop himself tearing the man's head off.

Borya shrugged. "Maybe he hit head. You check hospital."

Carter leaned forward, gripping his blade. "Here's what I think happened. You took him off the train, tortured him until he signed a contract, and then killed him." Just saying the words made his heart ache. He exhaled, looking down at the blade and thinking how one minute Marcus had the world at his feet and the next these creatures took everything from him.

When he looked up, Borya was smiling and his hand came up holding a pistol.

Dumb, he thought. The oldest trick in the book was to tape a weapon to the underside of a table, chair, or inside drawers. Carter didn't wait for the man to demand to be untied. A shot rang out, but he was already leaping to the side. He came up behind the near fingerless Egor.

Borya hesitated for just a blink, and Carter shoved Egor and in turn the table, ramming it into Borya's ribs. The Russian instinctively dropped his hands to cushion the impact. And then Carter dived.

He grabbed the gun hand and elbowed the man in the eye. The gun went off twice more, one of the shots taking the unconscious Egor dead center in the chest.

Borya screamed and went mad, but Carter held on, and finally bent the man's hand back so the gun was at his temple.

He hissed into the Russian's face as he strained hard. "Remember when I said it wouldn't be me that kills you, but your own stupidity?" He pulled the trigger and the top of Borya's head was blown off.

Carter let the body go. He knew it was always going to end this way. He knew it before he even entered their house. He already guessed his brother was dead, and he knew he came here to kill. This was just a letter in the mail to the Bratva—stay away, or there'll be a price to pay.

He checked his watch, and then began to move quickly, untying both men, placing the vodka bottle on the table. He picked up the severed fingers and tossed them onto the tabletop, and arranged the knife in Borya's hand.

The gun was still hanging on Borya's finger and his head was back. Carter stepped back and surveyed the scene, picturing it as a crime scene— two criminal brothers got drunk. They had a fight, a very bloody and torturous one, and then one shoots the other. Filled with remorse, he then kills himself. He snorted. Tough town they got here.

Carter knew it would fool no one with an ounce of intelligence, but it'd throw some dust into the air. He then crossed to the door and took the chair away and peered out—all was quiet, but he bet their neighbors were listening; gunshots usually meant people kept their heads down and didn't come out though.

He went out and shut the door, went down the stairs, and then headed back out into the night.

CHAPTER 15

The next morning, Carter and Sara met Yuri down on the dock at 8 am sharp. The Russian was already on his boat and waved, and then stepped onto the dock to greet Sara.

"The last times we went..." he puffed as he helped load the bags, "...we went by truck, because of ice."

"I'd heard you could drive over it once it was fully iced over." Sara jumped lightly onto the deck and walked to the rear to look out over the misted waters. The sun was just up, and the lake looked glass-like, serene, and magnificent.

Yuri came in close to Carter. "Here is your gun." He briefly looked over his shoulder at Sara and then from under his coat he produced a small cloth bag. "Full magazine, and a spare."

Carter took it and then looked inside. He nodded. "Good work." He looked up. "How much?"

"150,000 roubles." Yuri bobbed his head. "About 2,300 American dollars."

"No problem." He tucked the bag into his coat side pocket. "I'll throw another hundred in for you for your troubles." He smiled but there was zero warmth in it. "There'll be more business to do later."

Fact was, Carter expected to pay a lot more for a new Glock. He hoped he didn't need the gun. But if he did run into serious trouble, he wanted to be able to fight his way out. After all, he had already lit the fuse, so whatever would be would be.

"Thank you." Yuri nodded and then tilted his head. "Did you, *uh*, speak to the Orlov brothers last night?"

Carter zipped up his jacket. "Oh yeah, they were very helpful." His face became devoid of emotion. "Marcus is dead. I think they killed him and dumped his body."

Yuri paled for a moment, and then looked at the big American's hands. The knuckles on his right one were abraded and red.

"I see." He sighed and turned away. "Let's get started. It will take us most of the day to get to the mill." He paused, turned back, and lowered his voice. "Mr. Stenson, I know you have reason to be angry, but you have been here less than a day. Please remember the saying about an eye for an eye—eventually, revenge blinds us all."

"And doing nothing in the face of evil will just get you dead." Carter turned away and moved to the gunwale. He rubbed his bruised hand and stared out over the water for a moment before he went and sat with Sara in the rear of the boat. After a moment, she turned to him. Her face still looked strained and there were dark rings under her eyes.

"I've seen the mill; in pictures, I mean. Marcus did a wonderful job of cleaning it up."

Carter continued to face the water. "He was good like that. Smart, focused, and diligent. I'm looking forward to seeing it for real."

"Me too. Sort of," she said. "I know seeing it is going to make me see him in every single thing he has done to the place."

Carter just nodded.

Her lips drew into a crooked smile. "Did you know they say it's haunted?"

Carter turned to her. "Yeah, Yuri told me last night. Even before the paper mill was first opened, many people have gone missing. Just vanished in the night."

"Do you believe it?" she asked.

He shook his head. "Why not? Freezing, deep water, too much vodka, not enough light. I bet that's what snatched people, more than anything supernatural."

"Yeah, I guess." She inhaled and exhaled slowly. She turned to him again, her gaze level. "So, what did Yuri give you?"

Carter didn't hesitate. "A gun."

"Good." She nodded. "I want one too."

He leaned forward and took her hand. "Sara, I have to tell you that I think…"

"You think, you know, he's dead, don't you?" She looked up into his face and when he didn't refute her, she smiled ruefully. "I knew it. It's okay, I knew it deep down as well."

He sighed. "I'm so sorry. You have to think about what it is you want to do now, and going forward from here, I mean."

She nodded and drew in a deep breath. "I only wanted it because he did. Now that he's gone, I don't know anymore."

"Then sell it, leave all this behind, and go back to the sunshine, and the Pacific Ocean," he said. "We're not even in winter yet, and with everything else going on, it might turn out to be hell here."

"But I'm not a quitter." She faced him. "Neither are you."

He waited.

"Marcus wanted this farm to be a success. So do I. His legacy will be this successful operation. Besides, if I quit, they win." She gathered herself. "We won't be scared off." She bobbed her head for a moment. "But I can't do it by myself." She reached across to lay her hand on his forearm.

Carter felt a small tingle like a tiny electric shock run up his arm and he tried to dampen down some old feelings that still rattled around inside him.

"I'll be here for as long as you need me." He placed his large hand over hers.

"Thank you, Carter. Thank you for everything." Her head dropped.

"It's okay. This has been shit all around. And no one will think less of you if you do decide to pull out and never look at this place again."

She shook her head. "I'm not running from this. If we do, it'll mean Marcus' life was taken from him, from me, for nothing."

"They need you to countersign the contract so they'll come at you again," Carter said softly. "You know that, don't you?"

"I do." Her eyes narrowed. "But we know who they are, and we also know that they will be prepared to use violence." She turned to him. "We know the rules now."

He half-smiled. "And we can use them too. I can stay until this place is running smoothly, and until there are no more threats." He sat back. "I'm just glad you're okay."

She turned away for a moment but then back, and her eyes blazed. "No, I'm not okay, Carter. I want their fucking heads for what they did to Marcus."

Carter's voice was low and menacing as he looked back out at the passing water of the lake. "So do I."

CHAPTER 16

Nearly 12 hours later, Sara stood at the gunwale and watched as Yuri pulled them into the wharf at the mill. She felt a tingling in her stomach at seeing a place she had only looked at in pictures.

She turned to Carter and he nodded back at her as he also saw the small group of men gathering, and she assumed they were the staff Marcus had recently organized.

Yuri nosed in and Carter threw the rope over the bollard and lashed it down. He jumped up and turned to help Sara, but she had already leaped up onto the wharf and stood with hands on her hips for a moment, before striding up toward the large house.

Yuri pointed at the men. "Mrs. Stenson, do you want to meet people?"

She ignored him as there was something burning she needed to do first.

"Later," she heard Carter say from behind her.

Sara strode up the hill, smiling tightly to the young and old men as she passed by them and came to the large mill manager's house. She grabbed the handle and paused for a moment, gathering herself, and then turned the handle and pushed the door inward.

It was getting on sundown now and orange light came in through the windows. Dust motes glowed as they floated in the air, and she smelled cleaning polish, new paint, and old wood. On benchtops were blue and white bowls, some with new fruit in them. There were also vases with wild flowers that needed changing, and rows of books, some in English and some in Russian.

She headed for the stairs and bounded up them, hearing the squeak of protesting wood, and went straight toward the main bedroom. Inside was a huge bed with fresh linen laid over the top but not tucked in. She felt her throat catch—Marcus never could make a proper bed.

She went to the bedside table and saw a photograph of the pair of them, on a beach holiday from a few years back—tanned, salt-crusted hair and eyebrows, and laughing into the camera.

Sara picked it up and sat on the bed. Then slowly laid back, holding the memory to her chest.

"All gone," she whispered. And then. "Stolen." She closed her eyes and let the tears come.

She didn't know how long she lay there but a knock on the door downstairs snapped her out of her misery fugue. It was near dark now, and she turned her head to shout, "A minute."

She sat up and looked at the picture again. "I want to finish what you started, Marcus. I'll really try." She put the frame back where she found it. "If I can bear it." She wiped her eyes with the back of her hand, stood up, and then crossed to the window.

It'd be so easy to tell Carter that she would appoint a manager to run the mill in her name. *The Russian mafia could go to hell*, she thought.

She leaned on the windowsill, staring out over miles of bleakness. And what if she handed half over to them? Would all her problems go away?

"*Yech.*" It would be exactly the opposite of what Marcus would have wanted. She turned away from the window and headed for the stairs.

As she got to the bottom of the stairs, Carter was standing just inside the doorframe. He looked so much like Marcus it made her suck in a breath and stare for a moment. She knew all about his background and also knew that he was the dark to Marcus being the light. She had loved him once, but his life seemed to be one of chaos and war, where at that time in her life she wanted calm and predictability.

She stared down at him, seeing that look in his eye he used to have so many years ago. Sara didn't want anything to happen to him, but even if she tried to send him home, she knew he'd refuse. It was another reason for her to decide if she wanted to continue. It meant she wasn't only putting herself at risk, but also Carter.

He smiled up at her. She knew his love of his brother was paramount, and where she wanted to have her vengeance, he'd be the instrument to make it happen if she wanted it. For security, she could have no better general. *But as a friend, she could have no better... what?* she now wondered.

"Meet and greet time?" she asked, brows up.

"Yep. They seem a good bunch, and all waiting outside." He stood aside so she could step out onto the porch. She saw that her bags had been laid there and four men waited in a line, all eyes on her. On the other side was the bearish Yuri, still looking slightly morose.

She came to the edge of the porch and Carter stood looming at her shoulder. She nodded and smiled at each of them.

"Thank you," she started. "Thank you all for supporting my husband and getting this enterprise off the ground. My name is Sara Stenson. I know of you through my conversations with Marcus, and he spoke fondly about all of you."

She looked toward the first man, the youngest, and had a guess at who it was. "You must be Nikolay."

The young man half-bowed, and a smile spread across his face. He didn't seem to know what to do next, so Sara crossed to him and stuck out a hand.

"Pleased to meet you, Nikolay."

He grasped it and shook it while bowing again. Sara smiled. "Perhaps you can introduce me to your father and friends."

Nikolay walked her over to an older man with a grey mustache that bore a resemblance to him. "This is my father, Pavel."

They shook hands and then she was introduced to both Leonid and Dmitry. The first puffed on a pipe that looked whittled from a tree branch and the second man had his sleeves rolled up, displaying a fading tattoo of a wolf wearing a beret with a dagger through it that looked like an old military tattoo. She stood back and saw that all of them looked a little nervous.

"You all helped get the place started. And I want to assure you that I'm not here to shut us down, but instead move us forward. There'll be work to do, and strong hands and sharp minds will be needed."

Pavel turned to speak quietly with his son, who seemed to push back a little, but after some urging from his father, he turned to her and cleared his throat.

"There are two things, Ms. Stenson; one, will Marcus, Mr. Stenson, be coming back?"

She drew in a deep breath. "Marcus is not coming back." Just saying the words wounded her. She lifted her chin. "And the second thing?"

"The bratva, who came here..." Nikolay started.

"Unfortunately, they *will* most likely come back," Carter replied for her. "But I'll never let them harm anyone or anything here as long as I live. I promise you that."

The men spoke among themselves and then nodded. Sara could see that they weren't quite convinced. *Why should they be?* she thought.

She stepped forward, her voice now raised. "Marcus is gone," she said. "But his legacy will be this successful business. Will you help me finish his dream?"

They spoke as one: "*Da!*"

CHAPTER 17

It was morning, mid-spring, but Carter shivered as he stepped out of his bed. He had taken one of the cabins in the mill compound, and as yet, it wasn't one of the ones that had been fully repaired, and there was enough natural ventilation to let a nice icy breeze run straight through it.

Thankfully, the power was on, and armed with a hot water bottle and a Soviet-era kerosene heater that gave off a smell that made his eyes water, he was able to grab a few hours' sleep.

It was just gone 5 am and it'd still be a few hours before the sun was a pale-orange wheel on the horizon. He dressed quickly and stepped outside, flipping the jacket's hood up over his head and watching as his breath drifted away in little vapor ghosts.

They would come, the bratva, he was sure of that, but just not when. Even though the death scene he had created in town of the murder-suicide of the Orlov twins might fool the local cops for a while, he doubted it'd be too much of a coincidence for the Russian mafia to swallow, as they had eyes everywhere and would know he and Sara had arrived.

The holstered gun was at his back, within easy reach. They could simply come for payback for the twins. And if that was the case, he bet it'd be a single shooter from the tree line. Carter let his eyes run along the line of dark pine, spruce and birch—they were thick and at this time of the day, there were too many shadows for him to see in even a few feet.

However, Carter suspected they'd more than likely come to try and get Sara to countersign the deal they had forced Marcus into. Even though the bratva were experts at breaking the law or working around it, it was much simpler if they could operate within its framework. After all, death and bloodshed was messy and bad for business. And when it came to the mafia in any country, business always came first. At least to begin with.

He hoped they would come, as he wanted to see their faces—all of them. Get to know how they looked, talked, and moved; the best hunters, man and animal, got to know their quarry.

The ex-Special Forces soldier looked slowly over the compound—everyone was still asleep and it was quiet as a tomb. The ground was a little muddy after some rain overnight, and as he looked over the soil, he saw the tracks.

Carter frowned and craned forward—he'd been hunting many times and also been involved in tracking in Special Forces. He knew animal tracks—mammal, bird, and reptile—but these he didn't recognize at all.

They were about two feet width between the footprints, if that's what they even were.

He saw that they entered the compound from the high tree line, meandered about, and then exited close to where they came in.

The tracks weren't deep so whatever it was can't have been large. *Must be a fox*, he thought, *or something like a badger*; he made a mental note to ask Yuri later on.

Carter sucked in another deep breath and bit it off. The cold stung his throat and lungs, and he had to work to stifle a cough. They all had a lot to try and accomplish today. Sara would be beginning her work in the lab, getting the facilities in shape. And he and Yuri were heading out on the lake to the chosen pen sites. It was warming now, and the ice was breaking up and showing a lot of open water. There were many weeks of work ahead, and it all had to be completed before the cold came back.

Thankfully, Marcus had left detailed notes, a project plan with critical path areas identified, as Sara called it, which was literally a blueprint for them all to follow. The guy had been a genius, and it made Carter feel both proud and angry all over again.

They'd hire a local marine biologist to assist Sara with the scientific lab work now that Marcus' expertise was lost, but for the mundane and mechanical side of running the place, Carter and Yuri could take up most of the slack, and the kid, Nikolay, was as smart as a whip, so he'd also come under Sara's wing.

Carter ambled down toward the water where he met Yuri at the wharf. The Russian had a large, thick Russian cigarette jammed in the side of his mouth and waved as Carter jumped down onto the deck.

"A little cold, yes?"

"A little cold, very yes," Carter agreed.

"You know, some Russians go swimming in lake this time of year." He grinned.

"They would be the insane ones," Carter shot back.

Yuri pointed to the bollards and went to the small wheelhouse as Carter set to untying the ropes and casting off. With a cough and a growl, the boat pulled away.

There were several sites they had chosen. Each was about half a mile from the other sites, to ensure good geographical separation. If any one of the pens became infected by some sort of fungal or bacterial outbreak, then hopefully the other pens would be far enough away that they wouldn't be contaminated.

Carter stood at the stern, watching as the mill vanished in the distance. He felt nervous every time he left Sara alone—she was capable and smart, and now was armed, but the local mafia had added a new complexity that she wasn't trained to deal with.

But he was. He turned. "Yuri."

"*Mmm*?" The man sucked on his cigarette one last time and flicked it over the side into the pristine waters.

"I need a little more hardware." Carter walked toward the wheelhouse. "Something a little more... persuasive."

Yuri chuckled. "Oh, I see." He looked over his shoulder. "I don't suppose that it is a good fountain pen so you can write a strong letter to Moscow bureaucrats."

Carter chuckled. "Not this time. I need a snow uniform—extra large."

Yuri groaned.

"And a sniper rifle. I'll give you the specifications." Carter waited.

Yuri slowly shook his head. "You want to start a war... here, in Russia? You'll get yourself and maybe us all killed, Mr. Carter Stenson."

"Marcus was the man of peace. And look what that got him," Carter said. "My objective is to stop anything happening before it starts." He stepped in closer to Yuri. "I truly hope nothing starts. But if it does..."

"You will finish it." Yuri wouldn't look at him. "I don't like it."

"Some people play by different rules. Brutal and bloody ones. To have any chance of winning, sometimes you need to play by the same ones," Carter said evenly.

Yuri sighed. "Snow uniform, no problem; rifle, harder. You have specs, you say?"

"Yes," Carter said. "Same as before, money no problem, but to be untraceable and no questions asked."

Yuri scoffed. "You will make local black marketer very rich man. I see what I can do." He turned, his brow creased. "Last thing, *da*?"

Carter smiled. "Sure, for today."

Yuri snorted. "And last thing from me. You have no proof that bratva had anything to do with Marcus' disappearance. For now, law on their side. Remember that."

Carter ignored him.

In a few more hours, the sun was fully up and warming the water's surface. Vapor seemed to rise from it, and it was glass-smooth except for the occasional block of bobbing ice, most no larger than bowling balls that thumped against the bow as Yuri cut the water.

After another half-hour, Yuri slowed as he scanned the shoreline, looking for landmarks. And then he cut the engine.

"Site number one."

Carter nodded and lifted a red buoy with a pole and flag attached. It had hundreds of feet of rope attached to a small hook anchor and he pushed it all over the side. The anchor sank quickly, taking the rope with it, and in another few seconds, the buoy bobbed down as it struck bottom and then came back to the surface.

Carter then lifted one of the Perspex capsules that contained a small camera. It also had fins on each side that moved up and down for maneuverability, as well as a tiny propeller.

Yuri had his laptop open in the wheelhouse, punched a few keys, and sharpened the resolution. "Online and transmitting," he said over his shoulder.

"Dropping camera... *now*." Carter put it over the side, and the small propeller whizzed to life, the side fins angled to take the camera down.

Carter joined Yuri in the wheelhouse. "What are we looking for?"

"Snags," Yuri said. "Sunken logs, old shipwrecks, monsters of the lake." He turned and winked. "Basically, I look at the bottom surface to ensure it is fairly uniform so nets stay in place and remain anchored."

Yuri guided the camera capsule lower. "The sturgeon are bottom feeders, so if the lake is uneven on the bottom, the nest won't sit flat, and the fish get out."

"Or something gets in," Carter added.

"Correct; maybe local sturgeon that might be sick." He guided the small camera deeper. "Now at 50 feet. This lake is a rift lake, meaning it is basically a giant tear in Siberia. It can fall away very sharply, and so we cannot place nets on a cliff edge."

"Makes sense," Carter replied.

At 120 feet, Yuri leveled the camera off. "Here we are."

On the screen, there was an endless plain of brown mud. The occasional tree trunk stood upright on the bottom with hanging weed from its branches that made them look like the tattered masts from old schooners permanently frozen in time.

The water at this depth was crystal clear and as long as they avoided stirring up the silt on the bottom, they'd have excellent vision.

"Looking good," Yuri said.

They patrolled the lake depths for another 15 minutes, doing wider and wider loops, and then finally scouted the full perimeter. In an hour, they had nearly completed their task when down deep the camera suddenly became buffeted as if it was in a washing machine.

Then the silt exploded around the camera, and Carter had to dive for the tether and hang on as the small Perspex capsule tumbled and jerked in the water.

"What the hell is going on?" Carter yelled.

"I think... something... went by us." Yuri furiously worked the controls for another few minutes before he managed to get the camera out of the agitation zone.

"Is okay now." He shook his head. "Must have been big sturgeon."

"Let's confirm that," Carter said. "Bring her back around for another look."

Yuri nodded and turned the small camera about. He headed back into the clouds of debris. Most of the heavy particle matter was settling, but some of the finer silt remained suspended like gossamer veils in the deep water. Visibility was now down to about six feet.

"Around here," Yuri said, making the small capsule hover for a moment. He turned it 360 degrees. "Nothing I can see."

"Look down," Carter said. "Point it downward, at the lake bottom."

Yuri tilted the camera capsule.

"There... what's that?" Carter squinted at the image on the small screen.

"I don't know." Yuri carefully eased the camera a little closer to the muddy bottom, trying to avoid the tiny propellers stirring up more silt.

"Strange," Yuri whispered.

Cut into the silt, there looked as if something had been dragged over the bottom.

"Like tracks maybe?" the Russian asked.

"Could a big sturgeon do that?" Carter asked.

Yuri frowned. "Much too big and deep in mud; sturgeon glide." He held his hand out flat and moved it in an approximation of one of the large fish.

"Follow them," Carter said.

Yuri rotated the capsule and it traced the strange markings along the lakebed. Minutes ticked by and the strange tracks continued on. Even from the small screen, they could see the bottom was angling steeply downward the further they went.

"200 feet," Yuri said. "Maybe we dislodged something, and it rolled. Must be that."

"Yeah, right." Carter scoffed and noticed that Yuri was perspiring heavily.

"You saw that water agitation. It was something moving in a way that wasn't like a uniform rolling or sliding." Carter straightened as the camera came to an underwater cliff.

Yuri hovered the camera at the precipice. The darkness beyond was absolute, as the tiny dot of light in a Perspex box hovered in the water.

"We are at 250 feet. The camera cannot go much lower." He sighed.

Carter leaned forward and stared into the abyssal blackness. "How deep do you think it goes here?" Carter asked.

Yuri shrugged. "It is very deep, and in some places, the lake is over a mile deep, but I don't think it is that here."

The tracks or marks went over the edge and vanished.

"So, you're sticking with something sliding or rolling along the lake bottom, is that right?" Carter half-turned.

"What else could it be?" Yuri muttered. "Nothing that big lives in the lake. Nothing that's ever been seen." He faced Carter. "Once after heavy rain, a huge log was washed further in. It was already waterlogged, but it retained neutral buoyancy. When I took divers down, it loomed out of the dark, hanging mid-water. Scared them, very bad. At first, my divers thought it was a whale. Or something else."

Carter just stared at his worried expression for a moment, until something splashed on the surface a few dozen feet out from the rail of the boat and both men spun toward it. On the lake's surface, bubbles popped and ripples were spreading outward as it returned to calm.

"I think we should go. This might not be a good site for the fish after all," Yuri said just above a whisper.

"Why?" Carter turned to him. "Listen, big guy, I hope you're not going to get all jumpy and superstitious on me now, are you?"

Yuri just stared at him. "Did you know there is a place on Lake Baikal that is known as *the Devil's Crater*? For centuries, vessels have been disappearing there without a trace. Did you know this?"

Carter shook his head and waited as the man obviously had more to say.

Yuri went on. "Yes, is true. As recently as 2011, a boat called the *Yamaha* left the village of Buryatia in the Kabansk region. The conditions were calm, the crew was experienced, everything good, but it didn't matter. Contact with the vessel was lost shortly after their departure when they say a thick fog rose up from out of the lake itself and enveloped them. When the fog finally burned off, the *Yamaha* was gone."

"And?" Carter waited.

"And, all the crew had mobile phones and they were well within range of cellular services, but none of the crew could be reached. It was if they were completely outside of the network. After the fog lifted, many search-and-rescue operations were undertaken but all trace of the *Yamaha* had vanished."

"The Devil's Crater, *huh*?" Carter folded his arms.

"Yes, Mr. Stenson. It was as if the *Yamaha* was swallowed by the lake itself, and locals believe that the area occasionally produces horrific, sudden whirlpools that appear like a crater upon the water's surface, hence the name, *Devil's Crater*. It sucks in anything unfortunate enough to be caught in one of those vortexes, and be dragged all the way down to hell."

Yuri stopped talking, and his face looked drained of color.

"O-oookay." Carter could see the Russian was rattled and really believed the supernatural aspects of the tale. "Thank you for the story, Yuri, but I gotta tell you that every damn lake, sea, or large body of water in the world has tales of things from the deep or unexplained events. If we believed them all, we'd never leave dry land."

Carter had enough of local scaremongering, and he knew that if the legends were really let off their leash, then every bump, splash, or moan in the night would consume everything they did.

"Mr. Stenson, superstition has nothing to do with it. All I wish to say is that the lake should be respected." Yuri regained his composure.

"And that we will do," Carter agreed.

"And I still think we should not use this site for a fish pen anymore." The camera bobbed back to the surface and Yuri turned back to the wheelhouse. "You grab camera, and we go to second site."

Carter groaned and retrieved the boat hook. He knew that science and physical evidence would provide pushback against the myths, but that these legends became ingrained superstition and part of a culture's folklore the more they were allowed to exist.

He reached over to grab the camera box. *For now, he'd play along*, he thought and lifted it from the water.

Carter looked at his hands. "What's this crap?" They were covered in slime.

"Huh?" Yuri turned, cigarette now dangling from his lip.

Carter lifted his hand to his nose and recoiled. "Jesus. Smells like shit."

Yuri came and grabbed his wrist, and squinted at the clear mucous-like slime on his fingers. "Never seen it before." He dragged Carter's hand closer to his face and sniffed. He grunted and released the hand and shrugged. "Smells like something dead. Maybe some sort of algae from lake bottom."

Carter looked around and saw an old coffee mug of Yuri's, grabbed it, and scraped some of the mucous off the camera and into the mug. He then tied a rag over the top.

"We'll see what Sara thinks it is." He grabbed another rag to wipe his hands and also the camera casing. "Yech." He tossed the rag to the corner. "Let's get to the other sites and finish our work."

CHAPTER 18

Sara frowned as she changed magnification on the microscope, enlarging the spectrum and moving the slide a little.

"Interesting."

She sat back for a moment and folded her arms. The sample that Carter had brought her from the lake didn't really make sense. The viscous material was made up of a form of mammalian tissue—epithelium—one of the four basic types of animal tissue, along with connective tissue, muscle, and nerve tissue.

She looked across to one of the other lab rooms separated by glass partitions. Nikolay worked on one of the sturgeon incubation tanks; though she faced him, her gaze was turned inward as her mind ran on.

The baffling thing was the tissue sample wasn't from a single animal. The cells indicated several animal types, human being just one of them.

She knew that the epithelial layers contain no blood vessels, so they must receive nourishment via diffusion of substances from the underlying connective tissue—they basically absorbed nutrition from the base animal. *So what were they doing all mashed together over a hundred feet down in a Siberian lake?*

All she could think of was that after big storms, dead animal carcasses sunk to the bottom. Then the currents and lake tides moved them into eddies, crevices, and depressions where they all rotted down together, creating a biological soup.

"It's a theory," she mused.

At her side, her computer light blinked on, informing of a successful Internet connection.

"Hallelujah, welcome to the modern world."

She rolled her chair across the floor. In an area of crap communications, when a link was finally established, it was not to be wasted.

She first did a quick search in her medical journals for the form of liquefied epithelium tissue and found nothing. Then she tried biology forums, and even lakebed precedents, but again there was nothing.

Has to be an aberration unique to Baikal, she thought. She sat thinking about the material for a while longer before deciding to log it, but let it go, as there were several things that she had wanted to delve into about the area while she had the opportunity.

She typed in her search string and leaned forward to read. She blew air from between her pressed lips. "Good God."

She knew the lake was old, but didn't know just *how* old... and big. Lake Baikal was a mile deep and formed by the Earth's crust literally being pulled apart to create a giant tear in its surface around 30 million years ago.

Sara scoffed softly as she read of the many myths and legends—there were pages and pages of them. Of course they had their own Nessie they called the Baikal Water Devil. Sonar readings from over the past 100 years had indicated something large down there in the depths, but as recently as 2016, fishermen were complaining of having their nets torn to shreds by something in the lake.

She sat back, feeling she wasn't learning anything particularly useful, when she saw the last story on the page, and a fairly recent one. It also dovetailed in with something Yuri had mentioned to her. *Lights*, he had once told her. Coming from deep below the water. She leaned in, squinting at the article in the Siberian Times. She read quickly.

In 1977, a deep-water submersible called Paysis was undertaking a scientific research dive in Lake Baikal. The surface crew reported that they lost contact with the vessel and it was only later that they found out why.

The submersible was traveling at just 3 knots at a depth of 3,800 feet down in the dark and crushing waters when the crew reported that suddenly they lost all power and also their external spotlights, leaving them lifeless and slowly sinking in a blackness that was absolute.

But only for a moment because a green light shone on their submersible from an external source.

The lights again, Sara thought, as she scrolled the page.

The crew reported that the light reportedly remained fixed on the submersible for several seconds, making them feel slightly dizzy with a tingling in their bellies, before it suddenly vanished to once again leave them in the stygian blackness. In another second, all their power was restored.

There was nothing on their sonar and to this day, there had never been a satisfactory explanation for what the source of the light was. Given the lake's size, depth, and remoteness, much of it, even to this day, remained unexplored.

Sara felt a slight tingle run up her spine and folded her arms. "What the hell am I getting myself into? *Already gotten* myself into," she corrected.

*****

Three sturgeon pen sites were finally chosen and the netting was set to be laid. It was a huge, labor-intensive and expensive job.

In addition, Nikolay managed to find a newly graduated biology major named Stefan Koloshev who could help him in the lab. After a quick interview with Sara who liked his credentials, he was approved on probation and in no time, the pair was streamlining operations and had everything ready for acceptance of the fish and eggs.

Yuri, Carter, with the help of Dmitry, Pavel, and Leonid's boats, laid the cable netting that was strung from the water's surface all the way to the lake bottom. The buoys were designed to hang a few inches below the surface, and the floats were made from synthesized polymer that was tough, retained its buoyancy, and wasn't troubled by extreme cold and even freezing. In addition, along the mesh line were banks of sensors, some allowing the teams to locate the pens even when they were below the ice.

Sara worked with Stefan and Nikolay and together they not only managed to bring the laboratory and hatchery online, but just a week later, she also managed to convince the Russian administrators at the Federal Agency for Fisheries and Conservation to release the adult fish, plus the first batch of fertilized Beluga sturgeon eggs to them.

In no time, they had several huge tanks filled with tadpole-sized sturgeon fishlets that'd grow quickly to about eight inches and then be ready for release into the first fine-mesh nursery pens.

The adults came in individual tanks that were loaded with ice to slow down their metabolism and keep them calm. Carter had helped them guide them in as they were lowered by helicopter and then wheeled into the mill house labs.

He and Sara had marveled at the huge fish as they stared down at one specimen—it was close to 20 feet long, and along its back in three rows were the raised scutes, sharp bone-like knobs that were also present on alligators and some dinosaurs. The tiny eyes and upturned snout with dangling feelers added to the prehistoric appearance.

They'd both reached in and ran a hand down the flanks of one of the fish. The water was freezing, but the skin was slick and taut with muscle.

"You'll like it here," she said to it.

"Or we'll eat you," Carter added, to which Sara scowled.

The fish arriving meant Carter and Yuri would then have the daily chore of checking the water quality—everything from natural to synthetic contaminants would be monitored. Carter had no doubt that the bratva would show up again, and if they decided to seriously poison the water, then there was little chance of doing anything—you couldn't exactly move pens quickly that were anchored to the bottom.

Carter would also be patrolling the bank, but as the huge length of wilderness shoreline had to be traversed on foot, he knew he'd need extra eyes and ears soon. And he would ensure those eyes and ears came with some serious muscle.

CHAPTER 19

Moscow—Bratva, work-in-progress meeting

Arkady Tushino had been called to Moscow for a meeting along with other local bratva lieutenants to discuss their business ventures and opportunities in their regions. Their boss-of-bosses and chairman was Gennardy Zyuganov, and he terrified every single one of them.

Zyuganov was six-four and weighed in at 300 pounds if he was an ounce. In his prime, he was a wrestler and weight lifter. Rumor had it that once in a bar fight, he had physically torn the head from a man with his bare hands. Looking at the hulking brute, no one would dispute it.

Zyuganov sat holding a report in those head-tearing hands and read slowly. There was a large cigar in his mouth, unlit for now, that he rolled from one side of his thick lips to the other. The report was a summary of their moneymaking projects they were involved in; the costs, long-term cash flow, and risks. It was the company balance sheet, and he ran his criminal enterprise like any other big business.

Each of the delegates took turns explaining their projects in more detail, and it had finally come around to be Tushino's turn. The worry for Tushino was on his turn, the boss had dropped the report and turned his cold, pale gaze on him.

Tushino detailed his multiple projects, and also the opportunity of the part ownership of the Stenson sturgeon fish farm to sell high-value Beluga caviar. When he had finished, Zyuganov grunted and took the now very wet cigar from his mouth.

"When will this American woman sign your contract?" he asked in a voice that was slow and deep.

Tushino swallowed and struggled to remain outwardly impassive. "I expect any day now. The widow has only been in Russia for a few weeks now and she has brought with her the brother of the former owner. They do not have the expertise or contacts as Mr. Marcus Stenson did. She is helpless and has no choice but to work with us."

"Helpless, *hmm*?" Zyuganov's jaw worked for a moment. "Tell me about the Orlov brothers."

Tushino frowned for a moment, not comprehending how the big boss even knew about the pair of low-level thugs. He hiked his shoulders and his mouth turned down. "They were local muscle who drank and fought too much." He shrugged. "The idiots seem to have killed each other."

"Did they?" Zyuganov's eyes were like pale lasers. "Do you know who this elder Stenson brother is? Have you even seen him?"

Tushino shook his head slowly and could only stare, waiting. Something was happening that he hadn't anticipated, and he certainly didn't like it.

Zyuganov took the cigar from his mouth. "I have friends in America, and they have done some background checking for me. This elder Stenson is not just ex-military, he is *ex-Special Forces*. And whatever he did in Special Forces is sealed from my scrutiny. I don't think he was just the military cook, do you?"

Tushino felt his stomach sink as Zyuganov's jaw worked for a moment before he continued.

"And you killed his brother." Zyuganov never blinked. "He arrives and two of the men who were involved in killing this man's brother suddenly decide to kill each other. Really? And you still think this is all a coincidence?"

"We never killed his brother." Tushino licked his lips. "The police said…"

"*The police are idiots.*" The roar made Tushino wince. The group's eyes were on him now as Zyuganov bared his teeth. "You pull an alligator by the tail, don't be surprised if you lose an arm."

Tushino gulped but tried with every fiber of his being to maintain an iron-like composure. He knew that to show weakness now would mean he might leave the building in a potato sack… and in pieces.

"If there are loose ends, I will tidy them up, sir. You can count on me, you know that, Mr. Zyuganov."

Gennardy Zyuganov leaned forward on the table, his bulk making the entire oak frame squeak. "I don't care about this fish farm. I don't care about two morons getting themselves killed, or even that an American has caused you to lose face. But I do care about making money and losing control. Mr. Tushino, are you in control of your district or not?"

Tushino stood. "Yes, Mr. Zyuganov. Absolutely, sir."

Zyuganov continued to glare. "Go there, make a deal with the woman, and see this man. See if he will be… *reasonable*." He leaned back in his leather chair, making it squeal under his considerable weight. "When we next meet, you prove to me you control your district." His eyes narrowed. "Or I'll have someone control it in your place."

*****

"Heads up." Carter straightened as he heard the high-powered motorboat in the distance. He quickly felt for the gun at his back and eased it out and back in case he needed to draw quickly.

Yuri and the other men stopped what they were doing and watched the water, and even Nikolay poked his head from the huge loading doors of the mill laboratory to watch.

Carter wandered up to the main house and as he came to the bottom of the steps, Sara stepped onto the front deck and stood with hands on hips.

"Who is it?" she asked while still holding a screwdriver in one fist, obviously in the middle of repairs.

Carter watched the boat arrive. It wasn't like Yuri's or the other boats that tended to work the lake, and instead looked more like a pimp's boat. It was a sleek-looking motor cruiser, incongruous for these parts.

"Either we've got some visiting movie stars, or the local mafia has arrived to try and do a deal with you." He looked up at her. "You want me to take care of this?"

"Not a chance." She continued to watch the boat as it nudged ice sludge out of the way as it came into the wharf.

Yuri joined them and squinted down as the group of men alighted from the boat. "I can see our old friends, Drago and Volodin," he said as two big men waited for the others to disembark. "But no sign of Orlov twins." He glanced at Carter who gave him a flat smile.

Yuri looked over the rest. "Other man I don't know. But now comes Arkady Tushino. He is the local boss. These are the men that came and talked to Marcus."

The four men walked up the hill toward the main house, and Carter could tell at least two of them were armed because of the telltale bulge in their jackets. Lumped muscle rolled under their thick clothing, and they looked raw and intimidating. It didn't bother Carter one bit.

Carter stepped down when they got to within 20 feet of Sara. He held up a hand flat in their faces. "Stop right there, and state your business."

Tushino stepped to the front of the group and pulled on a wide smile, but his dead eyes never left Carter. "My name is Arkady Tushino, and you must be Carter Stenson." He held out a hand, but Carter ignored it. Tushino shrugged and looked around. "Where is the brother, Marcus?"

Carter heard Sara's intake of breath. Frankly, he wanted to kill them all, but he knew Yuri was right; he had no proof and he couldn't exactly cite the Orlov twins as witnesses for the prosecution. For now, the law was on their side. Carter would let them play dumb for a little longer.

"Not here. Like I just asked, what do you want?"

"Not here?" Tushino looked troubled. "I hope he's okay. Very bad country this; some bad people." He seemed to brighten. "So, when we last met with Marcus, he wanted to ensure that his business was never troubled by these bad people or circumstances again."

Tushino stepped around Carter to address Sara. "And you must be Marcus Stenson's charming and beautiful wife, Sara, I think." He grinned up at her, but she remained impassive.

"Is hard here for a woman. And dealing with Moscow is also very hard, and strains the patience, especially if you are a foreigner. We can help with that too. Streamline everything. Even find new markets for you, for the fish, and for the eggs."

"Eggs?" Sara frowned. "No eggs for sale. In fact, no nothing for sale." Her eyes were flat. "We can't help you and too bad you came all the way out to be told that. We'll be fine."

"You are mistaken, Mrs. Stenson. Mr. Marcus has already agreed to this. Your approval is only a formality under Russian law."

Sara bared her teeth. "Bullshit."

Tushino held out the contract. "I think you'll recognize this."

Sara and Carter leaned forward. Sara was first to ease back and her lips were drawn back in a snarl. "That's not Marcus' signature."

"I was there when he signed it." Tushino frowned back. "It is his."

"You really are as dumb as you look. That signature is not even spelled right—there's only one 't' in our name." Sara motioned with her head back to their boat. "Get outta here."

Tushino pulled his head back on his neck. "You're playing a dangerous game, Mrs. Stenson. I think you don't know who you're dealing with."

Carter stepped in close to the man faster than anyone else could react and pulled him close to hiss into his face. "You heard the lady. Get the fuck out of here."

Two of Tushino's men went for their guns, but Yuri drew a long knife and held it by the blade, ready to throw.

"No, no, let's all stay friends here, *da*?" Tushino waved them down but stared back into Carter's eyes. "This is the last time you'll see me... being nice."

Carter pushed him hard so he fell back in the icy mud. "And this is me *being* nice, right now."

One of Tushino's men obviously thought he saw an opening and darted in at Carter. He came in like a linebacker, but for a big man, Carter was extremely light on his feet and stepped back, dodging the huge roundhouse punch thrown at his head.

Carter then grabbed him as the follow-through took him past and yanked him sideways to use the tip of his elbow onto the Russian's temple. The big guy grunted in pain and went for his gun. Carter's expression was devoid of emotion or effort as he punched down again onto the man's jaw, and leaned down to rip the gun from his hand.

He then used the heavy iron revolver to smash it back across the man's face, eliciting a crunch of metal on cheekbone. The big guy went down onto his knees, and Carter hit him again, knocking him to all fours, and then held the gun to the back of his ear.

"There are two ways forward for you from here—one of them is you all getting on your boat and pissing off. The other is very bloody and painful." He looked up. "For all of you."

Tushino bared his teeth and spoke rapidly in Russian. Carter understood every word as the man was ordering his other men to pick up Drago, and they'd finish this later.

"Today, I just really came to look in your face." Tushino glared. "I promise you, we'll be back, Mr. Carter."

"You'll regret it if you do." Carter nosed toward their boat. "Now fuck off."

The Russians headed back down the hill toward the wharf, with Drago being more dragged than walking.

Yuri came and stood beside him. "This will not end well."

Carter turned to him. "They want total capitulation. Was never going to happen." He looked toward his team still watching and looking very nervous. "Get everyone back to work."

Carter walked up to the step where Sara watched the man jumping back aboard the boat. Tushino stood on deck, still glaring back up at them.

"Sorry you had to see that," Carter said.

"Forget it." She looked at him for a moment. "We sleep safe in our beds because rough men stand ready in the night to visit violence on those who would do us harm."

"George Orwell." He snorted softly. "Always liked him."

"This isn't over, is it?" she asked wearily.

He sucked in a deep breath and let it out. "Probably not."

"There's only one of you, and we're a long way from home," she said softly and turned to face him. "Well, here, even the Russian justice system is as bent as a banana. So we're screwed, aren't we?" She chuckled but with little humor.

"We're never screwed. Tactics 101—amplify your strengths and minimize your weaknesses." He turned to her. "If there's only one of me, then the solution is to get more of me." He grinned. "I have some buddies who would love a little Russian holiday."

He held up the Russian's weapon. "And now you have your own gun."

EPISODE 03

CHAPTER 20

INTERACTION: *Lake Baikal waters, 2 miles north of the Paper Mill—1972*

Sergei and Golkin sat in silence as the small fishing boat drifted. It was 3 am, a moonless night, and they were far enough from the paper mill that they couldn't smell the stink of the chemicals.

Golkin's large, rough hands detected the minuscule vibration on the line and he eased forward, just as the weight came on, heavy, and it dragged on his line, taking more over the side.

"Got him," he said, and his friend's head snapped around.

"Sturgeon?" Sergei asked while quickly reeling his own line in to ensure they didn't get snagged up on each other's equipment.

"I think so." Golkin pulled the line in that now felt like he had a sack of sand on the end. There was no intermittent tugging or swerving around that he usually felt from a large fish. Sturgeon weren't great fighters and came up slowly but gently, but they swam in circles, swinging the line. This just felt … *dead.*

After another 10 minutes, Golkin had a large pile of line at his feet, and he estimated the fish must have now been only another few dozen feet or so below him.

"Better get the gaff, I think it is of good size." He leaned over, straining to pull the last few feet in, but still not seeing any shape or hint of color.

Sergei grabbed the seven-foot pole with the wicked-looking steel hook on the end and leaned over. He rolled up his sleeve and laid both his hands and the gaff in on the water's surface, ready.

The fish *must* have been right under them, but as Golkin stared, there seemed to be a green glow or light. Suddenly from behind him, his friend screamed and that was followed by a loud splash.

"*What?*" He whipped his head around just in time to see Sergei's legs disappear over the side. "*Sergei!*"

He let the line go, the fish forgotten, and rumbled forward in the boat. But his old friend never came back to the surface. "*Sergei,*" he yelled, the words echoing back at him over the expanse of pitch-dark water. "*Sergei.*"

Golkin stood up in the boat, legs wide and braced, snatched the lamp up, and then held it out over the side. The water had returned to its glass-calm. He looked back to where he sat and saw that his fishing line wasn't feeding back out. Oddly, whatever he'd caught was staying just under the boat and not trying to retreat back to the depths.

Golkin stood, holding the lantern higher. "Sergei!" The calm and silence were unnerving now, and he held the lantern down over the water and looked into it. He frowned. *Was something there? Could it be Sergei?*

The small bobbing boat seemed to become glued in place as though he'd run aground. Then, to his confusion, something started to rise over the gunwale. It could have been a long, wet length of rope that quested in the air like a glistening, dark worm. Others quickly followed it, all along both sides of the boat.

"*Stop!*" The boat began to sink lower in the water, as if it was suddenly filled with a great weight—or a great weight was pulling it under. "*Stop it!*" he yelled again.

He picked up the net and whipped it down on one of the long slimy things, but it bounced off as if they were made of rubber. The boat sank another few inches lower.

Golkin tried to keep his balance as the wooden gunwales began to creak and strain as the things held on. The boat went down another few inches and was only just above the waterline now. He started to panic and tried to gauge how far it was to shore.

Could he swim it? Did he have a choice?

A green luminescence surrounded the boat and then water started to spill over the side. It told him his time was up.

"What are you?" he yelled as the boat began to submerge.

Golkin knew he had to be away from the boat when it went down or the suction would drag him with it. The last thing he wanted was to be in the water with that thing, but he had no choice now. *Maybe*, he prayed, *it only wanted the boat.*

Golkin drew in a deep, shuddering breath and simply stepped out into the freezing water.

He never made it more than six feet.

CHAPTER 21

Summer ended and autumn hit with the first snow flurries. Though a Siberian winter wasn't something to desire and in fact, in many aspects, to be feared, Carter looked forward to the ice returning in great thick sheets, as once the pens were submerged below the ice, then other than feeding the fish through ice holes, they'd be sealed in and be one less thing for him to worry about.

The days and weeks rolled on, and with no more contact from Tushino or his goons, his veiled threats receded into a back room of the mill house residents' memories—all except for Carter's.

Carter dropped the packages on his bed. He sat down next to it and rubbed hands up through his short, blond hair. He guessed he should be thinking that having the weapons was enough and he hoped he never had to use them. But the fact was, his thirst for vengeance hadn't been fully slaked, and he itched to use them now that he knew who to use them against.

Every time he thought of his little brother being murdered, his anger near overwhelmed him. Carter Stenson breathed in and out slowly, calming himself. He was a professional, and he knew that emotions made you reckless. And recklessness could make you dead, and there might come a time he'd need to be ice cool.

He turned to unroll the blanket and checked over the new rifle—it was an AK-101, a new-type Kalashnikov that could be fired in either semi-automatic or fully automatic mode. It had a huge optical scope on top, an effective range of 500 yards, and a 30-round capacity.

He held it to his shoulder and sighted along it. For a locally sourced rifle, it was a damned good one and he couldn't have hoped for better—Yuri had really come through on the quality.

The other package included the whiteout fatigues—a combat uniform in a speckled white to blend into snowbound environments. He was satisfied and rolled the clothing and the gun into the blanket, placing them in the back of his closet and in behind the false back. He hung his clothing back in front of the false back of his closet, closed it, and stepped outside.

He had a chair pulled up on the small porch of his cabin and had a blanket pulled around his broad shoulders. The evening was quiet and had been like this for weeks. Things were progressing well, and he even dared to believe that the bratva might have decided to give them some space after all.

Carter doubted that, so he kept to his plan of bringing in backup. He half-smiled as he remembered the call through to his buddies. He'd told them he was getting the band back together, and he had a job for them, paying twice what they were earning now. The bonus being, they got to spend time with him in Siberia, mostly spending their evenings playing cards, drinking vodka, and traveling into the town to annoy the local ladies.

When the laughter had died down, he also mentioned they might have to bump chests with a few of the local Russian mafia. As he expected, that got them interested. But when he told them about Marcus, they agreed immediately.

He rocked back in his chair. The sun was setting and a sky of the palest blue was just beginning to darken. It was so peaceful; he now understood why people came all the way out here and carved out a life in this wilderness.

I could live here, he thought, and his eyes moved to the mill manager's house, and the yellow glow of lights inside. He saw Sara's shape move past one of the windows and he continued to stare for a moment longer.

He felt a small flame of desire flicker in his chest, and he quickly got to his feet, turning away. "Nope, nope, nope. Don't even think about it." He went back inside to the warmth, the whiskey, and his memories.

CHAPTER 22

It was a bitter Sunday evening when they noticed that Leonid was late coming back from one of his last fish pen checks. Night came quickly this far north, and though the air was still and calm, it could get lethally cold as soon as the weak sunlight vanished over the horizon.

All the other boats came back in around the same time—4 pm—that was the rule. But 5 pm came and went, and there was no response back from his radio or phone. There was no excuse for this, as they had a rare period of communication clarity.

Then 6 pm came and went. And now the group had gathered around a fire, deciding what to do.

"Maybe he's had engine trouble and he's pulled in on the shore somewhere," Sara said. "Waiting for morning."

"She could be right. And now that the lake is beginning to freeze, it'll be dangerous in the dark," Carter added. "That's why we had this curfew to begin with."

Pavel looked up at Carter. "If it was your friend lost out there, or your brother, what would you do?"

Carter looked down and exhaled through his nose for a moment. He looked to the older Russian. "I'd go out."

"Then we go out," Pavel agreed. "Because if any of *us* was lost, that is what Leonid would do."

The men agreed, and Carter knew that even though it would be blacker than Hades out on the water, and would be just as cold, there would be no other option even listened to now.

Yuri took control of the search and decided that Carter and Sara would stay behind, as they couldn't leave the mill compound unguarded. And that job needed to be done by two people.

Carter and Sara complained but he knew this was a job for the Russians, and they saw it that way as well.

"Stay in constant radio contact. Leonid's roster said he was to head out toward the far northern pen, which is five miles north-northwest. Start there," Sara said.

"We stay in a wide line with plenty of light." Yuri's voice was deep and slow. "Remember, if his boat is in trouble, or sunk, then it could be laying low at the waterline, so be careful and vigilant." His jaw clenched for a moment. "And pray he isn't in the water."

*****

Yuri piloted his boat north and then steered a little to the west. He could still see a pinprick of light from one of the other boats, probably Pavel's, with Dmitry's already lost in the distance.

Yuri had a wheelhouse top spotlight that had a handle where he could swivel the beam just using one hand. It was enormously powerful and cast a long tunnel of light out into the blackness.

He traveled slowly at around three knots, just under walking pace, and for a good reason. Already his bow was shunting aside slabs of ice, and as it sat low in the water, a big one could stave in the front of a smaller boat. He should be okay as long as he took it easy.

Soon their entire lake surface would be covered over. And if Leonid had gone down, then he would be entombed until next summer... or more likely lost forever.

He suddenly remembered the tracks on the bottom he and Carter had discovered. Maybe it wasn't a log, but the impression from the keel of a long lost boat, sunk and then sliding along the bottom.

Or dragged by something, he thought, and quickly shook the terrible thought away. *There are no monsters of the lake, there are no fish-people, there are no haunted ghosts lighting up the deepest deep areas of the lake. Forget it, they're all just myth and legend of old Siberia, and I am modern Russian*, he scolded back at himself.

His modern logical mind urged him to believe that. But his ancient Russian mind was a mixture of deep superstition and fears, and he suspected his friend was gone now, drawn down by the Devil's Crater effect just like in the tales of old.

"There's nothing to fear but fear itself," he said softly and wondered who had said that. "Someone not out by themselves on this lake at night," he replied and chuckled nervously.

Yuri shut off the engine and let the boat drift for a while. Even though sound carried for miles over the lake's surface, this far out, there was no sound coming from the shore. There might have been the distant throb of one of the other boats, but it was more likely to just have been the blood rushing in his ears from his pounding heart.

"Blacker than witch's broom closet out here," he whispered.

He spun, as there came a bark or a cough a few hundred yards out over the water that he knew was probably one of the large nerpa seals. He turned the light in the direction of the sound but saw nothing. He panned it along the water's surface for a while and then sure enough found a pair of shining pinpricks of light reflected back at him.

"Hello, little one," he said and felt relieved that he wasn't out here alone, even if his company was seal and not human. He wondered whether he had any bait in his icebox when the cough came again but was then followed by a harsh scream that didn't even sound like it could have come from the throat of a seal. Yuri rushed the strong spotlight back to where he had seen the eyes. They were still there, staring back, but they were unnaturally high in the water and strangely green-tinted. The noise died away again.

"Was that you, little one?" he asked.

The luminous, unblinking eyes stayed fixed on him for a moment more and then to his surprise, they split apart and went in different directions.

"What?"

There was the sound of splashing and then both dots of light were gone. Yuri cursed and slowly moved the spotlight over the lake surface, trying to locate the eyes again.

Two seals? he wondered. He turned his boat toward where he had seen the eyes.

He switched off the engine and let the boat glide. There were a few basketball-sized chunks of ice. And then something else. Yuri came out of the cabin and stared over the side.

"*Ach*, no."

He grabbed a fish net and waited until the boat glided closer and then scooped the thing out. He unfurled the mesh and lifted the thing free.

It was a pipe, homemade, and undoubtedly Leonid's.

He lifted his chin. "*Leonid*!"

Yuri waited, with his head tilted.

"*Leee-oniddd*!"

He waited again, but there was nothing. Yuri looked at his hands. There was glistening mucus on his fingers that had come from the pipe. He reached down into a space on the gunwale and dragged out an oily rag to wipe his hands and also the pipe, and then placed it in his pocket.

He went back to the wheelhouse and started the engine, and then moved his boat in larger and larger circles out from where he had found the pipe. But after another 40 minutes, he cut the engine and came back out on deck. The lake now was a dark, endless plain, and there was nothing in any direction.

Maybe he just dropped it over the side, he thought hopefully.

Yuri lit a cigarette, dragged hard, and then exhaled the smoke in a large plume, and after another few minutes, went back into the wheelhouse again. He picked up the radio handset and opened the mic to the other boats—thankfully, both men came back immediately but reported seeing nothing.

"We give it another hour. Maybe resume again come morning." The men agreed.

He swiveled the light once more—there was nothing, no seal eyes in the dark, no unusual shapes or anything that might resemble Leonid's missing boat.

Yuri sighed. "Sorry, my friend. I hope you managed to get to shore and are waiting for us there somewhere. But if not, sleep well and be at peace."

The big Russian started up the engine. They'd come back out next morning, but he already knew he'd never see Leonid or his boat again.

CHAPTER 23

Carter waited on the wharf as the old, sturdy boat chugged toward him. It struggled to push aside the blocks of ice, and he could hear the thumps against its stained bow from hundreds of yards away. It would undoubtedly be the last of the season as within weeks or even days, the ice sheets would be absolute, and no boat would travel on the water.

As per his instructions, his two buddies had taken an indirect route to the mill, traveling separately in the event the airports were being watched by the bratva. They had taken to the water at Slyudyanka, the southern-most towns on Lake Baikal, and one that should be free from scrutiny.

Carter watched a huge figure step up on deck and throw him a casual salute. He nodded in return. Just like him, both men were ex-Special Forces and he knew the guys had been looking out for some extra work, and something to keep them interested.

They'd always stayed in contact, and as far as Carter was concerned, they were family, so they always looked out for each other as well. He'd drained his savings now, as there were things he needed—expensive things—and he'd be damned if he was going to cause Sara any financial pain.

Carter's lips quirked up when he remembered the look on Yuri's face when he gave him the shopping list; the big Russian had visibly paled. But the man also recalled the Russian mafia intrusion, and he knew that if, or when, they came back, it would be with violence in their hearts.

"My black-market dealer will be driving Mercedes car and have gold teeth after this," Yuri had said with a shake of his head.

"Good customers get good service," Carter had replied. But then he grabbed the man's shoulders and looked into his face. "You don't need to be involved in this," he had said to the man. "You have already gone above and beyond what was asked of you."

Yuri had nodded. "I made a promise to help Marcus and his wife. That promise still stands."

"Thank you," Carter had said, meaning it. And good to his word, in a week, Yuri had secured the order—every bit of it.

Carter's attention was drawn back to the wharf as the boat bumped up against it and one of the figures jumped down with a thump of boots. The other paid the boat's captain, and then also jumped down. Immediately, the boat reversed out and chugged away.

The men picked up their packs and walked up toward where Carter stood waiting. He grinned as they got to within a dozen feet of him.

"Well, you guys don't look a day over 25 years old."

"Yeah, but those are dog years, boss," the big guy with the red beard and crew cut said, grinning back.

"Smoking, drinking, and red meat is my secret." The other guy was just as big, and had a broken side tooth.

Carter shook the redhead's hand first. "Red, good to see you, buddy." They pulled into a quick embrace.

Then Carter turned to the next guy. "And nice to see your big ugly mug as well, Mitch."

Carter had known Red Bronson and Mitch Tanner ever since he had first started in Spec Ops. They were all recruited in the same week, and quickly became inseparable, all three of them sharing a love of adventure, risk, and too much booze.

From time to time, they had all put their shoulders to the wheel to help each other out. They didn't blink at any sort of request and saw each other as brothers rather than just friends.

Red looked around at the frozen compound. "Just how the hell do you find these types of places? And in a Siberian communication blackout zone."

Carter followed his gaze. "Come on, this is Russia's answer to Club Med! Welcome!"

Mitch laughed. "More like welcome to Club Hell."

A light snow began to fall, dusting their hair, and Red looked up and then exhaled, expelling a long gout of vapor. His lips compressed for a moment.

"Sorry about Marcus. That's fucked up, man."

Carter nodded. "Yeah. And we're gonna ensure it doesn't get any more fucked up."

Mitch picked up his bag. "A hot shower, a warm rum, followed by a debrief will be just what the doctor ordered."

Carter nodded. "I'll briefly introduce you around, then show you to your places. We can all get together in my cabin later and talk."

*****

Carter went over the equipment he'd obtained with his small team—he managed to get handguns, rifles, and snow uniforms and also some Gen-II monocular night vision goggles for all of them; they were a little dated, but a robust design, and still did the job.

Carter had been offered some position-mounted claymores, and though the chance of blowing up a bear, deer, or maybe some hunter who had wandered onto the property by accident was high risk, he still took four. He'd only arm them during nighttime hours, as there shouldn't be hunters out this far, and even they wouldn't be tracking at night. He just hoped the bear and deer wouldn't be wandering around either. The wolves, well, they were cunning enough to sense danger and usually avoided the scent of humans.

Carter also took some sensors and could program them to send a signal back to his phone if their beam was broken. It was fairly good modern Chinese tech so it cost him a small fortune. But it'd be worth it if ensured there was less chance of sneak attacks.

All up, Red and Mitch were happy with their armaments and they'd only managed to bring their own knives. Bottom line, if anyone turned up looking for trouble, they'd get it back double and either go home with a bloody nose, or end up in a cold, shallow grave.

The three men sat around and drank and talked for hours. Tomorrow, Carter would take them out to walk the line—tour the mill property to get a feel for the terrain, and possible places of egress.

They'd also build a few shelters out in the woods in case they needed to make some war in the forest or go to ground. But Carter seriously hoped it wouldn't come to that.

As far as himself, Red, or Mitch was concerned, they were happy to get down and dirty as events required.

Carter sat back and stared at the amber fluid in his glass. The crap thing was, he knew from experience that sometimes it was war itself that decided how things turned out.

CHAPTER 24

Carter and his team had fully taken over the security. Yuri worked well with the new Americans and he seemed okay, if not a little wary of them. Nikolay, Stefan, Pavel, and Dmitry just stayed out of their way.

Carter had also introduced them to Sara. She had shaken both their hands, as she looked them over. "Appreciate your help. You'll report to Carter, but I'm the boss," she said as she stared hard into their faces. "Just remember, you're in Russia now."

"We've all worked in Russia before, Mrs. Stenson," Red replied.

She raised one eyebrow. "Do the Russians know that?"

Red and Mitch both just grinned.

She shook her head and sighed. "Call me Sara, and thank you for coming."

The days came and went, and it was on the night before the new moon when it was darkest that one of the claymores detonated. Carter was out of bed and dressed in his snow gear in half a minute. He snatched up both his night-vision goggles and a large handheld mega-watt flashlight that he kept switched off for now. In another minute, Red and Mitch were with him, dressed and ready to go.

Sara was out on the porch of her house, dragging on a thick coat. "What the hell was that?"

Carter waved and yelled back. "Claymore detonation. We're on it."

"Claymore?" she asked, mouth agape.

"We're on it." Carter rejoined his team. "Far claymore, the one near the lakeshore on the track," he said. He flicked down the night-vision goggles and switched them on. "We stay dark until we get a little closer."

The three men headed out fast, low, and quiet. Carter knew exactly where every claymore was planted, and the one that had detonated was in his third quadrant and the one furthest out at nearly a mile along the shoreline and inland by a hundred feet.

It took them 10 minutes to close in, and Carter waved them down and spread his team out in a small skirmish line. Red was out to the left and Mitch to his right. They all had guns pulled in tight to their shoulders, eyes unblinking as they edged forward one silent step at a time.

Carter slowed even more, not caring if they came in at glacial speed as the pitch-dark forest had fallen into a deathly silence. The night-vision optics made everything a fluorescent green, and if there were any eyes staring at him, they'd be glowing back like silver chips.

He was just 20 feet out from where the claymore had been planted when he saw the large, ragged mound lying about 10 feet from the detonation point. It was well beyond the trigger thread, so had probably been up close when it had set off the claymore and then been blown backward.

Carter eased in a little more. The mound was much bigger than a man, and even though torn up now, he could see there were masses of bloody fur. He whispered into his mic.

"Got something here. But looks like we mighta just fragged Yogi Bear."

From out of the green gloom on the left and right, Mitch and Red appeared, guns pointed at the mound of flesh and fur.

Mitch grunted. "Make a nice hat and boots, I guess."

Carter joined them and stared down at it. He placed his foot against the great beast and pushed it over onto its back.

"Jesus." Mitch's lip curled. "Did the blast do that?"

"*Un-fucking-likely*. That ain't all the bear," Red said and shook his head. "Where's all the freaking guts gone?"

Carter came in closer and crouched with his rifle across his knees as he examined the carcass.

The thing hadn't just been eviscerated, but the inside of the body was totally empty, and there were no guts spread around. It looked like it had been cleaned in an abattoir, and the front wasn't blown open, but just looked... sort of... unzipped.

"Something's not right," he said.

Though the huge body was definitely from a bear, and a big one, probably once standing at about seven or so feet tall and weighing in at around 800 pounds, the thing now looked hollowed out.

Carter quickly looked about, trying to find the telltale glossy blackness of blood or viscera on the ground, tree trunks, or even in the branches overhead. But there was nothing.

"Where are the guts?" Red repeated.

"No idea." Carter got to his feet.

"Wolves, maybe?" Mitch nudged it with the toe of his boot.

"Nah, it's only been 20 minutes since the blast; hasn't been time for scavengers to feed on the organs." Carter still scanned the brush. *The thing was, if they weren't here, and weren't eaten, then what the hell happened?* he wondered.

Truth was, Carter had no idea. But he needed to see it in more light. "Spread out, and go to flashlight. Let's find those guts." He flicked his goggles up, pulled out the large light, and switched it on. The white glow immediately did as he expected it to: show the blood as glistening splashes.

But there should have been more.

"Got a trail here," Red said.

Carter and Mitch followed him as he tracked the trail through the frozen forest. Streaks of blood and deep gouges in the snow showed that something of considerable weight had been dragged through the forest,

Maybe some sort of predator had claimed the innards? Carter was now thinking. "Heading to the water," he said softly, and then, "Hold positions."

There was the sound of water movement where there should have been none. There was no breeze, and therefore no chance for the water to be producing waves or even ripples. But there was something agitating the water, and maybe moving in or out of it.

"Go dark," Carter said, switching out his light, and dropping his night-vision goggles over his eyes again. He pulled his microphone plug up in front of his chin.

The men shouldered their guns and eased toward the water. Carter estimated there was only about 50 feet of land before they hit the shoreline. Then, whatever it was would have its back to the freezing lake—it could cross the ice, swim, or come back at them.

He spoke softly into his mic. "Heads up, waterline ahead."

He looked down and could still make out the blood trail, but now up close he saw it also contained glistening streaks like mucous and also spiked tracks. He came out of the forest and went down on one knee beside one of the last tree trunks. The trail continued to the water without deviating an inch.

Red crouched beside him and looked through the scope on his rifle.

Mitch was still out in the dark and came in on the mic. "Got light," he said.

"Where?" Carter said, standing tall.

"Wait…" Mitch cursed. "*Nah*, gone."

"Where were they?" Carter said, straining to see out over the water and ice.

"Couple of hundred feet out—looked deep, and then they vanished. And it was damn fast."

"Shit. Okay, come on in." Carter looked down at the trail. Whatever it was, it never stopped at the waterline. The blood trail went in and kept going.

"This is some weird shit," Red said.

Mitch ambled in. "Hey, they don't have alligators here, do they?"

Red snorted. "Even if they did, you think gators would be swimming in that water? It's nearly solid ice now."

"What did they look like?" Red asked. "Could it have been some sort of Russian mini submersible?"

"It was a glow, greenish like phosphor-lights." Mitch snorted. "And yeah, the sub crew were just ashore loading up on some supplies. You know, like a couple of buckets full of bear guts." He barely stifled his laugh.

"Shut it, asshole," Red said and turned to Carter. "What do you think it was, boss? This is your patch."

"Don't know," Carter said and looked out over the lake that was freezing into a checkerboard of huge slabs of white. "I just don't know." He sighed, hating to ask the question. "Mitch, one thing: did the glow look man-made or natural?"

Mitch frowned. "I don't understand."

"Man-made or like bioluminescence?" Carter asked again.

"Wasn't no firefly." Mitch still frowned.

"Whatever." Carter waved them on. "Let's get out of here."

The trio headed back to the bear carcass and stood around it, staring down at the ruined animal. Evidence seemed to point to something just taking the innards of the bear. But why would anything just take the guts of the bear and leave all the meat? It didn't make sense.

"No guts, and something else," Mitch observed. "No blood either."

He was right. The huge carcass wasn't leaking blood, and it should have had buckets of it pouring out.

Red bent forward and used the muzzle of his gun to open one of the gut-flaps. "You know what? This fucking thing is gross being all empty like that." He peered inside. "It's hollow." Red's mouth turned down as he straightened. "You know what it reminds me of? A ghillie suit."

"Yeah, yeah it does," Mitch agreed.

Carter looked back down at the mutilated lump of fur and meat. "A ghillie suit." He felt a small knot tighten in his gut. "We take it back," he said.

"What? Even without its guts, it's gotta weigh 7–800 pounds," Mitch complained.

"*Nah*, it's empty," Carter replied. "5–600 hundred, tops. Between us, it'll be a piece of cake. I want Sara to take a look at it."

"Sheee-it," Mitch spat. "Well, I'll tell you one thing. If those old Russians decide to cook it, I'm not eating any."

CHAPTER 25

It took the men over two hours to drag the carcass back to the compound. By then, the body had stiffened more from the cold than rigor mortis.

"What now?" Red asked, putting a hand in the small of his back and stretching.

Carter turned about for a moment. "To the mill house; that's where we've got the labs set up. Sara and the boys can check it out in the morning."

Yuri came out of his cabin and pulled on a thick coat before crossing the grounds to see what they were up to.

"You find answer to explosion, yes?" He stared down at the thing. "Good hunting... is bear?"

"It was," Carter responded. "We'll let Sara take a look at it tomorrow."

Yuri leaned in a little closer and then drew back. "Is blind."

"What?" Carter turned back around to the bear. Sure enough, he now saw that both eyes were a milky white. And there was more; the tongue was shriveled as though dehydrated.

"Maybe why it walked into your bomb," Yuri pronounced, but then also saw the mouth. "Strange; looks like it has been dead for a long time, weeks maybe."

"No. It was walking when it blundered into the claymore," Carter responded.

"But no blood, or guts," Red added.

Yuri leaned closer, and then blew air between his lips. "An abomination. If I believed in God, now would be good time to start praying to him."

"Yeah, well, I don't think God has anything to do with this thing," Mitch responded. "More like the guy from down under."

Red grinned. "You mean from Australia?"

"Oh fuck off." Mitch returned the grin. "Come on; let's dump this big bastard so we can clock off."

The three men dragged the dead creature to the mill house loading doors, and Yuri jogged ahead to open them wide.

They tugged it inside. The mill house had been cleaned and converted into several laboratory rooms and offices, and it had more doors to pass through to keep the lab section and hatcheries clean, temperature-controlled, and secure.

The men left the dead animal outside in the main stock receiving area, which wasn't heated so the cold would stop it thawing out. Carter threw a tarpaulin over it and stood back with his hands on his hips.

"Weird," he said softly.

"Got that right; this *whole* thing is turning into one weird-ass trip," Mitch said.

"Is not even full winter yet," Yuri said ominously.

"Yeah, thanks for inviting us. I'm having a great time already." Red slapped Carter on the shoulder, as Mitch chuckled and nodded his agreement.

"Yeah, drinking cold beers in warm sunshine is overrated anyway," Mitch said. He looked down at his gloves that were covered in drying blood and glistening mucous. "Well, I'm fucked. So if there's nothing else, I'm gonna down a few shots, and then hit the hay."

"One minute." Carter crossed to a long wooden bench and searched around until he found a pen and some paper. And then hastily scribbled a note to Sara. He dropped it on the tarpaulin.

"Okay." Carter led them out and stared back at the mound under the tarpaulin for a few seconds before closing the huge doors.

"And weirder by the second," he muttered and locked the doors.

*****

Sara and Nikolay were first into the laboratory and immediately saw the huge mound covered over with a tarpaulin. They switched on all the lights over the cavernous building and wandered over.

There was a note on top and Sara lifted it, recognizing Carter's handwriting and then began reading.

Sara, we found this bear in the woods last night—dead—after it walked into one of our booby traps. I think there was something inside it. Can you guys look it over and give me your opinion? This might be important. Carter.

She folded the note and stuck it in her pocket. It was cold in the outer most room of the mill house building that was more like an entrance area they had created for supplies delivery, and so there was no smell emanating from the still-frozen thing.

Sara ripped the large blue plastic tarpaulin from it, and her brows immediately drew together.

"What the hell?" She looked across to the young Russian. "Have you ever seen something like this before?"

Nikolay's head jerked back on his neck. "I have lived in these parts most of my life when I'm not at university, and I've seen bears alive and dead. I've seen them as fresh kills, and also as very old carcasses in the woods. And this bear has not been alive for a long time."

Sara stared down at it. "Carter said it walked into one of their booby traps... last night." She pulled the tarpaulin all the way off the beast and then crouched beside it to get a better look. "I don't get it."

She knew Carter was level-headed and didn't think he made mistakes, so maybe it was dark and he didn't know what he was looking at. She turned to Nikolay. "Get me a probe, something... anything."

He quickly jumped up to look around for something he could use as a probe, spotted the pen Carter had used, and rushed to grab it. He then returned to hand it to Sara and crouched again by the mutilated mound of flesh and fur.

Sara held the pen up and half-smiled. "This is the best you could find? In a lab?" She sighed and then began to prod the carcass in several places.

The thing was still mostly frozen so it felt like rock beneath the fur. She poked at it with the pen and wished he had a magnifying glass. But this time, when she lifted the pen from the body, some of its fur came with it.

There was also something sticky at the base where the hair follicles were that reminded her of tar. She brought it close to her nose and sniffed.

"*Phew.*"

It smelled of spoiled meat and oil. Maybe remnants of the bear's last meal that might have even been exploded from its stomach in the blast.

"Hey."

"*Ach.*" Nikolay physically jumped at Stefan's greeting.

"Just in time," Sara said. "We need your local biology expertise."

"Oh yes. What have you got there?" Stefan came and leaned over him. "Big old dead bear?"

Nikolay shook his head. "Yes, at least most of it. Carter found it last night and wants us to examine it."

"Why?" Stefan leaned forward to look the remains over. "It's been dead for weeks, maybe months. It'll stink the place up."

Nikolay stood. "Carter said it was walking around last night. Walked into one of their booby traps."

"How?" Stefan pointed. "The eyes are sunken as their optical fluid has shriveled. The gums and soft palate tissue are discolored as well as dehydrated. Classic characteristics of necrosis."

"That's what I thought." Sara also stood and pointed. "Let's winch it onto a trolley and get it inside. When it thaws a little, we can have a better look."

Stefan grimaced. "This is not really why we are here."

"I know. But one thing about Carter is he doesn't make mistakes. And if this thing's got him spooked enough to want us to take a look, then I think we should," Sara said, still holding the pen. "He also said that he thought something was inside it. So we'll make time for it."

"Inside it?" Stefan put his hands in his lab coat pockets. "Well, I suppose it does give us a break from looking at fish and eggs." He peered inside the empty gut cavity and sniffed. "Thawing already. Let's get it on the steel bench before it leaks everywhere."

The trio used the overhead lifting winch to heft the huge dead animal onto a trolley, and then wheeled it into one of the vacant laboratories. They then moved it across onto a stainless steel bench that already had drainage holes for leakage.

Sara and the pair of young Russians donned aprons, rubber gloves, and paper masks over their faces. It was all they had. Then they stood on either side of the table looking at the mountain of flesh.

"I want to look inside first," Sara said. "Then I want to see how it is that this thing was supposed to have been walking around."

Stefan leaned over it. "Male, so we can rule out it being a pregnant female that somehow lost the fetus."

Sara kept her eyes on the thing. "Nikolay, come around this side and hold the flashlight for me."

Nikolay joined her, holding up a plastic flashlight as Sara used a long steel probe to push inside the open chest and gut cavity.

"*Hmm*, it's totally empty," she said. "And I don't think it was eviscerated by a blast as there is no bleeding, and no arteries draining out as there would be if the organs were torn free."

Nikolay lifted the flashlight higher. "They looked to have been sealed or cauterized."

"I agree, but I don't think by heat. There's no sign of burning or searing." She probed some more. "It actually looks like it was totally emptied out and then each vein, artery, and even capillary was sealed with some sort of biological adhesive."

"Hello." She craned in further. "There are holes in the cavity that aren't normal. Over the areas of the head, legs, and arms—over all the extremities."

"Wounds?" Nikolay asked.

"No, not really wounds." She frowned. "The lower colon is also sealed over. This thing couldn't shit even if it wanted to. It's impossible." She reached for a scalpel and extended probe, and then leaned into the beast, cutting around one of the holes. "Hold the light over here."

Nikolay leaned in, shining the light where he was asked.

She pushed the long probe in and could now see that the holes traveled all the way into the limbs as if they were also basically hollow.

She then turned her attention to the neck area, and when he probed, the hole there went all the way up into the skull.

"Interesting." She straightened. She tried to think what could cause what she was seeing, but nothing came to mind. She'd never even heard of anything that did this to an animal.

Sara shook her head. "Carter said this was moving around. And to do that it needed a brain." She quickly put the probe down, turned about, and then moved to open and close cabinet draws until she found a set of mechanical shears. She plugged them in and proceeded to shave the large cranial dome and when finished, she stood back with hands on her hips.

She grinned at Nikolay. "Don't suppose you have a spare bone saw in your pocket?"

Nikolay slowly shook his head and smiled. He snapped his fingers. "Hold on."

He ducked outside to the open area and rummaged around for a moment, finding the metal toolbox. He quickly grabbed up a large screwdriver, hacksaw, hammer, and chisel.

She nodded; they were heavy-duty, but they'd work.

He raced back in. "I don't think we need to worry about hygiene with our patient." He still bathed them in bleach, then wiped them down with a cloth and laid them out for Sara to use.

"Oh no, no." She held up a hand. "The heavy work is for younger muscles."

"My pleasure," Stefan said. "This has me intrigued now." He used a scalpel to slice away the fur on the head and then rolled it back like a cap, exposing the skull. It should have been a pinkish-white, but instead was a dull, yellow-grey.

He looked up at Nikolay. "We take turns." He then set to using the saw to cut right through the bone. It took him 15 minutes of sawing to go halfway around, and then he handed it over to Nikolay so he could catch his breath and rest his arm.

When Nikolay finished off the cutting, Stefan then used the hammer and chisel to bang along the cut-line until the top circle of cranium bone popped free. Stefan held it in his hand and stared.

Sara and Nikolay joined him, and Sara's brows came together in confusion.

"This… is not possible," she breathed out.

The skull was empty. And just like the stomach and chest cavity, it looked to have been totally cleaned out.

Stefan shook his head and rested his hands on the table as he stared down into the empty skull cavity. "Mr. Carter was wrong. This creature hasn't been moving around for a long time."

"There's no forebrain, midbrain, or even hindbrain. It could never have had motor functions, and as the medulla is missing, there is nothing to regulate the involuntary life-sustaining functions such as breathing, swallowing... even its heart rate," Sara said softly. "It could never have even been alive."

Nikolay shone his light around in the cavity. "Hey, there's some sort of excretion in there."

"Get me a sample," Sara said.

Nikolay went to a bench, lifted a swab, and came back to swipe it through the dark, viscous fluid, then handed it to her. Sara took it to one of the many microscopes in the laboratory, smeared it on a slide, switched on the reflection light, slid it onto the view plate, and then leaned over the eyepiece.

Stefan waited a moment and lifted his chin. "Well, what is it?"

She changed focus, and then lifted her head away, her forehead creased. "I've seen something like this before; it was something Carter brought back from the lake bottom. But this... this is different." She looked back down into the eyepiece. "There's something else mixed in there."

"Is it at least biological?" Stefan insisted.

Sara stepped back. "You tell me."

Stefan nodded and came around the table to lean over the microscope and adjust the focus to suit him. His brow creased deeply.

"I don't understand what I am looking at. I see a lot of mammalian cells in there from several species, and all dead. But there are also living cells in there... I think that's what they are. I see cytoplasmic fluid, but they have no mitochondria, nucleus, or ribosomes, and their cell wall is totally elastic. They are definitely not bear cells, and I have no idea what animal they could even be from."

"I don't know either. But like you said, it isn't bear." Sara exhaled. "Remember what Carter wrote? He thought there was something else *inside* there."

"Something *not* bear." Stefan slowly turned back to the creature on the benchtop.

A sharp noise from behind made the three of them spin around.

*****

Carter looked in through the glass door and saw Sara and the two young Russians crowded around the massive lump of dead bear. He rapped on the frame, making all three of them jump.

Sara waved them in and then straightened. "Thanks for your early morning gift."

Carter nodded toward it. "Sorry about that, but we found it last night, blown up by one of our booby traps. Not what we were expecting."

Nikolay pointed with his small light. "Not what anyone was expecting, I think."

"What can you tell us?" Red asked. "Because that bear is weird as shit."

"And inside it gets even weirder," Sara replied. "I've never seen anything like it, or even read about it in my entire life." She looked back down at the bear. "We were just wondering how it could have ever been alive." She looked back up at Carter. "Are you absolutely sure this thing was walking around last night?"

Carter held up his hands. "Well, we didn't actually see it walking around. But how else would it have stumbled into our claymore?"

Sara grimaced. "Claymores around our mill compound? Jesus, Carter, we'll talk about that later. But none of you actually saw it alive then?"

"We saw its tracks, and they were fresh," Mitch said. "The bear tracks headed into the kill zone… on its own two-fucking-feet. And the snow in that area had only fallen in the last few hours."

"Okay, cool it," she shot back. "I'm just laying out what the scientific evidence has suggested. And that is the bear has been necrotic for some time."

"Yeah, and maybe someone carried an 800-pound dead bear through the forest at night and threw it at our claymore." Red laughed.

"And where's the guts?" Mitch asked. "I've skinned and cleaned a bear before, and you end up with about 70 to 100 pounds of stinking organs. It was all gone, and the thing looked cleaned out."

"He's right," Red said. "Pretty damned sure this *thing* got the shit blown out of it. There should have been bits and pieces everywhere, but instead, all we found was a trail of blood and crap leading to the water."

Sara frowned. "How long from the explosion to when you arrived?"

"Thirty-five minutes, give or take," Carter said.

She nodded. "Enough time to drag the innards away. But not enough to thoroughly clean out the carcass."

"I know claymores, and I've seen some weird stuff happen—heads stuck up in trees, arms blown off still holding guns, and even some guy standing right in front of one when it went off and was totally untouched." Mitch raised his eyebrows. "So, could the blast have done that to the innards? Blown them clean and clear, I mean?"

"All the way to the lake? No," Sara said emphatically. "The internal organs of mammals are all secured in many places—the stomach to the esophagus and throat, the intestines lead to the colon and then the anus, and the heart's aortas have thick, branching veins and arteries that are like rubber cables. I've dissected plenty of cadavers, and they are as tough as boot leather. The innards could be decimated and the beast eviscerated, but not blown clear to leave a cavity like that."

"Damn," Carter said. "This is getting a little freaky."

"It gets freakier. Check this out." She waved him closer. "The missing internal organs weren't the only oddity we found."

The men crowded around the remains and Sara pointed into the open skull. "As well as no organs, there's no brain either. Basically, the total physiological infrastructure is all gone. There's not even any connectors for the organs; not anymore anyway."

"Not anymore? Are you saying it's been altered?" Carter asked.

"Possibly, but how, by who?" She pointed with a gloved finger. "There are other changes—there are holes everywhere. I think artificially made."

"What for?" Red asked.

Sara half-smiled. "You tell me." She held up a finger. "But remember that sample you brought me from the lake bed?"

"Yeah, you said the tissue sample was from many animals, and there might even have been human cells mashed in there," Carter replied.

"That's right." She folded her arms. "We found some more with the same jumble of necrotized animal cells. But there was something else in there—a biological trace, and the cellular structures weren't dead this time. But this stuff wasn't normal—not normal for a bear, not normal for anything."

Red snorted. "We can already see it's not a normal bear. Just what the hell is it then? An experiment, or a Russian joke?"

"Some joke." Stefan looked strained. "It just can't have been alive. There was no brain, no heart, no lungs, nothing."

"We need to know more." Carter sighed. "I don't like mysteries so close to our compound."

"It's the best we can do with what we've got," Stefan said. "This isn't a research lab, and Sara isn't an environmental or evolutionary biologist with extensive mammalian databases to work with."

"I need to know what the hell is creeping around the compound at night," Carter replied.

Sara lifted her chin. "Stefan's right; we just don't have the equipment or expertise. But we know someone who does, don't we?"

Carter smiled. "I'll bite, who?"

"We already have contacts within the Federal Agency for Fisheries and Conservation." She walked toward him. "Mr. Mikhail Ivanov, their chief scientist, is our contact for the sturgeon and eggs. He signed off on everything and is supportive of what we're doing."

Carter shrugged. "Great, then let's put a sample together and send it off to him."

"Ah, excuse me." Stefan held up a hand. "They might shut you down."

"What?" Sara turned to him. "Why?"

Stefan sighed loudly. "They panicked after Chernobyl and closed every business, shop, school, and house for a hundred miles. If they think this thing is some sort of mutation or infection from the paper mill, then wave goodbye to everything."

Sara groaned.

Nikolay opened his arms. "We just tell him we collected it well away from the water and the mill."

Sara turned to Carter. "What do you think?"

Carter stared at the ground as he spoke. "For some reason, this thing scares the shit out of me. Even more than the goddamned mafia." He looked up. "We need to know."

"I'll prepare the sample," Nikolay said.

"Thank you," Carter said and began to turn away.

"One more thing," Sara said.

"Yeah?" Carter paused.

"You said in your note you thought something was inside there, the bear. What did you mean by that?" She waited, watching him closely.

Carter narrowed his eyes for a moment as he stared at the massive pile of the bear's remains for a few more moments. He exhaled.

"You said that the bear couldn't have been alive or moving around, right?"

"That's right." Sara waited.

"When we found it, Red said something that got me thinking. He said he thought at first it was like a ghillie suit."

"A what?" Nikolay asked.

Carter spoke over his shoulder to the young man. "A ghillie suit is a type of military camouflage suit designed to resemble the background environment."

"I remember," Red said. "All that fur. Thought we bagged one of the bad guys." He nodded.

"Well, what if you were right, about the bear not being alive, and not moving around." He looked up but avoided her eye contact. "What if something else was moving it around?"

"Holy fuck, yeah, wearing it like a ghillie suit. Now I get it." Red's eyes were wide. "That *is* fucked up."

Stefan frowned. "You think there was a man hiding in there?"

"I don't know." Carter shook his head. "But those holes over the limbs, like where you'd put your arms in, and also stick your head up into. I'm just saying that something might have been in there, inside that carcass."

"Making it move around. Even after it was dead?" Nikolay breathed.

"Unlikely, Carter. Nothing like that exists now or ever." Sara's lips compressed.

"This lake is weird and getting weirder," Mitch said.

"According to the legends, it always was." Carter rubbed his chin.

"There's no record of anything like this I know of in Siberia," Stefan said. "This is an old country, plenty of word-of-mouth tales, but nothing written down."

"Maybe there is." Carter turned to Nikolay. "You mentioned a cave you and Marcus found with ancient drawings that showed the lake and something happening on it, right?"

"Yes, something hitting the lake we thought," Nikolay agreed.

"I need you to take me to that cave and those rock drawings. I need to see them myself."

Nikolay nodded. "When?"

"Today," Carter replied. "And I don't want anyone out after dark for a while."

"I should come with you," Sara said.

He shook his head. "We need to get that sample off to the Ministry as a priority. We can have Yuri run it down to Listvyanka."

He turned to Mitch and Red. "You guys go and check the other sensors and plant the rest of the claymores. I hope that this thing was the only one, but if not, I don't want any more of them lumbering into our compound."

"You got it," the pair agreed.

"Nikolay, I'll see you in an hour—wear your hiking gear." Carter was already heading for the door.

CHAPTER 26

Carter forged ahead, with Nikolay directly behind. The young man looked out of breath and had remarked a while back that Carter was much fitter than his younger brother had been. He immediately looked awkward and apologized, but Carter just waved it away.

Carter tucked his chin inside his collar, as it was cold—damn cold. There was plenty of deep snow on the ground and a biting coldness that hung all around them like the freezing vapor did in the air.

In several hours, they had made it to the small rocky uprising and began to climb.

"This way."

Nikolay skirted the areas that he said caused them trouble the last time and easily found the mouth of the cave. He went to wave Carter in.

"Wait," Carter said and pulled his rifle from over his shoulder.

"Oh, you're right." Nikolay eased back. "Just because there was no bear the last time, might be one this time."

Carter picked up a lump of loose rock and tossed it inside. It bounced and skittered deep into the cave, but after another moment, all was silent again.

"Okay." Carter waved him in. "Let's go."

The pair switched on flashlights, Carter's a huge spotlight that nearly illuminated the entire cave.

"Wow." It was as big and deep as Nikolay had said, and they quickly made their way to the smaller offshoot cave.

Nikolay pointed his light inside and then ducked his head to enter. "The bones, they're still as we left them."

He crouched and Carter came around him to pick up some of the coffee-brown bones, turning them over in his hands. He rubbed a thumb on the pitted bone and looked at the remains of the teeth in one of the skulls.

"Remains of several bodies here—adults and children. Age browned, and that only happens after a long time." Carter rested his forearms on his knees.

"Yes, Marcus said that he thought the bones could have been up to 100,000 years old." Nikolay shone his light beam around. "We think they must have been trapped by a rockslide. They all died in here."

He sniffed, detecting a faint odor a little like cinnamon. If the cave had been truly sealed up, then as the bones rotted and they turned to dust, the people would be now floating in the air as motes of dust. That odor he detected might be the spirits of the tribe's people.

"Looks like the entire tribe was sealed in and wiped out." Carter tossed the bones down like they were old sticks and looked around. "You said there were rock paintings?"

Nikolay backed out. "Yes, this way."

He led Carter further down along the cave tunnel to a long, flat wall. "Here, this is where they painted." He ran his light along the wall.

Carter followed the light. The wall was flat, at least 20 feet long, and covered in all manner of images.

"Already they seem a little less, colorful," Nikolay said.

"Exposure to the air. They're starting to degrade. Sealed up, it was like a time capsule. Not anymore."

Carter stepped in a little closer to where depictions of deer, bear, wolves, and also many other animals that were now long extinct like the mammoth, a giant antlered moose-like creature, and what might have been a rhinoceros with a branched horn sticking from its nose.

"Maybe they survived for a while," Nikolay observed.

"I think you're right," Carter said. "Look here." He moved to the far end of the cave, and his bright light lit up every crack, crevice, and flat space that had been used as a canvas.

"I haven't seen these images." Nikolay crowded close to him.

Carter nodded toward the wall. "That looks like a hunting or war party setting off."

Sure enough, there were several figures walking away from the cave, all carrying spears.

"You know what I think?" Carter crouched and lifted his eyes. "I think you're right about them surviving. Whatever it was that came down caused the monster wave, but that's not what killed them. Maybe days or weeks afterward, those damned big human brains of theirs triggered their curiosity. So they sent out a small team of warriors to go have a little looksee."

Carter moved a little further along, following the frescoes and did his best to decipher the artwork story.

"*Holy shit*." He lifted his light and stared at the wall image. "One came back."

Nikolay came closer and peered at the drawing. It was of a human figure standing with arms wide. But his belly was painted blood red, and streamers or rope seemed to emanate from his gut. And worse, what looked like spikes or spindly legs were rupturing from the core of his body.

"What do you think?" Carter asked and turned to him.

"I think…" Nikolay shook his head.

"Go ahead, say it, because I'm thinking the same thing." Carter waited. "Come on, say it, so I know I'm not the only crazy one here."

Nikolay looked down at the ground for a moment before lifting his head. He sighed. "The bear. Just like the bear."

Carter nodded. "Yeah. Something was inside the returning warrior. He came back to the cave, but with something in him."

Carter rubbed his stubbled chin, making a rasping sound that was loud in the near-silent cave. "Did it have something to do with the thing that struck the lake?" He turned to the young Russian. "And you said you could make out where the thing came down in the lake?"

Nikolay nodded. "I think so. The landmarks are all still here."

"Good." Carter checked his watch and then turned away. "Show me."

Nikolay took him higher to the lookout at the top of the outcrop. They had to pull their hoods and face coverings in tight over their nose and mouth, as the wind here was bitterly cold. It also stung the eyes and the pair had to close them to slits.

"There, and there." Nikolay pointed.

Carter immediately saw the landscape that was the perfect match for the cave art images. The artists had a good eye for perspective, and he could also make an estimation of where the thing came down.

"Right about... there." He pointed.

Now it was a white desert of ice and snow for as far as his eye could see. But by the coastal hills and bays, it was only about a mile or so down along the shoreline and maybe half a mile out.

It was roughly between where they were now and the first of their fish pens. They'd even taken soundings around these areas and found them useless as prospective sites as they were too close to the black depths of the rift, where the lake bottom fell away to over a mile.

"Well, I'm hoping that if something fell in there, it stayed in there," Carter said.

"Yes, down deep," Nikolay said softly.

Carter turned and Nikolay didn't meet his eye. But Carter knew they were both thinking the same thing: whatever fell into the lake all those tens of thousands of years ago and infected the long-dead warrior, and then what also crawled out of the belly of the bear, was undoubtedly connected.

Where they were was a great vantage point, and at night, it'd be a great place to watch out for those mysterious lights that Yuri and the men had mentioned. A curious thought jumped into Carter's head: could the deep lights be in any way connected to the crash here all those thousands of years ago?

Crash. He snorted softly at the thought. Not *impact* as in meteorite. He sighed. *I'm buying into the legends already*, he thought and turned away. He paused.

Carter bent to pick the small thing up and held it in his hand, warming the freezing object. He opened his fingers displaying the black Swiss army knife—*Marcus* was written on its side, and it was just like his own.

"This place is bad luck," he whispered and then turned. "Let's get back."

CHAPTER 27

The next morning, Carter stepped out of his cabin and the cold hit him like a slap. He coughed as it seared his lungs and he quickly hiked his collar up as high as it would go. He also rolled the beanie down to his brow line. But still, his remaining exposed skin stung like needle pricks.

The compound was dusted with snow, and it was hard to tell where the snow ended and the iced-over lake began.

He and Yuri were set to take to the bobsleds and head out to the pens that morning. It would stretch the limits of the small fuel tanks, but it shouldn't be a problem unless they needed to deviate.

He was about to head down to the wharf when he saw the markings in the snow. He recognized the tracks from right around here a few months back. He stared at them, trying to tease from their patterns the type of animal that had made them.

Carter had been game hunting and also tracking in the military, but these were beyond him. The double markings had a gait of about two and a half feet wide between the foot, hoof, or bug prints, if that's even what they were, as they looked more stilt-like than feet or legs. He turned his head to follow their path and saw that they entered the compound from the tree line again to the north, wandered about in the compound as if searching for something, and then finally exited close to where they came in.

Carter followed them for a while, seeing exactly where the creature went. He saw that the tracks led from cabin to cabin—but not all of them; just the ones that were occupied. They then headed toward the main house where Sara was and went up the steps. Due to the snow-free wooden steps and porch, they vanished for a while and he assumed they went right up to the door, but then reappeared back down the steps into the snow again.

The tracks weren't deep, so whatever it was couldn't have been very heavy. He still thought it might have been a fox. Last time, he had asked Yuri and the big Russian had just shrugged and held his arms wide, indicating it could have been a dozen different sorts of creatures. Also, things can get distorted in snow pretty quick if the temperature changes and there is even a miniscule thaw.

Once again, they vanished back up to the tree line, and this time, Carter followed all the way. It didn't take him long to climb the hill and when he got above the mill compound, he saw that there was a larger disturbance in the snow.

"*What the hell?*" he whispered. "Did you get eaten?"

The smaller tracks intersected with the greater disturbance and then only a larger set of tracks appeared like that of a deer or some sort of large hoofed animal. They moved quickly off into the freezing forest.

There was no predatory hoofed animal that he knew of; plus, there was no blood. Carter scratched his head and exhaled a stream of vapor as he stood looking around at the wall of trees.

"Siberia." He snorted and turned to look down over the compound again. There was so much going on, and so much of it out of his area of experience. He sighed, feeling a little overwhelmed for a moment.

Carter suddenly wished Marcus was here—he was the smart one. If only there had been a way for him to be here when his little brother first arrived, he never would have run foul of the bratva.

Carter stayed on the hilltop for many minutes, looking down over the range of buildings, all covered in snow and looking like something from a Christmas postcard.

He shifted his gaze back to the forest line—much of it was a solid wall of trees and impenetrable to his gaze. It was dark in there, and anything not wanting to be seen had the perfect hiding place. When on missions, he had a soldier's intuition when it came to a sensation of being watched... and he had that now.

"Fuck it," he said and headed back down.

By then, he could see the big Russian up and already down at the wharf, smoking one of his stinking cigarettes for breakfast as he waited for Carter to arrive. He'd pulled the two bobcats out and was ready to go out to the pens.

Carter shook himself. "It's goddamn freezing."

"*Pfft.*" Yuri waved him away. "This is nothing." He turned back. "You hear of place called Oymyakon?"

Carter snorted. "Of course not."

"Coldest town in Siberia. Some days gets down to 88 degrees below zero." Yuri grinned. "You know how cold it gets on Mars? Don't think, I tell you; only 80 degrees below zero."

Carter chuckled. "That's supposed to make me feel better?"

"No, warmer," Yuri shot back.

"Well, at least the fish don't mind." Carter stamped snow off his boots. "Let's go."

They sped out onto the frozen lake, sounding like two bikers on a desert highway, and throwing huge tails of crushed ice and snow out behind them. Carter loved the bobcats, as they were fast and fun, and if it weren't for the excruciating cold lancing any exposed flesh, he'd be out on them for relaxation every single day.

The pens were located by GPS bulbs embedded in the pen buoys that were sunk just below the ice, so finding them was by technology as much as using the coastal landmarks.

"Here." Yuri skidded his sled to a stop. He stepped off and hefted the chainsaw, shovel, and pickaxe.

Carter pulled up next to him and lifted another large box from his passenger seat that contained the underwater camera and diving equipment in the event one of them needed to go into the freezing water.

The Russian yanked the chainsaw to life and then set to cutting lines in the ice—six feet one way, then the other, creating a square. When he'd sunk the spinning blade down as far as it would go along all four quadrants, he cut more furrows within the square. When done, he put down the saw, grabbed up the pick, and set to digging out the chunks.

Yuri had to repeat this process twice as the ice here was already four feet thick, and by the time he struck water, he was puffing like a train.

"Not so young anymore." He grinned through a flushed face and beard specked in ice chips.

Carter laughed. "One day, you'll look back and wish you were as young as you are now. So enjoy it while you can."

Yuri threw his head back and laughed like a bark. "You can make anything sound good. Are you sure you're not a salesman?"

"Barman," Carter shot back.

Yuri straightened for a moment and lifted one bushy eyebrow. "I think you were not always a barman, yes?"

"Jack of all trades." Carter grinned. "Want me to take over?"

"Now?" Yuri puffed. "Is nearly finished." He shook his head. "I think you get to do next one."

The upside was they didn't need to fill it in as the ice layer actually created downward pressure on the water, so punching a hole in it made the water well up to the surface. Then the cold took over, freezing it back over again.

It was damned cold, so they'd need to pitch a tent over the hole to slow down the refreezing. But even then, they'd still need to keep the water agitated so it didn't get an ice skin over it and need to be hacked through all over again.

Carter just hoped there weren't any problems below, because if there were, then one of them would need to don the cold-weather diving gear and head down. He'd dived in the Arctic as part of his Spec Forces training, and no matter how many layers, or how thick or hi-tech the wetsuit was, it was damned unpleasant.

The size of the final hole became clear, as Yuri had cut steps on the way down to the water. Otherwise, he might be at the bottom of the hole when he punched through and end up getting swamped.

This way, he was on the bottom step when the icy liquid burst upward, rising slowly and giving him time to clamber out.

Carter took over, lowering the camera. This time, it was tethered and once it was in the lake, Yuri switched on the computer to track it and began to maneuver it away.

"Going down," he said and Carter went to crouch beside him and watch as the camera headed down into the inky dark water.

The tent over the hole was like a cocoon from the elements and the pair of men watched intently as the submersible camera descended. Yuri rotated it for a moment when they were only a few dozen feet down, so he could look back at the hole, and then—there was a glowing blue square amongst the sheets of white, and Carter could even make out the shadow of him and Yuri huddled next to it.

"Heading down."

Yuri righted the camera and pushed the small joystick forward, pushing it down toward the bottom. It took several minutes as there was about 150 feet of water depth in this pen area.

The pen was large, and it would take them a while to travel along the net line, first looking for breaks or tears, and then to locate their farmed sturgeon.

"Looking good," Yuri said as they traveled along the pen net-line. The water was so clear, the small headlamps on the robot camera picked up with crystal clarity the snags, nets, and their peg anchors into the lake bottom.

It would take them nearly an hour to patrol the perimeter, so Carter opened a thermos and poured a coffee for each of them. Yuri reached into his pocket for a small silver flask and held it out to Carter—*vodka*, he suspected. He shook his head and Yuri shrugged and tipped a good shot of clear liquid into his own mug.

He toasted Carter and sipped. The big Russian went back to the small screen and watched the dark water lit up by their lights go by yard after yard. All seemed normal.

"So," he asked. "The beast; what did you find? Was it really a bear?"

Carter inwardly groaned, remembering Yuri wasn't involved in the autopsy. "You heard about that, *huh*?"

He nodded. "I hear about everything. You are the owners of the business, but I am the manager. If something happens, I know about it. And the local Russians will come to me first."

Carter grunted. "Okay, and yeah, it was a bear... once. It's confounded us and the remains just raised more questions than they answered. We've sent some samples off to Moscow for them to do some analysis. We'll wait to hear from them."

"Good." Yuri acknowledged. "A bear that is alive, but not alive. Very strange." He raised one bushy eyebrow. "Let Moscow sort it out."

Carter half-smiled, now appreciating that the guy really did know everything.

"Hold on." Yuri squinted at the small screen and then paused to work the controls as his brow furrowed. "Water is being stirred up."

"The sturgeon?" Carter asked.

"No, sturgeon will surge if they are frightened. But I don't think it's them." He changed the camera angle. "Something is down there... with them."

"Maybe a seal." Carter leaned forward.

"Maybe." Yuri didn't look convinced.

The Russian maneuvered the camera into a new zone, and the water settled immediately. He swung the camera back, but there was nothing in the water behind them or to indicate what had caused the surge in currents.

Yuri bobbed his head. "This lake is so big it has its own tides and currents. But all looks good now," Yuri said. "Let's find our fish."

All their fish were tagged with electronic sensors that were the equivalent of being on a technical leash—they knew exactly where the fish were at all times. The computer plotted on them a schematic map as all being within a 200-yard space of the western end of the pen.

Yuri maneuvered the camera in their direction, and soon he found the first of them. The huge fish was on the bottom, resting; its eyes shone back silver from under the bony scutes of a brow ridge. On seeing the camera's light approaching, it gently flicked its tail and glided away, like a long aircraft taking off.

In another 30 minutes, they had found every one of their charges.

"All present and accounted for," Carter said.

Theoretically, they could have known that from the mill compound, as an alarm was set to go off if any of the fish moved beyond the netting wall. But the net needed to be checked, and one thing the sensors couldn't do was give an indication of the fish's health, only their location.

"Okay, bringing camera back." Yuri used the small joystick to speed the camera back toward them as Carter hauled in the line. It took another 15 minutes before the small camera's light began to illuminate the dark hole on the ice.

Carter didn't need to go down the ice steps, as the water had welled up to the surface, and the camera bobbed up right beside him. He reached out, grabbed the box, and hauled it in. Even through his gloves, he could feel the bitter cold from the water and thanked their lucky stars he didn't need to go in today.

The pool of dark water in the center of their tent suddenly welled up.

"Hey..." Carter lay the camera down. "What the hell?"

Then they felt something else—there was a thump from the ice sheets. The pair froze and Yuri slowly turned to Carter.

"What was this?"

"I think something just hit the ice," Carter said. "Could a sturgeon do that?"

"Maybe. But why would it?" Yuri licked his lips. "Come on." He stood and backed out of the small tent with Carter right behind him.

Immediately outside, they felt the bite of the wind chill, and the glare of the muted sunshine on the endless ice sheets made them squint.

Yuri took out a small pair of binoculars, put them to his eyes, and then turned about slowly. Carter put on his sunglasses from the glare and also looked out over the ice. *Did something just come down on the ice, or bump up into it?* he wondered.

There was another thump, followed by a cracking and vibration that tickled the soles of Carter's feet. He gritted his teeth. "I can't see anything, but it feels kinda close."

"I think is coming from underneath us," Yuri said and then nodded. "Yes, I think this is what it is; below the ice, not above."

"Shit." Carter spun about, and then looked down. "Underneath us."

Yuri walked forward a few paces. "Maybe not directly underneath us. The sound and vibrations could be carrying for a long way." He continued to turn about.

Carter looked down at the ice. He knew what freezing water could do to the human body, and it only took three minutes before internal organs could start shutting down. "Hey, are we safe here?"

"There." Yuri pointed just as there came another crackling rumble, and then a sound that was like huge trees splintering.

Carter followed his direction and could see several hundred yards further north and away from the shoreline what looked like an explosion of white happening—a geyser of ice and snow as it was thrown into the air.

"*Shit*, something is coming up." Carter backed up. For some insane reason, he thought it must have been a submarine breaching, but then had no idea why he thought that, as there were no subs in Lake Baikal.

With pounding smacks, the airborne slabs of ice came back to earth, and just as quickly as it started, it seemed over. The pair of men stood and stared for several more moments.

"We gotta check this out," Carter said.

"No, not a good idea." Yuri threw out an arm.

Carter slapped his shoulder. "I'll take the lead then, you can follow."

Carter turned and ran to his snowmobile, threw a leg over it, and started the engine. Yuri was close behind, muttering his warnings all the way as Carter took off and sped toward the disturbance.

He was traveling fast, eating up the distance in seconds. He had no idea what he was about to encounter, or what he'd do when he got there. But he could feel the solid weight of the gun in its holster at his back.

Carter slowed when he was just 50 feet out and turned off the engine, the bobcat sliding to a stop. He slowly got off and waited for Yuri to do the same.

"Take it slow," the Russian said and then turned. "You first."

Carter grinned and turned back to the huge mound of broken ice slabs, and the pair of men had both pulled their guns and held them in two-handed grips. Carter approached and Yuri was at his shoulder.

Even up close, it still looked as if a submarine had breached the way the slabs had been pushed up, some of them were broken into boulders and shunted aside. It had taken Yuri close to an hour with a chainsaw and axe to cut and hack through the ice. But whatever did this had done it in seconds, and it must have been big.

Carter waved Yuri to the other side of the breach. The explosion of ice was about 40 feet wide, and he wanted plenty of space in the event either of them had to fire their guns.

Carter stepped up on a slab, and then another, climbing the outer edge of the ice crater. When he was about eight feet up from the lake-ice surface, he peered over the edge of the broken ice, down into its center.

There was open water there, still not fully welled up from below. It swirled and boiled as if there was something moving about in there, but the water was inky black and impossible to see below the surface for more than a foot or so. But as he stared, he was sure there was a green glow coming from deep in its center.

Yuri's head came up from the other side. He looked down and then across to Carter. He shrugged.

Carter wished he had the camera to toss it in to get a look down there, but bet he'd lose it in seconds. Instead, he settled for picking up a fist-sized lump of ice and lobbing it into the agitated pool.

It splashed into the center and in response, there came an almighty explosion of freezing water. Carter cringed back, but nothing came up with the water. In a second or two, he lifted his head and looked down again. The green glow was gone.

The water was still and calm, and it began to slowly well up to the ice's surface. He watched it for a full five minutes, but there seemed nothing there but ice and freezing water now. He even tossed in another chunk of ice, but it splashed and sunk without any more response. Whatever had been in there was now gone.

Carter waved at Yuri and clambered back down. The pair met up at their snow bobcats. Carter exhaled and stared back at the explosion of ice.

"Any ideas?"

Yuri shook his head. "There are no whales here, no submarines, and no seal or sturgeon is going to be able to punch a hole through six feet of ice." He sighed and looked back at the crater of exploded ice sheets. "I have heard that sometimes the ice sheets can buckle and twist if there is a big storm somewhere pushing on the water and ice layers."

"That's not a buckle, but a freaking hole." Carter scoffed.

"Then I have no ideas." Yuri shrugged.

"I'd love to see what's down there." Carter placed his hands on his hips.

Yuri blanched. "Please, Carter, do not even think of doing that."

Carter stared at the crater for a few more moments. "*Nah*, not this day. But I don't like mysteries." He turned and grinned. "I mean *more* mysteries." He stared for a moment more, his mind working. "Hey, drop a camera in, and set it to auto-record. We'll get it later."

"Sure." Yuri paused. "Hover, or sink to bottom?"

"Put it on the bottom," Carter replied.

Yuri nodded and set to rigging the camera, and then, with Carter, scaled the broken ice. He handed it to Carter.

Carter carefully eased down toward the pitch-black water and tossed the camera in. It would auto pilot itself to the bottom, where it would land, and then watch the darkness until they retrieved it or it filled its memory chip.

"We'll come back in a few days." Carter clamored out of the crater.

Yuri just exhaled. Carter threw a leg over his snowmobile. "Okay, let's grab the rest of our stuff." He glanced back at the ice explosion. "Might be a good idea not to mention this to the others. There's enough things to worry about already."

"*Da*."

Yuri glanced back at the broken ice and then to Carter. For the first time, Carter noticed that the big Russian looked scared.

EPISODE 04

CHAPTER 28

INTERACTION: *Overlooking the Mill Compound—10 minutes ago*

Stanislov Borga was dressed in all white camouflage clothing and was a silent and near-invisible ghost as he moved through the snow-draped landscape.

Over his shoulder was an SVD Dragunov sniper rifle with a five-round magazine—it was reliable, light, and he was deadly accurate with it for up to half a mile. Though the tree coverage was still thick on the hill, the air was breathless and had a clarity that was perfect for a marksman.

Borga had been given his targets—two of them, the man and woman. Either one was acceptable as his job was to send a message. However, the American man, Carter Stenson, was the real priority target.

He found a perch behind a large tree and settled down to wait. It was still early morning and he had at least eight hours of light to wait for a perfect kill shot. But he also had light amplification equipment so if he had to camp out, he would.

It had taken him a day and a half to get to the lake and then wend his way circuitously through the thick forest, so he was determined not to head back without completing his mission.

He had been engaged by the local bratva, but he was a freelance assassin for hire. It didn't matter to him if it was a man, woman, or child, what their crime or politics were, or whether it was simple revenge or even the removal of an opponent. If the money was right, his target was as good as dead.

Borga lit a smoke and exhaled through clenched teeth, spreading the smoke. The smoke would dissipate quickly and the cold locked up odors so he wasn't worried about it being detected. However, if he were here in the dark, he'd have to dispense with smoking. But he suspected his job would be completed well before then.

He lifted his rifle, looking through the scope to scan the compound—

there was the main manager's house that his briefing notes had told him was used by Sara Stenson. Then there were about a dozen smaller cabins used by the workers, and one of them by Carter Stenson. The major building was the old mill house that had been turned into their laboratory, hatchery, and administration center.

Borga sucked in another lungful of smoke and eased it out again. He'd been freelancing ever since he left the Spetsnaz forces. He'd enjoyed his work there, but the pay was shit. Now, he only needed one good hit on a high-profile target to make nearly an entire year's wage. And a confirmed kill today would do just that for him.

Confirmed kills were never a problem for him. Borga specialized in headshots and with the Dragunov's 7.62mm caliber rounds and a muzzle velocity of 2,500 feet per second, the effects were a hole in one side of the skull and the other half blown off like a broken dinner plate.

He'd heard Americans had hard heads, and he couldn't wait to test that and see Carter Stenson's in pieces.

Borga stubbed out his cigarette against the tree trunk and waited. This was the hard part, what separated the professionals from the amateurs. Impatience and nervous energy were enemies that needed to be conquered. The right shot was worth waiting for. A rushed shot could mean a catastrophe, as the target not only lived, but also then made it impossible to get to them a second time.

Borga's neck prickled and he glanced over his left shoulder. Then a few seconds later, the right one, and continued to watch. He slowed his breathing so he could focus—a soldier's intuition told him when he wasn't alone.

The sniper crouched and carefully lifted his rifle to his eye, sighting through the scope and then panning it slowly along the wall of forest. A few flakes of snow drifted down but the air still had good clarity. Even so, the number of trees meant that further in, if anyone was hiding, they could be easily obscured.

Borga lowered the rifle and tilted his head to listen. Was there the soft scrunch of snow underfoot? He concentrated, but it wasn't repeated.

There was always the chance he could be discovered purely by accident. People could come hunting, gathering wood, or simply stretching their legs. He would always try and avoid killing innocent civilians, only because it might attract attention. Also, he didn't get paid for it.

He couldn't see anything and decided he might move from where he was currently staked out and shift a little further along the ridgeline. Borga turned away from the forest and put his rifle over his shoulder. He then began to rise to his feet.

The sniper took one last look down at the compound. Big mistake.

There came the rushed sound of something heavy moving through the snow behind him. He spun, reaching for his gun at the same time.

But his hand froze as the shadow fell over him. It wasn't a man, but seemed to be a massive bear. The thing didn't growl or even grunt, but he was grabbed by the throat with one massive, taloned paw, the pads or claws shutting down his windpipe. Borga was lifted in the air and his legs bicycled uselessly beneath him.

Like a child, he was tucked under a heavily furred arm. The stink of the thing clogged his nostrils as he began to beat at it. But he might as well have been striking a side of beef for all the effect he was having.

The thing was cold beneath the fur, and the stink was one of corruption rather than the cookie-like smell of a furred beast. Borga reached for the knife at his waist, drew it, and stabbed upward into the bear's armpit. The blade sunk in deep. But no blood spurted, there was no roar of pain, and the thing didn't even flinch. Instead, something like dark rope flashed out of the wound and pulled it closed.

The massive paw was taken away from his throat and Borga yelled. He knew when he was in the shit and needed help. The mission was over and only survival mattered now.

He yelled again, as he could make out now where they were heading—the frozen lake was in front of them. Was the beast planning to take him out onto the ice? Maybe its den was somewhere up or down the shoreline.

Borga still had his gun over his shoulder and knew he only needed a few seconds if he was released to put a bullet in the beast's head.

But when the creature got to the frozen lake edge, it didn't step onto the ice, but instead leaned forward to tear a hole in it with one enormous arm. Huge chunks were lifted and pushed aside, exposing water that was blacker and colder than hell.

"*No, no…*"

To his horror, Borga could see what was going to happen next. The creature burrowed into the hole in the ice it had made—*directly into the freezing water*.

The assassin sucked in a deep breath, but as soon as he entered the water, it was like being punched in the gut and the cold against his skin felt like it burned. In just a few seconds, his lungs exploded to force him to try and gulp air, but instead he sucked in the terrible, black water.

His last thought was how much the freezing water hurt his teeth before the darkness took him.

*****

Red saw Mitch lift a hand and he held his position. The pair had been tasked with patrolling the perimeter of the mill compound, and even though it was daytime, the light was a muted washed out grey from the heavy cloud cover that extended all the way down to the treetops.

"I don't like this," Mitch whispered.

Red scoffed and looked over his shoulder. "What? You mean the cold, the food, the being stuck out in the Russian boonies, or the fact that there could be some sort of weird-ass creatures running around out here, climbing inside dead bears, and making them act like giant puppets?"

Mitch grinned. "Yeah, that last one... and also the food."

"Makes two of us," Red said. "Come on. The sooner we're done, the sooner we're back drinking vodka and eating barbecued reindeer."

The pair continued on, rifles ready, and even though both men were highly experienced and normally cool as ice cubes, both of the ex-Special Force's soldiers had nerves that were currently strung wire-tight.

Red hadn't felt this edgy since their last tour of Afghanistan where they were on night patrol in a Taliban-controlled zone. Just like then, he had the feeling of being watched and of imminent danger.

There had been a snowfall an hour or two back and the effect was powdery dry snow that squeak-scrunched underfoot—it was also virgin snow, meaning it was unblemished by tracks of any kind.

The cold, and the snow had other effects—it damped down sounds so the only noise came from their own plodding footsteps in the powder that pressed all the way to their calves.

"*There*—tracks—not human," Mitch said.

"Shit," Red hissed.

"What do you wanna do?" Mitch crouched behind a tree trunk.

Red crouched beside him and looked again at the tracks. "Yeah, big sucker." He pointed with the barrel of his gun. "Came from out there and headed further into the forest, over that way."

"Follow?" Mitch asked.

"Wait." Red held up a hand and tilted his head. "Did you hear that?"

Mitch turned and the pair crouched in silence for a couple more minutes before Mitch slowly shook his head. "Something... a bird maybe?"

"*Nah*, thought it was a yell." Red checked his wristwatch—it was only mid-morning. "We got time to check this out. Priority one, we make sure whatever this sonofabitch is, it doesn't wander into our camp."

"I heard that, compadre," Mitch agreed.

The pair stood and began to follow the tracks.

"That bear..." Mitch spoke without turning.

"What about it?" Red asked.

"... you think it's as Carter said; you know, it being like a ghillie suit?"

"Impossible." Red blew air between his pressed lips. "That's just dumb."

"What do you think happened to all those bear guts then... and the brain?" Mitch frowned. "That was some weird shit—I don't even think it was a real bear."

Red snorted. "'Course it was a real goddamn bear. Wolves must've got it—got some huge ones around here; Siberian wolves are big suckers... get to 150 pounds." He chuckled. "And guess what? They don't hibernate, so there's your suspects, not some dumb-ass mutant bear."

"Yeah, sure, okay." Mitch nodded. "Wolves I can deal with."

The pair continued to follow the tracks. The prints curved inland about a quarter-mile and then headed back... toward their compound.

A light snow began to fall again, dampening the last sounds of the forest and also slowly filling in the tracks. In another hour, they were beginning to close in on where they started out.

"I don't believe it; this fucker is heading right toward our base," Mitch said.

"Well then, we better head it off. Come on, let's move it." Red picked up the pace, forcing Mitch on as well.

They tracked it all the way back to the small hill overlooking their compound, and soon located an area where there were multiple indentations in the snow that made it look all churned up.

Red saw how the prints seemed to become closer together before the area of disturbed snow. "Whatever it was, it sped up." Red walked in a little closer. "Then something went down here."

He turned, slowly scanning the surrounding forest, and then noticed something on the tree just in from the skirmish of marks. He quickly crossed to it and lifted a finger to wipe it across the mark, then brought it to his nose.

"Ash. Someone was smoking here." He turned about and then pointed. "Hang on; more tracks leading in." He walked toward them and crouched. "Human, single person, probably a guy in boots." He rested his forearms on his knees. "It all came together right here, and went bad for someone or something."

Red stood up and turned. "Then the big tracks go that way."

They followed the bigger tracks all the way to the frozen lake. They didn't stop. But at the water's edge, there was a broken-open hole in the thick ice as if something had burrowed in.

"It went swimming? After it punched a big hole in the ice." Mitch shook his head. "Why would it do that?"

Red exhaled, blowing a long cloud of steam. "Fucked if I know. But remember what we found after the bear guts went missing? Same thing." He turned back. "What worries me more is that this fucker was up at the tree line watching us."

Mitch turned. "A scout?"

"What do you think?" he replied.

Mitch gritted his teeth. "Fuck me. Gives me the willies thinking these things are watching us."

"We need more kit," Red said. "Let's get that fat Russian, Yuri, to order us some motion-operated spy cams we can plant around the camp perimeter. If they're watching us, I wanna be watching them right back."

"Works for me," Mitch said.

"We can put it on Carter's tab." Red took one last look around. "Come on, we've been out long enough."

CHAPTER 29

Federal Agency for Fisheries and Conservation—Moscow

Mikhail Ivanov whistled an old Russian folk tune as he opened the package from the mill house fish farm in Siberia. It was sent from Carter Stenson, the brother of Marcus Stenson who had mysteriously disappeared.

He was glad when the wife and brother had decided to take over, and more so when they brought in some good people to assist them with the technical side of the breeding program.

For the most part, breeding and raising sturgeon was expensive, time-consuming, complicated, and given there was no return on any investment for at least five years, no one wanted to be involved. Having the American couple invest was a stroke of good fortune.

Besides that, he liked them and wanted them to be successful, so he gave them his full support. Mikhail was a proud Russian, and he knew that Beluga sturgeon caviar was a national treasure and must be preserved for future generations. If it took an American to help them do it, then so be it.

He was the lead fisheries' scientist at the department and took charge of the program personally, so when anything arose, he ensured it was forwarded directly to him so he could smooth out bureaucratic hurdles or any action requests for assistance before they landed in some administrator's top drawers where they simply went to gather dust and die.

Mikhail finished opening the package, working slowly as his fingers suffered from a little arthritis now, and then held up the small test tube sealed with tape and wax. There was a freezer pack included to keep it cool and he quickly discarded that. He frowned and shook the tube, seeing the glutinous dark liquid slop back and forth.

He opened the accompanying letter, saw it was from Nikolay Grudinin, and began to read.

Good morning or afternoon, dear Mikhail,

I have enclosed a sample of some biological material we retrieved from the carcass of a bear in the Lake Baikal Forest. The bear was not healthy—far from it—and we found some unusual characteristics that warranted further investigation.

This sample was extracted from its cranial cavity and could not be identified with our limited resources.

Hope you can shed some light on it. Thank you for your assistance.

P.S. The bear was found far from the lake, and the fish and the compound area are not contaminated, and we simply wish to know if the substance might be rabies.

Your friend, Nikolay Grudinin

The Mill House, Lake Baikal, Siberia

"*Hmm.*" Mikhail closed the letter and held the tube up again. "Well, what are you? Not bear bile, and not Arctic rabies. Maybe some necrotized brain tissue from a form of meningitis type infection, perhaps?"

The department had a complete laboratory that extended to electron scanning microscopes, gene sequencers, and a DNA database of nearly every creature on the planet.

The unfortunate aspect of this sample was that Mikhail lacked important information, like how long was the bear dead? What was the state of the brain? And most importantly, how long was it exposed to the external environment? This could itself have contaminated the sample.

Mikhail prepared a glass dish and stuck a label on the top, marking it "Sample 01*: Siberian*" and the date. He then used a scalpel to cut the seal open as he walked to a standard microscope. He first upended it into his dish and used a long, glass rod to pick up a drop on its end for him to smear on a tiny glass pane. He sealed the dish and then pushed the slide pane into the viewing aperture of the scope.

He lifted his glasses to his forehead and looked down the eyepiece, gently moving the focus for a moment. He concentrated as he increased the magnification.

There were certain things he was expecting as it didn't really matter how diverse the cells were because they had certain parts in common—cell membranes surrounding a cell, forming the physical boundary between the cell and its environment. Then, inside the cell's skin, there was the cytoplasm, which was the watery substance called cytosol, which contains other cell structures such as ribosomes, where proteins are made. Finally, there was the DNA, a nucleic acid found in all cells holding the genetic instructions cells needed to make proteins.

These were the things that were parts of all cells and the characteristics Mikhail expected to see. After all, they were in the cells of organisms as different as bacteria and human beings, and in fact, all known organisms had such similar cells, and these similarities showed that all life on Earth had a common evolutionary history.

Mikhail lifted his head, blinked a few times, and then looked back down into the scope. The problem was the cells he was looking at had none of those characteristics. That in itself was outstanding and a little alarming, but what was even more astounding was the cells were still alive.

"What the hell are you?" he breathed out and straightened.

Options flooded his mind that worked a mile a minute. He took the sample from under the microscope and prepared it for the spectrometer and the electron microscope. He also used some in the DNA sequencer, even though there seemed no evidence of nucleic acid for it to test.

It took him several hours before the full results started feeding in, and all of them just left him more and more baffled. There was one final analytical tool at his disposal, and it was when he used the images and analysis results from the sequencers and spectrometer in the global gene database, that he finally got a hit.

Mikhail stared at the screen for many minutes, almost trance-like, before his lips formed the single word: "*Tunguska.*"

He sat down slowly, before his legs gave way. All Russians knew of the event that occurred near the Stony Tunguska River in Yeniseysk. It was in 1908, over the sparsely populated Eastern Siberian Taiga, where 770 square miles of forest was flattened.

The explosion was generally attributed to the airburst of a meteor, and even though it was classified as an impact event, no impact crater had ever been found. The suspected object was thought to have disintegrated at an altitude of around five miles over Siberia rather than to have hit the surface of the Earth. To this day, the Tunguska event was and is the largest modern impact occurrence on Earth in recorded history.

All Russians were aware of the event, but only a few scientists knew of the analysis done in 2013 of the micro-samples taken from a Siberian peat bog near the center of the affected area, showing fragments that may be of meteoritic origin.

They also showed up something even more interesting—biological material. Not truly cellular, as there was no defined internal structures as we knew them. They were an anomaly and a paradox, and to this day, they remained unique and a mystery.

The known data was kept in a secure file named: THE SIBERIAN INCIDENT—TUNGUSKA. And another thing the researchers did was they entered the biological analysis results into the genome database, in the event more of the material was ever found. And Mikhail had just done that now.

Tunguska was nearly 1,000 miles from Lake Baikal so there was no way they could be from the same event. So something else had occurred there. Something new… or perhaps something very old that'd just reappeared?

Mikhail got to his feet, his eyes still staring. Professional scientific curiosity burned within him.

The scientist grabbed up the packaging Carter Stenson had sent and read the phone number attached. He lifted the phone and his fingers flew as he dialed. He waited, listened, then hung up and dialed again, and again—it was the same every time: no connection.

Mikhail slammed the phone down and quickly glanced at his watch—he had a hundred things to do, and if he hurried, he could still make the midnight flight to Listvyanka.

The Russian scientist spun on his heel and headed for the door.

CHAPTER 30

Carter came to the door of his cabin rubbing his eyes and looked out over the frozen compound. Last night, Red and Mitch had come to see him and babbled about following some tracks, and then seen some sort of skirmish area up at the tree line. For a few moments, he could barely focus. And *that*, he knew, could be deadly.

For the sake of himself, Sara, the business, and every person at the mill compound, he needed to be laser-focused and razor-sharp.

Carter wanted to pool what they knew, so he had called a get-together down at the mill house for this morning and had Mitch send word to Yuri and all the Russian workers —it was time for a good old-fashioned management meeting.

As he headed down along one of the snow trenches they'd dug as pathways, Sara caught up with him, so heavily rugged up her arms stuck out from her side.

"What's happening?" she asked him.

"Just getting everyone together for a general update. Share what we know." He snorted. "What little we know."

"Good plan; we should do it often, maybe twice weekly," she declared, and then looked up at him. "Got a message back from Moscow; they're coming. Then lost comms before I could ask any questions."

"Really? What did they say?" Carter stopped just outside the heavy double doors.

"I'll update everyone." She nodded to the door. "Thank you."

Carter pushed one of the heavy doors inward and Sara went through.

"Everyone," Carter said as a greeting to the group.

There were nods and muttered replies to both him and Sara.

There was coffee on, and Pavel had made some pryanika, soft cookies spiced with honey and cinnamon. The group stood or sat around the large entrance room that they had originally brought the bear carcass into. It was large enough for all of them, but the downside was it wasn't fully heated.

Dmitry, Pavel and his son, Nikolay, plus Stefan, all stood on one side; Yuri, Red, and Mitch closer to Carter and Sara. Their combined body heat began to warm the room.

"Okay, it's time to share information. It's no secret that there is something out of the ordinary going on."

Yuri's eyes widened for a moment and his lips hiked up at one of the corners.

Carter grinned and waved him down. "Yeah, yeah, I know; that's an understatement. But I believe we have everything covered for now." Carter half-turned to Sara. "As our company president is here, it's a good time to share what we've been doing, progress, and any other things the group should know about."

"Everything? About time." Stefan's gaze was flat.

"If it's relevant to the group, then yes," Carter said, knowing full well that gave him an out not to share anything he thought might *stampede the horses*, as they say.

Before Stefan had a chance to question him, Carter pointed to the big Russian. "Yuri, why don't you give us an update on the pens?"

Yuri grunted. "All good so far. The ice has covered over the pens so they are safe... from above." He eyed Carter knowingly before going on. "The adult fish are bedded in, and the sprats are feeding, growing, slowly, but growing. I think we have good progress here. No problems." He stopped and waited.

"Very good, Yuri, thank you," Carter said.

"Yes, that's very good to hear, as they're the foundation of our entire business, so thank you," Sara said.

Pavel raised his hand.

"Yes, Pavel," Sara asked.

"We are running low on meat. Dmitry and I should do some hunting again soon. There are seal colonies to the north and reindeer herds still in the forest. Is good time." The older Russian waited.

"How far in the forest?" Sara asked.

Pavel bobbed his head. "Depends what we hunt."

"No seals," Carter said. "Two days, hunt together, do not split up, and not near the lake. Only hunt inland for now, okay? The, *ah*, bratva may still be hanging about. Doubtful, but best to be careful."

Carter bet no one in the room thought it was the Russian mafia he was concerned about, but no one pushed him on it. The men nodded, and Pavel said something quickly in Russian to Nikolay who nodded.

The young man turned to Carter and cleared his throat. "My father wants to know if there are still booby traps in the forest."

"No," Carter said. "We've taken down the claymores in the forest, but there are several along the lake line. So you must avoid them. At the perimeter, we have installed motion and thermal sensors, and Red and Mitch requested motion-triggered cameras so we've got them to install as well. So like I said, stay away from the lake, and we're all good."

Carter saw Red raise his eyebrows, maybe asking should he share why they wanted the motion sensors, but Carter almost imperceptibly shook his head. Red nodded and just continued to watch the group.

"Sara," Carter asked. "Moscow development?"

Just saying the Russian capital's name focused everyone.

"Thanks, Carter." She looked across the group. "And thank you, everyone, for the progress and hard work."

Sara stepped into the center of the group. "A while back, we sent a biological sample to the Federal Agency for Fisheries and Conservation for analysis. Well, they've answered us, more emphatically than I expected." She half-smiled. "They'll be paying us a visit."

The group muttered and shifted their feet. Stefan tilted his head.

"They? Who is coming?"

Sara turned to him. "Mr. Mikhail Ivanov, and he's also bringing another scientist as well, this one an evolutionary DNA specialist."

Stefan's eyes widened slightly. "It is unexpected, and highly unusual that Mikhail Ivanov, the lead scientist in the ministry, will be coming in person. Is this a good thing?"

"I thought we'd just get some sort of report back on what was in that stuff we sent. This might be a problem? What did he say?" Carter asked.

"Not much really," Sara replied. "But he seems a supporter of ours, and I can see in Marcus' notes that he worked with him before."

Carter sighed. "So he wants to take a look for himself, *huh*?"

Sara nodded slowly. "It'll be fine."

The group shuffled and many of the Russians muttered amongst themselves about not liking Moscow bureaucrat's onsite.

"I'm sure it'll be okay," Carter added loudly.

"Sure it will. Told you we should have burned or buried it." Mitch sneered. "Now we've got the Russian authorities breathing down our necks."

"No, he simply has an enquiring scientific mind and is coming to investigate the sample, and probably where it came from." Sara turned to him. "He'll help if we need it."

Carter glanced at Mitch. "We might be able to get some government assistance with our potential mafia problem as well. Nothing makes the local authorities more responsive than a visit from Moscow."

"This would be a good thing," Yuri said.

"Okay, we'll show him around, and I'm sure he'll want to see the bear and where it came from." Carter rubbed his chin. "If he plans on going wandering around near the lakeshore, we'll definitely need to take those claymores down... all of them."

"Yeah, I hear that blowing up Moscow officials might just get a black mark in your ledger," Red sniggered.

"When's he arriving?" Yuri asked.

She shrugged. "As soon as he could get transportation. But I think he'll be here by tomorrow evening."

"Fine. Red, you and Mitch take the ordnance down and store it. I want no trace. And get those cameras set up—in and outside the compound. Everyone else, let's clean the place up before the brass arrives."

*****

Carter walked up the slope with Sara, stopped at her front porch, and looked up at the leaden sky. The cloud was thick and heavy as usual, but today it was so low that he could see it moving through the treetops.

"Snow again soon," he murmured.

"Another day in paradise." She sighed and then looked up at him. "Everyone is wound up pretty tight, huh?"

"Yep, and I just think that right about now a single thing could push them over, and then they'll run for the hills." He jammed his hands in his pockets.

"I might just run with them." She gave him a watery smile and then sighed. "This place certainly has its own unique blend of problems." She counted off her fingers. "Foreign country, remote, mafia gangs, weird bears, legends about things in the lake." She held up another finger. "Oh yeah, and we live in a place that's called the haunted mill."

He laughed softly. "Yeah, but that's my point. Everyone has their limits and if something else weird happened, it might push us all over. Collapse everything."

"Not a chance; we're tougher than that." Her brows knitted.

"That we are." He gave her a small salute. "Let's just hope this haunted mill has thrown the worst it has at us."

"Sure." She snorted softly. "Good luck today, Carter."

*****

That evening, the dark and silence was only broken by the tiny red lights of the motion sensors detecting movement. The cameras turned on and watched. They also had motion-sensitive target-following and swiveled on their bases to track the movement.

This time, they followed the moving object all the way into the camp, and with their unemotional electronic eyes, watched as it went from door to door, and then to Dmitry's cabin house. His door slowly opened and then closed.

It was an hour later that the man exited, standing naked on his front deck for a moment, before walking up the snow-covered hill to then vanish into the forest where the disturbance first arrived.

CHAPTER 31

Mikhail Ivanov looked down from the snow plane's window as they flew over the frozen lake. The plane was a small six-seater with a combination of floats, wheels, and snow skids for all cold-climate terrain landings—perfect for the Russian winters.

On the other side of the plane was his best biologist, Anna Ledvedev, who specialized in genetics. She seemed lost in thought as she stared out the small window at the frozen landscape below. Anna had a formidable mind, encyclopedic knowledge of DNA characteristics, and was one of the few experts to have had the opportunity to review the Tunguska samples. She had achieved all this and was only 28 years old.

In the front of the plane, the pilot turned to yell back into the cabin, "Coming down." He held up a splayed hand. "Five minutes."

Mikhail nodded, and he saw Anna straighten as well. The pair buckled in tight, as coming down on ice was always a risk. Though the sheets were usually uniform, in some places, the pressure of fast-growing ice could cause folds, ridges, and holes that could be catastrophic if the plane were to strike one on landing.

Mikhail felt his stomach flip a little as the plane came down fast and then began to bank. The pilot had obviously sighted their destination and perhaps a potential strip of long, flat surface ice to come down on.

As the plane tilted, Mikhail caught sight of the mill house and its compound—one large warehouse-sized building right on the waterline, and possibly a dozen houses, big and small, dotted about. A few people had come out to stare up at the approaching plane.

Anna leaned across to him. "They are all Americans?"

He shook his head. "No, the owner is an American. Her name is Sara Stenson. The original owner, Marcus Stenson, vanished, and now his brother, Carter, is helping out. The rest are Russian citizens." He shrugged. "Mostly locals."

"Friendly?" She tilted her head.

"Yes, yes, I think so," he said uncertainly.

"And do they know what happens if the samples turn out to be what we suspect they are?" She tilted her chin.

He smiled sadly. "No, they don't."

She raised an eyebrow. "Then let's hope they stay friendly." She turned back to her window, and Mikhail did the same on his side.

He hoped so too. Because if there was evidence that another Siberian incident had occurred in the past like that of Tunguska, then the entire site would need to be sealed off, especially from the public. Unfortunately, Russia had a habit of evicting people from their land, and their only redress was the courts that were labyrinthine, mostly acting under orders, and worked at a glacial speed. By the time any adjudication was handed down, coincidently, any *cleansing* work that was being undertaken had long since been completed.

"Hold tight," the pilot shouted back at them as they dropped and came in fast.

The plane came down smooth and level, but soon as the skids touched the rock-hard ice, it was like they were traveling over corrugated iron. The vibrations made Mikhail's back teeth hurt, and he clamped them together and gripped his armrests so hard his hands became claws.

It felt like it went on forever before they finally slowed and the pilot revved the engine one last time and turned the nose of the plane back toward the mill house. They taxied in closer, and then he cut the power. The single, large propeller stopped spinning almost immediately.

He flipped off his seatbelt and turned to look out his small porthole window. Several people were coming across the ice to greet them, and the pilot came down the cabin to unlock and open the side door. He stuck his head out, shouted a greeting, and then flipped the stairs down.

"This is our stop." Mikhail got to his feet.

The pair grabbed their carry-all bags, and the pilot helped them with their larger luggage. Anna looked out of the door.

"How long do you think we'll be here?"

Mikhail shrugged. "Not long; a few days at most to do the onsite analysis. Just enough time to get a feel for what we are dealing with."

The pair came down the steps, and a large man waved. Mikhail waved back.

"Mr. Stenson?"

"*Nyet*, Yuri Revkin, *menedzher*," Yuri responded.

"The manager, good," Mikhail replied and turned to the next man, a youth. "And?"

The young man grinned widely. "Nikolay Grudinin, and it is a pleasure to meet you at last, Dr. Ivanov." He stuck out his gloved hand.

Mikhail took the hand and pumped it. "Please call me Mikhail." He stood aside. "My colleague, Dr. Anna Ledvedev."

Even under all his furs and wraps, Mikhail saw Nikolay's eyes light up. He seemed to nod, bow, and maybe blush all at once.

"Dr. Ledvedev, it is my pleasure."

"Anna..." She smiled and held out her hand to shake his.

Behind them, the pilot had finished unpacking their large cases containing their equipment and climbed back into his cockpit.

Mikhail waved him off and then turned toward the compound. "And now…"

"Of course, of course." Yuri ushered them to the slope of the land.

Mikhail was amazed at the size of the site. He'd seen pictures of the old mill complex during its working days back in the '70s, and then it just looked dirty and cramped, a collection of old industrialization-type warehouses that seemed like no one ever bothered to clean up.

He always suspected there might be toxins hidden beneath the soil, as many older companies used mercury to keep the logs free from algae and bacteria, but their testing over the decades had shown nothing above background normal, so he was hopeful they were clean.

Mikhail pulled the knitted scarf he had over his chin up a little higher. He was looking forward to analyzing the samples that had been found, and also seeing the source material—the animal—that they came from. It might just turn out to give them answers to a century-old mystery.

Yuri dropped the cases on the wharf where another couple of men waited, and gave them instructions to take the personal bags to two cabins close together for Mikhail and Anna, and to also take the technical equipment to the laboratories.

"Mrs. Stenson and Mr. Stenson are looking forward to meeting you," Yuri said. He leaned closer. "They are not married, and it is very complex, as—"

"I know, I know." Mikhail waved it away. "I'm sorry for the loss of Marcus Stenson. And I know this is his brother here now."

Yuri nodded. "Okay, good." He pointed. "This way."

They trudged up the hill to where a man was waiting on the front porch of the main house. Mikhail had seen pictures of Marcus Stenson, who was slightly bigger than an average-sized guy, handsome, and enthusiastic-looking. He could immediately tell this man was related to him. But he was larger, more menacing-looking, and held himself with a calm authority that the scientist found a little intimidating. He bet his last rouble this Carter Stenson had some sort of military history. And not one where he sat at a desk.

"Mr. Stenson?" Mikhail asked as they stopped at the bottom of the few steps up to the porch.

"Carter," the man said in a deep American voice. "Come on up, get warm. Sara is waiting for you inside."

They climbed the steps and stamped snow off their boots. The door opened and Sara Stenson stood there smiling back as Mikhail and Anna crowded the doorway.

Sara ushered them inside. "It's a pleasure to meet you at last. I saw in my husband's notes that you personally were of great help to him in procuring the correct testing sites and also facilitating the fish and egg batches."

Mikhail nodded. "It was a good project plan and for a long time, we in the scientific community had raised a flag about the dire situation the Beluga sturgeon were in. Your husband was the first person to actually have a well-thought-out plan to arrest, and eventually reverse, the decline."

"And he, now, you all seem to be doing it," Anna added.

"Thank you," Sara said. "I'm sure you're both tired and if you like, Yuri will give you a quick tour. Tomorrow morning, we can then meet at the mill house and share what we've found."

"Perfect," Mikhail said.

Carter then walked them to the door. "I'll show you to your cabins and get you settled in." He turned back to Sara. "Anything else?"

The woman seemed to think for a moment, and then turned to Mikhail.

"My instructions to everyone were to be open and honest with you. I hope we can have that courtesy returned."

"Of course." Mikhail gave her a small bow but felt Anna's eyes briefly flick to him as they went out the front door.

CHAPTER 32

Central Irkutsk, Siberian south

Arkady Tushino sat with the small cup of coffee in front of him that was so dark it could have been crude oil. He stared straight ahead at the blank wall in front of him but his mind was hundreds of miles away at an old paper mill compound on the shore of Lake Baikal.

His sniper, Stanislov Borga, had vanished. He had worked with the man too many times to think that he had failed or had simply quit and left the job. For him to disappear meant he could only be dead. He went to Lake Baikal and never came back.

He grit his teeth; this Carter Stenson was proving more tenacious and formidable than he expected.

He just prayed Gennardy Zyuganov never found out, as his big pumpkin head would break into its normal grinning sneer at how Tushino was once again underestimating his target and fumbling his duties. It would be seen as another failure, and Tushino didn't think he had many more failures left in him before he'd be bundled into a sack and dropped in some cold river on a moonless midnight. His lips turned down cruelly. Or maybe as the ultimate insult, he'd be dropped into Lake Baikal.

It seemed that his chances of fully acquiring a stake in the Beluga caviar business were close to zero while Carter Stenson was there. Tushino's only real option was to remove this Stenson *mudak*, and then force the woman to countersign the contract. Or maybe remove her too.

Tushino steepled his fingers and sat back, still staring straight ahead. There was one unforeseen risk; if they acquired the business without the Stensons fronting it, then the bureaucrats in Moscow might not want to continue supporting them.

His lips curved up at the corners. There was another option—a delicious one: burn everything to the ground, kill everyone there, and just walk away. This would mean a significant human capital and financial investment already expended would be lost, but it was the choice that brought the greatest satisfaction to him, and one he could sell to the big boss as him sending a message to the people to not mess with Arkady Tushino.

His hand curled into a fist as his appetite and desire for chaos filled him to the brim. This bastard American had caused him to lose face amongst his peers and his boss, and only blood and pain would ever restore it.

He bit it down hard and resolved it would be the final option. There was one last chance—he knew that the woman was the weak link. And American women were soft and pampered. If he could get her by herself, with a little bit of encouragement, she would agree to anything. He bet he'd only have to remove an ear or maybe one or two of her fingers.

Tushino's mind worked on his plan, trying to think through the variables. What if the woman held out? Thinking her hero would save her? *Simple*, he thought. *Remove the hero*. If Carter were taken out of the picture, she would have no choice. She would be alone then.

Tushino smiled. The fact was, he always wanted to kill Carter Stenson, and any plan he came up with had his death sitting right at the center of it. His grin widened as he leaned forward to pick up his phone and dialed one of his lieutenants.

"Stavros..." His eyes burned with intensity, but his lips had curved into an oily smile. "I have a job. Get the men together—all of them."

CHAPTER 33

The next morning, Carter was first into the mill house before anyone else was awake. There was a breeze coming off the ice sheets that felt like it could strip the flesh right from his bones so his skin would then fall to the ground as frozen flakes.

However, the previous night had been as still as a graveyard, and he rewound with interest the last evening's surveillance footage. On the walk to the mill building, he noticed more of those weird spindly tracks coming into the compound. Whatever those little bastards were, they were still hanging around, and still avoiding detection. But now, he hoped to finally see exactly what their late-night visitors looked like.

The footage from all the compound's cameras fed into a central online folder and the computer software then organized it into a single, logical, time-organized stream as the motion sensors were each activated. As a sensor was triggered, the associated camera came to life and it'd record until it was handed over to the next sensor. In effect, it should act like someone was following the intruder with a single lens and tracking it right throughout their camp.

That was the plan, and it was one that Carter had used on night surveillance when they were guarding outposts and ammo dumps in the Middle East.

He started the footage thread and underneath was a position ID that identified a designated camera so he could work out which was being triggered and when. This was largely unnecessary, as he could see from the clarity of the images where they were pointed. But the time was critical, and it told him that whatever entered the camp did so at about 1 am.

"Okay, let's see what we got here."

He leaned on his hands as he watched the camera footage play out. The sensor light came on first at the tree line. Then a few seconds later, the next sensor light came on a little closer to their group of cabins.

Carter frowned and leaned forward. Another light switched on and its associated camera in among the cabins came to life. But strangely, there was no sign of what it was that might have triggered them.

"What the hell?"

Carter stopped the film, backed it up, and then ran it again. But no matter how many times he did that, there was nothing showing on the film.

What happened—malfunction? he wondered. *Were the cameras pointed in the wrong directions? Was the recording too slow or was the creature too fast for them?*

One after the other, the sensor lights and the cameras came on, tracking something that it wasn't recording.

Until they got to Dmitry's cabin.

Carter squinted at the screen as the tracks went up to the door, and then after a few seconds, the door was slowly pushed inward as if by a breeze and then gently closed.

He waited and watched. The small time counter in the corner progressed but nothing happened. Carter sped the film up—10 minutes, 20, 30, 40, and it was only after 55 minutes that the door was opened again.

To Carter's surprise, it was Dmitry who stood there. But he was stark naked.

"You gotta be shitting me."

Carter knew that even though the air was calm, it was still around zero degrees and would have been near unbearable on the bare skin, no matter how tough the local men were.

"Crazy-ass Russians," he whispered.

The older man walked stiff-legged down the steps and then trudged off into the snow. The cameras followed him as he walked up the hill, with a strange stiff-legged gait, arms hanging dead by his sides.

After another few moments, he vanished into the forest.

"Got something?"

"*Jesus!*" Carter jumped at the voice from behind and turned to see Red and Mitch entering the mill house.

"Bit jumpy, *huh*, boss?" Red grinned. "Or did we catch you watching porn?"

"Idiot." Carter sighed and went back to looking at the screen. "I've got something and nothing. We had a visitor into the camp again last night, wandered around but damned if we caught it on film." He scoffed. "But then I got one of the Russians coming out buck naked and walking off into the forest."

Red shrugged. "*Meh*, in Sweden they cut holes in the ice and go swimming in it."

"They do that in Australia too—they even have swimming clubs where they throw ice in the water. It's traditional," Mitch agreed.

"It's madness," Carter added. "Maybe Dmitry..." He sighed and paused. "No, I don't know. Bottom line is, I'm no wiser on what has been triggering the sensors."

"Maybe the cameras aren't looking in the right place. Did you ever think it might have flown in?" Mitch asked matter-of-factly.

Hmm, no. Carter hadn't thought of that. "Good point." He straightened. The door opened again as Stefan and Nikolay entered and bade everyone good morning. By then, Red had coffee on and they waited on their Moscow guests to make an appearance.

Carter glanced back once more at the camera feed, and his brow remained pinched. There was something he was missing, and it set warning bells off in his head. He folded his arms and continued to stare at the small screen for a few more moments.

"You know what?' He turned to his men. "Why don't we take a walk up there and see what that crazy Russian has been up to?"

*****

Carter was first to Dmitry's door, with Red and Mitch at his shoulders. The first thing he noticed was a speckle of frozen blood on the wooden porch. It immediately put him and his team on alert.

The door was closed but unlocked and he pulled his handgun, and then turned to his men, counting down. Red and Mitch also had their weapons ready.

Carter shouldered open the door and went in quick and low. Red and Mitch came to the door and each leaned around the frame, pointing their weapons inside, one low, one high. They knew the room was too small for all of them, so they just covered the room.

It was empty, and Carter quickly darted his eyes over every surface, dark area, or open door. He quickly went to the small washroom and eased around the corner.

That's when he saw it.

"Goddamn." He narrowed his eyes and gripped his gun a little tighter. He quickly looked about. "Clear."

"What you got?" Red and Mitch entered and leaned into the washroom.

"Ah, shit." Red's mouth turned down in disgust.

On the bathroom floor was a pile of viscera—ropes of green, grey, and red intestines, bright red liver, heart, pink lungs, and the small bluish-green bag of the stomach.

"What the fuck," Red repeated. "That's fucking human."

All three men had seen the insides of people, so they knew immediately what was laid out before them.

"Disemboweled," Carter said. "And more." He crouched beside something that looked like chopped oatmeal. "That's brain matter."

"Boss, this is bad," Mitch said. "Real bad."

"No, this is bullshit. We saw Dmitry walk out of here," Red fumed. "Maybe he murdered someone."

"I don't think so." Carter holstered his weapon. "I think *this* is Dmitry."

"But we saw…" Red began and then his face dropped. "*Ah fuck*. Just like the damn bear."

"Looks like it," Carter said and went to the door, peering out. "We'll put this on ice." Carter turned to his friends. "Then we need to work out what the fuck is going on, fast."

CHAPTER 34

Mikhail pushed on the large doors of the mill house and held them open for Anna. "Good morning," he said loudly as he dropped his bags.

"And to you." Yuri came forward, already beaming. "Mr. Stenson is just doing another job and should be with us soon. Mrs. Stenson is in one of the laboratories. Let me get you both some coffee and you can warm up a little."

Mikhail and Anna went to talk to Stefan and Nikolay. Mikhail shook hands again. "So, our resident science team... things are well?"

Nikolay gushed a little and seemed to have trouble keeping his eyes off Anna, but Mikhail was impressed with his competence. The older of the two, Stefan, was a little more reserved, to the point of sounding a little bored. Together, the pair related their work with the sturgeon breeding program, the hatchings, and other details of their work.

Mikhail nodded patiently, and though he was a supporter of their program, it wasn't why he and Anna had flown all the way down here.

"And so," he announced with a clap and rub of his hands. "The sample you sent me. First, I would like to examine the carcass of the animal you caught where the sample was taken from."

"Caught?" Yuri raised a bushy eyebrow. "Blew up more like." He held out an arm toward the inner laboratories. "Stefan, Nikolay, please take our guests through." He shrugged. "It is limited space, so I will wait for Mr. Stenson out here."

"This way please." Stefan paused. "There is no real need for biologically sealed garments, but we recommend gloves and masks only as we think the cellular material is still viable."

"We have our own equipment," Mikhail responded.

Mikhail and Anna then followed Stefan and Nikolay into one of the side laboratories, and through the glass partitions he saw Sara Stenson who turned and waved.

He and Anna donned their full disposable bio-suits regardless of what Stefan had told them. He looked back and saw that Sara had slid out a gurney containing a huge body covered in a sheet from the freezer. It was still an amazing sight as the sheeted mass lumped on the steel table was nearly to her chin. Nikolay then took them in.

"Mikhail, Anna, welcome." Sara had a paper mask over her face, and her eyes looked wearied.

He nodded and then walked toward the massive lump. Sara

immediately drew the sheet away, revealing the mass of dark fur with the huge rent down the middle. The bear was lying on its side, and the top of the skull was placed beside it like a stained porcelain bowl.

Sara stood back. "The strangest thing I've seen in my life."

"Indeed." Mikhail walked around the table and Anna moved to the top to peer into the empty skull cavity. Even though it was kept extremely cold and the smells were locked up, for the moment, Mikhail held his breath, not wanting to inhale the thing's fumes

Anna straightened and turned to Sara. "In your report, you said the brains were already removed, yes?" She raised her eyebrows, watching her.

"Yes, removed, but not by us," Sara replied. "The cranial cavity was empty when we opened the sealed skull."

Anna's eyes narrowed a little as she looked back down at the empty cavity. "And it was ambulant, you said. Without a brain. You saw this?"

"No," Sara replied. "According to Carter, it wandered into an explosive. When they got there, it was torn up. The stomach cavity was already empty as well."

"So, it could have been killed by another predator? Maybe a pack of wolves who ate the innards," she asked.

"It's possible." Sara shrugged. "And they did find a blood trail of something that led from the carcass to the frozen lake, where it kept going all the way into the water."

Anna stared for a moment before shaking her head. "I know of no animal around here that would take the offal back to the water. The biggest aquatic creature is the male nerpa seal, and though they can get to 140 pounds, they would not drag away a bear's intestines."

"We don't think it was a seal either." Sara might have grimaced behind her mask. "This might sound dumb, but it looked to us like something else was in the body, something *not* bear, and once forced out by the explosion, made its way to the water."

Anna fixed Sara with her gaze for a moment before turning to Mikhail. The Russian scientist just grunted without saying a word. "Let us begin." He moved to the torso cavity, gripped it with two hands, and pried the ribs apart. "Could I get some light here please?"

Nikolay brought a flashlight and held it up over his shoulder. He stared inside for many minutes and then backed up. He took off his gloves and dropped them in a bin, and then went to one of his cases, where he took some more gloves, placed a headlamp on his forehead, and switched it on. He returned to the carcass.

"Into the belly of the beast," he said softly.

Mikhail breathed evenly. He had seen the holes in the flesh. They weren't wounds but looked more as if they belonged there. He reached in with a probe, feeling their depths, and saw they sunk right to the ends of the extremities—as if they were spaces to insert hands or fingers. *Ridiculous*, he thought. But then he remembered... *Something in there. Something not bear*, Sara had said.

Mikhail felt his heart rate pick up a little. He then probed the hole leading up to the skull that they claimed had already been empty. The idea that something had been inside the huge beast filled him with both professional curiosity and base human revulsion.

Exactly what could have been in there? he wondered. That question and the dozen others forming in his mind were exactly why he was here.

"Anna, the lights—the special ones."

Anna nodded, went to another case, and opened it out. Inside was another box that contained what looked like flashlights and bulbs, but had weird funnels and the globes were a dark purple.

"Bring it here and hold it up as I open the body cavity." He turned to Nikolay. "I need a strong arm to open and hold this ribcage wide."

"Yes, sir." Nikolay gripped the bear's flesh and lifted. Stefan crowded in behind them as Anna flicked on the light.

It was a weird purple.

"Wow, blacklight," Sara observed.

"Yes," Mikhail said while leaning into the cavity. "Ultraviolet radiation is invisible to the human eye, but it has other scientific uses."

He leaned further into the carcass. "And the most striking example of fluorescence occurs when the absorbed radiation is in the ultraviolet region of the spectrum, and thus invisible to the human eye. We humans can't see it, but we can get it to reveal itself when we use black UV lighting."

"Good thinking." Sara strained to see.

"Some things can hide from our primitive vision." Mikhail turned to Stefan. "Quick, my bag, there's some forceps and a collection tube."

Stefan went and opened the bag that had multiple slots for medical equipment and test tubes. He grabbed what Mikhail has asked for and returned to hand it to the chief scientist.

Mikhail reached in and grabbed something. When he pulled his arm out, in the blacklight, it looked like a glowing blob of gristle. He dropped it into the test tube.

"Now, watch this." He turned to Anna. "Turn off the UV lights."

She did as he asked. The glowing blob of flesh vanished before their eyes, leaving a greasy but empty glass tube.

"Amazing." Sara's mouth dropped open.

"Now you see it, now you don't," Mikhail said with a smile. He lifted the empty tube up and gave it a shake as he stared into it. "We've been waiting for you for over a hundred years."

The Russian scientist lowered his hand and the tube, and then turned to the group. His face became serious. "What I am about to tell you is of the utmost secrecy. And I only tell you because I need your assistance with what's about to happen next."

Anna stiffened and quickly turned to face him with an expression that held a warning.

Mikhail waved a hand gently in the air. "It's okay, Anna, we'll truly need their help, and they must know what we all are potentially dealing with here."

She nodded but Mikhail could tell she wasn't really convinced. Mikhail handed the tube with the blob in it to Sara.

"I'm sure you'll find this is similar biological material with identical genetic structure as the black fluid you gathered. Except it only reveals itself under UV light."

Sara held up the now empty-looking tube. "You know what it is, don't you?"

"You said you believed that something was inside the cavity. And all evidence points to that being true." Mikhail turned to look again at the massive carcass. "The bear was moving around, even though its extremities seemed to be necrotizing. Like it had been dead for days, weeks, or maybe even years in this freezing climate, yes?"

"That's correct," she said.

"All mammalian bodies function through chemical processes—fluids, sugars, adrenaline, and hormones actually drive our muscles." Mikhail began to pace. "Blood is the fuel for our bodies that keeps our physical machine working. But when the heart stops beating, the blood stops flowing. No blood, no fuel, and the machine breaks down." He paused. "That black fluid was a manufactured substance to keep the bear carcass fed, mobile, and I guess you could say, lubricated. So, to answer your question, Sara, that black substance is like blood, but just not the bear's."

"Stefan, do the honors." Sara handed the sample to the young Russian.

"Excellent." Stefan prepared the sample as Anna came and held the blacklight up over the microscope. He then slid a sliver onto the microscope plate and bent over the eyepiece. Nikolay watched, looking transfixed.

"Mikhail, what do you mean when you said you've been waiting for this for a century?" Sara asked.

Mikhail sighed, moved to the edge of the room where there was a single chair, and sat down heavily, clasping gloved fingers together.

"In 1908, there was an *incident* in Siberia… a massive explosion about 100 miles from here over the Tunguska region."

"I've heard of it," she replied. "It flattened hundreds of miles of forest."

"A meteorite explosion," Nikolay added, now listening over his shoulder.

"That's right," Mikhail said. "An object exploded in our atmosphere. It was some sort of astral body we believed, but thankfully, it never made landfall; otherwise, it might have left a crater the size of Moscow."

"But what has that got to do with us?" Nikolay clicked his fingers and turned to Sara. "The big wave. From the cave."

Mikhail turned to him. "The *big wave*? What is this?"

"They found a cave," Sara answered. "With some early human remains, possibly tens of thousands of years old. They were sealed in by a rockslide. But before they were entombed, they created a pretty vivid cave art story telling us what they saw."

"A time capsule," Mikhail whispered.

She nodded. "It showed their land being inundated by a huge wave from the lake..." She looked into Mikhail's eyes, "...generated after the lake was struck by an object from the sky."

Mikhail snorted softly. "Of course—the lake." His eyes lit up with excitement. "The Tunguska region was flattened and nothing remained of the object. Or so we thought. Under blacklights, just like the ones we are using here, we found something—biological samples from the crash site that didn't match up with anything known in our massive genome databases."

Sara's mouth turned down. "But I bet they matched up with what we just dug out of this bear's gut cavity, right?"

Mikhail nodded slowly and turned to her with a flat smile. "What we found at Tunguska was merely fragments; little more than scattered specks. And what you have found is something else entirely. Something unique to our planet, or perhaps, not of this planet at all."

"Not of this planet? An alien?" Nikolay chuckled. "Seriously?"

"Maybe," Mikhail said without humor. "Maybe the detonation over landfall was a failure. But over the water, it was a success. A successful touchdown."

"The lights under the water. The legends." Nikolay drew in a breath. "Something crashed, or landed. And it's still down there."

"This is just conjecture," Sara observed.

"Of course. We have more to learn before we call it one way or the other." Mikhail turned to Stefan. "What can you tell us?"

Stefan leaned back from his microscope. "The material is certainly biological, but it seems to be free of bone or cartilage, and nearly all striated muscle mass." He leaned back over the eyepiece and moved the slide a little. "However, there is something a little more solid in there, and if I had to guess, I'd say it's a little like chitin."

"What's that?" Nikolay asked.

Stefan looked up. "Exoskeleton, shell, like on a lobster or insect."

Sara tilted her head. "What would that be doing inside the bear?" She looked to Mikhail. "Could it have been a scavenger? On the corpse?"

"Interesting." Mikhail stared at the floor, his eyes not quite focused.

"Bears eat insects, and insects eat bears—there are plenty of beetles and other insects that scavenge on flesh. But not in this type of cold, and also none that I know of that are invisible to the naked eye or glow under ultraviolet light," Nikolay said.

"Yes, there are," Anna replied, turning to him. "Scorpions—all of them fluoresce under ultraviolet light, such as an electric blacklight or even natural moonlight. The blue-green glow comes from a substance found in the hyaline layer of their shell."

"So that blob of flesh was from something like a scorpion?" Nikolay's brows were up.

"I didn't say that." Anna turned to Mikhail. "I didn't even say it was from a land-based organism."

"You might be on to something there." Stefan leaned back. "There was something else in the sample—zooplankton fragments. Mainly *Filinia rotifers*, and also *Epischura* bacteria—from the lake."

"Is that good or bad?" Sara asked.

"Hmm, not exactly something I'd expect to see inside a bear." Mikhail turned away as though thinking.

"Everything comes back to the lake," Anna said. "I think whatever failed to come down at Tunguska, seems to have successfully arrived in the water."

Mikhail nodded and faced Nikolay. "How old did you say that cave art was again?"

The young Russian shrugged. "Marcus Stenson was the caving expert, and he thought it could have been up to 100,000 years old, based on the weathering to the surrounding rock."

"Paleolithic period." Mikhail tapped his chin with a knuckle for a moment. "So, the lake arrival was before Tunguska and was actually the first." He sighed. "I'd love to see those pictures, but no time now. I'll send a team in later if you give me the map coordinates."

"So what now?" Sara folded her arms. "All we have is a spoonful of weird flesh from inside a bear. The thing that was in there is gone, and I'm afraid the bear isn't talking."

Mikhail smiled. "It's actually telling us a lot, Mrs. Stenson." He pointed at the bear carcass. "That empty gut cavity certainly has lacerations from the blast, but I can also see a definitive line in the fur and flesh indicating it was already open. Like a flap."

"Yeah, I saw that," Sara said.

"You were right to think something was in there. But I think the thing was living in there, riding around inside," Mikhail said as he turned briefly back to the bear before facing her again. "Maybe like some sort of opportunistic parasite."

"The idea that something was in there is extremely alarming." Sara grimaced. "But the size of the cavity indicates a significant creature. That's not any parasite I know of."

"I agree. And no parasite I know of either." Mikhail cocked an eyebrow. "Intriguing, yes?"

"Intriguing, and horrifying." She exhaled loudly. "Why now? Why after 100,000 years is this happening?"

"No, I don't think it has only just started recently." Mikhail sat forward. "Think of all the legends, all the stories dating back centuries from this area. This has probably been going on for hundreds, thousands, and perhaps tens of thousands of years. Maybe the numbers were so small so as to not create too much of a panic."

"The haunted mill," she said. "They knew about it."

Mikhail turned to Stefan. "Thank you, Stefan and Nikolay, you may return the bear to the freezer." He began to pull off his gloves. "Let's get another coffee and…"

Through the glass partitions, he saw Carter Stenson enter the outer room with two other men. They were all armed.

Carter spoke briefly to Yuri and then turned to point at Mikhail and waved him out.

Sara headed for the door. "Something's happened."

CHAPTER 35

Carter paced, waiting for Mikhail to join him. Sara was first out and rushed to him, her face twisted with concern.

"What is it? What's happened?"

Mikhail joined them, his eyes going from Carter then to Red and Mitch. "Mr. Stenson?"

Carter exhaled through his teeth. "There's been an incident; I think. Dmitry…"

"What has happened to Dmitry?" Yuri closed in on him, followed by Nikolay.

Carter eased the big Russian back a step and faced Mikhail. "We've been having some intrusions into the camp. And given our problem with the bratva, we installed some surveillance lights, sensors, and cameras. Last night, they were triggered and came on, looked like they followed something, but recorded nothing."

"They were blank?" Yuri's huge brow furrowed.

"No," Carter replied. "The sensors registered movement and told them to record, but they didn't pick up the thing that had turned them on."

"Carter, we think now we might know why," Sara said. "Mikhail…"

The Russian scientist cleared his throat. "We found some biological material inside your bear that is not visible within the normal spectrum. But shows up under ultraviolet light—blacklighting."

"Bullshit," Red said from behind them.

"Is true." Mikhail folded his arms. "It may well be that the thing that was inhabiting the animal carcass might be the same; so for us, totally invisible."

"Oh shit." Carter shook his head. "Well, that's just great."

Yuri reached out and grabbed his arm. "Mr. Carter, what about Dmitry? Is he okay?"

Carter rubbed his forehead. "We went to his cabin and found, ah, evidence he might have been killed."

"What?" Yuri gripped him again. "What happened to him?"

Carter tugged his arm free and stared at the ground. "Like the bear."

"I don't understand." Sara came in closer to him. "What do you mean, like the bear? Is he in his cabin… his body?"

Carter turned to her and lowered his voice. "Yes, no… not all of him."

Nikolay turned and raced for the door, and Carter spun. "Stop him."

Red moved across in front of the door and held a hand up in the young man's face. He shook his head. "Sorry, buddy."

Nikolay spun back to Carter. "He is my friend. I must see what happened to him."

"Not yet," Carter said. "It might still be dangerous."

"Dangerous?" Sara scowled. "Carter, you're scaring everyone. What the hell is going on?"

Carter tried to organize his thoughts. "Okay. Like I said, the security tapes told us nothing last night. Except for it showing Dmitry coming out of his cabin, naked, and then heading up into the forest. We went there to check it out, and found his... insides."

Nikolay's face twisted and he cursed in Russian. "You said he walked into the forest. He's alive. Remember, this man is a hunter."

"He hunts naked?" Red scoffed.

"I don't know, Nikolay," Carter said softly. "I just don't know."

"Show me the tapes," Mikhail asked.

Carter nodded, went to one of the computers, and restarted the camera recording from the beginning, displaying the first sensor light coming on and then passing down the line. The footage went light-to-light, and the associated camera-to-camera was triggered, but there was nothing showing.

"It's tracking something it can't see," Carter said.

Until it got to Dmitry's cabin.

The door was gently pushed inward. And then the time ran on.

"What's happening?" Mikhail asked.

"Wait for it..." Carter sped it up.

Sure enough, the door was pulled inward and then Dmitry stepped out, naked. He stood on the small deck for a moment, stock-still, and with what appeared to be a totally blank expression. He then walked stiffly down the steps into the snow and then headed up to the forest line.

"Very interesting," Mikhail said.

Mitch looked over the top of the group. "We thought that whatever it might have been could have flown in. Avoided the cameras somehow."

"Not flying and not empty," Mikhail said. "Bring it back to the beginning, and then take it frame by frame. I'll show you where I want you to zoom in."

Carter did as he was asked. "Rolling." He played it forward again.

Mikhail squinted in at the footage as the sensor lights were triggered on the snowbound compound. One after the other, until he suddenly lunged forward.

"*Stop.*"

Carter froze the footage, and Mikhail practically had his nose pressed to the screen.

"Enlarge this section and play it forward from now, slowly, frame by frame."

Carter fiddled with the computer, enlarged the screen, and did his best to improve the image clarity. It was still a little grainy, but it held together. He played it forward at an extremely reduced speed motion.

The footage quadrant shown displayed the snow as the lights came on and the different cameras recorded the perspective and angles as it moved between the camp's geographic positions.

Mikhail pointed. "Got it. Did you see?"

"No, nothing. See what?" Carter asked.

"Back it up and play it again." Mikhail stood aside, but kept his finger on the screen. "Watch down here."

Carter played it again, stopping at each frame this time, and the group all crowded around. There seemed nothing to see, until Mikhail tapped the screen. Marks began to appear in the snow, one after the other; small, but they were there. They were the exact same marks, or spindly tracks, he had seen before.

"Holy shit," Carter said.

"*Now* do you see?" Mikhail grinned.

"I see it, but I don't believe it. One of those bastards came right into our camp and wandered around." Carter rewound and played it again.

Red straightened. "What was it doing?"

"What was it doing? What was it looking at, or looking for? And how long has it been doing that? Too many questions." Mikhail's brow was furrowed, and he slowly straightened.

"You were right; the fucking thing is invisible," Mitch said.

"No, not invisible. Or at least not anymore if we used your blacklights, right?" Carter turned to Anna.

She nodded slowly. "Theoretically, if your motion sensors had our UV bulbs installed, then you might finally get a look at one of these things. It could work."

"Good." Carter grinned. "Then I hope you brought a lot of them." He turned to Mikhail who seemed lost in thought.

"You okay?"

"Show me the footage again," Mikhail said softly. "Where the man emerges from his cabin."

Carter reset the film and replayed it. When he got to Dmitry emerging, he stopped it.

"Zoom in on him." Mikhail leaned on his knuckles.

Carter enlarged the naked figure, and then allowed the computer to clean it up and improve the clarity.

The group stared. Dmitry's face was slack and the eyes looked milky. But what was the most alarming was it looked like there was a line up the center of his belly that looked like a huge wound only just being held closed.

"Oh no," Nikolay whispered, and Yuri turned away.

Mikhail made a deep sound in his chest. "Take me to this man's cabin." He turned to Anna. "And then I think we assist in installing blacklighting for Mr. Carter's sensors."

CHAPTER 36

Carter first led the group to Dmitry's cabin where Mikhail confirmed what Carter already knew: the remains were human. He watched as Anna used the blacklighting and they were then able to see that mixed in amongst the blood was the familiar viscous fluid.

"This is where they met—Dmitry and the, entity," Mikhail intoned. "Then both of them left, but I think only one was alive." Mikhail's face was stony as he turned to Carter. "Let's see where he went. And upgrade your sensors."

On the way, Carter led the group from sensor light to sensor light, and the ones he deemed strategic, he had Anna replace the normal bulbs with blacklight fixtures. It was a somber procession, with Carter, Mitch, and Red keeping their eyes on the forest line, alert for anything now. *Anything they could see*, Carter thought.

Mikhail then asked to be shown around a few other areas of the compound where they experienced anything unusual, and Red then took them up to where he and Mitch found the skirmish area at the tree line.

It was on the hill just overlooking their cabins and just inside the first stand of trees where they found all the snow churned up, tracks, and the sign of a cigarette being stubbed out on the tree bark... but then nothing else.

Mikhail then used a portable blacklight wand to shine over the snow, tree trunks, and surrounding foliage. There were myriad traces of the fluorescing material having been splashed or sprayed around.

"So, it was in here too," Carter said.

"It, or them?" Red asked.

"Good question." Carter turned to Mikhail. "What do you think?"

Mikhail switched off his light. "We still know next to nothing at this time. But my guess is there's more than one." He turned to Red. "You followed the tracks?"

"Yeah," Red said. "They led all the way to the lake, and then kept on going. This smoking sucker just burrowed into ice over five feet thick... with his bare hands."

"Maybe it wasn't him. Or wasn't him anymore." Mikhail looked back out over the mill house compound. Yuri joined them and stood silently, listening.

Carter saw where he was looking. "Yeah, and if I was on a stakeout,

I'd think this was a good vantage point as well."

"Yes, it is," Mikhail agreed. "Very good for observing… life."

Red talked to Anna as she continued to investigate the surrounding brush, and Carter turned back to the Russian scientist. "When we found the bear and saw that something might have come out of it, my initial thought was it was a ghillie suit… a camouflage suit. Being worn by someone or some thing. A little like what you said about it being a type of parasite. Do you think… that's what happened to Dmitry? He was taken to be turned into some sort of suit of clothing?"

Mikhail turned pale eyes on him for a moment before nodding once. "I have a theory." His lips pressed into a flat line for a moment before responding softly.

"Remember when I postulated that it successfully arrived this time, in the water, instead of exploding over land like it did in Tunguska?" He turned away and exhaled, blowing a trail of vapor into the air. "Do you know how we, humans, enter the water? I mean deep water?"

Carter nodded. "Of course, in diving suits, submarines, submersibles, things like that."

Mikhail nodded. "Yes, correct. Human beings can enter the water and dive down without any problem for short times. But for longer periods or for greater depths, we need to have a special suit around us and our own mix of air to breathe."

Mikhail turned to look over his shoulder. "What if these things need suits to get around on dry land? They can tolerate it for a while, but to really move about for extended periods, they need something else."

"The animal bodies… *us*." Carter felt like someone was grabbing his chest as his heart started to beat a little faster.

Mikhail nodded. "For years, the people have been disappearing as well."

"Ah, shit," Carter said softly and felt a little nauseous. "These things have been watching us, and using the animals, and now us, as skin suits to get around. That is really fucked up."

"Not just now, I think," Mikhail said. "You know of the legends of this place?"

"Yes, it was called the haunted mill," Carter replied.

Yuri grumbled into his beard for a moment, but his face looked pale and lined. "Remember when I told you about everyone vanishing here all those years ago? I think now we know what happened to them."

"People go missing here, and have been for hundreds of years, and maybe even thousands of years. But there was another reason it was called haunted," Mikhail said. "And that was because it was rumored that they used to see the specters of the dead here."

Carter blew air from between his pressed lips. "It was them, wasn't it? In the bodies of the missing people, and maybe coming back to watch some more."

"Maybe watch, but who can really know what they want," Mikhail said.

"I know what they want," responded Yuri. "Us; our bodies, our souls."

Anna, Mitch, and Red wandered toward the group. "There is another reason they watch us." She lifted her chin. "Perhaps the reason they come back is to try and talk to us?"

"Why?" Mikhail shrugged. "Are they sentient? That is the question we need to find out. Because if they are, then they do not regard us as something to be valued, acknowledged, or even something on an equal footing with them."

"They just see us as raw materials to make their potential diving suits," Carter growled. "They haven't even tried to communicate."

"We don't know that," Anna shot back. "For all we know, they've been trying to speak to us for years. Maybe even hundreds of years." She folded her arms tightly across her chest. "These things might be so different to us, that for all we know, us trying to communicate with them would be like playing music to someone who can't hear." Her eyes bored into Carter's. "Before we declare war, I think we should at least try."

"Seriously?" Mitch bared his teeth. "Lady, they just cut the guts and brains outta one of our people. I know how I'll be communicating if one of those fuckers tries to get close to me."

"That's enough." Carter sighed. "Step one, we determine what it is we're supposed to be communicating with. Right now, we're at an extreme disadvantage."

Mikhail nodded, but Carter noticed that Anna's lips were pressed into a hard line and her eyes blazed back at them.

Behind them, Red chuckled evilly. "*Then*, when we can see them and have evened-up the advantage line, we kill 'em all."

Carter didn't disagree.

On the way back down to their compound, Mikhail grabbed Carter's arm to slow him down.

"Mr. Stenson…."

"Carter," he replied.

"Carter, thank you. We must capture a live specimen. It is imperative we examine it, and yes, try and communicate with it if possible."

Carter looked at the Russian scientist for a moment. "Have to tell you, Mikhail, my first priority is keeping everyone alive and in good health. I think we both know that what happened to Dmitry wasn't exactly their version of trying to communicate with us."

"I know, but we need to try. At least once," Mikhail said. "Please."

Carter exhaled through bared teeth for a moment. "I'm pretty sure these things regard us as some sort of lower form of life. We don't spend too much time on trying to talk to cows or chickens. They might not even want to communicate." He shook his head. "But we can try and take it alive." Carter held up a finger. "But if it looks like it's going to put any of our people at risk, then you get second prize—to examine one that's dead."

"Agreed," Mikhail said. And then. "So, how will you capture it... alive?"

"Cargo netting. We bury it under the snow and rig a trap," Carter said. "Should work, as long as you're right about them not flying."

"*Hmm.*" Mikhail thought on it for a moment. "They might be very fragile. That's why they need suits to travel in." He kept hold of Carter's arms. "Might I suggest you try and capture it before it has left its... suit?"

"*Suit.*" Carter snorted. "I'm starting to hate that expression, and I'm sorry I ever mentioned it. Yeah, we can try and capture it while it's still driving around in its mobile corpse. But that thing looks at any one of us sideways and we send it straight back to hell."

CHAPTER 37

The group stood around the large table, eyes downcast and minds drifting in a fog of despair.

"So, it *was* him," Sara said softly. "I hoped that…" She never finished.

"Yeah, me too." Carter nodded. "Somehow, someway, these things are co-opting animals…and people.

"As a biologist, I should be intrigued. But I'm not. I'm just sickened, and worried." Sara's jaw clenched momentarily. "So, the plan is we're supposed to try and catch it, or one of them. Talk me through it then."

"We will net it," Yuri said. "We have several large nets we use to lift cargo from the holds of the supply ships in summer. We can join them together and rig a spring-trap to catch and hold it."

"Catch the thing inside the compound?" Sara asked.

"*All* of the thing," Carter added.

"What does that mean?" She turned to him.

"Usually, once it's in the compound, it's outside of its… skin suit," Mikhail said softly. "We…"

Sara snorted. "Skin suit."

"Yeah, it's all screwed up, but we can't agree on the right term. But the bottom line is if it's outside of its skin, then it's invisible. Mikhail also thinks it might be fragile," Carter said. "We know they've been coming to the far tree line before entering the camp. We rig the trap up there. We want it inside the suit—we want all of it."

Sara's jaws worked as if she had a bad taste in her mouth as she tried to take in the revolting concept. "Then what?"

"We catch it." Carter frowned.

She shook her head. "Yes, I know that. But after you've caught it, then what do you do with it? Are you going to keep it in the net?"

The group looked at each other, and Mikhail started to chuckle. "She's right. We need to have something or somewhere we can corral it, when or if we catch it so we can study it properly."

"Yuri?" Carter turned to the big Russian. "Can we rig something up?"

"Like a cage?" He shrugged. "Sure, what size?"

Mikhail rubbed his chin. "If we are planning on capturing the host animal, then it must be able to accommodate that as well. Maybe six foot square."

"Iron or wood?" Yuri asked.

"Iron… in the event the host animal is a bear," Anna added.

"If it is bear, need to be 10 feet square." Yuri blew air through his lips. "And need to be very strong. We have some iron left over from the fish tank construction. I can weld something. Give me a few hours."

Carter portioned out the tasks required, and then glanced at his watch. "We've got eight hours until sundown. The cameras have been triggered around 1 am, but in the event we're being watched as soon as it's dark, I want everything in place before then." He clapped his hands. "Let's do this."

Carter oversaw the work going on and noticed Pavel move his bedding gear into his son's cabin. He guessed that given what happened to Dmitry, the father and son wanted to be close to each other for security. And he couldn't blame them.

Sara talked quietly to Mikhail and Anna, and he knew he wouldn't let her out of his sight. He remembered from years ago that she could be a little stubborn, but if it came to bruised egos and a few choice swear words, he'd take it all on the chin rather than see her put at risk.

By mid-afternoon, up at the tree line, they'd rigged the netting in a shallow pit and covered it over with snow. It was at the end of a natural pathway through the forest. The tree corridor was what they believed the things had been using to get to their vantage point above the compound.

Though the ground had been hard to dig into, most of their work had been in preparing the net—there was now a set of pulleys and weights they'd use to spring the trap. The one other thing they'd need was some bait, and Carter had volunteered to be the dummy standing out in the cold with his back to the forest corridor.

Yuri continued with his welding of the cage, a massive cube of bars and mesh. At this point, they had no idea of the exact size and shape of the thing when it exited the host and so the mesh was kept to three inches squares—not ideal as it made reaching in a problem. But the upside was, it also stopped the thing *reaching out*.

"How we doing?" Sara asked, standing close in beside him.

"We're on track. The blacklights have been installed in selected cameras and sensors, the trap is being laid now, and the cage is in its final stages of development," he responded.

She shivered. "This is like being caught in a nightmare. We came to Siberia to open a fish farm. Marcus got killed by the local mafia, and now we're getting ready to try and trap something that might not even be from our planet."

"After this, nothing will ever seem hard again," he said softly. "Don't worry, we'll win."

"I guess they'll sing songs about us one day." She half-smiled up at him.

"Yeah, but they'll all be in Russian," he added and liked that she at least seemed still able to joke with him.

"I'll just be happy if we're around to sing about it," she added.

"We'll be fine. The real question is what do we do if we catch one and we can't talk to it?"

She nodded. "If it's intelligent, and there's more than one, they might think we're taking it hostage."

"Or prisoner," he agreed and then began to quickly think through the implications. He made a mental note to discuss the potential for retaliation with Red and Mitch.

"They might believe we've declared war on them," she added. "I'm nervous about this whole thing."

"Sara, considering what they've been doing to us, I doubt they even think we're intelligent beings. They might view us as no more than we see chickens or cattle."

"So they started it, huh?" Then she scoffed. "I guess they did."

Mitch and Red joined them. "Where do you want us?"

"Down here," Carter said. "I don't want us all scattered all over the forest. And I want everyone equipped with blacklights just in case it gets past us."

"Or there's more than one," Sara added.

"Seeing as you're our stalking horse, we'll need to be close enough to give you cover," Mitch said. "If we're too far away, you get in trouble and you're toast."

"Jesus, man." Carter threw his head back.

"What?" Sara spun to him. "Where are you going to be?"

Carter sighed. "I'm just going to ensure we steer it into the trap is all."

"You're going to act as bait, aren't you?" Sara shook her head. "This is why everything went to shit between us before. You were always too quick to stick your own neck out. There's no risk too great for you."

"Sara…" Carter went to place a hand on her arm, but she batted it away.

"Idiot." She stormed off, but then half-turned. "You're a fool, Carter Stenson. You keep trying to leave everything behind."

Carter watched her go for a moment, knowing she was probably right.

"No you're not, boss," Red said. "Civs just don't get what needs to be done sometimes."

"The sheep rest easy, because the dogs of war are there to protect them from the wolves," Carter muttered.

Red held out a gloved fist. "Here's to all us dumb dogs of war."

Mitch and Carter bumped knuckles, and Mitch grinned.

"And we'll be out howling tonight."

*****

The watery Siberian light was beginning to fade as Carter took one last look overhead. His mic crackled to life.

"Good luck. We got your back, big guy," Mitch said from his place of concealment. "Just one thing...."

"What is it?" Carter asked.

"If you get skinned, do we still get paid?" Mitch sounded like he was talking through a wide grin.

Carter chuckled. "No, so you better damn keep me alive. Out."

Carter shook his head. "Graveyard humor; gotta love it." He began to trudge up the snowbound hill, feeling like he was walking to the gallows. As he passed by one of the sensor lights, it triggered, bathing him in the blacklight, his white camouflage uniform glowing purple until he had gone by.

After several minutes, he reached the top of the ridge and scanned the tree line. It was already dark now and near-impenetrable just a few feet in. A light snow had begun to fall. There was a natural track between the trees, possibly an old game trail, or maybe something that had been once carved out by the previous mill owners.

Right now, it looked like a black tunnel that was bored into a snow-covered green mountain. It was from within there that they expected their visitor to arrive.

Carter turned to look back down on the compound. Lights had come on and the roofs were coated in white. It was almost like a picture from a postcard or the cover of a fairytale book. Except it was a dark fairytale where something weird and deadly was stalking them, and as night took hold it was inflicting unspeakable brutality on them.

He ground his teeth. It was worse, as it killed them and then wore their bodies like some sort of foul suit of clothing or armor against the environment. So, no fairytale...more a nightmare straight from Hell itself.

Carter checked the gun at his hip and the knife on the other. He kept his hands free and open; he didn't know if the beings could understand what a weapon was, but for now, he wanted to seem as unthreatening as he could manage.

Carter turned away from the warmth and light of the compound and looked along the shadowy tree line again. The snow was unbroken, and there were no strange tracks appearing.

It was rapidly darkening as full night took hold and in a few minutes, it would be a cold, bleak, and lonely night. Carter sucked in a deep breath and turned his back on the forest...and he immediately felt the sensation of eyes on him.

"Ready," he said into his throat mic.

"All clear," Mitch said in response.

Carter knew that Mitch, Mikhail, Anna, plus Yuri, Nikolay, and Stefan would be crowded around the camera monitors. There were now new cameras spaced around him—one on a pole, two at the tree that were focused on the dark forest, and another pointed at Carter. All were remotely controlled and could be swiveled if need be.

After several long and excruciating minutes, there was nothing, and Carter hiked his collar up a tad, exhaling and letting his breath escape as a long cloud of vapor that hung in the air for a moment. The temperature seemed to be dropping and he moved his feet, trying to keep the circulation going. The last thing he wanted was for his leg muscles to freeze up if, or when, he needed to move quickly.

"Come on," he whispered and again fought the urge to continually look over his shoulder. *Trust your ground team*, he kept telling himself.

Bait. He chuckled softly. That's what I've made of myself; no wonder Sara was pissed at him. They broke up before because he always took the hard missions in the most violent places on Earth and was always one of the guys that took too many risks on behalf of other people. She said that, and she was right.

"*Boss*."

The word was soft in his ear, but it still startled him.

"Go," he said.

"Movement," Mitch said in the familiar emotionless speak that was adopted by both pilots and Special Forces soldiers when the hammer was about to come down.

"Keep talking to me, Mitch," Carter said softly.

"Just in behind the first line of trees, something's moving in there. Can't make it out yet." Mitch sounded like he shifted. "No need for UV lights as it's got a physical presence right now. Must be still in its skin suit."

"Good; that's what we want," Carter said, and his hand automatically went to the butt of his gun to feel its reassuring presence.

His neck prickled, and then so did his forehead, scalp, and even his ears. Every atom in his body was screaming at him to turn around, but he held it in check. They needed the thing to be drawn out from its hiding spot. They needed it right up behind him.

Carter bet that by now it had seen him and was taking a little look before deciding on whether to have a run at him.

But he also wondered why it would? If it was already in a skin suit, why would it attack him? He guessed that as they had found that the bear's body was actually rotting, then even though they could animate the beast's infrastructure, they couldn't stop it from breaking down. Maybe they needed replacements from time to time. Or maybe they needed the *fresh* flesh for other things.

Carter let his eyes slide to the left and then the right without moving his head, just using his peripheral vision. But he saw nothing.

Come on, do it. Just come down the track and into the open. I'm nice and warm and you've got nothing to fear, he whispered.

More minutes ticked by.

"It's still holding its position, boss," Mitch said. "Just staying in behind the tree line."

"Shit, this is killing me." He grimaced. "Okay, going to try something."

Carter started to walk a little toward the compound and away from the forest. The effect was immediate.

"*Movement*. It's coming out," Mitch advised.

"What is it? Can you see it?" Carter asked and slowed his pace to little more than a shuffle.

"*Ho-le-y* shit," Mitch said. "It's a fucking huge wolf. Gotta be 120 pounds."

"Ah crap." Carter pulled his gun and held it in front of himself. "But is it... is it a *real* wolf though?"

"Can't tell." Mikhail took over the microphone. "It's holding its position just before the trap."

"You think it knows?" Carter asked.

"Maybe. A real wolf might sense the trap. But if it's one of the things, it might not and is just being cautious." Mikhail *hmmd*. "Unless when it's inhabiting a certain animal, it can adopt all the extra senses of that animal as well."

"That doesn't help." Carter exhaled through pressed lips.

"And why we need to capture one... alive," Mikhail said. "Carter, without turning, shuffle a dozen feet to the left. See if we can entice it to come forward."

"Okay." Carter eased to the left, keeping his eyes on the compound.

"Stop," Mikhail said.

Carter did as asked and gripped his gun tighter.

"Hold," Mikhail said suddenly.

"What's happening?" Carter gripped his gun so hard now his knuckles ached.

"Ho-*ooold* it." Mikhail's voice was softer as if not wanting to be overheard.

Carter stared straight ahead, feeling the blood pound in his ears. He'd kick Mitch's ass for letting Mikhail take over the comms now. A scientist didn't appreciate the time it took for reactions or have the anticipatory skills that a soldier had when facing an adversary.

Mitch would have been able to instruct him on what he should be doing, not a damn desk jockey scientist. Carter let the air hiss from between his bared teeth.

"Fuck this," he whispered.

"Now!" Mikhail yelled.

Carter spun and looked dead on at the biggest Russian grey wolf he had ever seen in his life. The thing started to run toward him, but it only took about three steps before the trap was triggered, and the sides of the net were flung up around it.

Carter dived out of the way as snow exploded in a huge cloud around him that obliterated anyone from seeing what was happening. But in another two seconds, it dropped to reveal the net bulging with its special cargo. It then began to whip and jerk, as the final snow was shaken free, leaving just the wolf inside.

CHAPTER 38

Carter slowly approached with his hand still on his gun. The weirdest thing was the wolf never made a sound—no growls, snarks, yips, or even rage or fear-filled breathing at being constrained. He'd seen snared wolves before, and the damn things were furred furies and fighters to the bitter end.

"We got it," he said and went in even closer.

"On our way," Mitch said.

"Carter, do *not* get too close," Mikhail said. "We have no idea of what it's capable of. You have your UV light?"

"Yep." Carter felt for the blacklight wand in his pocket. If the thing exited the wolf, he wanted to be able to see it. He switched on the light, bathing the wolf in purple, but for now, it was just a wolf. A big one, but normal—normal-*looking* anyway.

No, almost normal, Carter thought, as he brought the blacklight closer to its face. The mouth hung open, showing the huge and strong teeth of a carnivore, but he also saw that the gums and tongue were blackened and dry, and there looked to be no moisture in the mouth at all. Also, the eyes were milky orbs, as though the thing was blind. However, as he moved around it, the head turned, so it seemed to still be watching him.

"So, maybe not blind after all, huh?" he said softly.

Carter crouched lower and tried to see underneath the animal, but the net webbing and how the beast was lying made it impossible. He stood and turned as Mitch came jogging up the snow-covered slope, followed by Yuri and then Mikhail, gasping and wheezing.

"Stay back," the Russian scientist puffed.

Mitch and Yuri stopped 10 feet back, and Carter, already in close to the captured animal, turned to them.

"Somehow, it had the ability to eviscerate Dmitry, so we mustn't underestimate its ability to inflict damage." Mikhail turned one way then the other. "We need to get it back to the laboratory, urgently."

"It's not going anywhere," Mitch said. "That net is strong enough to hold an elephant."

"Yes, but we have no idea whether it came alone," Mikhail replied.

"Oh, yeah." Mitch turned to scan the tree line, his gun lifted.

"Okay, get it down Yuri, and let's drag it back. I'm very interested to see what our passenger looks like." Carter gave him space.

Mitch bent closer and peered in at the wolf's head. "Just like the bear;

looks dead."

"Yeah, not exactly the most lively of creatures, is it?" Carter said.

Yuri cut down the net and it fell in a heap in front of them. He grabbed the lead rope, keeping it taut and the purse-end of the net closed tight. Carter also called Red back in to lend a hand.

"Everyone grab hold." Yuri started to drag the 120-pound animal, leaving a rut in the snow.

It took them 30 minutes to maneuver the animal down to the mill house laboratory where Sara was waiting for them. Once inside, they used the hoist to lift it over the open cage. Timing was going to be everything— they needed to tip it, open the net, and let the animal fall into the fortified cage, and then quickly seal it, all seamlessly.

"Well done." Her eyes were wide as she stared at the wolf.

"Good to see I can still attract something at my age." Carter grinned.

"I still think you're an idiot." She turned to give him a half-smile. "But good job."

The animal, still in its netting, was lowered into the cage, and Carter was waiting to slam the lid closed when the net was removed. Mitch waited with a long steel pole to give it some encouragement to behave. Behind them, Anna, Nikolay, and Stefan watched with wide eyes.

"Ready?" Yuri asked.

Carter looked into the hanging bag of netting. The wolf's head was turned to him, and its milky eyes still staring, seemingly sightless, but he felt it was watching him closely.

Carter gripped the cage top and braced himself. "On my 3... 2... 1... *go!*"

Yuri cut the netting, and the tight loop rapidly opened. The wolf began to fall, and it immediately spasmed. Its legs began to kick and then spread as though trying to stop itself falling fully into the cage. For a few seconds, it looked like it was going to be caught up, but Carter reached out a hand and punched down on it, forcing it in through the cage top.

The wolf fell with a thump and lay like a corpse. Carter slammed the top shut, locked it, and then jumped down and backed up with the others. He stood breathing hard, hands on hips.

"Well done, everyone."

"Something else to tell my kids—I caught a monster," Mitch said through his smile.

Carter grinned. "You're having kids?"

"Yeah, one day." Mitch looked indignant. "Just need to find a woman who's smart, good looking... oh, and rich."

"If I was you, I'd just settle for desperate." Carter grinned and slapped his shoulder. He looked back at the wolf lying in the cage. "So, now what?"

"Magnificent," Mikhail said, keeping his eyes on the beast and rubbing his hands together. He crouched to get a better perspective.

As if sensing him, the wolf finally came upright and sat on its haunches staring straight ahead. The group slowly walked around it, examining what they could while staying several feet back from the cage bars. Even though the bars were woven with a finer mesh so nothing could poke through, no one trusted the creature.

"Creepy as fuck," Mitch said as he stared into its face. "Those dead eyes."

Anna craned forward. "After death, the eyes drain of blood and the pigments are also leached away. That's what makes them look that milky blue-grey."

"Like I said, creepy as fuck. It's dead, but still looking at us." Mitch straightened.

"We should kill it and burn it. Now, while we can." Yuri's voice was a menacing rumble.

"Gets my vote," Mitch agreed. "Burn it all."

"No, we have an opportunity to study it." Mikhail scowled. "We need to take it."

Nikolay got down at ground level and then grimaced. "I can see dried blood on its stomach. I think there might be the open wound there just like the bear."

Mikhail lifted one of the hand-held UV lights and switched it on. He moved it over the beast and then on every corner of the cage. But the blacklight showed nothing.

"I think for now our friend is staying inside its nice, warm suit of fur." He switched off the light.

"Then we need to coax it out," Carter said. "We won't learn anything new by staring at a huge wolf."

"I agree. But I don't want to damage it." He scratched at his short beard for a moment. "Maybe it is shy from all the attention. Maybe we should switch off the overhead lights and leave the room—observe it from a distance." He turned and raised an eyebrow to Carter.

Carter smiled and nodded. "I think you're right. After all, it rushed me when my back was turned. Switch on the cameras and also the UV lights." Carter looked back at the immobile creature. "Then we'll see what happens."

*****

The silent darkness now filled the room. The creature waited for many more minutes just sitting and watching, using the senses of the carrier being to inform it of its surroundings.

It sensed the bipeds were still in proximity, but not so close now. The confinement it found itself in was beyond its capability to break out of quickly. But not beyond its ability to escape if it exited the carrier. It knew it could also simply take another host once outside of the barrier.

It would be vulnerable, but only for a short period, as it knew it could survive for an extended time outside of its carrier host. But it wasn't a problem, as there were many more creatures it could adopt when it got close to one. It simply needed to empty them to make room for itself.

Slowly, it withdrew its sensory feelers from the limbs and also drew back its eyestalks from the cranial cavity. Lastly, it released its hold on the torso flaps in the belly and they swung open to let the creature slide to the ground.

The rush of new sensations was abhorrent—it immediately felt the dryness and the sensation of weakness. But it wasn't totally defenseless.

The being slowly began to patrol the outer edge of the cage, coming to one of the welded seams, pausing to examine it further. It began to work on the knob of welding solder holding the cage bars together.

CHAPTER 39

"You have got to be shitting me." Mitch's mouth hung open and he turned and pointed to the screen.

The creature looked a little like a caterpillar in that it was segmented and had a soft looking body. Two eyestalks were on one end with bulb-eyes that constantly moved independently of each other as it examined its surroundings. From its front, or possibly its mouth, small tentacles waved and flexed.

Mikhail grinned like a schoolboy, and Anna beamed as she pushed in below everyone else to stare at the video feed from the makeshift containment room.

Sara began to speak softly. "Multipedal, binocular vision, segmented, perhaps with a form of chitinous armor, but also has tendril-like motility filaments or, limbs, or maybe they're something else entirely."

Anna beamed. "It's so... alien."

"It's a fucking nightmare," Mitch said. "That thing was in the wolf's body driving it around."

"And inside the bear," Carter said.

"And also in Dmitry," Nikolay added softly.

"But is it the same one?" Mitch looked at Carter.

"It doesn't matter; it is an abomination," Yuri replied.

Carter noticed for the first time that the big Russian held some sort of talisman in his hands and rubbed a thumb against it as he watched the monitor.

"Perhaps and perhaps not. It is strange and that's all. It has been created in a place far different from here, and so reflects the biology and evolution of wherever that is." Mikhail began to scribble notes in a small pad. "Perhaps to it, we are the abomination."

"No, I agree with Yuri; *that* thing in there is the abomination." Carter felt his stomach flip a little as he looked at it. It was only around two and a half feet long, up on about a dozen spindly legs.

Stefan looked queasy. "Do you think... it is intelligent?"

Behind the creature lay the wolf, immobile and seeming deflated. Anyone coming across it would believe it was just like any other dead animal, desiccated and beginning to decay.

Except the skin flaps of its chest and stomach were opened out like a door left ajar, waiting for the occupant to return.

"Intelligent? Possibly," Mikhail answered.

Mitch snorted. "How? It's just a fucking big bug."

Sara was wide-eyed. "See down its back? I think that dark mass running down like a spinal cord is a form of brain stem. If I'm right, then given its overall size, the brain to body ratio is far superior to humans. After all, we think it came here in some sort of craft, right?"

"Right, so definitely an intelligent species," Anna said softly. "We just need to work out the best way to communicate with it."

"Impossible," Nikolay whispered.

"No, if both species are intelligent and *want* to communicate, then it must be possible." Anna turned to Mikhail. "One of us should go in there."

Mikhail held up a hand. "We need to think about this."

She grimaced impatiently. "This is the greatest opportunity mankind has had since...."

"The Aztecs encountered Cortez," Carter finished. "And got wiped out."

"No, that's not what I meant, and I don't believe that," Anna said a little breathlessly. "Think of what it could tell us."

"I agree it *is* an enormous opportunity. But with enormous risks." Mikhail raised an eyebrow. "So, the question is, *how* do we talk to it?"

"Mathematics, geometry, symbols, lights... we can try anything and everything," Anna said, her words pouring out in a rush.

"I guess it's like you said: if it wants to understand, it will." Nikolay joined them.

Mikhail nodded thoughtfully. "Have either of you ever heard of a Polish philosopher and writer by the name of Stanislaw Lem?"

Anna shook her head, and the older scientist went on.

"He postulated that communication between alien species might deliver nothing but frustration." He turned to look at her. "It's not just the words and dialogue, but the very thought processes might be so different to our own as to be incomprehensible."

Mikhail continued to watch the strange being. It now seemed to be examining a single place on the bars of the cage, the two eyestalks with their bulb ends bent forward as long legs tapped against the metal.

"Fascinating," Mikhail said.

"What do you say to something like that?" Nikolay asked.

"What could we say?" Mikhail turned. "To return to Stanislaw Lem, in one of his examples, he brings up the point that in every known human language, we would be able to translate a message, say something as simple as, 'My grandmother is dead. Her funeral is on Wednesday.' As well as being translated, it will be understood, right?"

Anna nodded.

"But this translation is only possible because biologically and culturally, we share the same reference points needed to understand the words. You see, we humans all die, so we understand death, and therefore funerals. We reproduce between two sexes, so have mothers and fathers and also grandmothers, so we know what a grandmother is. Plus, we all mark the passing of time in terms of the dark and light periods caused by the rotation of our planet."

He kept his eyes on the unearthly being. "But now try and imagine an alien from a world of permanent darkness, so it has no days. And reproduces asexually like an amoeba. Therefore, it would have no parents or grandmother, so it would have no concept of what one is, let alone have any attachment to one. And just think, beings that divided at the end of their life rather than dying and decomposing would not even understand the notion of death and especially of funerals."

Anna folded her arms. "So you're saying we can't, so we shouldn't even try?"

"No, no, we can try. I'm just marking out the expectations we should have." Mikhail turned to Carter. "Mr. and Mrs. Stenson, what do you think we should do?"

Carter's jaw was set as he looked at the weird creature. He turned to the older man. "There's an old saying about how wolves don't waste time negotiating with sheep." Carter drew in a breath and looked back at the thing, and then to Sara. "Right now, I feel we're the sheep."

Sara nodded. "After Dmitry, my first instinct is to kill it, immediately. But, there may be more of them out there. As a scientist, I say that for now, we've got it in a cage, and we put it there so we could get a look at it and analyze it. But can we manage it?" She looked up into Carter's face. "Carter, you manage risks. Can we control it?"

Carter looked across from Red to Mitch. "We're soldiers, and right now, we see this thing as an adversary. So I want to know its weaknesses and strengths, and an effective way to eradicate it, or them. While it's alive, we observe it, and you guys can try and speak to it if you want. And when it's dead, we cut it up and find out what makes it tick."

Mitch nodded his approval but then frowned. "Hey, what are you going to feed it?"

Carter looked back at the cage, immediately wondering how long it would survive—it was a good question.

"I have a theory on that," Mikhail said. "My suspicions are that the bodies they, inhabit, they also use for sustenance. That's why they dry out and necrotize so quickly; they're draining them as they inhabit them."

Yuri groaned and rubbed his face.

"Oh, poor Dmitry." Nikolay turned away and started to gag. He slapped a hand over his mouth and rushed from the room.

"Aw Jesus, doc, that is fucked up." Mitch's lips turned down. "They're moving the bodies around and eating them at the same time? Damn."

"Please, please," Mikhail said. "Remember, they may be as different to us, as we are to…"

He seemed to be searching around for an example, so Carter gave him one.

"Sheep."

Anna spun back. "No, they just don't yet know that we humans have a sophisticated civilization." She rounded on Mikhail. "I want to go in… by myself," she declared.

"No chance," Carter intervened. "Somehow, one of those things, or *that* very thing, disemboweled Dmitry and wore him out of his cabin like a suit of clothing. We don't yet know how it did that. I cannot allow you to be in there unprotected."

"I won't be; it's in a steel cage of bars and mesh and you're right here in the next room." She turned to look at the monitor of the creature still investigating the bars on the cage. "I think if we all go in there, it'll retreat into the wolf, and we'll learn nothing. But it might not if just a single person goes in. Someone needs to gain its trust."

"I'm against this," Sara said. "I'm for observing it, but from a safe distance."

Mikhail's mouth was turned down and he folded his arms. "Science is about taking risks, not staying safe."

"You're kidding, right?" Carter's mouth dropped open.

The Russian scientist turned to him. "We must know. We must try."

"Sorry, I can't allow it." Sara came and stood beside Carter.

Mikhail nodded. "Please remember, you called us, Mrs. Stenson. And though this is your business, this is our jurisdiction. In this, we outrank you."

"Then I'm the one who should go in there," Carter declared.

"*Carter.*" Sara scowled.

"No." Anna held her hand up flat. "I'm the smallest and least intimidating."

Nikolay eased up closer to Anna. "I would like to be in there with you. Just to help you."

She smiled and shook her head. "Thank you, Nikolay. But I should go in first. I'll stay well back from the cage, and the creature cannot get out."

"What do you need?" Mikhail asked.

She shrugged. "Flashlight, whiteboard, and pens to draw geometric shapes." She smiled up at him. "And my wits. That's it."

Mikhail took one last look at the screen and then stood back. "Let her through."

"This is a really dumb idea," Mitch said.

"I agree, and I'm putting on record that I'm against this," Carter said and waited for a second or two, but saw nothing but steely resolve in the young scientist's eyes. He grabbed the door handle ready to open it, but holding it closed while he continued to look at Anna who had all her equipment under one arm and a large pillow under the other. "That thing makes one aggressive move, and it's toast."

She half-smiled. "Welcome to our world, spaceman."

"That ain't no spaceman," Mitch said from behind her. "You got that bit about it gutting people, didn't you? Oh yeah, and also draining them like a can of soda."

Anna ignored him, and her face became calm. "I'm ready."

Carter turned to his men. "Red, cover us from the outer room. I don't want this thing silently calling to its buddies."

The big man had been staying well back and his jaw was set. "On it." He racked his gun and left.

Carter stared back in through the glass panel at the thing, which had moved its investigation to the top of the cage and once again to the steel bars.

"Good luck," he said and pushed the door open.

CHAPTER 40

It was just gone midnight when Arkady Tushino waved the trucks into the shoreline a mile down from the mill house compound. The three vehicles were jammed with two dozen men. All of the bratva soldiers he had chosen were experienced and ruthless, and they could be trusted to carry out his orders to the letter.

The trucks would wait, and not for long, as they expected the entire operation to be over within a single day. He'd split his 24-strong army into three teams—two teams would approach from the left and right flanks of the mill compound, with one objective: flush out Carter Stenson and take him down.

This order had one caveat—his face must not be marked. This was because Tushino needed the head intact and recognizable.

The third team, his team, would approach the mill manager's house where Sara Stenson resided. She'd be taken and then persuaded to sign the contracts. If needed, Carter's severed head would be used as a little more incentive.

Tushino grinned as he gave out final orders. He'd love to be the one delivering the death stroke to Carter, but taking him alive was deemed too dangerous. However, it would be enough reward to be able to look into his cold, dead eyes.

The men busied themselves checking ammunition, explosives, and weaponry, and then stood ready.

Tushino nodded to the freezing forest. "Go."

The group shouldered rifles and trekked off in amongst the trees. They'd march together for most of the way and then split up when they were a few hundred yards out. They all had GPS trackers and had plotted their routes well before they even boarded the trucks.

Tushino hoped his teams caught Carter Stenson out by himself. But he wondered whether the local Russians at the mill would be prepared to fight for him, and therefore die for him. He doubted it. At the setting of the sun, he was a foreigner, and they owed him nothing.

In another 20 minutes, the group split up—his team of eight would approach the mill compound from the rear and head directly to the large main mill manager's house.

The other two eight-strong teams would surround the site and move into ambush positions. Their orders were simple: no negotiation, no taking hostages, but shoot to kill. They were to take no chances.

Tushino grinned at the thought of being able to slap the signed contracts down on Gennardy Zyuganov's large oak table—*deal done*, he would say.

The great ogre would grunt, but nod, acknowledging that Tushino got the job done. Maybe he'd get a promotion; maybe he'd become Zyuganov's right-hand man in Moscow. The opportunities and rewards were near limitless.

In another few seconds, Tushino began to smell wood smoke drifting through the forest. Bulukov, his team leader, started to go into a crouching walk and half-turned to wave the men to quietness—they were getting near.

It took them another 10 minutes to get to the high tree line at the rear of the compound. Tushino straightened behind a trunk and looked down on the encampment.

He'd been here before, but now the entire scene was coated in white. Snow was thick on the ground and building roofs and the freezing temperatures kept it in a powdery form—except where it was trodden into furrows back and forth between buildings and also the huge warehouse-sized mill house at the lakefront.

In the darkness, the lake itself was now an endless plain of nothingness, and without seeing where the wharf ended, it would have been impossible to know where the land ended and the mighty iced-over lake began.

Bulukov came in close to him after doing a quick reconnoiter and pointed to the largest house closest to them. The other men crowded around.

"Manager's house. No rear door, front only; lower ground windows on all sides, not shuttered. But no sign it is occupied right now."

Tushino nodded. "She must be in there somewhere." The front door could be seen from the compound, so the windows it was. "We break into three groups and enter via back and both side windows all at once—there will be nowhere to go." He checked his watch. "Our other teams should nearly be in position. We enter in... 20 minutes, from... *now*."

"*Mark*," Bulukov said and calibrated his own watch. The other men did the same. He split them up into three-three-two teams, circled a finger in the air, and then the three groups began to creep through the heavy snow.

With minutes to spare, they were at the windows and each one was easily opened by sliding the blade of a knife in to open the latch. They waited, counting down the seconds. They needed to time it right, and go in fast. An open window in winter dropped the temperature in a house in seconds and was an immediate telltale of an intrusion.

Tushino waited at the tree line with a small pair of binoculars to his eyes. He would follow a few seconds after they breached the house. He expected to be let in the front door —he couldn't wait to witness the look on the American bitch's face when he walked in.

He saw his teams in place and took a quick glance around the compound. The heavy trees ringing the huge compound grounds gave no indication of where his other two teams were, but he knew that there were over a dozen men lying in ambush and waiting for Carter Stenson to make an appearance.

He grinned and checked his watch—seconds to go. So far, everything was going to plan.

"*Wait.*" Bulukov's word froze Tushino and the teams. "*Someone's coming… yes, the woman.*"

Tushino's grin split his face. "Perfect," he breathed out.

****

Igor Stavros, leader of Tushino's left-flank team, moved his group along the tree line, maneuvering them into place. He had just minutes until he was to be ready.

He would place his best shooters out in front, and as soon as the American was spotted, they were to take him down—headshots preferable, but as long as he went to the ground, then the killing shot could come later. The only stipulation was not to obliterate the face.

He lifted his own gun, bringing the scope to his eye, and ran it along the far line of trees—he could just make out the other team in behind their own set of snow-patterned trunks. He grinned, his white teeth showing behind the bushy, black mustache. He was going to enjoy this.

Stavros then moved his perspective to the house and saw the third team's men at the side windows and knew they would also be around the back. All was good, and all teams were in place.

"Hey."

Stavros frowned and turned at the call from one of his group.

"Look."

He followed where his man was pointing and could make out the solitary figure standing in the snow, watching them—naked.

CHAPTER 41

Anna went in through the door to the mill house's large entry area where the cage was set up. The group crowded around the video feed screen, watching so they could zoom in and out. All except Sara and Carter, who stayed at the door, observing her through the glass panel set into it.

"This is a mistake," Sara whispered.

"Yep." Carter had his gun in his hand and stared into the room with such intensity his head ached. The blacklights illuminated the thing to make it seem a phosphorescent apparition, and its horrifying physical characteristics weren't softened by the ghostly halo.

He remembered what Mikhail had said about it being so different to them that it may never be possible to communicate. He thought that about it as well. Carter had fought adversaries that thought different than him. He had looked different and his values, customs, and language were strange and unusual, and in some cases repugnant, to other peoples of the world. But they were still people.

So what of a truly alien species? It might not even recognize us as thinking entities. Humans never gave a second thought to the ants on the pavement, or worried about the deep thoughts of barnyard hens.

Mikhail came and joined them, sharing the window. Carter turned to him. The older scientist nodded.

"I know, I know, you both disagree with me letting her in there."

"No, it's not your fault." Sara continued to watch the room. "If we really wanted to stop her, we could have."

Carter's lips pressed into a line for a moment. "So what do you think?"

The Russian scientist shook his head. "I don't know what to think. But in a few minutes, we will know more. And Anna is being very brave; scientists like her who are prepared to take mortal risks advance human knowledge. I admire her."

Carter just grunted.

"Look," Sara urged.

As Anna entered the room, the being moved unnaturally fast back into the belly of the wolf. The skin flaps on the stomach closed and the animal seemed to reinflate. The wolf's head then swung toward her. The eyes that were like milk now had a slight darkening behind them.

"It's using the eyes," Mikhail said. "Its own eye stalks must travel up into the animal's cranium."

"Biological periscopes," Carter said softly and felt his stomach roil at the thought.

Anna dropped her pillow onto the ground about five feet from the cage and sat down cross-legged on its center.

"Anna." She pointed at her chest. "I'm called Anna."

She placed her bags and other items beside her, and first drew out a small whiteboard and pen. She drew a shape and turned it around. Carter opened the door a crack so they could hear.

"Square," she said.

She then erased it and drew a circle, and repeated the show and naming. She then drew some simple mathematics symbols and calculations. The opaque eyes of the wolf stared and it remained as still as a statue.

Anna then pulled out a flashlight and began to flash it into the wolf's eyes. So far, there was no sign that anything was registering. She brought out a small radio, turned it to a Russian music channel, and played something with lyrical guitar solos. Once again, the wolf only stared.

Carter sighed. "For all we know, the thing is deaf."

Mikhail nodded. "For all we know, it has senses that we cannot even imagine." He looked at Carter. "For all we know, it sees in four dimensions, or in some spectrum we can't even envisage. Or perhaps it is simply pulling the thoughts from her mind."

"Better not do that with me; it won't like what it sees." Carter turned back to the small window.

Anna stopped for a moment and grabbed her crossed legs with her hands and just stared back. Carter could hear her talking softly but couldn't make out the words. The wolf seemed to sit back, and then almost imperceptibly at first, the skin flaps of its stomach opened and the creature eased out. It was just by a few inches at first, and then a few of the long spindly legs came, followed by its soft but segmented body.

"Oh my God, she did it," Sara breathed out.

"This is extraordinary." Mikhail quickly turned. "Stefan, are we...?"

The young man nodded. "Recording, yes."

"*Phew.*" Mikhail turned back to the window. "They'll be analyzing this film for generations."

"Depends on what comes next," Carter said softly. "Hey."

"What?" Mikhail turned.

Carter nodded to the room. "Something else is happening."

The pair of men stared. The thing was fully outside of the wolf whose body once again collapsed like an empty sack. Now, its size could be properly judged as it approached the bars closest to Anna. It was roughly two and a half feet in length and two feet high, although most of that height was the long legs, about six on each side, and stilt-like with multiple joints.

The body reminded Carter of a long, pale, loaf of bread and there were definite segments, but the way it moved didn't give off an impression of a shell or carapace, more like softened leather, like that of a spider.

The two eyes on long, thread-like stalks were never still. One remained trained on Anna, while the other turned one way then the other, constantly on the lookout, maybe for ambush attacks... or an opening to escape.

"What's it doing?" Carter asked.

The creature moved back and forth in front of Anna, as though pacing. Its eyes never left her, as she turned her head, following it.

"I don't know." Mikhail's brow furrowed, but then his eyebrows rose. "Unless... unless it's watching her watch it."

"Maybe it's surprised that Anna can even see it." Sara turned to Carter.

"You might be right; maybe its invisibility was one of its defenses, now stripped away," Carter said.

"It might not like being seen," Mikhail responded.

"Good; it's worthwhile showing them that we have the technology to even things up —we're not just another dumb creature that makes up part of their clothing inventory."

The creature then paced around the entire outside of the cage, even around behind the wolf. It stopped from time to time to survey the surroundings beyond the cage. It then slowly came back to Anna and became motionless.

From the front end, what Carter assumed was the face, and from in between the bloom of writhing, tiny tentacles, extended a long, flat thread. It snaked toward Anna.

Carter began to open the door, but Mikhail put his hand on his arm. "Wait."

The thread extended further but reached toward Anna's writing pad. It stopped and hung in the air several feet short. It tried again from a different angle but again found the pad and pen too far from its reach.

"You've got to be shitting me." Carter shook his head.

"It wants the writing equipment." Mikhail grinned and clasped his fingers together as if shaking his own hands in congratulations. "She's done it; it understands and wants to talk to her."

Anna turned to them, her brows up as if asking the question. Mikhail didn't hesitate and nodded, making *hand-it-over* gestures.

Anna picked up the pad and when the thing was at the closest point to her, she held it out. The creature stopped.

There was an instant when the small woman was sitting before the strange being, and it had frozen with both its bulbous eyes on the swaying stalks now fixed on her. Eyes met eyes and the human and alien creature seemed to share a moment that even Carter found astounding.

Anna smiled and spoke softly to it. It seemed to crane forward and the long, flat, ribbon-like tongue gently eased out about two feet, but still wasn't close enough, and it withdrew.

Ann left her pillow and got up on her knees to crawl forward a little more and held it out again, this time only a few feet from the bars of the cage.

"Come on, here it is, take it," she said softly through her smile. "Talk to us…"

The ribbon-like tongue shot out and curled around her wrist. Anna screamed, and Mikhail yelled something in Russian. The woman's eyes were wide and she looked like she was receiving an electric shock as the thing braced its spindly legs.

She began to be reeled in; it should have been impossible, as even though Anna was a small woman, she still undoubtedly outweighed the creature by more than two to one. But slowly and surely, she was being pulled closer.

The room full of people behind Carter erupted in yells and horror.

"Fuck it." Carter dragged the door open and brought up his gun. The creature let Anna go, but the tongue shot out faster and longer than anyone expected. This time, it didn't strike at Anna, but at the blacklights, smashing each one with lightning speed.

With the lights out, the creature vanished beyond their visual spectrum. Then to Carter's horror, the single bar the thing had been investigating earlier fell outwards with a crash.

"It's fucking out," he yelled with his gun up.

Mikhail yelled for the portable UV lights, and Nikolay responded, lifting one of the small handhelds and running into the room. Mitch and Red, who also had their guns up, and Yuri, who held a crowbar, quickly followed him. Stefan waited at the open door, watching nervously. Sara stood just behind him.

Nikolay held up the light and for one brief moment, the thing was illuminated, out and standing right beside Anna. But before Carter or Mitch could get a single round off, it went for Nikolay and smashed his portable blacklight.

"Shut the door," Carter yelled… too late.

As Stefan blinked and hesitated for just a few valuable seconds, the young man's eyes widened as a red line went from his groin to his left shoulder. Then he simply fell in half.

The creature's tongue was obviously used for more than grasping things as Stefan was surgically cut from between his legs to just beside his neck. Blood splashed as his body opened like a flower and then collapsed on either side of the doorway… wedging it open.

"*Fuck*!" Carter yelled and rose, leaving Anna with Mikhail and Nikolay as he raced to the open doorway. "Sara!" he yelled.

Sara stood with her hands over her face, drenched in Stefan's blood. Carter grabbed her and she lowered her hands.

"It killed him," she said softly and looked down at Stefan's mutilated body. Her jaw set. "Get it."

Carter nodded once, and he and Mitch went after it.

Yuri and Red went to follow but Carter yelled over his shoulder for the pair to stay on guard with the scientists.

"Blacklight." Mikhail got to his feet.

"Bring it," Carter said as he and Mitch were already outside the door.

CHAPTER 42

The thing was easy to track, as there were bloody, skittering, knitting needle-like prints leading down the corridor, but so far, the main cargo entrance chamber doors to outside remained closed.

"It's still in here," Mitch said, swinging the barrel of his gun one way then the other.

"Yep." Carter crab-walked toward the external doors, planning on putting himself between them and the outside. The tiny blood tracks had vanished, and Carter wished he had body armor.

Mikhail came to the door and held up the handheld blacklight, and both ex-Special Forces soldiers moved to have their backs to the walls, holding their guns on the expanse of the room, ready to take a shot.

After a moment of Mikhail waving it around, there was no sign, and both men became aware of how fast the temperature was dropping in the outer room. Then Carter looked up and saw why.

"Stand easy. Look." He nodded to the roof. "It's out."

There was a small, skylight-type window high above them that was now broken.

"Sonofabitch. So it can climb as well," Mitch said. "Or maybe it can fly like I said ages ago." He turned to glare at Mikhail. "Finished *communicating* with that fucker yet?"

Mikhail lowered the light. "It outsmarted us. It got out of the cage and past all of us."

"No shit. This thing is no dumb animal. To it, *we're* the dumb animals." Carter sighed and lowered his gun. "And now we know how it opens up its victims. It performs a little do-it-yourself surgery with a built-in scalpel."

Mikhail reached to switch off the blacklight.

"Keep that light on," Carter demanded. "It might still be hiding in here."

Mikhail shook his head slowly. "Why? It could have killed us. Could have killed *all* of us, in the cage room, but didn't. It just wanted out."

"Saving us for later." Mitch still seethed. "Maybe for dessert."

"Maybe you're right." Carter lowered his gun. "It had sawn through the cage bars and probably could have gotten away earlier if it wanted. I think it was observing us as we were observing it."

The three men stood in the center of the room, turning slowly. Mikhail had his portable blacklight held high, but after five minutes he lowered his arm.

"We are alone."

"Yeah." Carter holstered his gun. "Let's go see how Anna is doing."

They entered the room to find Yuri crouched beside a bloody sheet that had been thrown over the remains of Stefan. Nikolay had an arm around Anna, propping her up as Sara, still streaked with blood, talked softly to her. Anna nodded as she held a hand to her head and still looked shaken.

She turned when Mikhail entered, her eyes widening and beginning to speak in machinegun rapidity to him. Carter only caught a few of the Russian words but didn't like what he was hearing.

"Help her up," Mikhail said and pulled a chair closer.

Nikolay did as asked and guided her to the seat. She sat down, but reached out to hold onto Mikhail's arm, her hands gripping like claws.

She began again in Russian and Sara frowned. "No, in English. This affects us all."

"Yes, Anna, slowly please, and in English," Mikhail said calmly.

Anna blinked a few times and swallowed, her eyes round and a little wild. "I saw it," she said and swallowed again. "When it had hold of me; I saw into its mind."

Carter came and crouched in front of her. "Tell us. Tell us what you saw."

"They've been sleeping for thousands of years. They send up scouts to take, *samples*, every few years..."

"*Samples*. The animals and us, you mean?" Mitch said.

"Yes," she replied. "But now, they're all waking up." She tugged on Mikhail's arm and shot to her feet. "They're going to call for others—they're ready now."

"What?" Carter got to his feet as well. "Others?"

"What do they want?" Mikhail's eyes were half-lidded.

Anna's face crumpled for a moment, and her eyes flooded. "The wolves, the bears, the fish... us. They use biological entities like we use machines. *We* are their raw materials; their building blocks, their glue, their fuel."

"I told you," Yuri said softly. "They want us."

Mikhail patted her hand and eased her back down. "Good, good, rest now. We learned a lot today."

Anna shook her head. "It did too. That's why it knew to smash the UV lights. It pulled the information from my head. It didn't like being seen."

"How much time have we got?" Mikhail asked her.

"They will call on the next full moon to take advantage of the strong gravitational effects to boost their signal—five days. Then the others will come. And when they do..." Her face was bleached of color and her lips worked for a moment. "The oceans... the oceans are where they'll arrive. In the deepest trenches; they now know it's where we can't get to them."

"They're getting ready for an invasion," Carter said. "Establishing a fortified base."

"Those motherfu..." Mitch shook his head. "Kill 'em all."

"Thus ends the interspecies communication." Carter turned to Mitch. "Get Red, tell him to suit up. These things want a war, then we'll give 'em one, and before their main forces arrive."

"No." Anna jumped from her chair to scrabble at his arm. "There's still a chance we can talk to them. It could have killed me but it didn't. It was surprised to find we had intellect."

Carter frowned down at her. "No, it used you. That's all."

"They're different to us and don't think like us." She grimaced and crowded him. "They have no concept of pain or loss. We just need..."

"Stop it." Carter pushed her back a step and then walked right up into Mikhail's face. "We're going to cleanse the site, but your buddies in Moscow better come up with a plan to root out those ones down on the bottom of the lake before we, and everything living thing on this planet, end up next year's suits of clothing."

Sara used a rag to wipe some of the blood from her face and arms but her hair was becoming sticky. "I need to get this off."

"I'll walk you up there," Carter said. "Just in case that thing is still looking for another ride."

EPISODE 05

CHAPTER 43

INTERACTION: *Lake Baikal Forest—right now*

Igor Stavros scoffed as he stared at the naked man standing in the snow. "What is this fool?" he whispered.

"Sentry duty on wash day?" One of his men laughed. "Or maybe he lost a bet."

Stavros put binoculars to his eyes. The man was of average height, bearded and middle-aged, or maybe even slightly older than that as his beard, chest, and pubic hair were mostly a grizzled grey. On his arm was a fading tattoo, possibly of a wolf wearing a beret with a dagger through it. He recognized it—military.

What is he doing? he wondered. *Did he come up here to shit, or was he mentally impaired?* He had no time for this. Though his brief was to try and avoid taking out the Russian citizens, this idiot might put his mission at risk—one shout from this man, and they'd all be exposed.

Fuck it, he thought. Why wait? He turned to one of his bratva at the rear and first put a finger to his lips, made a cutting motion at his neck, and then pointed at the lunatic.

The bratva nodded his understanding and slung his rifle over his shoulder. He then drew forth a huge hunting knife that he kept at his back and headed toward the naked man.

The guy was facing them and hadn't moved a muscle. The bratva approached, his knife hand behind his back, casually holding up his other hand in a friendly wave.

Stavros watched, hoping he could be taken down quietly and efficiently. His man got in striking distance, and then the hand holding the knife lashed out, stabbing deftly into the chest, just between the ribs over the heart—an immediate kill stroke.

But the naked man stood straight, his mouth still gaping open and face blank. He didn't fall or even react. He didn't even bleed. But then the weirdest thing Stavros had ever seen occurred.

The naked man's stomach opened, like it had been slit, and the two sides of the gash hung there, wide, showing an absolutely empty gut cavity, like his man had somehow disemboweled him.

There was a puff of snow from just in front of the naked man, who stood there, eyes vacant as if he was in a trance.

His bratva recoiled a few paces from the gutted man, held his knife up to him, and spoke a few words that were lost to Stavros. But then in another moment, he turned to look over his shoulder at the bratva team leader, his face pale and confused.

That's when it all went insane.

There was movement, not from the naked man, but from the snow between them, and then his bratva soldier looked like he had been shocked or struck. He doubled over, and then threw his head back, clutching his front.

Even from where Stavros was, he heard his man's grunt of pain, and then from between his clutching fingers his jacket opened and his stomach poured out wetly into the snow before him. The heat of the internal organs rose in curls of steam and the pile of guts quickly melted into the snow.

"*What the fuck?*" Stavros's mouth hung open for a moment.

His man toppled face-first into his own hot gizzards and stayed down. Stavros now only had six men at his disposal and swung to call three of them from their stakeout positions.

Stavros circled his hand in the air and then pointed to his man who had fallen back into the snow. His three team members pulled rifles in tight to their shoulders and headed over, wading through snow that came to their knees.

Stavros stuck the field glasses into his pocket and instead put his riflescope to his eye to get a closer picture of what was unfolding while having the naked guy in his crosshairs—but he still just stood there, immobile, immutable, his stomach open like a trapdoor.

As he watched his three men cautiously approach, Stavros scowled into his scope, and then his brows drew even tighter together—something was happening in the gap between the men. There seemed to be marks, tracks, being made in the snow. And they looked to be headed directly toward his men.

"Look out, you fools," he hissed.

It was too late. The first of the three men yelled and spun as though he had been struck. His rifle fell into two pieces as half of his face was cut away. The red line of blood also traveled all the way down his coat.

What the fuck was going on? Stavros felt a cold hand of panic on his neck. His head whipped around. *Was someone throwing something? Some weapon he couldn't see?* he wondered.

His next man in line did the same, except his arm fell from his shoulder with the hot blood spurting, staining the snow a brilliant red. He yelled and kept on yelling as he turned to stagger away.

This was too much for the final man who turned and started to run in a plodding gait away from the killing zone. Behind him, his one-armed man held the spurting stump and yelled a string of Russian curses.

Stavros pointed his gun at the bellowing man and fired one round into his head, dropping him and immediately cutting off his screams. It was all going to shit, and Stavros had no idea why.

"Tosco," he yelled after his last man who ran and kept on running into the forest. "Get back here." And then, "*You fucking coward!*"

The man never slowed or even turned, and then he was gone. Stavros hit himself in the forehead with a gloved fist. "*Mugda!*" he cursed. Tushino would have his head for fucking up.

They'd made too much noise now. He quickly looked over his shoulder at the mill compound but didn't see any movement or people coming to investigate the yelling—*a small blessing*, he thought and then swung back to the ruined bodies of his men.

Stavros could only guess that somehow the American had rigged some sort of booby-trap—razor wire or something. But strangely, the naked man still stood there, like a clockwork toy that had wound down.

See how you like this, he thought and raised his rifle, sighting dead center on the naked man's forehead. He breathed out and gently squeezed the trigger.

A red spot appeared on the man's brow immediately followed by an explosion of blood and bone out the back of his skull. The naked old man's body fell back into the snow.

"Fuck you," Stavros whispered and then lowered his rifle. He turned to where his three remaining men were secreted on the hillside tree line. He called to the first… nothing. The second and third… also nothing. Not one of the men showed themselves or answered his call.

After a few more moments of absolute silence, he knew he was alone. Stavros had braved many tough and bloody times in his life, but it had been a long time since he had felt the cold hand of death at his neck.

He turned slowly, letting his eyes run over the snow, over the tree line, and he even glanced up at the branches overhead. But there was nothing now except the cold, silence, and solitude.

Maybe they had all run off. That must be it. He didn't really blame them after seeing their comrades be sliced up by nothing but thin air. Stavros came to a decision—he would leave his position and join up with the other team on the far flank. If any of his missing team were there, they'd answer to him.

Stavros shouldered his rifle, and as he turned, he noticed something strange. In the snow were weird tracks made by what looked like some sort of spikes. Following them back with his eyes, he saw they traveled circuitously from the killing zone of his men, all the way to stop just six feet beside him.

As he stared, another indentation appeared in front of the others, and then another. His mouth dropped open. It was as if something was taking slow and careful steps... toward him.

"Fuck you." He swung the muzzle of his gun down, but there was a whipping sound in the air and he felt a burning pain from his genitals to the center of his chest. The burning suddenly became ice cold.

Stavros gritted his teeth and dropped his rifle. He placed a hand over his stomach, but even through his gloves he felt the warm slipperiness as his insides spilled out into the snow.

The Russian killer began to weep with fear, pain, and confusion. "How?" He sunk to his knees.

The last thing he felt was something gripping the front of his shirt, something he still couldn't see, beginning to push inside his belly.

CHAPTER 44

Sara dried her hair last, better now for the soap and scalding shower but still feeling unclean from being bathed in the young man's blood. Things were getting out of her control—even more out of control—and right now, all she wanted was for the sun to come up and get through the night. *Everything would look better in the morning*, she kept telling herself.

Right now, she wished she could just lie on the bed and drift away. Everything in her body ached with fatigue and there was a pain behind her eyes from tension, tiredness, and also raw fear.

She had sent Carter back down and wouldn't call him back as her escort, but instead would head back down to the mill house herself to see if there was anything else she could be doing.

She pushed the last box of Marcus' personal items under a cupboard, and then took a quick glance around the house and all the changes she had made—blue china on dark antique wood dressers, long, settler-style table with fresh fruit, and dried flowers. There were now comfy leather chairs near a fireplace and couches with colorful cushions.

There was still work to do, so there were paintbrushes, screwdrivers, and hammers on every tabletop both upstairs and down. It all looked so normal; a different world to the one of chaos and horror down near the water.

Sara turned, just hearing the deep tick-tock of the mantle clock up against the far wall. The one thing she'd need to get used to in a Siberian winter was the absolute absence of sound—snow falls dampened down everything, and there were few animals wandering about, or owls hooting, and even the rustle of leaves in a breeze.

The thing she missed was the night sounds of Florida, where there was a gentle shush of tiny waves on golden sand.

She made a mental note to switch on the radio. There were a few stations they could sometimes get out here that played a few hits, mostly Russian, but a few European ones she recognized—hello again, ABBA. She smiled flatly and headed toward the kitchen.

Sara stopped in her tracks, tilting her head. One thing about the absence of sound was it magnified any remaining noises. And unusual ones stood out like a red cherry on a white cake. She waited, frozen to the spot, concentrating her senses.

Then the windows blew inward.

Sara dropped her coffee cup and spun toward the closest window as huge men in white, bulky outfits crashed in and continued to pour through.

Her body locked up for just a moment, maybe only a second, but by the time she turned to run, she was cornered, as from the back of the house was more smashing and more figures breaking in fast.

They were armed, faces covered in white ski masks. *Where was Carter? Where was Mitch, Red, or even Yuri?* she wondered, as the noise the intruders made should have carried all across the compound.

She was immediately grabbed by both arms and held to the spot as the others raced through the house, obviously looking for anyone else.

One of the men crossed to the front door and opened it. A single man stepped inside.

"You." She bared her teeth.

Tushino grinned, bowed theatrically, and straightened. "Yes, me. I told you I'd be back. And now here I am."

Sara wrestled with the iron grip of the men who held her. "You son of a bitch, I'll see you in…"

Tushino quickly crossed to her and punched her in the eye, rocking her head back on her neck. Sara saw stars but worked hard to not black out. She felt dizzy and her left eye was now hot, wet, and blurry. But she managed to stay upright.

"What do you want?" She had never felt such hate toward anyone in her life, and if she had her gun, she would shoot him in the face, dead center, without even blinking.

"A signed contract, of course." Tushino produced some folded paper and held it up. "Unfortunately, as negotiations have been protracted, expensive, and a little messy, the original deal has had to be altered to include compensation to reflect those conditions."

Tushino smiled sympathetically. "So, you give us control of 75% of the mill house sturgeon business, and we will be on our way." He placed a hand on his heart. "And I promise you will never be bothered by us or anyone else again." He held out the papers.

She spat on them and wasn't surprised to see some blood in her sputum, as she could taste it. The punch to her eye must have ruptured her socket.

Tushino half-turned away but then spun back to punch Sara in the other eye. She fell and the men let her drop. But the blow wasn't as hard as the last time, and she looked up through blurry eyes, but not at Tushino; instead, her eyes went to the tabletop.

In a blink, she launched herself at the table, grabbed the screwdriver and staying low, swung it back at the man, catching him in the front of the leg. The small flat blade of the screwdriver only sank in about half an inch, but the howl of pain was worth the beating that came after.

The punches and kicks immediately rained down on her. Sara managed to cover up at first, but the fists were like iron and the boots were large, hard, and ice cold from the snow, and they stomped and kicked with a ferocity that ruptured muscles and fractured bones.

"Stop," Tushino hissed. "She's no good to me dead or in a coma."

Sara lay on the ground, feeling like she was at the bottom of a long, dark pit of pain, sticky hot blood dripping from her nose. She barely heard the man say, *bring her*, as it all felt like a dream now. But in the next few seconds, she was being dragged out through the back broken window, feeling the sting of the bitter cold as the blood froze on her face.

CHAPTER 45

"Shots." Red spun to Mitch who had his head tilted, listening.

"Sniper rifle." It was Carter who broke first. "Ridgeline."

"*What?*" Mikhail blanched behind his beard.

Carter was already heading for the door and pulled it open, allowing Red and Mitch to speed through.

Carter turned to the group. "Mikhail, keep working on more ways to locate or track those damned creatures."

Yuri waded through the smaller group members. "Bratva? Here now?"

"Probably." Carter seethed. "You cover the mill. We'll be back soon."

"Da." The big man reached up to slap the gun in the holster at his hip.

Red, Mitch, and Carter sprinted for their cabins, zigzagging and staying low. Carter was already looking along the tree line.

"Gear up. Outside in two minutes."

The whizzing and soft *splut* of bullets striking the ground beside them ensured all three men dived to the snow.

"Fuck," Mitch yelled. He looked up. "Eastern tree line. 10 o'clock."

"Then that's where we'll meet—see you there." Carter bullocked and burrowed his way to the cabin, then launched himself from the snow to the door, shouldering it open as he dived inside to quickly roll back to his feet.

Bullets continued to hit the building's wooden frame so he kept going fast to his closet. He yanked it out, dragging the clothing out of the way to get to the false back and his weaponry.

In 100 seconds, he had pulled on his snow camo-gear, and had his rifle and other weapons ready. The last thing he did was put the communication plug in his ear and switch it on. He was thankful to get the electronic handshake that told him his men had already done the same.

He didn't bother going out the front door where he expected dozens of scopes would be homing in—after all, he had no doubt that he was their main target.

Carter went to the back of the cabin and kicked out some of the rear panels. He dove outside and grinned as he saw his two men kitted up and doing the same.

He leaned around the corner of his cabin and held the rifle and scope to his eye. He saw the figures on the ridgeline trying to conceal themselves. Even though they were in whiteout camouflage fatigues like his own, he knew they weren't professionals—they'd already fired dozens of rounds and not hit any of them yet.

"Our Bratva buddies—I count eight targets, but probably more scattered up at the eastern tree line."

"Got 'em," Mitch said.

"I see 'em; orders?" Red added.

"I'll draw their fire. After all, I'm betting they're here for yours truly," Carter said. "You two get up to the tree line and come at them from behind." He leaned out again and a bullet whacked into the wood near his head.

"We got no time for this shit." Carter pulled back. "Take 'em down. Unless it's Tushino. I want that gold-toothed asshole alive."

"Roger that; total threat removal, but capture the king. Out." Both Red and Mitch sprinted up the hill as Carter swung around and fired several rounds into the tree line. One man fell out of his position like a sack of sand and then stayed down.

"That's one down already, assholes," Carter said through clenched teeth. He kept on firing, with bullets smacking into the cabin as he drew their fire.

In another few minutes, his men had vanished and he knew they'd be rapidly working their way along behind the line of trees to get into an attacking position. He had no fear that his guys would be worth two or three of every one of Tushino's goons they came up against.

More minutes passed, and Carter smiled cruelly as he thought through how he was going to enjoy getting his hands on the Russian boss.

Then he heard the scream. His head spun to Sara's house. There came the sound of breaking glass.

It was a fucking diversion, his mind screamed. Their target was Sara all along.

Carter broke cover, praying his men were in position.

CHAPTER 46

Carter ran hard. He had to trust that his two men would take out any snipers, or he'd catch a bullet any second now. Already, he had that weird feeling of anticipation in the side of his face and ribs that made him feel exposed, waiting for the massive impact of a high caliber slug.

The weird creatures from the bottom of the lake were an adversary that was impossible to understand. But the Russian mafia gave him something to focus on, something he *could* understand. Carter knew how they thought, what they wanted, and could anticipate them. And Carter also knew that if he could anticipate them, he could get ahead of them, and then he could kill them.

He went into Sara's house fast and hard, rolling and coming up aiming his gun. He immediately saw the multiple points of entry—the smashed glass and the broken furniture... it would have been terrifying. There were also spots of blood on the ground that made him grind his teeth and want to roar with rage.

They hurt her, and it would have only happened just minutes ago. He headed for the back of the house and found the broken open window surrounded by large boot marks. Carter went straight out into the coldness.

The tracks in the snow behind Sara's house told him there were several men, possibly up to eight, and they dragged something with them—he knew that was undoubtedly Sara.

He had to hope they had no reason to take a dead body with them. So she was either unconscious or bound. And that meant he still had time.

*****

Red and Mitch went hard and low, staying at least 200 feet back from the tree line. In another few moments, they were coming up on an expected intersect position where they knew some of the shooters would be.

Red lifted a hand and Mitch stopped. Red turned to his friend, put a finger to his lips, and then drew a long blade from a thigh scabbard. Mitch grinned and did the same.

Red then pointed out to the left with a flat hand and Mitch nodded and headed off, while Red took the right side. The men moved silently into the snow-laden forest like a pair of hungry wolves.

Red saw his first target—a big guy in camo pressed up against a tree trunk, an expensive hunting rifle with scope pressed to his eye. His absolute focus was on the compound, and he suddenly braced, leaning out slightly as he prepared to fire at something that had drawn his attention down in the valley.

Red was up on him in three quick strides, and his blade whipped up to enter his neck—he had several good killing areas on the neck to choose from depending on what he wanted to accomplish: the first was to simply slow them down or incapacitate the target—that was accomplished by a simple stab into the neck beside the larynx. If he caught the jugular and opened the esophagus, it meant the lungs and gut rapidly filled with blood. If the guy got medical attention, it wouldn't be fatal.

But instead, Red chose a much more lethal strike—go into the neck's flesh at the side, deep, and then sweep the blade outward, severing the larynx, jugular vein, and carotid artery. The carotid was the real sweet spot as it fed the brain with blood. Cut that, and the fucker was dead in seconds.

Red stabbed in hard and swept to the side. A fountain of blood and steam sprayed the air, and Red ducked out of the way.

The guy placed a hand over the gaping wound, his eyes wide and mouth gaping. As he turned, Red saw that already the color was draining from his face. There would be no words, no yell of warning or surprise.

Red gave him a small salute as the guy went to his knees and was about to head off to find his next target when he paused. He quickly reached into the snow to lift the guy's expensive hunting rifle.

Nice, he thought and laid it up against the tree so he could find it later. He then sped away.

Up ahead was a hint of movement. Red went into stalking mode once again. He tightened his grip on the blade, his eyes never blinking. Red knew that he and his buddy Mitch wouldn't stop until every one of the would-be assassins was dead.

CHAPTER 47

Carter entered the tree line, and slowed. Tushino would undoubtedly expect to be followed so he would probably leave a few men behind in ambush.

The men were certainly killers but Carter knew they would be nothing but brutal amateurs. Sure enough, as he edged forward among the snow-muffled quietude of the forest, he just caught the sound of whispering coming from up ahead—*amateurs*, he thought again.

Carter went down behind a tree and eased his head around. He had on his snow camouflage, and he would have been invisible within the nighttime white landscape.

He didn't move a muscle and even held his breath for several moments. Then, sure enough, he saw the steaming puff of an exhalation from behind a tree trunk—*there*—one of the ambushers.

After waiting several more minutes, he saw the other man positioned 50 feet away, creating a potential crossfire kill zone either side of a natural pathway.

Carter knew time was against him, and he had to be past these guys and back to following Tushino before they vanished. He had no idea how they were going to get Sara back to one of the main towns or try and spirit her back to Moscow, but his money was on them having some sort of transportation waiting for them on the frozen lake.

Tushino's group was headed down along the shoreline and about a quarter-mile inland for now, but he still bet he could run them down given the chance.

Carter drew forth one of his smaller blades and sighted a tree corridor in through the forest. He flung the blade out hard and it traveled a good 100 feet before thudding into the cold trunk of a Larch tree just out to the side of the killers.

In the near-silent forest, it made a sold *thunk* that dragged both men's heads around, and their rifle barrels flicked up. As expected, both men stepped out to aim.

Stupid amateurs, Carter thought again and fired.

His first round drilled into the temple of the closest guy. He was thrown to the side. The second guy immediately swung back at the noise, and not being a professional meant his first instinct was to look to his buddy… instead of covering himself.

In that split second, his eyes went from his dead comrade to where

Carter was now up on one knee and aiming directly at him… it was the last wrong decision he would ever make. Carter doubted he could even see the small round circle of the muzzle pointed between his eyes, but the next thing he knew, a dinner plate-sized piece of skull was blown out the back of his head, taking half of the guy's brain with it.

Carter immediately got to his feet and started running hard again. The tracks were easy to follow and surging adrenaline gave him a burst of energy that drove him forward like a machine.

*****

Mitch wiped down his blade as Red joined him. At his feet was a still-twitching man with vivid, pumping blood staining the pristine snow.

"That's number three," he said emotionlessly.

"I've taken down five; you're slipping, brother." Red grinned.

Mitch snorted and then looked about. "There's nothing living on the other ridgeline. Means the last group is the one that Carter has gone after. Why don't we join him?"

"Sounds like a plan." Red nudged him. "Maybe you'll get a chance to even up your tally."

"Only if Carter leaves any alive." Mitch chuckled for a moment, but then raised a single brow. "Hey, make it interesting?"

"Sure, buck a head—let's go." Red waved him on and the pair of ex-Special Forces soldiers sprinted into the freezing darkness.

CHAPTER 48

Mikhail paced slowly, lost in thought. Things were going bad—the bratva had arrived and he'd heard shots fired. Given Carter and the two other American ex-soldiers had headed off into the forest, he expected that something had also happened to Sara Stenson.

Mikhail had been trying to call Moscow to let them know what was happening, and to call in help—he managed to get through, but wasn't sure he was understood... or believed.

Anna gave him a watery smile as she sipped coffee. Color had returned to her face.

"How are you feeling?" he asked.

She nodded. "Better, now."

"Tell me again..." He dragged a seat closer, "... about what you learned when the creature had hold of you."

She sipped and stared at the wall for a moment, as she must have taken herself back to being seated before the cage.

"They don't understand," she began. "To them, we human beings were not really sentient creatures. Instead, we were deemed nothing but resources, just like the other animals, and were simply biological stocks to be used at will." She looked up at him, her eyes glistening. "These strange creatures have supreme intelligence, but no emotions or feelings or compassion; they were more like insect automatons."

"It is as we thought; every man, woman, child, and every other living thing on the planet would be used and consumed." He leaned closer. "Where do they come from, Anna? Did you see?"

"Darkness. The depths." Her brow creased. "A place that had been used up, leaving nothing but emptiness. I don't think it was their home world, but somewhere else."

"I think they're travelers; like interstellar locusts." The idea made his skin crawl. "For all we know, they had been jumping from planet to planet for countless millions of years, using and consuming as they went. Time means nothing to them, as they seem to be able to hibernate for many millennia at a time."

"I just couldn't..." Her lips pressed together as though she struggled with her thoughts for a moment. "I just couldn't get them to see who we really are. I still believe they only need to be educated about human beings." She looked up at him. "It could have killed me but chose not to. I was so close."

Mikhail patted her shoulder. "Rest now." He could have laughed out loud, but it would have been with no humor. The bratva had proved countless times that they were happy to mistreat, maim, and kill their fellow people. *If you couldn't change the mafia's characteristics, then what hope did you have of changing a monster's?* he wondered.

Yuri had been pacing around the room and finally threw his hands up. "I cannot stay any longer, I'm going," he announced.

Mikhail got to his feet, staring for a moment. Then he said something that even surprised himself. "I'm coming with you."

Yuri shook his head. "No, I…"

Mikhail turned to Nikolay. "Look after Anna."

"What?" The young woman's eyes blazed. "I'm not your daughter." She sprang to her feet. "Something is happening this night. Something that may decide the fate of our entire species, and I refuse to cower in an old mill." She folded her arms. "I'm going with you."

Yuri gaped at Nikolay who just shrugged. "You don't expect me to stay, do you?"

Yuri sighed. "This will be dangerous." He looked to the covered body of Stefan and then back at Mikhail "Very, very dangerous."

"Right now, so is sitting here doing nothing," Anna shot back.

Mikhail shrugged. "She's right."

Anna quickly grabbed her jacket. "We won't slow you down."

Nikolay rushed to his father, who was sitting down in the corner just looking at his hands. The young Russian spoke rapidly but softly to him. After a while, the old man looked up, and to Yuri, he seemed to have aged a decade in a day. He nodded and kissed his son on the cheek.

Nikolay then grabbed a portable acetylene torch and a scalpel. "Ready."

Yuri shook his head. "Put that down." He went to turn away but then paused. "Bring the torch."

CHAPTER 49

Tushino urged his men to greater speed to meet their waiting trucks. He had a team of six remaining and after hearing a gunshot from so close behind, he knew that his two men left in ambush positions had prevailed. Or they had not.

If they did, then they would bring him Carter's head. If they didn't, then it could very well mean it was Carter closing in on them, and he was more formidable than he had ever imagined.

Tushino gritted his teeth and looked across to the unconscious woman, only just resisting the urge to reach across and strike her again. If the dumb bitch had only just signed his contract, none of this would have happened.

He only just fought down the urge because as long as he had her, he was insulated from a direct attack. But he needed to be on his own turf quickly or he'd be caught out in a frozen Siberian forest in the middle of the night.

His group leader, Bulukov, eased up close to him. "GPS puts us at only 500 yards out. Be there in five minutes."

"Good." All of this team could fit in a single truck now. He'd leave the other teams behind so if the next group came back in, they could take another waiting vehicle, as there was no way he would be waiting for stragglers.

He grabbed at Bulukov's arm. "As soon as we get there, we load the woman and take off."

Bulukov nodded. "Yes, sir."

As they approached the frozen lake, the temperature seemed to drop. Tushino's lungs burned from the freezing air and his mouth became sticky. He spat into the snow, the gobbet freezing before it traveled two feet from his mouth. This was a godforsaken place, and he'd be glad to leave it behind.

Bulukov held up a hand and the group stopped. He turned. "You hear that?"

Tushino frowned and concentrated. "No, I don…" Then he did.

It sounded like something huge being torn apart and a deep cracking like distant thunder. In among the noise, there might just have been a scream.

"What is it?" he asked in a whisper.

Bulukov slowly shook his head. "Sounds like a rockslide, but we're a long way from any cliffs. What do you want to do?"

Tushino looked over his shoulder. "We must get to the trucks—no choice; we go on."

The bratva boss gritted his teeth. He fucking hated this place more by the second.

The haunted mill, he remembered someone telling him. He felt the chill on his neck, and now he knew why it was called that.

*****

Carter could tell they were headed back to the ice now, and he also bet there would be trucks waiting to speed the group away the moment they arrived.

Though Tushino and his men were in the lead, after being here for over a year now, his advantage was he knew every shortcut there was. Carter branched off and took a more direct path to the lake. He knew he'd arrive in just a few minutes and as he ran, he started to load more cartridges into his gun.

He slowed, listening. That noise—the cracking and tearing—he recognized it, and it was the sound of massive ice sheets being torn up.

"Oh no, no, no." He held his gun in one hand and started to sprint.

CHAPTER 50

Bulukov was first through the tree line onto the lakeshore. He slowed, his arms dropping to his side, looking one way then the other. He then turned to Tushino.

"Where are they?"

Tushino's mouth was open and the other men piled up behind them. Two of them placed Sara's unconscious form onto the ground. They all stared—at what wasn't there.

There were no trucks, no men lounging beside them smoking thick cigarettes, and no ice sheet meeting the frozen shoreline.

Instead, in a huge disc, the ice was broken open, and they could all feel the bone-numbing cold emanating from the impenetrable black water.

"They left us?" one of the men asked. "Why would they leave us?"

"No." Bulukov walked a few more paces forward. "The sound we heard before, it was this; the ice breaking up."

"They broke through... or sunk?" another of the assassins stammered.

"Impossible," Tushino spat. "It was over six feet thick. They'd need dynamite."

Bulukov shook his head, walking right down to the edge of the black water. He pointed out to where the ice started again and turned back. "It's folded up, as if it was broken upward from the water side... from below."

The big Russian fumbled in his pocket for a moment and then withdrew a flashlight. He held it up and pointed the beam down to illuminate the dark but crystal-clear water. He craned forward.

"No, look." He began to shake his head. "They *are* there. Under the water." He frowned and craned forward even more, stretching out his flashlight arm. "Wait... something moving."

"One of the men?" another of the team asked.

"I don't..." Bulukov took another few steps closer, his boot now actually in the water. He slowly moved his light around.

"*Svoloch!*" He leaped up, as the bear's head broke the dark water's surface. He tried to keep his light on it but his hand wobbled.

Tushino's lips pulled back in a frightened rictus and he pulled his revolver, trying to aim at the huge animal as it lifted itself from the water. But then immediately to one side of it, the antlers of a deer showed, then on its other side another, and then another. Then a wolf began to rise from the inky water.

The bratva leader's mind became confused and scattered—their transport was gone, and now they had an army of animals surfacing. Some of them large and dangerous beasts.

To Tushino's horror, a man came next, his long hair wet and matted to his shoulders. Bulukov yelled his fear and shone the flashlight into his face, illuminating milky-white eyes that belonged on a corpse.

"They're dead. They're all dead," Bulukov screamed at Tushino. He then spun back and immediately shot at the bear, once, twice, and three times. But it took the bullets without flinching, or worst of all, not even making a sound.

Tushino's gun hand wobbled as he backed up, and his teeth began to chatter. He realized now what was so terrifying was that none of the beasts made a single sound—not a snort or a sneeze, a growl or even a whine.

He'd had enough. "Fire! *Shoot, shoot!*"

The men opened fire and their bullets zippered the animals and people rising from the icy lake. Many of the wild rounds splashed in beside them, but hitting them or not, none made a difference.

"Cease firing." Bulukov waved a huge arm in the air. "It's Stanislov Borga."

Sure enough, Tushino saw the mustached sniper he had engaged to kill Carter also rising from the water. He still had on his white camouflage fatigues, but now the front hung open, and there could have been the dark, washed-out remains of blood there.

Now he knew what happened to him. But just like the animals, Borga's face was dreary and slack and his eyes were the deadest of white, but there was just the hint of something dark behind them. He rose up from the depths and headed straight for Bulukov.

Tushino began to shake his head. "No, don't let him, there's something wrong." He lifted his gun and fired. With more luck than skill, his bullet struck Borga in the shoulder, the impact punching him back half a step. But even though there was now a ragged hole in the clothing and undoubtedly the flesh beneath, Borga never made a sound and continued to approach Bulukov.

Bulukov in turn turned and yelled to stop firing, but when he turned back, Borga was now only a few feet from him.

"Borga, what's happening?" Bulukov stared into his face, but the assassin never said a word, and instead lifted an arm. In turn, Bulukov reached out to take the hand, thinking he was asking for help.

The hand gripped Bulukov's, and Borga simply began to turn back to the water.

Bulukov was dragged forward a step.

"Hey, no, brother. What...?" Bulukov was bigger and yanked and jerked at the hand gripping him, but it made no difference and he was slowly being pulled into the freezing water.

One of Tushino's men went to break ranks, but the Russian leader screamed at him to stay where he was. Tushino knew it was turning into a madhouse and he quickly looked up and down the coastline. To the south were hundreds of miles of frozen nothingness. He turned back—to the north, in just over a mile, was the mill compound.

He looked back toward the water as the animals and strange people were reaching the shore now. He saw Bulukov still struggling as he was dragged, screaming, down into the depths.

Tushino knew he should try and help, but he also knew none of his men would obey the order. When that happened, chain of command would be destroyed.

"*Madhouse*," he whispered as the huge and tough Bulukov started wailing like a small child as Borga, still expressionless, took them both down into the stygian dark water.

"*Mad, mad, madhouse*," he whispered again. Tushino decided. "Grab the woman. This way."

CHAPTER 51

Red and Mitch caught up with Carter as he belly-crawled toward the chaotic sounds at the shoreline.

"Something big going down," Carter whispered.

"Sounds like a full-on fire-fight," Red said. "And it ain't against us."

"Yuri?" Mitch asked.

"No, something else." Carter increased his speed. "Nearly there."

The three men crawled through the last trees and saw the Russian men gathered at the shoreline. But then they saw what they were firing at.

"Sweet jumping Jesus." Mitch's mouth hung open.

Like a scene from a portal of hell, the dead animal hosts were rising from the water and stepping up onto the land—bears, wolves, antlered deer, and even several people, some in clothing, others looking bloated and mottled, as if their flesh had started to corrupt.

Red blew air between pressed lips. "That answers the question about if there's more than one of those ugly little critters."

Beyond the Russians, the inky water held a distinct green glow down in the depths. Carter spotted Tushino, and then Sara being held up by two men.

"That bastard," Carter hissed, seething.

He dispatched Red and Mitch to different positions, and moved along the tree line behind Tushino and his men while they were preoccupied.

After another few seconds, he saw that the Russians looked to have decided to head up along the shore—back toward the mill.

Carter yelled from his concealment. "*Cton*—stop!"

The Russian hitmen looked panicked at the new voice, and their guns swung from the approaching corpse-like animals to Carter's position. One fired, perhaps on instinct, as there was no way he could have spotted Carter.

Carter returned fire and hit the man in the heart dead-center, dropping him like a stone.

"Bring the woman here." Carter drew a bead on the man holding her. "Tushino, last chance. Or I shoot another of your men."

"Carter Stenson." Tushino suddenly looked wracked with indecision. The animals were edging closer, and he seemed to have no choice. "A truce."

"Bring the woman, *now*." Carter ground his teeth, as they seemed to be conferring. He fired above their heads. "*Fucking right now*."

One of the men looked to try and steal his way into the forest to try and work his way behind Carter. A single shot from either Red or Mitch rang out and the Russian fell backward from the trees.

"Don't think we won't kill you all," Carter yelled. "Three seconds, or you're all dead." He aimed. "Two seconds."

"All right, all right." Tushino spoke rapidly to his man who held Sara. In turn, he dragged her along the shore toward Carter's position and then went to lay her on the frozen ground. Carter spoke to him in Russian.

"No! Bring her to me... closer."

The man's eyes burned with anger and also a hint of fear, but he brought Sara into the forest. He spotted Carter, and saw his armaments, and quickly laid her down, raising his hands and straightening.

"Now fuck off."

The man backed up, but by now the animals had reached them, so instead of rejoining his group, he turned and sprinted down along the shoreline. Another man broke ranks and also sprinted into the frozen forest.

Tushino's eyes bulged as he yelled for them to hold their place.

Carter quickly drew Sara to him and immediately saw the beating she had taken. He felt the surge of anger in his chest.

Tushino seemed to have made a change of plans, held his hands up, and began to walk toward Carter. "I surrender."

In turn, Carter fired a single round into the snow at his feet.

"Your men can do what they want. But *you* stay right there."

"What?"

His men looked one way then the other, and as one lowered their guns and then ran at breakneck speed into the freezing forest.

"Bastards!"

Tushino bared his teeth and spat a stream of Russian curses, first at his fleeing men, and then at Carter. He spun back, bringing his gun around, but Carter fired first into his leg. Tushino screamed and went to one knee, grasping his leg.

One of the bears reached him and looked down with its milky eyes and gaping, desiccated mouth for just a second or two before leaning forward and gathering him up as if he weighed nothing.

The merciful thing would have been for Carter to put the Bratva leader out of his misery. But Carter had no mercy for this creature.

He stared as the screaming Russian was carried to the dark water, beating against the sodden hide of the enormous animal. In another few seconds, his screams were cut off as he vanished below the lake's dark surface.

Red and Mitch rejoined Carter, and they watched as many of the beasts that had risen from the freezing water were going after the fleeing Russians. Unfortunately, another group was heading toward them.

"They're dead," Red breathed. "They're dead, and being driven around like fucking zombie suits."

"When the gates of Hell are opened, then the dead will rise," Mitch added. "Boss, time to go."

"Yep." Carter brushed hair from Sara's face and saw she was still only semi-conscious, and he worried about a serious concussion. However, for now, perhaps her being oblivious to what was going on was for the best. He stood and lifted her. "Let's get the hell out of here."

Red and Mitch turned to take shots at the closest animals but other than blow chunks of flesh from some of them, it didn't slow them down at all.

The trio pulled back into the forest and quickly moved along the trails Carter knew to speed them back to the mill compound.

*****

In another 20 minutes, movement from up ahead had the three men take cover. Carter held Sara close with one arm and lifted his rifle with the other. But soon, the flashlights and noise the group were making gave them away.

"Yuri," Carter said.

The big Russian lifted his gun above his head. "Hold your fire."

Carter came out from behind the tree trunk as Yuri and the scientists all came in. Yuri quickly crossed to Carter and took Sara from him. "She's alive." He exhaled with relief. Then he looked up. "Tushino?"

"Dead... sort of." Carter turned to Mikhail. "The creatures came out of the lake; lots of them. They grabbed most of Tushino's men and they're heading our way. We gotta get back to the mill and create a defendable position."

Anna looked over his shoulder.

Carter pointed to the dark forest. "Red, Mitch, take point. Mikhail, Anna, communicating time is over. And let's light 'em up as we go."

Mikhail nodded. "Yes, yes." But then bobbed his head. "We didn't, ah, bring any blacklights."

That meant they only had the portable one Carter had with him. "Then let's hope they stay in their skin suits." He shoved them. "Move it."

CHAPTER 52

The group ran hard. Red and Mitch sped out ahead, next came Nikolay and Anna, followed by Yuri carrying Sara. Mikhail puffed his way next, and Carter covered the rear, while also putting his hand in the center of the old scientist's back to give him a shove along.

Though the animals never moved quickly—as if the creatures riding around inside them had trouble moving the limbs at any speed—he knew that the alien creatures themselves moved like lightning. Added to that, without a full contingent of blacklights, they were now invisible.

The entire time Carter moved through the dark forest he had the tingling feeling up his spine from his imagination conjuring something lashing out of the dark like a razor whip, slitting him open from one end to the other.

It took them another 30 minutes to begin to head into the compound. "To the mill house," Carter yelled from the rear. He knew it was the largest and most solid structure they had. Plus, it was where all the blacklights were stored. Bottom line: they needed to see their enemy.

As they left the tree line, Red out in front held up a hand. He then flattened his palm and waved them down.

The group crouched and Carter and Mitch came up to join the Special Forces soldier.

"What have you got?" Carter asked.

"The waterline, which used to be an ice line. Check it out." Red nodded toward the icy shore.

Sure enough, the ice was broken open in front of the wharf. There was also the tell-tale green glow emanating from deep below the water.

"Ah shit, here too," Carter said and exhaled in a hiss. "No choice; we got to get to the mill house. We can't afford to be stuck out in the open."

"Got it." Red turned back. "Then lock and load; we're going in hot."

"I heard that." Mitch wracked his gun and got to his feet.

Carter turned and waved Mikhail closer. "The creatures are coming to shore here as well. We've got to get inside." He looked to the small group. "We're going fast and hard. Stay in a line—just focus on the back of the person in front of you. Don't stop for anything. Got it?"

The group nodded, and Carter turned back to Red. "Mr. Mitch Tanner and Mr. Redmond Bronson, take us out. Gentlemen, stop for nothing and nobody—dead or alive."

"*HOOAH!*"

The pair slapped their guns and turned back. Red charged first, gun up, immediately followed by Mitch.

"Okay?" Carter asked Yuri. The big man still cradled the unconscious Sara.

"Yes, I've got her. I will not drop her."

"I know you won't. Let's go, big guy." Carter waved him on.

Yuri started to lumber forward followed by Nikolay, Anna, Mikhail, and finally Carter.

Carter put his scope to his eye and could see the animals and people coming up the shoreline—they looked ghostly, and in among them, he thought he might have seen Leonid. He hoped not.

Carter sucked in a breath as it came his turn to run. One thing was for sure: he wasn't going to let that happen to Sara, himself, or anyone else on his watch.

*****

Red and Mitch fired as they ran. They aimed for the animals' gut cavity, and many times, the beasts crumpled to the ground, meaning that the men's high-powered rounds had passed all the way through the dead flesh of the animal and into the creatures within.

"Not too many," Anna yelled.

Carter's brow furrowed as they closed in on the mill. *What did she mean? Did she mean not too many more steps to the mill? Or not too many more creatures killed?* If she was still hoping to communicate or make friends with these horrors, then she was out of luck, as that bus had come and gone hours back.

In another few minutes, they came to the mill and Red slammed his shoulder into the large set of doors. And then bounced back.

"*Fuck!*" He glared. "It's locked."

"I left it open," Yuri said and shifted Sara in his arms who seemed to finally be coming around.

"Look." Mitch pointed toward the waterfront where the ice had broken open in a massive circle over 100 feet around.

Carter turned and saw the creatures coming ashore. But there was something else—the deep green glow seemed to be emanating from a large object just below the water. It could have been a whale, but he knew that was impossible. Same again for a submersible.

He quickly lifted the scope to his eye and saw that it was a single object, but seemed to be a conglomerate of pieces—*no*, he thought, feeling his gorge rise—not pieces, but separate animals. The larger object was constructed of seals, and wolves, and deer, and there also looked to be a small, naked, human body pressed there, possibly a child.

"What the hell is that?"

It breached the surface and dark holes gaped open on it like orifices—it was a submersible, or some type of vehicle, but it was made from the living flesh of scavenged animals. There were long tendrils waving and whipping the surface and undulating below the waterline—obviously its primary means of locomotion.

Carter thought it was just as Mikhail had hypothesized that the creatures saw us, and every living thing, as raw materials. Where we used machines, they used... *us*. If they won, then this was the future of the human race.

Carter fumbled in his pocket for a moment and grabbed out his blacklight. He switched it on and pointed it—the light only just reached the weird submersible. But it now illuminated what was coming from the dark orifices—dozens of the many-legged creatures were pouring forth.

"I don't think they've seen us yet," Red said hopefully.

They, and the other beasts, were all heading in one direction—toward them. Carter pushed toward the front of the group.

"No time for this shit."

"Got that right." Mitch went to kick out when the sounds of the door being unlocked came from inside. The door was suddenly pulled inwards.

"Papa." Nikolay rushed in and grabbed his father.

The old man looked confused. He hugged his son back, and then looked from him to Carter. "I saw Leonid. But he is sick."

"I know." Carter nodded and helped everyone inside. He quickly pushed the door closed and locked it. "Okay, everyone, let's lock this place down. Secure every window, door, vent, and crack you can get to."

Mitch pointed upward. High above them was still the broken skylight that the original creature had escaped through.

"Got a 50-foot ladder?" Carter shrugged.

"So we batten down what we can, and for the rest, we just defend like hell."

"For how long?" Red asked.

"Mikhail?" Carter asked. "Will the cavalry arrive in time?"

The older scientist grimaced as he hiked his shoulders. "I don't know if my message got through."

Carter checked his watch. "Then in about five hours, it's sunup. We can only hope that by morning..." He looked up, "... I'm hoping that by morning, we're back in control."

"I think you're right," Mikhail added. "Remember the legend of the haunted mill, where all the people who worked here simply vanished one night? Everyone assumed they simply all went home. I think it's obvious that something similar to this happened. But by morning, it was all over."

"Either the sun coming up forced them back to the depths..." Red smiled but with zero humor. "Or they went back because there was no more meat for them to harvest."

"That is *fucked* up." Mitch scoffed. "Thanks for that, buddy."

"Think positive," Carter said. "Besides, right now, it's all we got." He pointed. "Quick weapons check; see what you've got left." He slapped both men on the shoulder. "Nothing can be allowed to get in here with us."

"You got it," the pair replied forcefully.

Carter then crossed to Yuri. The big Russian had carefully placed Sara in a large chair, and she started to mumble. Her eyes fluttered.

"Water," he said and reached out to grab her hand.

Sara winced. "Ow."

Thank God, he thought. *She could have had brain damage.*

Sara's eyes were still closed, and she lifted a hand to her swollen left eye. The right one was almost as bad. "Where…?"

"It's okay, you're safe now," he whispered. He rubbed her hand, holding it in both of his.

"What happened?" Her eyes opened as slits, and she winced again. "Oh God, my freaking head." She sat forward. "That bastard Tushino." Her eyes opened and were shot through with spidery veins of blood. "I'll kill him."

"Already dead," Carter said.

"Good." She eased back. "Good."

Yuri returned with a beaker of water and handed it to Carter. He carefully held it to her lips but she reached out to take it and drink. She drained it.

"Thanks." She blinked and then looked around, squinting. "Why are we all in here? And why is it so dark?"

"Hey, yeah." Carter noticed for the first time the main lights were out and Pavel had been sitting in the shadowed darkness. "Can we get the lights on?"

Pavel shuffled closer. "I turn them off as I think it hurt Leonid's eyes… when he came."

Carter frowned. "When he came? How close were you to him?"

Pavel bobbed his head.

Nikolay stood straight. "Papa, where is he?"

Pavel turned and stared. In the darkest alcove of a far corner, and standing inhumanely still, was the form of Leonid. The old man crossed to him.

"He no talk; he is very sick, I think." Pavel motioned. "Come, Leonid."

Leonid shot an arm out and grabbed Pavel's shoulder.

"*Shit.*" Carter's stomach knotted as what was happening clicked into place. "*Eyes on; armor up*," he yelled.

Nikolay put his hands to his head. "Papa, come away…"

"Get the fuck down." The old man blocked Carter's line of sight.

From the front of Leonid's sodden shirt, the material rippled as if in a breeze and then began to part. Fluid leaked out and then the cavity started to bloom open.

"It's coming out," Mikhail yelled.

Red sprinted in and dove, taking Pavel down.

"*Fire.*" Carter, followed by Mitch and then Red, opened up.

Dozens of rounds poured into the figure of Leonid that danced and jumped from the bullet impacts. The room quickly filled with smoke and the smell of gunpowder, sulfur, and a hint of saltpeter.

"Cease fire," Carter yelled. "Blacklight."

Mikhail carefully approached, holding up the purple beam. There was no blood from Leonid, as the body's flesh was like wax. The Russian scientist carefully lifted the light, following spindly tracks as they raced up the wall.

"It got out," he said softly.

He kept lifting the light beam until they saw the tracks head toward the broken skylight overhead.

"*Fuck it*," Carter roared. "And now they know where we are."

Sara got unsteadily to her feet and hung onto Carter's arm. "They'll get in here. They're smarter than us."

"We'll be overrun," Yuri grumbled. "By the creatures."

"We can defend it," Carter replied.

"All night?" She held her head for a moment. "How many are there?"

Carter looked away.

"Carter, how many?" she persisted.

He turned back and gave her a crooked smile. "A lot."

"Then we need a fort." She quickly turned about for a moment. "We should all move into the center of the lab. If push comes to shove, we can seal ourselves in the refrigeration room—it's basically a steel box." She turned. "Once in the central labs, we fortify every room on the way there. We create firewalls and defend each from the center."

Carter turned to look where she indicated—the central lab rooms were at the center of a nest of smaller rooms. All had heat-resistant and shatter-proof glass walls. It wasn't exactly bulletproof, but they were certainly solid enough to create a good level of resistance.

"That might work." Carter nodded and grinned.

"It *will* work." She pointed. "Mikhail, Anna, Nikolay, see what we can rustle up in the way of extra weapons, blacklights, or anything else we can use. Everyone is going to have to pitch in." She motioned at Pavel. "Pavel, find us some water. I hope we won't be here long, but if need be, we'll also be eating the sturgeon eggs in the chillers."

Carter grinned. "That's my girl." He grinned. "Glad to have you back."

She stumbled a little and Carter held onto her. Sara worked her mouth for a moment, her tongue running along her gum line. She frowned. "Chipped teeth; that bastard."

"Don't worry, he got everything that was coming to him," Carter said ruthlessly.

The huge wooden front doors of the mill creaked ominously as something large pressed against them.

Sara clapped her hands. "Okay, everyone, let's fall back."

CHAPTER 53

The group pulled back behind the individually sealed doors, locking each of them as they went. They gathered in the center laboratory that acted as the main hatchery and where the huge refrigerators remained. They gave off a gentle hum, and Carter looked across to them.

"Could they cut the power?"

Mikhail shrugged. "They're probably smart enough."

Carter walked along the benchtop tables, looking at what the group had gathered up. Red and Mitch were quickly doing ammunition checks, and had also been tasked with determining their defensive weaknesses.

Carter saw that Nikolay still had his portable blowtorch; there were also large knives, multiple scalpels, and a few glass bottles of hydraulic acid.

Carter called Nikolay over. "Keep the blowtorch ready—I think fire is a good option. As for the acid, put it out of the way—I don't want a bottle of that smashing and splashing anyone in here."

Nikolay nodded and then looked from Mikhail to his father, who was filling water bottles. He turned one way then the other, and then back to Carter.

"Where's Anna?"

"What?" Carter turned about. The central room they were in had several partitions, steel benches, large vats, and refrigerator units, but there wasn't really anywhere to hide, and the refrigeration doors hadn't been opened. There was nowhere to go unless she managed to fold herself into a small cabinet.

Inside with them was the huge form of Yuri, also Mitch, Red, Pavel, Mikhail, Nikolay, Sara, and himself—eight adults. It was crowded so it was easy to lose one small woman.

"We're one short," he said loudly to get everyone's attention. "Anna!" he yelled her name, hoping she'd pop up from behind a desk or somewhere where she could have secreted her tiny frame.

No one answered and Sara turned to him, her gaze level. Carter cursed softly. "Damn. We gotta find her."

The group set to opening cabinets, storage rooms, and looking under benches. Carter turned, looking out through the glass walls, trying to locate her.

"There," Mikhail said, pointing out through the multiple glass walls.

Carter's head whipped around. Sure enough, there was the small frame of the female Russian biologist, still out in the main entrance room.

She held up a blacklight and stood before the huge wooden double doors.

"What is she doing?" Yuri frowned and walked closer to the glass partition.

"We have to get her," Nikolay said.

"She's waiting for them," Sara said softly and turned to Carter. "She still thinks she can talk to them."

"No, she's not just waiting for them," Carter said as he watched her walk toward the huge doors that were now bowing inwards. "She's going to goddamn let them in."

"The hell she is," Red yelled. "Once they're in, they're in for good." Red spun back to Carter. "We need to stop her—take her down if need be."

"No." Nikolay burrowed under Yuri and reached the door, dragged it open, and sprinted out through the warren of rooms toward her. Red lifted his gun, aiming it at the young Russian.

"*Stand down, Red.*" Carter went after Nikolay. "Give me some cover."

Red charged after him.

"Hey," Sara yelled.

Carter turned back at the second door. "Yuri, Mitch, cover the home base."

"Bullshit." Mitch racked his gun and went after them.

"You heard him, Yuri." Sara sprinted out the door.

Mitch caught up. "Permission to disobey that last order, sir." He bared his teeth for a moment. "They get past you guys, we're all just fish in a big glass barrel."

*****

CHAPTER 54

Nikolay unlocked and pushed open the last door to the main loading area. He slowed.

"Anna."

She spoke over her shoulder. "Go back; they don't know you."

Nikolay approached with his hands up before him. "Please, Anna." In one hand, he clutched both the small blowtorch and the cigarette lighter.

Carter, Red, and Mikhail, followed by Mitch and Sara, came into the room. Red and Mitch moved to either walls, guns up and pointed toward the groaning front doors. The wood now bent inward in a huge belly and the metal locks started to squeal and pop.

Sara approached, hands up in front of her. "This is not the way, Anna. This is not controlled."

"Nothing ever is." She smiled dreamily. "I felt it, felt its intellect." She turned back. "I can talk to them; I know I can."

The door groaned louder, the bend in the center of its stout beams becoming impossibly huge.

"They're coming in—Sara, get back!" Carter yelled.

"Anna," Mikhail demanded. "Please, come back inside. Come with us."

Mikhail also held up a blacklight and switched it on. Carter still had his in his pocket but for now just had his rifle pointed. Nikolay edged even closer to the young woman.

"Boss, we need to be out of here," Mitch said over the top of his gun.

"Sara." Carter waved her closer, and she edged toward him. He couldn't wait anymore. "Grab her," he yelled to Nikolay.

Nikolay rushed forward—just as the huge doors exploded inward.

Like a vision of the gates of Hell, animals and people poured in, vacant milky eyes, gaping mouths, dry and black inside, and fur draped in lake weed or missing patches as the skin rotted away.

"*Engage*," Carter yelled, and he, Red, and Mitch fired, aiming for the core of the torso. Even Sara pulled out the handgun they had taken from one of Tushino's men and held it two-handed as she fired.

Some of the animals fell like empty suits, but it wasn't the beasts that worried Carter. Instead, in the glow of the blacklights, they saw in among the paws, feet, and hooves, or even crawling on some of the larger creatures' backs the spindly creatures looking like obscene spiders that glowed phosphorescently as they were bathed in UV.

"Friends! We're friends!" Anna yelled, still holding up her hands.

But if they knew, cared, or even understood, it didn't matter, as there were far too many and in seconds, Anna was engulfed as she stood there with her hands up in a universal sign of friendship, or perhaps surrender.

"*No*," Nikolay screamed as he saw she was tucked under the arm of a huge ursine beast and carried from the door.

"Don't you dare," Carter yelled at Nikolay who looked like he was about to go after her. The young man held his ground, but his expression told Carter he was in torment.

Carter gritted his teeth; he knew these things didn't arrive here for talks—they came for more raw materials.

"Fall back," Carter yelled.

Nikolay lit the blowtorch and set it on long flame. The tongue of blue flame with its orange-yellow tip still only shot out about 18 inches, but the creatures shrunk away from its heat.

"Give 'em hell," Carter yelled.

Carter's team yelled warnings or war cries, the blasts of machineguns filled the air, and the door's wooden frame groaned and cracked as beasts forced their way in. The animals themselves were deathly silent, which added to the surreal nature of the event.

Red and Mitch got to either side of the inner door and waited for Sara, Mikhail, Carter, and Nikolay to pull back. Then Nikolay screamed.

At first, he seemed to be in some sort of contortion with the hand holding the blowtorch stuck out straight in front of him.

But then when Mikhail shone his light toward the young man, they could see one of the many-legged creatures had its long tongue wrapped around his wrist and began to drag him forward.

It continually changed its position, its stilted legs moving almost in a blur and making it impossible for Carter to get a clean hit on it.

"No shot," Carter yelled.

Nikolay screamed as a line of blood showed at his wrist, and Carter guessed the thing was using the cutting edge now, with the intent of removing the blowtorch hand altogether.

Just then, Pavel burst into the room, calling to his son. In his hand he held a beaker of oily-looking fluid and he rushed toward him, tossing the liquid on the glowing creature and also splashing some of the animals.

As it sprayed in the air, the blowtorch ignited it, and the liquid exploded in an orange thunderball.

The creature holding him became a fiery comet as it skittered around the room, all the time making a squealing sound that was like screeching nails on a blackboard.

The animals in flame also fell back; perhaps for the first time ever, the many-legged things from the lake depths felt the touch of fire.

Pavel rushed to Nikolay who had dropped the blowtorch and was holding his wrist. He dragged his son backward while Red and Mitch lay down cover fire, and Carter also supported Mikhail as he backed up while holding up the blacklight to pinpoint the invisible creatures.

In another second, they were all inside the next door, but Carter still urged them on.

"This ain't gonna hold," Red said. "We should burn them all; that worked best." He nodded at the still-smoldering corpses out in the larger area.

"Yeah, it worked." Sara urged everyone toward the next inner door where the huge form of a morose-looking Yuri waited for them. "The problem is, gentlemen, we're basically inside a giant wooden barn. We set it on fire, we're screwed."

CHAPTER 55

They backed into the center laboratory room, and Sara stuck her gun in the back of her pants. Yuri came and hugged her.

"I saw Anna."

Sara nodded up at him. She suddenly felt the enormity of what was happening to them, and shuddered at the horror of what lay in store for the young Russian woman.

"A waste; a waste of everything. She dreamed of some sort of interspecies dialogue. But that isn't going to happen with these things while they don't see us as even something crudely intelligent." She rubbed at her eyes with the back of a forearm. "And now, she'll pay a terrible price."

Carter put a hand on her shoulder. "Maybe they do see us as intelligent, and just don't care."

"And that just makes me hate them even more," she said.

Mikhail rubbed a hand up through his hair that was in wild disarray. "That... large biological machine thing in the water. Did you see?"

"Yes, I did. And if it was a machine, it was one conjured in Hell. That thing was made up of the bodies of damn animals... and people," Carter spat.

"What did you just say?" Mitch frowned.

Mikhail turned. "I think we, and the animals, are of use for more than just transportation or some sort of environmental suits. I think they use, *flesh*, like we use iron, and wood and plastic. We are the building blocks for their machines, their transport."

"And their food," Red said.

Red laughed cruelly. "Well, you can forget that *take me to your leader shit*. More like, *take me to your larder*."

"They need to be wiped out," Sara said evenly. "Anna said that they were just waking up, thousands of them. And they were planning on calling home so they could call for more of their kind to come here." She turned to Carter with narrowed eyes. "It'll be the end of all of us, and everything else."

Mikhail walked forward toward the glass as the creatures broke through into another of the outer rooms.

"They're in the lake, down deep and hidden. But can you imagine if they get into the ocean trenches? They'll be beyond our reach." Carter came and stood beside Mikhail. "We don't have much time."

The older scientist nodded. "Hopefully, we make it out of here so we can tell someone. Find where they are."

"Good idea." Carter went to his kit and rummaged for a moment. He withdrew a pistol-like gun and a black plastic box. He flipped it open and inside were three special red-tipped rounds.

"Trackers," he said, loading all three into the breach. "I was going to use them to track the bratva's cars or boats." He snapped the pistol closed and looked up. "Red, Mitch, give me cover."

"Hey," Sara said. "What are you going to do?" She came and grabbed his arm. "You are *not* going back out there."

He smiled down at her. "Only for a second. We've got to be able to find where these things are hiding."

She talked through clenched teeth. "You better be goddamn back in two seconds, you big moose... Or I'm coming after you."

He lent forward and kissed her quickly on the mouth, and then nodded to his men.

Sara put a hand to her lips, her eyes wide as she watched him go.

*****

They exited the lab, and Carter jogged out in front through the rooms with Mitch and Red just behind until they got to the final door that held the beasts from them. Carter got down low and held the pistol in two hands. He nodded.

Red gripped the door handle. "On the count of 3... 2...1..." He yanked it open.

Carter fired, aiming at three different animals—a bear, wolf, and deer, striking all three of them.

"Good hits," Mitch yelled.

The beasts surged toward them and Carter fell back. "Close it," he yelled and lay on the ground, kicking at the door, just as something invisible lashed in and split his body armor all down the front.

"Shit." He rolled away, and Red and Mitch shouldered the door closed and locked it.

"Boss, you okay?" Red asked as Mitch held the door.

Carter felt his front and felt that the body armor was cut open, but there was only a graze on his flesh. "Yeah, yeah... just." He exhaled. "If I was wearing normal clothing, I'd be in two pieces right now."

"Two Carter Stensons?" Red grinned. "Now there's a freaking nightmare." He held out his hand.

Carter grabbed it and hauled himself to his feet. "Let's get out of here."

The three men backed into the center laboratory. Sara shook her head and grinned at him, and he gave her a small salute.

Carter turned back to the glass as Sara approached. He put an arm around her shoulders.

"What now?" she asked.

Carter snorted softly. "Got everything crossed?"

"Even my toes," she replied.

Carter knew that all they could do now was watch the glass partitions as animals threw themselves against them. The entire building shook as an 800-pound bear hit the glass. For now, the shatterproof panes held, but they all knew they wouldn't for much longer.

It was the silence that made Carter's skin crawl. There were no roars, screeches, or bellows from the animals, or even cries of torment from the people in among them. And the humans had expressions as slack as sleep-walkers, and their milky eyes, gaping dry mouths, and bedraggled appearance made it all a scene straight from an asylum.

Carter felt Sara tremble beside him, and he looked down and saw that it was from fury rather than fear.

"We need to burn it all," she whispered.

He saw that her eyes blazed with hatred. "We're in a big barn, remember?"

"I do." She looked back at the monstrous crowd, throwing itself at the windows and doors. "We can't let them take us alive and end up like that."

"No, we can't," Carter replied.

She was right. There was no way they could keep them all at bay, and eventually, one of the invisible creatures would get at them, and perhaps open them up right there and take control like they were shells of meat to be cloaked in.

Or maybe they'd be grabbed by one of the beasts or people, and dragged down below the freezing black water, perhaps to become another slab of material for a biological vehicle that waited there.

He reached down and kissed her and then held her face. "But before we go, we'll damn well make sure they know pain."

She nodded and smiled up at him. He let her go and turned. A deer rammed the glass and for the first time, a crack appeared in its length.

"Ah shit." Carter sighed and then turned. "Armor up, everyone; this is about to get really hot."

"Oh yeah." Red slapped in a fresh magazine and Mitch did the same. They checked their sidearms and knives, and then stood ready. Sara also pulled her handgun from her pants and held it tight.

Nikolay had a knife and his small blowtorch, and Pavel had a scalpel in one hand and a broomstick in the other. The huge form of Yuri held his handgun in one hand, and the other grasped the tiny silver medallion around his neck as he mumbled softly.

Mikhail moved around, putting all the remaining blacklights on benchtops and walls, switching them all on. The UV illuminated their surroundings, and the glow emanated out into the ranks of the animals.

"Jesus," Carter whispered.

In among the beasts, they saw the many-legged creatures, eyes high on the ends of stalks like some sort of crustaceans, watching the last group of humans inside.

More of the spidery things were riding on the backs of the larger animals like alien jockeys, and one was even hanging round the neck of a vacant-looking human being.

"She-*iiit*," Red said. "We are totally screwed."

Carter turned to Mikhail and sighed. "You know, Mikhail, now would be a good time for your Russian buddies to save our butts."

"If they got our message, they will come." He shrugged. "If they believed it."

The final door exploded inward and the wave of horrors poured forth.

"*Fire!*" Carter yelled and then opened up.

CHAPTER 56

"Back to hell, motherfuckers," Mitch yelled as he sprayed bullets into the surging creatures.

Red and Carter also fired high-powered rounds into the beasts, shredding them, and they also tried to pick off the glowing many-legged creatures. Some they hit; most they missed. They delivered belly shots into the animals, and many fell down, returning to the dead state prior to their reanimation.

Nikolay held the burning blowtorch up, and Yuri fired his gun. Sara also fired, screaming her anger, and shots that missed exploded windows outward, which just allowed more of the beasts to pour in at them.

After a few seconds, the ex-Special Forces soldiers had to change magazines, and around them grew a wall of dead beasts.

"Above," was all Mikhail yelled.

Carter looked up to see one of the spider-like creatures scuttling along the ceiling beams, and Nikolay extended the blowtorch flame to make it leap away.

Gradually, the group was forced backward into a tight knot of humanity. Outwardly, they bristled with guns, knives, and other sharp objects, but Carter knew that they'd exhaust their ammunition and strength soon.

His eyes slid to the huge tank of CO_2 they kept for oxygenating the fish tanks. A single bullet into that while Nikolay held a burning torch and the entire mill house would go up in an engulfing ball of fire. Ending them, and ending everything.

Sara saw where he was looking and placed a hand on his arm. Her mouth was turned down but she nodded.

"I'm out." Mitch dropped his rifle and drew his handgun. In seconds, Red did the same. The pair picked their targets now, as they ran down their ammunition.

Time was up. Carter started to bring his muzzle around toward the oxygen tank. He quickly looked at Sara who had her eyes shut.

"I love you," he whispered, but not loud enough for her to hear. He then turned to aim his gun at the huge silver cylinder.

The explosive *thump* made the entire structure shake. It was followed by another and another. There were no windows to the outside where they were; only the now torn-open front doors that gave a view to the hellfire that was raining down.

The nighttime landscape outside was transformed by a furnace's heat and brilliance, and the many-legged creatures first froze, and then as if on command all scuttled outside, followed by the zombie-like beasts.

"*Thavmásios*—fantastic!" Mikhail threw his arms up. "They came."

Carter started to shake his head. "Never have I been so glad to hear the Russian military was dropping bombs on me."

"Should we go out?" Nikolay asked.

"Not yet," Carter said. "I'm hoping they'll avoid the mill house and structures, but I think they'll be targeting anything moving for now. Let them mop up first." He walked closer to the glass. "Grab the blacklights and let's see what's happening."

****

"Oh my God," Sara breathed out as she stared out at the hellish chaos.

The ground, the air, and the sky alternated between darkness and flashes of hot red flame. Sara held up an arm as the bomb impacts shook the ground that they felt right to the bones in their bodies as they stood in the doorway.

Among the maelstrom of destruction, the monstrous animals lumbered about as if lost, and in the soft glow of the blacklights, the group could see the dozens of scuttling alien creatures.

"When there is no more room in Hell, the dead shall walk the Earth," Carter murmured.

The snow had all been melted from the heat of the explosives, and above, dark military helicopters hovered overhead as they threw down columns of brilliant white light over the blasted landscape.

A bomb landed in the center of a group of animals, plus a human that had one of the segmented creatures curled around his neck. There was the flash of the impact that was followed by rotting limbs being spread over 100 feet of the compound. Time and again, the precision strikes targeted the beings as they tried to head back to the safety of the water.

"*No*," Sara screamed. "No, no, no."

Carter spun to where she stared. The blast smoke cleared for a moment and caught in one of the helicopter's spotlights was a single figure with blond, matted hair and still dressed in a tattered, orange SeaWorld jacket.

"Marcus." Carter felt light-headed from shock at seeing his brother. Or what he had become.

The ghostly figure seemed to stare for a moment, and in that single glance, Carter wondered if there was any remnant of his brother being held captive in that shell now co-opted by the alien insect thing inside him.

Sara went to sprint forward, but Carter caught her around the waist.

"It's not him, Sara."

The next explosion hit Marcus like a thousand fiery hammers. One second he was standing there, and the next, he had been obliterated.

Sara screamed and Carter held her tight. Above them, another helicopter flew low out over the water where the ice was broken open and rained tracer rounds down from a 50-cal rotating machinegun, probably into the biological craft that had brought the beasts to shore.

After another five minutes of bombardment, it cut off and one of the choppers circled for a moment before coming in to land. Commandos were disgorged, and Carter, Red, and Mitch faded back a few steps.

The stink of gunpowder, churned earth, and rotting meat filled the compound. Carter looked out to where he had seen his brother, but nothing remained, not even a scrap of orange material.

Thank God, he thought. *His soul was now free.* He looked down at Sara, who looked ill.

"Are you okay?" he asked softly.

She shook her head.

"Mikhail, you take it from here," Carter said.

The scientist nodded and walked out with arms up, but holding a blacklight. A soldier approached, a captain, who saluted and called him by name.

Carter put his arm around Sara's shoulders.

She looked up at him. "I want to go home."

"So do I," he replied. "I think Lake Baikal has given up enough of its secrets for now. Besides, I'm pretty sure they're not going to let you stay even if you wanted to."

"Good," she said.

Carter watched as Mikhail talked to several Russian commandos who carried long pipe-like weapons he didn't recognize. Two more appeared, holding huge flashlights that emitted broad blacklight beams.

Amongst the debris, there were several of the segmented aliens. Some were clearly dead but others limped or tried to scuttle away. Under Mikhail's guidance, the commandos approached, pointed their weapons, and fired. Fine netting shot toward several and they were quickly bundled up.

Carter watched with satisfaction as a couple of the commandos carried what looked like large Perspex boxes. Mikhail peered inside and held up his blacklight, making the several many-legged creatures visible.

"Good," Carter said. "Time for them to be the lab animals."

CHAPTER 57

Carter stood watching the last of the helicopters disappear into the watery dawn light. A low mist hung over the mill compound that was a mix of smoke from the explosions plus steam rising from the rapidly cooling bomb craters.

Red and Mitch sat on the front deck of one of the cabins where they smoked and clinked small glasses of amber fluid. Carter watched as Mikhail wandered toward him and Sara. The Russian scientist still held a huge military radio.

"Is it over?" Sara asked.

"For now," Mikhail said. "We still have much to do, much to learn. We need to be ready for anything, now."

Carter looked over the compound. The grounds were bomb-scarred, the mill house was torn up, and many of the cabins had been reduced to splinters.

"Not much left. Not much to show for all the blood, sweat, dollars, and time."

"We have our lives," Sara said and turned to the Russian. "What about us?"

Mikhail straightened, and Carter knew that in Russia, they had a tendency to lock up their problems in an *out-of-sight, out-of-mind*-type strategy.

Mikhail looked about. "We had a choice; either we detain everyone here for questioning." He turned back. "Or we buy their silence and send them home." He smiled through his beard. "I have talked to Moscow and told them how you defended Russian citizens with your lives. They are appreciative. They have decided to compensate you, but you must go home, immediately." He nodded toward Red and Mitch. "And I think it best you take those two with you."

"Thank God." Sara leaned against Carter and closed her eyes for a moment.

"When?" Carter asked.

"Today. Your helicopter is already on its way," Mikhail responded. He turned to look out over the frozen lake. "We also thank you for pinpointing where these things are hiding. Tomorrow, I fear there will be a Siberian earthquake, with its epicenter emanating from the bottom of Lake Baikal."

"You're going to nuke 'em?" Carter asked.

Mikhail faced him. "Wouldn't you?"

"In the blink of an eye," Carter replied.

Mikhail grunted. "I know, not very science-minded of me, but I don't believe we have anything to learn from these creatures. They are like a revolting plague that will infect everything on our planet if given the chance. So we won't give them that chance."

Mikhail removed one of his gloves and stuck out his hand. "Goodbye, Mr. and Mrs. Stenson. This Siberian incident is now over for you."

They shook hands, and Mikhail then wandered down to the wharf to clasp hands behind his back and stare out over the frozen water.

Carter and Sara wandered over to where Yuri stood with Pavel and Nikolay. Yuri got to his feet.

"You are leaving?"

"Yes, within a few hours," Sara responded. "Thank you all, for all you've done. For working hard, fighting for us, and risking everything." She hugged each of them.

Carter shook Pavel's hand and the small man looked up at him. "I'm glad you go home, safe. We also will leave here." He gave him a crooked smile. "I don't like the lake so much anymore."

"Yuri, I want each of you to get a final bonus to compensate you for everything. If I wire the money to you, will you ensure Pavel and Nikolay get their share?"

"Thank you, and of course." He looked at Carter from under bushy brows. "If not, you might come back and pay me visit, da?"

Sara was about to turn away but paused. "Nikolay, there'll be many more fish farms in the future. I could certainly use a bright young man with an economics degree and lab experience."

The young man beamed. "In America?"

"Yes, or at least somewhere warmer than here," Sara replied.

"Yes and yes." His grin split his face.

In the distance, they could hear the whoop of approaching chopper blades, and Carter listened for a moment.

"Mi-26, Russian heavy transport chopper; military." He turned to Red and Mitch. "Yo, we're bugging out. Just bring anything that'll make it through customs. On the double." He turned back to Yuri. "Dispose of any remaining hardware."

Yuri nodded. "Into lake."

*****

18 hours later, Carter and Sara were still traveling, but now safely on a plane over the Pacific Ocean and heading back to Madeira Beach, Florida.

30,000 feet below, the sun made the water sparkle like diamonds on a blue blanket. Sara held a glass of orange juice and turned from the window.

"We were lucky."

"Hmm?" He turned to her.

"We always thought that the first contact with another species would be an opportunity for a meeting of minds. No one expected that visitors would see us as nothing more than raw materials. Or food."

"It was a nightmare," he replied.

"The last night at the mill house, it was a full moon." She continued to stare straight ahead. "Do you think... they got their message out? Called home?"

"I don't know. I doubt it," he said softly. "I think Mikhail got them in time."

"I hope so." Sara looked up into his face. "So, what now?"

He reached across and took her glass, sipping the cool juice. "Back to the bar, I guess. By now, there's probably nothing left but a smoking ruin." He laughed softly.

Sara didn't return the smile and instead just sighed. She faced the window again.

After a moment, he held her glass out to her but she didn't take it. She turned to face him. "You don't have to go back." She continued to look into his face.

He smiled down at her. "We made a pretty good team, didn't we?"

"You have your moments." Her mouth quirked up, and she finally took her juice back. "Stay with me."

Carter felt a little lightheaded as he stared down into her beautiful eyes. "I can do that; stay with you. But what will I do in Florida?"

She smiled and looked heavenward for a moment. "Well, I need a good gardener, and a maintenance guy. And a security guy."

He laughed and then leaned toward her. "Anything else?"

"Oh yes." She leaned across to kiss him deeply.

EPILOGUE

Pacific Ocean Approximately 124 Miles East of The Marianna Islands

The object struck the water just after midnight and created a tsunami that swamped several miles of the Philippines, Papua New Guinea, the Japanese coastline, and also devastated most of Guam.

At first light, spotter planes were dispatched, but no debris was seen on the surface. There would be no search of the seabed as the water here was far too deep. After all, the Marianna Trench was over 36,000 feet in this area.

The search was called off quickly as the international authorities knew that anything down in those depths was going to stay down there.

But down in that dark and crushing abyss, a green glow pulsed with life. Nearly seven miles down on the seabed, something the size of a city block that was smooth and organic bloomed open like a flower. The call had been answered, and the harvesting would begin.

CHECK OUT OTHER GREAT SCIENCE FICTION BOOKS

MAX RAGE
by Jake Bible

Genetically Engineered. Physically enhanced. Mentally conditioned.

Master Chief Sergeant Major Max Rage was the top dog in an elite fighting force that no one in the galaxy could stop. Until, one day, someone did.

The lone survivor, Rage was blamed for the mission failure and court-martialed.

With a serious chip on his shoulder, Rage finds himself as a bouncer at the top dive bar in Greenville, South Carolina. And, man, is he bored with his job.

At least until he gets a job offer he can't refuse. Now, Rage is headed halfway across the galaxy to the den of corruption known as Horloc Station.

With this job, Max Rage may have a chance to get back to what he was: an unstoppable Intergalactic Badass!

WARNING: THIS NOVEL HAS GRATUITOUS VIOLENCE, SEX, FOUL LANGUAGE, AND A LOT OF BAD JOKES! YOU MAY FIND YOURSELF ENJOYING HIGHLY INAPPROPRIATE PROSE! YOU HAVE BEEN WARNED!

RECON ELITE
by Viktor Zarkov

With Earth no longer inhabitable, Recon Six Elite are sent across space to scout promising new planets for colonization.

The five talented and determined space marines are led by hard-nosed commander Sam Boggs. Earth's last best hope, these men and women are the "tip of the spear". Armed with a wide array of deadly weapons and forensics, Boggs and Recon Elite Six must clear the planet Mawholla of hostile species.

But Recon Elite are about to find out how hostile Mawholla truly is.

CHECK OUT OTHER GREAT SCIENCE FICTION BOOKS

LOST EMPIRE
by Edward P. Cardillo

Building on their victory in the last Intergalactic War, the imperialist United Intergalactic Coalition seeks to expand their influence over the valuable Kronite mines of Golgath. Reeling from their defeat, the warrior Feng are down but not out. The overextended UIC and the vengeful Feng deploy battle groups and scramble fighters as they battle for position in the universe, spinning optics and building coalitions. Captain Reinhardt of the Resilience and the elite Razor's Edge squadron uncover the Feng Emperor Hiron's last ditch attempt to turn the tables with a new and dangerous technology. With resources spread thin, the UIC seeks to exploit Feng's weakened position through a very conditional peace accord. Unwilling to submit, Emperor Hiron must hold them off and quell the growing civil unrest of his starving, warrior people just long enough to execute the mysterious Operation: Catalyst. Commander Massa and his Razor's Edge squadron race against time to stop Hiron's plan, and a new race awakens, led by a powerful prophet set on toppling the established galactic order through violent acts of terrorism.

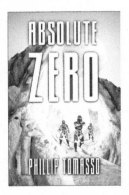

ABSOLUTE ZERO
by Phillip Tomasso

When a recon becomes a rescue . . . nothing is absolute!

Earth, a desolate wasteland is now run by the Corporations from space stations off planet . . . A colony of thirty-three people are part of a compound set up on Neptune. Their objective is mining the planet surface for natural resources. When a distress signal reaches Euphoric Enterprises on the Nebula Way Station, the Eclipse is immediately dispatched to investigate.

The crew of the Eclipse had no idea what they were getting themselves into. When they reach Neptune, and send out a shuttle party, they hope they can find the root cause behind the alarm. Nothing is ever simple. Something sinister lies in wait for them on Neptune. The mission quickly goes from an investigation into a rescue operation.

The young crew from the Eclipse now finds themselves in the fight of their lives!

Made in the USA
Las Vegas, NV
08 August 2023

75826326R00146